# Since
# Daisy Creek

# W. O. Mitchell

SEAL BOOKS

McClelland and Stewart-Bantam Limited

Toronto

*This low-priced Seal Book
has been completely reset in a type face
designed for easy reading, and was printed
from new plates. It contains the complete
text of the original hard-cover edition.*
NOT ONE WORD HAS BEEN OMITTED.

SINCE DAISY CREEK

*A Seal Book / published by arrangement with
Macmillan of Canada*

*PRINTING HISTORY*

*Macmillan of Canada edition published October 1984*

*A Literary Guild of Canada Selection
Seal edition / October 1985*

ISBN 0-7704-2064-8

PRINTED IN CANADA

COVER PRINTED IN U.S.A.

U  0 9 8 7 6 5 4 3 2 1

# FOR WILLA

## WITH GRATITUDE TO THE UNIVERSITY OF WINDSOR

### IOU's

Mildred Mitchell — Haig Elementary School
Emily Murray — St. Petersburg Senior High School
Rupert Lodge — University of Manitoba
F. M. Salter — University of Alberta

"Act as if the maxim of thy will were to become, by thy adopting it, a universal law of nature."

IMMANUEL KANT

# CHAPTER 1

It did help some to keep his eyes closed, let his mind limber up before starting out through the arctic dark to discover what had been caught in the body trap-line overnight. There'd be no surprises; all the joint snares would be full and kicking: high and stubborn between the shoulder-blades, the ache that would never, never die; in the right shoulder, shrill pain, the right elbow much the same; then down to the right hip, the thigh muscle shuddering but the calf not cramping yet; back to the right forearm, numb along its underside; finally the third and little fingers, alive with rodent nerve jerks. Return to base camp. We've got to get you up and out of bed, Dobbs!

Open the eyes. Aha! Excellent beginning! You've been sleeping on the *left* side, so you're not going to have to roll over, just slide the knees up. Easy! Easy! Get the left elbow underneath you. Hold it! Don't try to run before you've learned to walk, as that cliché-spawning son-of-a-bitch Arrowsmith always says. Now—slip both feet over the cliff edge of the bed for lever help so the elbow push can roll you up to sitting. Wait again. Hey-hey! That third vertebra behaved; no spasm, no head float or drift or eddy at all! Praise God! Both hands down now to either side. Get the torso weight balanced forward precisely right because we don't want to have to do this more than once. "Still with me up there?" Grab the bedpost—aah-haaa and hah-hup you go with all the speed of rising bread dough!

Oh, my! Missed that one, didn't we! Hiding in wait up there just behind the balls! In therapy next time we're going to have to make allowances for the bike saddle's iron spine, slide off a little more to one side so the inner edge of one cheek can cushion better.

Into the bathrobe, take down the cane from the head rail, get the feet into the slippers. Next target: the thirteen steps to the bathroom door.

"Good morning, Professor."

"Don't sing it, Miss Bews. Say it."

"Had a bad night?"

"They're all bad!"

"Aw—I'm sorry!" She really was; that was the important thing about Velvet Bews; she was truly sorry for them all. "Maybe we'll feel better after breakfast and therapy."

"Nobody feels better after breakfast and therapy!" With her bonnet and short-skirt uniform, she could have run right off a Dutch Cleanser can. And she could also have stepped right into a *Playboy* centrefold!

"How would you like it this morning, Professor Dobbs? In bed or on the table?"

Soft and lovely as her given name. "On the table, and after I've been to the bathroom."

"Can I help you there?"

"No thanks. This morning all by myself."

She set the breakfast tray down on the metal table at the head of the bed.

"And standing up."

She stopped wheeling the table towards the chair by the window. "Oh—do you really think you should, Professor Dobbs. . . ."

"It is for girls to sit—for boys to stand and often miss."

"Hey, Professor!"

"I don't want a repeat mortification of yesterday."

"Huh?"

"Miss Pickersgill had to help me up off the thing."

"Well—I can check back. . . ."

"I'll be all right, Velvet—I think."

"Good luck, Professor."

What a dear little bum-sprung student nurse she was too! "Shut the door after you, please, Velvet."

He had wondered how she had been given a name like that, until she had told him that her father had just loved the film and hoped his little girl would grow up beautiful as Elizabeth Taylor. He had not been far off the mark.

Damn it! Why had he waited till he was balancing with feet apart in front of the toilet to remember the neck brace that would permit not a fraction of an inch of head movement sideways, up, or down! Lowered eyes could give him a glimpse only of the end of his nose but not the end of anything else below. Stooping did afford him a clear view of the bowl's oval target, but it withdrew his crotch further out of sight. He'd *have* to sit to do it! No, sir! I will *not* sit to do it! I will aim by sound alone, and if I miss, then sorry, Velvet Bews.

Now, still with me, are You? Where is it! No dizziness, please! Where is the thing! Not down there! Or there! Where in hell has it got to! Glory! Glory! Hallelujah! It has risen! First time in three months!

Lean forward and push it down and wait and pray. Pray to that Great Urinator in the Sky!

Bull's-eye!

Now—"Please Flush and Wash Your Hands," as each square of Kathleen MacNair College toilet paper advised. And do not look into the mirror on the wall, which will tell you who is the ugliest of them all, for after her walk in the woods Mama Bear turned one side of your face into porridge before you could jump down out of bed and run all the way home. Don't waste wit on yourself, Goldilocks; save it for Miss Bews or Miss Pickersgill or Miss Learmonth or Dr. Arrowsmith. Especially for Arrowsmith.

But of course he did look, just as any young German student would look every morning to check his duelling scar trophies with Heidelberg pride. The analogy did not wash worth a damn, for he hated the right side of his face, with the claw track lifting the corner of his mouth and pulling down the under-margin of the right eye socket so that it was permanently skewed into sadness. Thank God for the neck brace that kept him from seeing bear and surgeon tracks over his chest and stomach! Maybe when they let him out of here he could do lots of sunbathing for a masking tan. Wasn't there special make-up that birthmarked people used to cover grape and cherry facial stains?

Now—out of here, back round the end of the bed, and over to the chair for limp toast, the coffee you could read through, and a forkful or two of that cleverly reconstituted yellow stuff they call scrambled eggs.

Rest for an hour to recover from breakfast and to gather strength for Miss Nelson down in therapy. Arrowsmith wouldn't be visiting today, but maybe tomorrow. Then he could tell him more than he cared to hear about the miraculous erection.

Oh, bless you, loving-hearted Velvet Bews!

It was a good two hours since he'd got out of the pool and been wheeled back up to the room. The pain still echoed. The preliminary ice and heat applications had not been all that analgesic through the tense-and-flex and stretch exercises. Miss Nelson denied that she had increased the traction pull, but she was not to be trusted. The ultrasound *had* been turned up too high because he *had* felt the nettle sensation burn the skin between the shoulder-blades, and she *had* made an adjustment when he mentioned it. She admitted that she was adding five more sit-ups, but that he really must leave the decisions to her for a change. He said he would, just as soon as she had proved to him that she could call them a lot better than she had been doing so far. Just his luck to draw a medieval bitch like her!

He did not often think of her as "Miss Nelson," but as "Irma the Great." During therapy sessions as "Irma the Uncompassionate." Less frequently as "Irma the Beautiful." With her blonde mane, violet eyes, porcelain skin, corn-cob-even teeth, she was a fair and unflawed woman, Britannia without trident. A helmet she did wear, for twice a day through city traffic she made a knees-up charge on her quarter-ton Triumph Bonneville to and from the hospital. Each morning and each evening in spring and summer and fall, rhythmic and regular and powerful as any traction machine, she also sculled five miles. She was ranked third in singles nationally. In spite of the incredibly active life she led, she smelled quite nice, a little like clover. With her, he imagined, intercourse would be an Olympic event. Every time.

After the exercises she had said, "Men can take pain much better than women can—generally."

"You going to give me a neck—back rub?"

"Massage doesn't really do you any good, Dr. Dobbs."

"It *feels* good."

"And that's all it does."

He supposed he was a disappointment to this iron nightingale, expert in measured pain and controlled suffering. Sooner or later he must tell her she had been given bad vocational guidance. Before it's too late, Florence, shove your heat lamp up your ass!

Forget the long journey down the hall to the sunroom today! He simply did not have the energy left for it. Back into bed and try for a nap. Maybe then. Just maybe.

Getting into was so much easier than getting out of. Remember—the *left* side and the knees up in the foetal position to take tension off the spine. He'd started out so great this morning and now—it wasn't the best of times, it was the worst of times!

He supposed he was beginning to understand how a woman must feel after rape. From now on, asleep or awake, he must live always with apprehension; he could never again hide from himself the possibility of sudden attack. When the grizzly sow up Daisy Creek had taken him into her embrace three months ago, she had educated him in terror. In correcting his foolish innocence she had not quite destroyed him, but she had killed trust for him. He knew now that savagery had no geographic limits, that civilization excused no one from horror. Her cruel lesson had been instant as *trompe-l'oeil*, but with no return to first image; the stairs went up; the stairs went down down down down. Duck to rabbit rabbit rabbit rabbit rabbit forever. She had taught him something he should really have learned long before reaching the age of forty-seven: the capsize quality of life.

And he was indeed a self-pitying bugger. Insensitive to others' suffering, too. No shortage of that in here. He must remind himself more often of those rheumatoid arthritics with their knees and elbows like footballs, of Louis, Mrs. Gatenby. . . .

God damn that goddam bear!

Now—why had he climbed back into bed? Sleep

would not be blessed, only sometimes gave escape.
Which was really worse: pain or nightmare? Dilemma,
Dobbs. Take your pick: those ivory combs or the long
and slender lavender tongue that seeks and finds and
touches you with fire! This time the horizon may close
right in and suffocate you with despair! Please! Not this
time, please! Not the empty eye, the socket that grows
and nears and becomes a horror vortex that will suck
you down and end you!

Oh, God, he and Descartes had been wrong all
along! Because he thought, it did not guarantee he was!
At all! Or ate or screwed or shit or hungered or woke.
. . . Only nightmares were true. . . . And pain. . . .

"Hi, Elmer."

That was strange. Usually the dreams were sound-
less.

"Hi, Elmer." The voice was no longer distant. This
time he could place it: behind him and right by the
bed. And familiar. That had been her name for him
ever since he had first paraphrased Socrates' caution:
"The unexamined life is not worth living." She'd been
about five then, and often in later years he had warned
her, "Don't you eat that stuff, Elmer. It's horse-shit!"

"Annie!"

"Poppa!"

"Annie—Annie! Come round the bed so I can get a
look at you!"

Oh, Annie, dear Annie, won't you marry me!

It really was his Annie, and what did you say to
the daughter you hadn't seen or touched or hugged or
kissed in five years? "My God, you're tall!"

"I'm a big girl now, Poppa."

So many years he had wondered and worried about
his little lost girl. In his mind he had kept her small and
vulnerable, recalling her in a play-pen, in nightgown
before a fireplace, or grasping swing ropes. Even now
he could feel himself stepping back on one foot, the
other out ahead as he raised his arms high to lean
forward and thrust her out and up, to wait for her
return to him. He had never been able to push her long
enough or high enough to suit her.

"It's been so long, Annie!"

"Me too, Poppa."

How old had she been? Sixteen—seventeen? The last time he'd seen her. No—that was her age when the separation had happened, and before Sarah had taken her out to the coast, there had still been the occasional weekend rendezvous in parks and rinks and zoos and theatres. Also, just before entering university out there, she had come back to him for the five September days they'd camped in Paradise Valley. So—*that* must have been the last time. Nineteen?

Early in March the divorce had become final. Sarah's hysterical phone call had come just after. "She's with you! I know she is!" She wasn't. "She's gone! Left for good! Right in mid-term! Says she's got to find herself! You let me know if she shows up there!"

He had promised he would if Annie did. She hadn't. No more blue and gold days in Paradise Valley. Five years. Three letters.

"How did it happen, Poppa?"

"Help me onto my back. I pretty nearly need a block and tackle to get turned."

She leaned over him.

"Slide an arm under my shoulders and lift when I tell you." When she still had her arm round him, her cheek warm against his own, "You might as well kiss me while you're . . ."

After she had and he had and she'd withdrawn her arm and straightened up, she said, "I thought you'd never ask!" She sat down. "What did you do? Break Baby Bear's chair all to pieces?"

"You first."

"I guess I do owe you an explanation."

"If you want."

"Oh, I want. I came just as soon as I heard—what happened to you."

"Three months ago!"

"I found out just a week ago. I'd have come to you three months ago if I'd known then. Do you think I wouldn't?"

"I did wonder. I have also wondered—for nearly five years—where you were."

"A number of places."

"I also wondered whether or not you'd been destroyed, but I suppose your mother would have let me know. What places?"

"The States most of the time. Couple of years on the desert. New Mexico. Then Oregon for a while with the Space Feather family. I wrote you from there."

"You didn't mention any Space Feather—"

"I didn't think you'd be interested."

"I am now. What the hell's the Space—"

"A sort of one-crop agricultural community. Bare-bum baby on the hip style."

"Your hip?"

"No!" Her eyes blazed.

When would he ever learn! Just couldn't wait to blow it! There had never been anyone else in his whole life who could warm or chill the world for him as well as she could.

She had relaxed back into the chair again. "I stayed just long enough to realize I'd made a wrong decision. Last year and a half—Palo Alto. I'd still be there if somebody hadn't squealed on me, so two fellows visited me and suggested I return to the country of my birth, then apply properly for a visa. Like the geese—I flew north last fall."

"Where did you light?"

"The Island."

"And you didn't know till a week ago!"

"That's right."

"But your mother's in Victoria."

"It's a large island. May I smoke in here?"

"Sure."

She opened her purse. "I've been out of touch with her for almost a year."

"If your mother didn't—"

"Peter Ducharme in Campbell River. I ran into him when he was out for the spring salmon and he told me." She lifted the lighter to her cigarette, put it back into her purse. She exhaled. "I came."

"And when do you go back?"

"Ashtray?"

"Saucer on the window-sill for that."

"I wrapped the Island up. I'm looking for a job here."

"What doing?"

"Whatever I can get, and that generally means waitress, or if I'm unlucky, hostess. I already have a possibility. I'm to go for an interview at one."

"What are your chances?"

"About fifty-fifty. Depends on how I look in an off-one-shoulder Grecian gown. Ever heard of the Parthenon?"

"I think I have. Why is being a hostess unlucky?"

"No tips. Oh, something else that might interest you. I'm going back to school."

"That's great, Annie!!"

"Visual arts. Seems I paint, Poppa."

"How long have you been doing that?"

"Off and on—with a sort of inconsistent consistency—ah . . . three years. I've even had formal instruction. Drawing. Design. Art history. Painting. That's what I was doing at Stanford when the CIA came after me. Also I had a job part-time in the Flower Path, doing floral arrangements."

"Wouldn't that be better than being a waitress?"

"Nope."

"Why not?"

"Not as much money, and I prefer pimps, middle-aged lawyers, accountants, and other hustlers trying to make me."

"Prefer to what?"

"To me making funeral sprays and wreaths and crosses. Now—you, Poppa."

"I think—maybe I better sit up now."

This time he did not have to ask her to kiss him. She held him in her arms much longer. When she had returned to the chair, he said, "You know I've been grizzly-hunting the past five years. . . ."

"No—I didn't know that."

"Well, I have—and without much luck."

"So I can see."

"Late March or early April, depending on when the Easter reading break would come. This time it was April. Paradise Valley. Archie Nicotine's guided me every year. We took an old grey horse up Daisy Creek—he would have gone for dog food anyway. He shot him up there for bait and we gave him about ten days to get high enough for some bear to wake up and come looking for whatever hadn't made it through the winter. They're mostly carrion-eaters after hibernation, you know."

"No, I didn't."

"Well—one was enticed by the rot smell, and it came to the dead horse and I shot it and it did—ah, *this* to me."

"Just what did it do to you, Poppa?"

"Damn near disembowelled me—and this to my face. I've got a new ball joint in my right hip. Plastic. My right arm was smashed—the elbow—that's where the four-inch aluminum pin is—collar-bone—two cracked cervical vertebrae."

"Three months ago."

"Mmmh. I've had visitors, flowers, get-well cards. People from the Department—the odd old student . . ."

"But not your daughter—"

"Oh, don't, Annie! You're here now! Actually, during the first month—more than I cared for. They're down to just a trickle now. Dr. Lyon's been pretty faithful."

"Has he. How is he?"

"Most Sunday afternoons. Forgetful. More than he's been most of his life. Arthritic. Unpredictable. Old." He grimaced. "Like me."

"Oh, Poppa—you're not!"

"I am now!"

"Come on! Dr. Lyon's in his seventies! You're only forty—uh, something!"

"Ever since what happened to me up Daisy Creek I've had a lot of time to think about it. By my calculations, that grizzly robbed me! Robbed me of just about the difference there is between me and Dr. Lyon!"

"Take it easy, Poppa."

"One whole *generation* of years she owes me!"

"Was it a female?"

"She *was*, but I got all hers!"

"Her what?"

"Years!"

"Maybe you shouldn't talk—"

"Oh, Annie, Annie, Annie—it's awful nice to see you again!"

"I only wish it could have been sooner, Poppa."

"Not all bad. That it's later. I'm just as glad you didn't see my face the way it was at first. They've done a lot of work on it—"

"It isn't so—"

"The hell it isn't! The eye! It will close only halfway—or open! Even when I sleep. Always that red meat sickle. . . ."

"All right, Poppa."

"She just about three-quarters scalped me, too. Archie could have used the hanging flap on a coup stick. Do you know he's visited me at least six times, whenever he comes into the city from Paradise, I guess. I wouldn't be alive if it hadn't been for Archie. He got her off me—shoved my guts back in—"

"You sure you want to—"

"—cut and tied together a travois—with his boot-laces—dragged me out through snow up to his ass to the four-wheel and then drove half-way to Shelby, where we met the ambulance he'd phoned for from the agency. Oh, I tell me he came with me into Emergency here. Oh, I owe Archie, Annie!"

"Me too, Poppa!"

"There's Kleenex there somewhere. . . ." He heard it whisper off to his right. "He went back in. He skinned her out for me and salted her hide."

She said something but it was muffled in the Kleenex.

"Huh?"

"Who gives—" Her voice broke. ". . . Huh—who gives a—huh—good goddam!"

"Whaaat!"

"About a *skin*!"

"I do!"

"Oh, Poppa—why! Why would you! Last thing I'd ever want to see again! Why!"

"Because—because it's—hell, I shot her!"

"So? Look what she did to you! Why would you—every time you looked at her skin—you want to be reminded of—?"

"Why do you think I went after her in the first place?"

"Damn good question!"

"Five seasons! At dawn, nightfall—I lay out there

and waited, my heart in my throat! And then—then
this! Why do you think I *wouldn't* want that hide!"

She stood up. "Too bad you couldn't have the
other trophy as well."

"Huh?"

"But of course—Archie shot that one, didn't he?"

"Damn you, Annie!"

"Old grey horse's head mounted over the fireplace—"

"Drop it, for Christ's sake!"

"Sure." She put her hand on his shoulder. "Sorry,
Poppa."

"Are you really?"

"Well—no." She laughed. "Oh, Poppa—didn't take
us very long, did it."

"No."

"Yelling at each other just like in the good old
days. We really are back together now—aren't we."

"Mmmh."

"And just where will you lay her down?"

"My den. You're not leaving?"

"I have to. That job interview. Don't worry. I'll
come to see you tomorrow and the next day and the
next—if you still want me to." She bent over and kissed
him on the forehead. "After you get out of here, too.
Funny."

"What's funny?"

"When I was little you used to have to kick me out
of that study. But not any more you won't have to,
Elmer—not with that great white hunter icon in there."


Just as Annie went through the door, Velvet Bews
showed up with his lunch. The two of them must be
about the same age. They'd approve of each other.
Slice of white turkey, an ice-cream scoop of mashed
potatoes with a thin suppuration of pale gravy and the
familiar BB-shot green peas. He had not introduced
them to each other, though. Interesting omission.

"You didn't eat much, Professor," Velvet said when
she came to take away his tray.

"Don't bother to give the chef my compliments."

"I won't. Was that your daughter?"

"Good guess, Velvet."

"First time she's been in to see you?"

"She just heard—found out I was here. She's been out at the coast."

"Even without the shouting I could tell right away she was your daughter. Easy. Good-looker."

"I think so."

"Classy."

"I agree there too."

"Like you."

"Oh—back off some, Velvet."

"I mean it."

"You're just saying that to be nice."

"I don't—just say things to be nice very much, Professor. You are a good-look—"

"Quit it, Velvet."

"Honest."

"Velvet, I don't know just how we got into this. . . ."

"Oh—I got us into it. I said your daughter was good-looking and she probably got it from you. You are a good-looking guy—"

"Not any more."

She had shifted the tray to one hand and with the other was pointing at his face. "I been waiting for chance to tell you that for quite a while because somebody should have told you that before now, the way you are pretty uptight about what that bear did to the side of your face. And I am telling you not to let it bother you as far as us women are concerned, Professor."

"All right, Velvet."

"Guys I can't speak for. Like Miss Learmonth keeps harping at me all the time, maybe I'm not very professional, but I bet you could even turn her on. And I think you're going to find out—that women are really going to go for you more now than they ever did before."

"Oh, come on, Velvet."

"I'm right. You'll see. And if you were my dad that nearly got killed by a bear and I was out on the coast, you wouldn't catch me taking any three months to get to you." She took the tray in both hands again. "Sorry if I've been unprofessional again."

"Maybe, Velvet, but you keep right on being what you are. Classy."

"Mine died two years ago. We shouted at each other quite a bit, too." She walked to the door. "You got yourself another visitor. I asked him to wait until I got your lunch stuff out."

"Who?"

"The noble redskin. I didn't tell him he was good-looking too, but he is. I guess I do go for the older men—most of the time, anyway."

"You say that to all us older men."

"No," she said. "Mainly to the young ones."

The fall smell of camp-fire and buckskin entered the room ahead of Archie Nicotine.

Now that she had mentioned it, he supposed that Velvet was right. Archie was taller than most Stony men and lean. No paunch. Hard to tell how old he might be, for there was no grey, and the face had character but not age yet. There were brief fan lines at the corners of his eyes, quite deep creases from well above the wide nostrils and down past the corners of his mouth. His totem could have been cheetah. He might be in his early thirties; he might be in his fifties. Whatever his age, there was little of life, red or white, that had not been examined by Archie Nicotine.

"You goin' to use that chair or keep on the bed?"

Especially white.

"You take it, Archie."

He settled down, stretched both legs out. He removed the black hat and placed it on the floor beside the chair. He took a Sweet Harvest tobacco packet from his shirt pocket.

"I'm not very fussy about hospitals, Dobbs."

"Nice of you to visit me anyway."

"A lot of us people die in them."

"Death has never been segregated, Archie."

He was intent now on arranging the fine-cut on the cigarette paper. "Also—they could smell better."

"That's the antiseptic."

"Killin' the germs smell."

"That's right."

"Hey-up." He shook his head. Had he not, it would not have been clear whether the short sound clipped deep in his throat meant yes or no. He looked up to Colin as he lifted the cigarette to his tongue. "Bony Spectre. Smell him in here. Strong."

"Really?"

"Hey-up."

"Is that what he smells like—antiseptic?"

"Like tea been boiled a long time—or his hide just been tanned. You ought to know, the way he come close to you up Daisy, so you had a pretty good chance to smell him."

"I guess I did, but I was pretty busy at the time."

"Hey-up. When my girl, Magdalene, was sick bad—she was maybe twelve then and he was comin' after her and he smelled kind of sweet too, that time. Rotten sweet."

"You may be right, Archie. He certainly rides through here frequently."

"Whites wouldn't likely smell him so good anyway."

"Sure."

"Also it could be just superstitious horse-shit."

"How is she? Magdalene?"

"Fine. I guess. Wherever she is now."

"Oh."

"Hairdressin' someplace. She just comes back to Paradise once in a while."

"My Annie showed up today. She just left."

"She got kids?"

"No."

"Magdalene—two. That's why she comes back to Paradise when she does. They're with us now." He stubbed out his cigarette in the saucer on the sill.

"Archie—what's the score on that bear hide? Two months now."

"He said two months anyway—maybe more."

It *had* been two months ago—a good month after he had been brought into Emergency here. He had mentioned his concern about the hide to Archie.

"I took care of that," Archie had assured him then. "Thanks."

"I didn't say about it when I was in here before. I didn't figure you would be too interested in it before. Second day after I got back to Paradise, I went back up Daisy. Then I skinned her out and I sloughed the fat off. Wasn't much of that on her and I salted her hide good for you."

"That's quite a while ago. . . ."

"I got it in the agency root cellar—near freezin' in there still, but outside it's warmin' up pretty good now. What you want me to do with it?"

"Next time you come in—if you could drop it off at Wild Trophy World—over Spitzee Bridge, the other side of the railroad—"

"I been there before."

"Tell them I want her head mounted."

"So you can put up on the wall."

"No—not separate from the hide."

"For on the floor."

"That's right—but with taxidermy on the head."

"Hey-up."

"They make a mould—plastic form—then stretch the skin over it. I want her jaws opened and snarling to show the teeth. Glass eyes . . ."

"Don't cut off the head separate for on the wall like sheep or deer or moose, because you want her for on the floor?"

"Yes."

"All the rest of her for out flat."

"That's right."

"Snarlin'."

"Mmmh."

"Not grinnin'."

He decided he would let that one go by. With Archie it was often wiser to do that.

"She'd take up a lot of room—"

"No more than a rug would."

"—if they stuffed all of her for you."

"Why in hell would I want a full mount?"

"I don't see why in hell you want what you just said to me you wanted. Me."

"Well—seems to me you people took scalps?"

"Not so much of that goes on any more now, Dobbs."

"You really make your visits interesting, Archie."

"Hey-up."

And he was in good form today as he expanded on what he called the white problem.

"Havin' a lot more problems in those places where they made those campin' grounds and they opened up more lodges and hotels and hot springs in all the parks. Didn't you notice that?"

"I have, Archie."

"Look a few years back, those two girls got killed sleepin' in their tent on the American side when one of them made a bad mistake, campin' the wrong time the month for her."

"I read about it."

"Maybe a grizzly can't see worth a damn, but he can smell real good. You got whites—you got garbage, you know. Last summer was bad for both."

"I noticed a lot of garbage lying around Paradise Reserve too, Archie."

"Fellow and his wife taking pictures of two grizzly cubs in Wapta Park."

"On the national news—"

"The sow the other side the huckleberry patch didn't like that, so she did him about as bad as yours got you."

"Thanks for reminding me, Archie."

"He didn't die either, because his wife went up the lodge-pole pine and she yelled so the bear left him to go over and shake her down out of there and then took off." He paused to lick the new cigarette. "He didn't end up with no pictures of those cubs either, because she broke up his camera on him. Every year gets worse, and that's the whole situation."

"Grizzlies."

"Hey-up." Archie shook his head and the match. "Whites."

"If you say so, Archie."

"You know that too, Dobbs. Up there now you can read licence plates out of every province and out of every state there is. Used to be just a few to fish—to hunt—or to maybe just rustle some cattle out the forest reserve. I can understand that all right. Rainbow—cutthroat—bull trout. Big game. Okay with me if they like to do that. Makes some sense."

"And what doesn't?"

"That white game."

"Which white game?"

"Golf."

"What about it?"

"All the parks now. Hell of a place to do that in."

"I guess I agree with you."

"Chop out the bush. Plant short grass. Dig little weasel holes into it where there's a lake or a creek runnin' through it."

"That's for a water hazard."

"Hey-uh?"

"To make the shots more interesting—harder."

"For the wardens too. Lots of work for them, shootin' bears with those shells don't kill them."

"Tranquillizers."

"Hey-up. Then fly them away to another place so they won't get hit by one of them little white golf balls. I'd do it different. Me."

"What's your solution?"

"Not the bears. Tran—trans-kill-size the whites, then net them to take them out of there to where they belong, and that's the whole situation."

"Great solution, Archie. Write your member of Parliament."

"We already did that three years ago—the band council sent a pedition to the Premier and the Prime Minister and the natural Cabinet Minister but they did it anyway and to hell with the envirement and all us red originals." He stubbed the cigarette in the saucer. He leaned over and picked up his hat. "Million dollars a hole." He stood up. "I won't be comin' here for a while. I am a duly elected band councillor now."

"Congratulations."

"Meetings. Maybe a month fencin' for Moon and after that, hayin' the band and then green-feed Moon again. Maybe you won't still be here after that."

"I hope not. About that hide, Archie . . ."

"He said he had a lot of stuff to do piled up. He said maybe more than two months. Maybe four. If you're in a hurry—after everything I got to do in here I can go into there for you on my way out."

"That would be nice, Archie." He opened the drawer of the night table and took out his wallet.

"That ain't necessary, Dobbs."

"For your time and trouble, Archie."

Archie shook his head. "This time stuff it up your favourite white charity."

"I'll always owe you, Archie."

"Hey-up." He had stopped at the foot of the bed and pointed down. "Look nice here." He indicated the floor at the bathroom side of the bed. "Maybe over there."

"What?"

"In the mornin', warm for the bare feet."

"Hospital floors aren't cold in the mornings."

"Hey-up. I'll phone to you what he says about that bear hide."

# CHAPTER 2

It had been almost daylight before he could fall asleep, but this time it had not been pain or nightmare fear that kept him awake until his window had lightened.

She stood in the back line and he could tell that she was still in shock, quite unprepared for the explosions of laughter, the volleys of applause that had come at her from beyond the stage edge. They had forgotten to blindfold her!

She was looking down now and away from all the frightening unfamiliars out there. Though the stage was infested with the very young, the other starred angels and the Santa's helpers were no comfort to her at all.

She was still looking down. It must be her feet she was trying to find. Just as soon as the clerk had taken the lid from the box, Annie had fallen passionately in love with the slippers Sarah had bought for her. Now she tried to move back for a better look at the black velvet with the heart-shaped gold buckles, but this caused her to bump a brown boy elf with his cap point over one ear, so that he fell against the angel to his left, who staggered into the gauze-winged fairy queen, who slapped the adjacent reindeer. The elf also retaliated by turning and punching Annie, who pitched backwards but caught her balance. The silver star band slipped down and under her chin.

Colin saw her lower lip come out and the corners of her mouth go square, which meant that she would either cry or swear.

"You dummy son-of-a-bitch!"

The line, delivered with shrill feeling, was not part of Miss Partridge's script, nor was Annie supposed to run to the shallow stage steps and down the aisle and into his arms.

She would not stay even for Santa Claus.

"Count! To yourself! Count two—stop it—fly-rod straight up! Then count two again!"

"Don't flail it! Up and stop at twelve o'clock! One and two and snap it forward! Stop at nine o'clock! Like cracking a whip."

"No! Not your whole goddam arm! Keep your elbow down! Use the *elbow* for a hinge—not the shoulder."

"Here." He lifted her elbow and slipped the beer bottle between it and her side. "Now don't let it slide out. Do ten casts with it, then take it out and see if that elbow still comes up."

"Got one! Got one, Poppa!" Downstream he could see it jumping and jumping again ahead of her as she ran down the shallow curve of pebbled beach, her rod held high and out from herself as she tried to take the tension off the line. He had just started towards her when he saw her stumble, catch her balance briefly, then pitch forward. Her rod flew from her. When he reached her, she was curled up and clutching one knee. She was crying. He kneeled and took her into his arms.

"I ran out of line! He's a big bastard and he took all

my backing. . . ." She pulled away from him to reach out for the cork handle of her rod, but then fell back on the river edge to hold her knee again. He picked up the rod, reeled in the slack line, went back to her.

She was sitting up now and rocking with her knee cradled in her hands. "He would've gone five pounds, easy!"

"I saw him, Annie." He could also see the pain, the disappointment and the freckles stark upon her face.

"He just socked it—wet—the caddis . . ."

Nothing broken. They had straightened out her leg and he had rubbed most of the pain out of the knee. She was hardly limping when they got back to camp.


"Work upstream if you can. Always. Cast *up* and mend your line. Strip back and drop it and reach up again and feel for the pull of the current so you haven't got a belly in your line, so when he strikes, you have to suck up a lot of loose line and can't set the hook instantly. Your jerk reflex has to beat his spit-out reflex. Don't mend your line so the fly rips through the water faster than the current drift. Do it so it looks natural. A brown is the hardest to deceive. A brook is the most innocent of all. It's easier to get a cutthroat to willingly suspend his disbelief than it is to fool a rainbow."


"What's so interesting?"

"I was just trying to figure out—you know those nymph flies. . . ."

"Mmmh."

"They don't work worth a damn."

"For you."

"Do they for you?"

"Nope."

She was still squatting down at the end of the table and looking up through the bottom of the aquarium she had pulled over. "I was just trying to figure out— what does a fly look like to a fish? They can't tell colour."

"So I've heard."

"So—in fly patterns why is colour so important?"

"Maybe fish don't see colours—the way we do, but that doesn't mean they aren't getting colour signals all the same. Black . . . grey . . . intensities of shade and light."

"Those nymph flies. I bust my ass on them. I do wing pads and egg sacs, legs, setae. I can do nymphs now that look realer than any nymph ever floated up, but I have yet to get one single strike on a nymph. Well—except for a caddis worm and that's what's funny. A trout would have to be retarded to think it was a caddis nymph. Look at the peacock herl, green and gilt collars, then a fat, woolly middle made out of that . . . ah . . . whatever that stuff . . ."

"Chenille."

"Yeah. Fish must be pretty stupid to think peacock herl and chenille is the real thing."

"Mmmh."

"Or a Paramachene Belle."

"Dumb too."

"Actually pretty though."

"Intended only for Eastern trout of good taste," he said.

"Like pink popcorn. Take a Royal Coachman. Peacock herl again and scarlet silk body and those phoney white wings! Come on! That's what got me to thinking about what fish see. About what they think they see."

"So?"

"So I pulled this tank over and I got down here to figure out what Ethel sees."

"What's your conclusion?"

She stood up. "Don't have any. For sure."

"Just because you get down and look up doesn't mean you'll see what he sees."

"I know that."

"You are a human so you haven't got his fish eyes."

"I know I haven't. Also the water's up against a fish's eyes and not against mine. I already figured that out. She."

"Huh?"

"Her. Ethel. I've come to a sort of a conclusion anyway. Fish don't see all that clearly and that's why the nymphs won't work—won't fool them—if they have all the exact detail and form that makes them look more clear than a fish would see them, and all that does is to tip the fish off that the nymph isn't really real."

"Mm-hmm."

"So—maybe something that wasn't so exact might work better. What do you think?"

"Maybe."

"Just tie flies that are small or medium or large, short or long, grey or black or blue dun or brown or green. Just *suggest* they might be some kind of nymph. Let the trout do some guessing."

"You may be on to something, Annie."

"Just a shape and a colour and a movement."

"Uh-huh."

"What would I use to suggest juicy nymph stuff—flesh?"

"Something that's generally under water."

"Like what?"

"Fur."

"Fur!"

"Dubbing."

"What's that?"

"Take a length of thread—patch of fur. Cut off the hair in little bits and then put glue or wax on the thread so that when you roll it in the fur bits, it picks them up to make a sort of fur thread. You wind that around the hook shank and there you are. A number of fly patterns have bodies of dubbed fur. Mostly from water animals."

She had gone back to the fly vise then, using muskrat belly with its grey under-fur and guard hairs, dyed for black or green, otter for dun, mink for brown. He called them the Annie flies, shapeless fur lumps generally with a fluorescent red tag, to be cast, to sink and drift downstream, then to rise with the delicate jerk movement that would allure and seduce.


"Poppa?"

"Mmmh."

"Aren't any other animals use fire, are there?"

"No."

"Just us."

"Yes."

That would always be his clearest remembrance of her: leaning forward with her arms around her knees, chin forward, the light flickering now strong, now soft upon her face. She had withdrawn deep within herself, but she had not left him really. It was the fire spell they had often shared, the magic amalgam of close-apart.

"Not so much *discovering* it—fire—it's discovering you got power over it. Discovering you can *use* it." Not bad thinking for a twelve-year-old.

"That's the real discovery, isn't it?"

"I guess it is."

"But as soon as you use something—as soon as you have power over something, then something else happens."

"What?"

"You *need* it, and when you need it then you depend on it, so before fire you were independent of it—didn't need it—after, *it* has power over *you*."

"I guess so, Annie."

"I wish to hell you'd given me a good brain."

"I thought I had."

"I know I'm not dumb, but the way it is—what happens with me is I start thinking about something and my brain goes only part-way. It sort of gives up on me. Does yours do that?"

"All the time."

"So what do you do?"

"Try to make it go back to work."

"It isn't that easy."

"I didn't mean to suggest it was, Annie."

"Sure you can shove it, but it won't shove anywhere *important*. It just gives up and you shove it and it doesn't go anywhere important for you and it gets confused and it just trickles away into the sand. Or else—it all flies apart all over the place and then says what the hell. You ever wonder if you were going crazy?"

"Often."

"Was there anybody in our family—back a ways— that went crazy?"

"I had an aunt. Down east—one I know of."

"Did Mother?"

"I don't know. Let's get back to that brain I gave you. That's the way brains generally work. Anything else is the lightning-stroke-of-genius approach, and don't you eat that stuff, Elmer."

"I won't."

"Maybe I didn't."

"Didn't what?"

"Give it to you. Maybe your mother had something to—"

"I don't want hers!"

"Oh, come on. Isn't a matter of choice."

"It's a matter of what I've got! And I sure as hell haven't got hers!"

"Oh, Annie!"

"Let's talk about something else!"

"You brought it up!!"

"And I'm dropping it—right now!"

"All right, Annie. In legend they did."

"Huh?"

"Animals had fire. Bear had it first. Kept it tied to his waist."

"Uh-huh."

"And the—I think it was magpie—maybe raven— stole it from him and carried it back to people. So I guess we fluked it—with magpie's help."

"I'd rather have yours is what I was trying to say, Poppa."

"Okay."

"It's not all that great, but I'd rather have it than Mother's. I'm turning in."


"She's a dirty fighter! She's a bush-whacker! She's a back-stabber! She's a welsher!"

"All of those, is she?"

"She said I could go out tonight if I cleaned up my room and I did and now she says I can't!"

"She must have a reason why you—"

"She hasn't!"

"Any at all?"

"She always has reasons but her reasons aren't the true reasons!"

"If she thinks they are—"

"Thinking they are doesn't make them real reasons!"

"Now, hold on, Annie—"

"She doesn't trust me!"

"Oh."

"At all! On anything!"

"Do you give her reason to trust—?"

"And you don't either, any more!"


"Are you angry with me, Sarah?"

"No."

"I keep getting signals that you are."

"Oh. Do you? I wonder why?"

"I don't know. That's why I'm asking you."

"Have you any reason to think there's some reason I might be angry with you?"

"No, I haven't."

"So."

"God damn it—why are you? Just let me know!"

"Have you done something I should be angry with you—for?"

"No. Not to my knowledge."

"Then I must have no reason to be angry with you. I must not *be* angry with you."

"Level with me! For once!"

"All right. The doorbell."

"What about it?"

"You don't ring it like other people do."

"And what is so inflammatory about the way I ring a door—"

"I've told you. I've asked you. Push it. Just once. Not—ding ding ding ding ding ding! Better still, stop losing your key so you won't have to ring it at all!"

"I hadn't realized—"

"Also, this morning—again—you did not put water in the porridge pot after you'd dished out your porridge. I've asked you a hundred times—explained how it hardens to glue if you don't."

"Anything else?"

"Your pants—all your clothes—you just leave them on the floor where you drop them—"

"And everything I eat turns into faeces! Come on,

Sarah. Let's just peel these silly things off and get down to the—"

"Annie!"

"What about her?"

"And you! The way you—what you're trying to do with her!"

"What am I trying to do?"

"She's a girl."

"I know that."

"If she were a boy would you want her to play with dolls and tea sets and skipping-ropes?"

"I—I don't—just what the hell are you driving at?"

"I am driving at the way you are driving *her* into doing things that are not girl things. You are forcing her—"

"I am not forcing her into anything!"

"Yes, you are! Fishing, camping—"

"Only because she wants to."

"Only because you make sure she wants to! She's a girl and she has the right to be a girl—"

"She has the right to be Annie!"

"She has the right to do girl things and realize herself as a girl and not as a boy!"

"God damn it—she is a little girl and she'll grow up to be a lovely—"

"Not if you have your way, she won't!"

"We'll see."

"When it's too late!"

"I'll watch for it. If her voice changes or she starts to shave."

"That's another thing. She's just as sarcastic as you are—as well as foul-mouthed."

"All right, Sarah. All right. Now I'll level with you. I hate your purse!"

"Whaat!"

"Especially in the car, the way you plock it down beside you and practically in my lap! Or ask me to hold it for you! I hate all your fucking purses!"


"Please, Colin. Give me a chance to be her mother— once in a while. Don't exclude me! Both of you!"

"I—*we*—are not excluding you."

"Yes, you are."

"Sarah, I have no intention—you can be with her whenever you want to be. I'm out at the university all week. You're here at home with her. The two of you have all the time in the world to be together."

"Last Reading Break."

"What about it?"

"All ten days of it—you were out at the university."

"I had to be. It's just as important for a teacher to catch up as it is for a student."

"You do not have to explain Reading Break to me. All you have to explain to me is why you took her out there with you every single—"

"Because she wanted to come. Because the university grounds and all along the river bank are perfect for cross-country skiing and she hadn't had a chance to really use the skis we gave her for Christmas—"

"Wouldn't it have been nicer for us to have spent Easter together! As a family!"

"I guess it would."

"For once! It's been the same all our married life! 'I've got papers to do.' 'I want to finish this short story.' God, how I looked forward to that second sabbatical—the one you screwed up for that novel you never finished!"

"I'm sorry you feel that way."

"No, you aren't! You're not sorry at all!"


Those later years must have been hardest of all on Annie; though the marriage was no longer an active battleground, it was dangerous still with unresolved conflicts and differences beneath the family surface like live shells, mortars, and hand grenades unspent. No place at all for a child to wander into, to play and grow in, where the smallest false step could set off old emotion mines.

He supposed that both of them had wounded her without knowing it then, but she had found her own weapons. She had learned to sulk well. She had mastered sleight-of-hand rudeness. She had perfected the unfriendly stare, the cold look. How much self-control it must have taken, never to answer a direct question.

And then there had been raw disobedience and the confrontations that ended up regularly in screaming scenes. He began to leave for the university earlier and to come home later. He lied and said he was trying to get back to his writing.

"*You* get her up in the mornings! *You* talk to her! *You* do something about her!"

To finally shake her and throw her against the wall in the upstairs hallway, then to the floor, and then to pick her up and to slap her and slap her again, had been his final act of helplessness.

Early in September that year, the Lockheed L-1011 lifted into the sky, made a slow arc over the city, then headed east to carry Annie off to Brocklebank Ladies' Boarding Academy.

Great life warmth had been stolen from him.

Magpie was a disgusting thief, actually.

# CHAPTER 3

He looked up to the clock over the sun-room door. Twenty to five! Just the dregs of visiting hours left and she hadn't showed yet! If she were going to show at all!

"I'm cold!"

Mrs. Gatenby said "cold" as though she were clearing stubborn phlegm from her old throat. No need to look at a clock with her in the room; she marked the passage of time for you with her croak-plaint every thirty seconds.

They'd ring the end-of-visiting bell in twenty minutes! Annie Annie, Annie—you haven't changed a bit! Your first rendezvous promise to me—broken!

Slowly he engineered his waist and his shoulders to get his head towards the right. Not carefully or tenderly enough, both his neck and shoulder told him. Shit!

Mrs. Gatenby had slid down and canted in her wheelchair, at a loll angle made possible by the seat-belt they kept buckled around her middle under the chocolate-and-yellow afghan. Frail, bird skeleton on daily display either here or in the hallway. Sun-room to hallway to sun-room to hallway; Mr. James Bentley Marsh, Fergus Moffat, the hydrocephalic child, Mrs. Gatenby, Louis Muhlbiere. He had thought it so heartless, moving them about like tumbleweed, until Velvet Bews explained to him that the purposeful flow of nurses, aides, cleaning staff, ambulatory patients, doctors, and visitors past the neurological reception centre seemed a beneficial stimulation to the submerged ones. They slept and they were wakened and they were fed and they eliminated with all the privacy of unclothed mannequins in a department-store window.

"I'm cold!"

His neck was really killing him now, and getting turned round so that he could be facing front again caused him even more of what Arrowsmith called "discomfort." Euphemistic son-of-a-bitch! Slowly, slowly he eased himself down and out so that he could just catch the under-ledge of the head brace on the back of the chesterfield to relieve the goddam third-vertebra pressure on the pinched nerve. He closed his eyes.

So she was untrustworthy now as she had been untrustworthy then! Never depend on our Annie! She has no sense of time or any other convention invented by man!

"Hi, Poppa."

He opened his eyes. Correction: he opened one and a half eyes. "Have you ever been on time for a single goddam thing in your whole goddam life?"

"Not even my own birth—as Mother must have told me at least a hundred times."

"I'm cold!"

Annie looked over to Mrs. Gatenby, then quickly back to him.

"They'll be wheeling her out for feeding in a minute."

"Poor old thing!"

"She has lots of company on this ward."

Annie was not really listening to him.

"Only about ten minutes' visiting time left," he said.

"Mmmh." Her attention was on something above his head.

"What kept you?"

"Rush hour." Now her calculating look had shifted to his left. What could be so interesting up there! "Loaded buses went right on by me at both stops."

Velvet Bews entered the sun-room and headed for Mrs. Gatenby. "Supper time," she sang.

Now Annie was looking up to the wall opposite him.

"Couldn't you have allowed for that?"

"Allowed for what?"

"Rush hour."

"I thought I had but I guess I hadn't, and I'm sorry." She was still looking at the walls.

"What's the matter?"

"Nothing."

"You're not listening to me."

"Sure I am."

"I'm cold!" Mrs. Gatenby said more or less to Velvet Bews, wheeling her past them.

"Why don't you straighten her up!" he said.

"She'd just slip over sideways again." Velvet pulled the wheelchair back and to one side of the French doors. "Afternoon, Dr. Arrowsmith."

"And how are we today?" the doctor said as he crossed the room.

"Annie—this is Dr. Arrowsmith. Dr. Arrowsmith, this is my daughter, Annie."

"How do you do." He said it with even formality that belonged to his round and intent eyes under an arc of very flat, black hair. The formality did not go with the plump, boyish cheeks or the genoa jib ears. Colin had seen Dr. Arrowsmith for the first time from below, ten days after surgery and intensive care, the young, ventriloquist's-dummy face tilting down upon him. There had been instant distaste for this boy stranger, who without his consent had surgical knowledge of him. Then and now Dr. Arrowsmith's face was serious but not really solicitous.

"And how are we today?"

"I am Dr. Arrowsmith's first truly grisly case," Colin said to Annie. The doctor took up his right hand and considered the palm. He turned it over. "And we are the shits today."

The doctor lowered the hand to the chesterfield arm. He released it. "Still some discomfort in the neck . . . shoulder . . . the elbow . . . the right hip?"

"Just when I'm in pain."

"Dizziness . . . giddiness?"

"If I sit up or get up too quickly. And during your visits, of course."

"I've asked you to do it in stages." He turned to Annie. "I wonder if I could have a moment with your father, Miss Dobbs. If you could wait out in the reception area. You can come back in when we're done."

When Annie had left he said, "I want a little more co-operation from you. In particular, I don't want you to overdo it."

"Why don't you tell that to Miss Nelson?"

"We must not try to run before we have learned to walk."

"How about intercourse?"

The doctor squatted before the coffee table.

"An interesting thing happened to my penis on its way to the bathroom yesterday morning."

"Let's have that right foot."

"I feel I should let you know about it so that you can assess its neural significance."

The doctor picked up the right foot by the heel and lifted it to the coffee table.

"First time in over three months—not even a wet dream, then bang: hard on."

The doctor dropped the slipper, began to remove the sock.

"A real rock-dandy."

The doctor picked a pin out of the lapel of his jacket.

"Might even call it a resurrection of an erection."

"You haven't felt anything yet?"

"No. Nor have I had a response from you in regard to the fact that—hey!"

"Oh—you did feel that one, Dr. Dobbs?"

"Goddam right I did!"

"Until we finish I want you to speak only whenever you feel the pin prick."

"Ah—you're interested only in the *pin* prick."

"That's right."

Colin stared down at the pale hair-part. "Yes."

"Are you sure?"

"Maybe not."

"Please do not look, Dr. Dobbs."

He closed his eyes.

After a moment: "Yes."

A longer moment: "Yes."

Many moments: "You through?"

"I will tell you when I am."

"Thanks."

The doctor stood up. He replaced the pin in his lapel. "Still numbness. Tomorrow some tests."

"CAT scam again?"

"Scan. Possibly." He picked the slipper up from the floor.

"I can put on my own sock and slipper while you get my daughter back in here."

The doctor returned with Annie. "Even though you have difficulty accepting it, I've been telling your daughter, you are doing—not too badly. A little more co-operation and you could be doing quite nicely."

The end-of-visiting bell began to ring.

"Your father is a very lucky man, Miss Dobbs. Don't worry about that bell. I seem to have broken off a large part of your visit time."

When the doctor had left them, Annie said. "You could have been nicer to him."

He managed to stop himself before he said, "Not easily." There was really no point beyond self-indulgence in explaining to her that Dr. Arrowsmith was a real "discomfort" in the ass, without a mote of a sense of humour. He had diagnosed this severe malnutrition of wit very early in their association; it was most evident whenever Arrowsmith trailed three to seven interns behind himself and into the room to conduct half-hour

seminars in which he would use Colin for illustration,
just as though he'd forgotten his goddam projector and
slides.

"He seems like a nice man."

"It's an illusion."

"I hope you stopped being rude to him after I
left . . . ."

"I did a lot better after you left."

"I'm glad to hear that."

"I *really* let him have it."

"Oh, Poppa—"

"Punctured his pompous balloon with my erection!"

"Whaaat!"

"First time in three months, so I told the prudish
bugger all about—"

"All right, Poppa!"

"—stabbed me with his pin. I don't think it was in
anger so much as jealousy—"

"He's trying to *help* you! Wouldn't it make sense
for you to make an effort to help *him*—help you? What
have you got against him!"

"He has no sense of humour."

"Oh."

"Into the bargain—he lacks irreverence."

"That's what I've always liked about you, Poppa—
first things first."

"Humour is a serious matter."

"Yeah. Probably what broke up your marriage."

"That wasn't nice, Annie."

"I'm sorry." He could tell she meant it. But he had
meant it too. Just how creative a diagnostician could
the man be without the leaven of humour? It was so
annoying to have made again and again the unselfish
effort to be funny for him, only to be met with those
wide, boarding-school eyes, empty of appreciation or
even comprehension.

"No wrath like that of a comic scorned," Annie said.

"That's right." Arrowsmith was literal-minded as a
born-again Christian. Therefore dangerous. No. Not
true. Not true at all, for neural surgeons and other
practised performers, high-wire or trapeze, could not
handicap themselves with distracting humour; devout
concentration was essential to the next step, the next

swing-and-catch, the next nerve thread, or they would miss! No life net! And in Arrowsmith's act it was always the patient who fell to earth.

Once he had discovered that Arrowsmith was not only incapable of appreciating humour, but was in fact annoyed by it, the urge to abrade him became irresistible. He punished the doctor with slapstick, then with vulgar, with black, with dry, with ironic and sardonic, only to achieve the final corruption of raw sarcasm.

"So do you think you might co-operate with him a little bit more?"

"Mmmh. You get that job at the Acropolis?"

"Parthenon. They said yes. I said no."

"Why?"

She had got up from the chesterfield and stood before him. "Waitresses were not expected to be Athenian in dress style. I was wondering about—"

"I don't get it."

"Cretan."

"Oh."

Slowly and deliberately she turned with her arm extended and her finger pointing. "Who vandalized these walls?"

"Ah—you don't appreciate our paintings."

"They ever catch the person who did it?"

"They're pretty sure it was an inside job. A doctor. He donates all his Sunday paintings to the hospital."

"And to hell with his Hippocratic oath." She grimaced. "How could anyone get well in here."

"I have often asked myself that very same question, Annie."

"What chance of recovery can there be for a bunch of poor, trapped, sick patients forced to look every day at a bunch of sick paintings!" She began to turn again. "It's hard to decide which one of them is"—she stopped in mid-turn to face the patient in short hospital gown and slippers—". . . the most offensive."

"Mr. Muhlbiere just materializes from time to time, Annie. I'd like you to meet my daughter, Louis."

Mr. Muhlbiere licked his lips, his charcoal eyes fixed on Annie.

"He can vanish just as well."

Annie continued to look at the chalk face under the dead dandelion of white hair.

"He likes me, I think. Louis is—was—a cellist. Once. A very fine one. Concert professional. Have you a cigarette?"

"What?"

"Have you cigarettes with you?"

"Oh yes."

"Would you get them out?"

"Since when did you take up smoking?"

"I haven't, but Louis depends on me for one—every day, about this time of day. Just before supper. I generally carry a pack and lighter with me so I can give him one but today I forgot them—in my room."

She had already picked up her purse from the chesterfield. She took out a package.

"Put one in your own mouth and light it. Then put it into his for him."

Mr. Muhlbiere's tragic eyes were drawn to the lighter flame and his slippers hissed as he shuffled a few steps closer with his face tilted up and his mouth open. "Go ahead. Put it in for him."

She took out the cigarette, reversed it and pushed it towards Mr. Muhlbiere's asking mouth. His lips closed over most of the cork filter end. "Can he handle it all right from here on?"

"Yes."

"But he doesn't seem to have the use of his hands—arms."

"If I don't do it for him, Velvet Bews does. She's the singing nurse, who wheeled Mrs. Gatenby out of here. I think Louis likes her a little more than he does me. For Velvet he even moves an arm if she turns away from him."

"Why would that make him—"

"He likes to give her ass a pat."

"Oh!" Annie's voice was deep with compassion.

"Actually," Colin said, "she turns her back to him almost every time she lights him one of her cigarettes."

"How nice for both of them."

"Miss Bews has a pretty nice ass."

"I think all of Miss Bews must be pretty nice."

"I agree."

"What's he—Louis—"

"I owe her. Especially after yesterday morning."

"Mmmh?"

"The remarkable . . . ah . . . revitalization of . . . of my sexual—"

"Tell it to her—not me, God damn it!"

Now, in the still sun-room Mr. Muhlbiere's head and shoulders were wreathed in blue smoke, the end of the cigarette a half-inch of pulsing glow-worm.

"Poppa, what's he suffering—"

"Alzheimer's disease."

"And what is Alz—oh, God, it isn't right to talk in front of—"

"Don't worry. Louis's main tube is badly scrambled. Alzheimer's causes a sort of premature senility. Louis is only forty-three, Annie."

"Oh, no, Poppa!"

"Take the cigarette out for him before he burns himself."

She plucked it from his mouth and as she pulled it away, his head followed.

"In the planter. All right, Louis, I'd like to visit with my daughter now."

Mr. Muhlbiere was watching Annie push the cigarette butt into the earth at the base of the Chinese jade plant.

"I think Miss Bews might be waiting for you out at the reception centre now."

For the first time there was a ghost of change in the aged face.

"I won't tell her you had your cigarette for today."

Mr. Muhlbiere turned and whispered from the sun-room.

"Oh, Poppa, those eyes!" She came round the end of the chesterfield. "Like he'd lost his crown of thorns!"

"This is a very sad place, Annie."

"And you've had three months of it."

"Most of them fully conscious."

"When do you think they'll . . . release—"

"Laughing Boy says a few weeks more. Maybe. I guess it depends on whether he thinks I've stopped running before I can walk—how much discomfort I'm

feeling—whether these paintings give my ass the heartburn. Hey—you started to ask me something about
them, just before Louis."

"Oh—yeah." She turned away, then back to him.
"Three months you've been in here, so you've had
plenty of time to decide."

"Decide what?"

"Which one on the wall—is your favourite of them
all?"

"You're the painter. You tell me."

"Want a crit, eh. Weelll—it's hard to say, though
I'd rule that one out right away."

He looked to the painting she was pointing out,
just left of the French doors.

"Why?"

"Hectic-eclectic."

"Ah—they taught you big, dirty words like that at
Stanford, did they?"

"Yep. Only one possible title for that work: *Nude
Kidney Descending the Stairs.*"

"Not bad. Now—the second from the right of the
doors?"

Cupping an elbow, she raised a finger to her chin,
leaned slightly back for a few contemplative moments.
"You still go for the Romantic school, don't you? Me—I
never could take vaguely Venetian. *Sunset Over the Is-
lets of Langerhans.*"

"Still a lot better than that one: *Still Life with Enema
Can—*"

"*—Tubing and Catheter.*" She turned back to him
and looked up. "And the winner is . . ." She swept her
arm grandly aloft and pointed above his head.

"Stunned me! Every time I've come into this sun-
room!" Oh, God! This was like their old and silly game!

"Quite painterly indeed," she said.

The same sort of pretend game they had played
together when she was little. I am Wendy, sir, and I
am your waitress. Let me take your order, sir. Windy?
No, *Wendy*, you dummy!

"Undeniably Les Fauves. Here."

He could clearly hear her child voice. We're all out
of eggs and the Red River Cereal is yucky today.

"A little disturbed perhaps."

Windy Wendy, the yappy waitress! She was making the magic teacup and laughter game happen for them all over again!

"*Explosion in the Blood Donor Clinic*. Quite rich. I would place this winning painting in the artist's bloody period."

Now and then were instantly joined for him as her deep delight laugh went off like firecrackers. "Poppa, you said a doctor did them. It wasn't a *woman* doctor, was it?"

"We mustn't be vulgar, Wendy."

"You all right, Poppa?"

"Yes." He got it out with difficulty, for now his throat was disobedient.

She bent over him. "Oh, Poppa!"

"It's—all right. Had a little trouble—with . . ." He laid his head back. He closed his eyes. ". . . My . . . ahhh, my . . . emotional control—ever since . . . since . . ." From the bad eye first, and then from the other, the first ones were born, then began to slide down his cheeks. And the neck brace would not let him lower his head!

As he felt her arm circle his shoulder, his throat closed off for good.

"Here, Poppa."

"Aaaaaw . . . uh . . . aw," now his voice was shuddering. He clamped his teeth. "Shuh—sheee—yit!"

"That's better." Her arm tightened. "Nothing like that good old useful word, eh, Poppa?"

"Quit it and give me another Kleenex!"

When he had finished blotting, she said, "Think you can take many more weeks here?"

"I don't know."

"What are we going to do about it, then?"

"I don't know."

"Let's give it a little thought, shall we?"

He sighed.

"In a few weeks—"

"I don't trust him."

"Dr. Arrowsmith?"

"People without a sense of humour generally lie a lot. Probably more like months."

"Maybe it wouldn't have to be. What if—think you could manage, if you got out of here?"

"I don't know."

"Couldn't really be much worse, could it?"

"I don't think I have any choice."

"Or want to have." She got up without warning.

"God Almighty!"

"Oh! Did I—sorry—sorry, Poppa! Did I hurt—"

"You could not—have hurt me—"

"I'm sorry!"

"—more expertly if you'd trained in graduate physiotherapy at Stanford!"

"I said I was sorry." She waited. "Still hurting?"

"Yes."

She picked up her purse, slid her arm under the strap.

"You leaving?"

"Only if you want me to." She looked down to him for a moment. "Do you?"

"No."

"That's nice." She walked over to the entrance. "I think—the sooner you get out of here, the quicker you're going to get better."

"That's hardly a professional opinion."

She didn't seem to have anything to add to that as she looked closely at one of the paintings. She moved over to examine another of them. "He doesn't seem to have signed them, though there is something in the lower right-hand corner. Like a logo."

"It's a brand."

"Huh!"

"The artist who did all those was ranch-raised. He's branded each of them."

"Kind of. Looks like an arrow . . . and a duck, the outline of one . . . or a goose.

"It's an anvil."

"You're right." She walked back to him. "What do you think?"

"About the paint—"

"About you. Could you leave here? If there were somebody to—with you?"

"I don't know."

"I think that's the third time you've said that."

"It's up to them, isn't it? Mainly Arrowsmith. I have to have therapy every morning . . . traction . . . ultrasound . . . the pool."

"Are there out-patients who come in to get that?"

"Sure."

"All right then. If you had a way—worked it out with someone to drive you out here every morning and take you back? Why not? Until you could do it yourself. You'd be a lot happier, Poppa."

"I'm not arguing with you."

"Then why don't you find out?"

"I don't think it's all that simple, Annie. I'd pretty nearly have to have someone living in with me. Full-time."

"Now—why didn't I think of that?"

"And where would I find—who would—"

"Me."

"Oh—Annie!"

"Why the hell do you think I came back here? As soon as I heard. I love you, Poppa! I want to help you!"

His throat was acting up again.

"Talk to him tomorrow." She waited. "Will you?" She waited again. "If you cry again I'll bust your jaw."

"I won't. You won't have to."

"Well?"

"I will."

"Probably turn out to be hell for both of us, won't it."

"Your mother would agree."

"What's she got to do with it?"

"She once told me—we deserved each other."

"She could be right. I think I'd better go now—way past visiting hours." She pointed towards the opposite wall. "I got it, you know."

"I thought you would."

"Clever of him. The arrow and the anvil." She walked towards the door. "You'll talk with him tomorrow? Promise."

"I promise."

"Supper time," sang Velvet Bews from the doorway. "How do you want it, Professor?"

"Don't you answer that question," warned Annie as she went through the French doors.

"Let's just do it right here in the sun-room tonight, Miss Bews."

"Oh—you're crying, Professor Dobbs!"

"I'm sorry—I juh-just can't help it!"

"Poor Professor Dobbs!"

"Every time—sex—ual harrah—harassment drives me to tears!"

# CHAPTER 4

He had kept his promise to Annie. The tests and CAT scan results had been reassuring, Arrowsmith told him, and if Colin had someone to look after him at home, to drive him daily to and from the hospital for therapy and observation, there was good reason to be optimistic about early release. Exactly when would this parole be granted, Colin had asked. In possibly a week's time, the doctor had promised him.

"Do you actually mean that? Just one more week?"

"Unless some unexpected complication should turn up, of course."

"Of course. And is it likely to?"

"I'll know that better by the end of the week. These things aren't open-and-shut simple."

"Not with you. Do you expect some . . . unexpected complication that is not open-and-shut simple to turn up?"

"Just possibly. We'll have to wait and see what transpires."

"I *am* in quite a sweat to get out of here."

"We're both anxious for that."

"Could you give me the just-possibly odds—on this unexpected complication transpiration?"

"Let's just see. I assure you we both want the same thing. We can always use another bed here and we will do everything possible so that you can become an out-patient. After that you will come in daily. I will be checking you regularly. One thing—that neck brace can come off now."

For once he'd kept his word. The brace had been replaced that afternoon with a much less restrictive collar from which, if he were careful, he could take brief holidays. It was so much easier not having to shave through a metal crate. Also taking an accurate leak was simple now.

"I'll miss you, Professor."

"And I'm going to miss you too, Velvet."

"It's been nice having you for my patient."

"Well—it's been nice having you for my nurse. You've done a lot for me. More than I can possibly— tell you about."

"Like they say in the insurance commercial—you'll be in good hands now."

"Huh?"

"Your daughter's."

"Yes."

"I had a talk with her. Matter of fact I had a couple of talks with her."

"Did you."

"Mainly about you. Long ones."

"Then that must explain why my ears were burning."

"We pretty well see eye to eye about you."

"Uh-huh. Looks like I've got two daughters now, doesn't it?"

"Just you remember what I told you about what that bear did to your cheek."

"I will."

"And your eye. I really meant what I said."

"I believe you did, Velvet."

"And I'm going to miss you. A lot. Both of you."

"Both?"

"Louis died last night."

"Oh—I—I didn't know that."

"They don't generally broadcast that kind of thing around here." She turned to the young man in white

who had come into the room. "He's ready. This is
Warren, Professor. He'll be taking you and your stuff.
She's down there waiting for you."

"Thanks for everything, Velvet."

"Don't get me wrong, Professor. You still got only
the *one* daughter."


At some time while he'd been in the hospital, stair rails
and banisters had been invented; certainly he had not
been so aware of them before. From now on, going up
or going down, it would have to be grab and slide and
grab and slide again. Not too bad going up, but going
down was dangerous, especially the stairs to the basement. He could find no sensible reason to justify at-
tempting them at all, just that he wanted to.

He didn't care to ask Annie to help him down, and
she certainly wouldn't approve of his trying to make it
on his own. He could tell her the basement den was *his*
part of the house and had been ever since he had firred
and panelled the outside walls, framed the partition,
hung up the ceiling squares, put in the fluorescent
lights, and laid the green indoor-outdoor carpeting over
the concrete floor. She knew all that. No point in men-
tioning the matter at all.

He put off his descent for a week, then waited
until she had come downstairs in her buckskin blouse,
kerchief, fringed cowgirl skirt and riding boots, to leave
for her evening shift at the Saddle and Sirloin.

As soon as he opened the basement door and
looked down, he knew that he had made a foolish
decision. The stairs were narrower and they were steeper
and they were darker than he'd remembered them to
be. He flipped up the light switch. Damn it all! He was
certain he'd screwed in a new one just before the reading break and now—dead bulb! General Electric Alzheimer's! No way!

Half-way back to the kitchen he changed his mind;
if he were to hold both rails, he might be able to lower
himself to half-mast on the landing, then try going
down stair by stair in the sitting position.

He hung the cane on the doorknob. He grabbed

the rails. He concentrated. He tightened his grip. He concentrated harder. He sat.

It turned out to be a lot easier than he'd thought it would be. He rested for a moment on the next-to-last step; first time he'd known there were sixteen of them. Oh, shit! Very smart of you, Dobbs, leaving your cane up there! Without it, you cannot take one step through this shadowed basement. So just what the hell do you plan to do now! Boost yourself all the way up those sixteen steps?

No. Get yourself up and onto your feet. Grab both rails. Go up. Get the goddam cane. *Then* hiccup your ass back down the stairs again. No great matter at all. Just a physiotherapy bonus for today; thirty-two extra sit-ups. Irma the Great would approve of that! Gold star!

Once he'd waited long enough for his eyes to become used to the basement dusk, it was not difficult to find his careful way round the hot-water heater and the furnace, past the washer and the drier, then over to the den. He turned on the switch by the door and stepped inside. He leaned on the cane to take some weight off the hip, and looked to the end of the room where the desk stood under the foundation window.

Now he was home!

Sarah had found it in an East End second-hand store and given it to him for his twenty-second birthday present. Made of heartwood walnut, eleven feet long and four feet wide, it had hogged a third of the space in the living room area of their basement suite during his M.A. year. Except for his first pair of tube skates or his sixteen-inch red CCM bicycle, it was probably the most delighting gift he had ever received. More than a hundred years ago some Victorian bookkeeper must have stooped over the slope top to do his ledger entries, probably with braces broad as britching strap over his hunched shoulders. He'd have a high celluloid collar and black cloth arm-cuffs, as he dipped his nib again and again into a squat ink bottle on the level section that ran along the back under the spindled shelves for bills and receipts.

After removing the rack, he had sawed eight inches off the legs, stripped and sanded the whole thing,

filled with shellac and refinished with four coats of
rubbing varnish. It had taken two months of his evening spare time, but he had finished it before Sarah
would abort from methyl alcohol and varnish fumes.
Late that winter Annie had been born too.

The slope of the top was gentle as that of the
elementary school desk of his childhood, so that papers
would not slide off; the tilt it gave to his typewriter put
the sheet in the roller at a good reading angle. On this
desk he had finished his M.A. dissertation: "John Steinbeck's Use of Prophecy"; here he had prepared lectures, lesson plans, and conference papers; here he had
written eleven successful short stories and one third of
a novel that was to have been as great as *Of Mice and
Men*.

Here he had tied flies and loaded shells.

In here during the last two years of the marriage,
he had slept on the hide-a-bed plaid couch against the
wall.

He looked down at the fly-tying vise clamped to
the left-hand corner of the desk, the silver tube slanting
up like a miniature telescope. At the beginning of Reading Break he had tied up some flies, after he'd got his
gear together, taken the Weatherby magnum down
from the gun rack over the couch, and buckled it into
its case. That had been the night before he drove down
to Shelby to meet Archie. Even now, months later, the
vise held a fly between its jaws.

It was an Invincible, with its fat body clipped into
bug shape from tufts of brittle buck tail he'd wound
around the hook shank. Rayed with Plymouth Rock
hackle, holding white goose-feather tips upright for
wings, it was a beautiful floater on the angriest water.
A length of black nylon thread with a spring clothes-
pin hung from the eye end of the hook. Still! That night
four months ago, he had not whipped the fly or touched
its head with an enamel drop to finish it off. Now it
was as though the vise pinched four months in its
mouth, reminding him once more of the dreadful ellip-
sis that the grizzly sow had torn in his life.

With a fingertip he set the clothes-pin swinging.
He turned the swivel chair to face himself and sat
down in it. Whenever he had been blocked in his

writing, he had so often found escape in tying flies. It seemed to anaesthetize failure pain for him. As loose feathers stirred and lifted and drifted over the desk-top under his gentle breathing, and one by one the flies were freed from the vise to rest high upon their hackle tips, his tension would loosen more and more to release his mind and his imagination. In this basement cave he could forget that winter stunned outside. Down here sunlight disced and danced on water; river rings slowly widened and spread to grassy banks; foam and bubbles were borne circling by; grasshoppers leaped clicketing; mosquitoes whined; blue darning needles darted, held, and darted on again in their capricious flight.

How often down here he had broken off a warm and humming fragment of August for himself.

He'd had such great luck with Invincibles, especially on cutthroat; the fat body of hollow deer hair kept the fly afloat so much longer than other patterns could. Dries had always been his favourite. Annie showed no preference; wet or dry made no difference to her. Pragmatic Annie. Platonic poppa. No doubt about it, he had once told himself, Plato would have been a dry-fly man; his patterns would be floaters with feather filament so spirit light they could lift and carry the heavy dross of the material hook, ideal camouflage fanning from the barbed and lethal matter. No specifics for that Greek purist, just the simple and wingless bi-visibles likely, drifting over slicks and riffles where universal truth might lie.

Yet, at twelve she'd come up with her own fur abstracts, the Annie patterns. Annie, the unpredictable! Annie, the contradictory; Annie, his child, who wondered so often. They'd spent a lot of time together here, he at his typewriter and she with her crayons, on her stomach in the centre of the carpet, going through his bond paper like a hungry young beaver through cottonwood chips.

He tipped back the chair and looked up at the drawing to the left of the window. She had graduated from pencil and crayons to charcoal when she had done that one. Ten? Eleven. He had used a new nickname for her carelessly, and she had been so upset and he had been so sorry and said it was untrue and intended to be loving anyway, and that her nose was the best part of her face. To prove it, he had taken the Edith Sitwell anthology down from the shelf.

"See, darling? It's what they call a Plantagenet nose. It's a *royal* nose."

"She's got a beak like a fish-hawk!"

He had gone back to the bookcase again, for Virginia Woolf and finally for Leonardo da Vinci. "Look, sweetheart, people with big—bigger—noses are smart people. There is a definite co-relationship between the size of the nose and the size of the temporal lobes."

She had believed him, but a week later she had asked him if he thought she had a weak chin.

"No. Not at all."

"Then why does it seem that way to me?"

"I don't know. Like everything else, the size and shape of a person's chin is relative. Sure—there are chinless people and also there are lantern-jawed people. You are not either one of those—"

"Yeah, but when I look in the—"

"All right. You have got a big chin. Your chin is bigger than Dick Tracy's chin. Look, sweetheart, the size of your chin or your jaw or your nose doesn't mean a goddam thing anyway!"

She glanced down.

"What did you say?"

"What about boobs?"

"For God's sake, Annie, let's talk about something else!"

"I got a better idea."

"Yes?"

"Let's not talk at all!"

Two weeks later, for his birthday present, she had given him the large charcoal drawing of the moose's head. Whether that meant she had forgiven him for calling her "Moose Nose," he was not sure. But he did know that with her black hair and eyes and cream skin she had turned out Modigliani-beautiful.

The unfinished fly disturbed him now. He pulled out the shallow desk drawer; he reached inside for the fly-head enamel and the nail scissors. He whipped the eye end, did three half hitches on it, touched it with enamel, snipped the thread, then unscrewed the vise till the fly dropped free into his palm. He tossed it onto the desk-top.

How long had it taken him to know that he could cast and cast again, but no keepers would rise to his hook? How many thematic and narrative and character backlashes had he failed to pick free? How ironic it was that he had gone right on telling his creative-writing classes that they must course the stream every day, every week, every month, so that they would be there to take their limit if a caddis or a mayfly hatch happened.

With all the Christmas yearning of his childhood he had yearned for that second sabbatical. That would be a clear, pure year, when he would do the novel he had hoped to write if he could only find the untripped time to write. No more polished shards of short stories. *Jude the Obscure* and *Heart of Darkness* time! *Moby Dick* and *Huckleberry Finn*, here I come!

Every day, up and over the top to meet the foe! Obey without question that inner officer with the revolver in his hand! Face that typewriter again and again and again and again!

Painting the outside of the house had taken the last two weeks of May. He had used the first five days of June to do the living room and the kitchen and the downstairs hallway. By the first of July he had finished the rock garden and the lily pond behind the sun-porch.

That year, for the first time ever, he had almost enjoyed making out his income-tax returns. He had taught Annie to fly-cast. By Christmas time he had come to realize that he had been poorly trained for literary combat. His stored past was not unique; his life had not been exotic or dramatic, had not blessed him with hazards of love or passions of war. What stupid, amateur, arrogant ignorance had ever sucked him into thinking that any stranger would give away one moment of his life to read what Colin Dobbs had written!

He had come to accept that though he wanted to play the concert grand, about all he could master was the mouth organ. He had tied many fine flies that year. He had given up trying to saw the lady in half when he realized he couldn't even palm a quarter. He had shown the white feather. Finally.

Some day he might even swear off metaphor.

He got up and pulled out the top drawer of the filing cabinet. Something simple. Maribou streamer would do. The Black Leech pattern worked great on the big browns.

He had no trouble with the chenille, but he barely managed to spiral the rib tinsel, and when he tried to clip quill from the maribou, his right thumb began to twitch. Then the whole hand cramped. He freed the nail scissors and fired them across the room.

He leaned back in the chair and looked over to the gun rack above the couch. Even at this distance the claw marks she had gouged in the stock showed clearly. Goddam bear! Why was he compelled to carry blame back to her again and again and again? Childish! Like kicking the chair that barked your shin or stubbed a bare toe. Yet he did, with every twinge, every spasm, every arc of pain. And now the scarred rifle tolled him back. Four months. Didn't seem that long ago since he'd taken it down from the cloven elk feet.


He'd left the city outskirts about midnight, driven south the thirty-nine miles to Shelby, where Archie had waited for him in the Gateway Hotel lobby, and transferred his gear to the back of the agency jeep. A brief stop at Archie's cabin for bacon and eggs and coffee, then past Pile of Rocks, west on the Spray Road to Storm Creek Bridge, and south on the bull camp road till Archie stopped the four-wheel and they got out and took the forestry trail on foot. By then it was almost daybreak.

Archie led the way. He stopped only when Colin had to ask him to, several times during the earlier part of the trail, which was always up and often quite steep. Although Archie had said it was about a mile to the dead horse and Daisy Creek valley, it had seemed like five. A short while after the trail relented and started down, Archie stopped.

"How much furth—"

Archie shook his head, put a finger on his mouth, pointed down.

There was enough light now to see the tracks.

Heel to toe, he could have got both his own into one of them.

"All right to whisper?" he whispered.

"That's all."

"Is it up ahead of—"

"Hey-uh." Archie shook his head. "Old shit—old tracks."

Even before they had reached the hide, he heard clear high hoots, the almost school-yard sound of ravens.

"Bear's been comin' to it couple days now. Maybe."

They lay side by side in their snow nest, looking down the slope through a screen of leafless buck brush and spruce boughs Archie had set up between them and the horse. He had never before seen so many ravens at one time; they came and they landed on the carcass, speared beaks in meat, jerked free, and carried off across the broad valley and into the bush on the far side.

"What do you think, Archie?"

"It's comin'. Sight on the horse bait. Wait till I say. Smart to shut up now. Complete."

He and Archie must have caught first sight of her at the same moment, for as he saw her emerge from jack pine on the far side and well up the valley, he heard a sudden release of breath beside himself, then an exclamation. In Stony. The ravens had been startled too; it was as though the dead horse had tossed all of the birds into the air to hang briefly in shrill chaos, then to unravel up the valley towards the bear. As they swooped round her, she lifted to her hind feet, turning in a slow pirouette that followed their circling. She dropped to all fours and moved in casual slow motion, further out into the open, the ravens harassing her all the way. She rose again to bat at the flutter wreath as though annoyed by blackflies.

She dropped and began a leisurely and shouldering saunter further out. Now her hump had declared itself. My God, she was big! She stopped and came up again into the grossly human posture, snout high and turning now to one side, now to the other.

"Smellin'!"

The air was still, so it was impossible to tell, but surely Archie would have made certain they were downwind and safe from scenting. Just how far from them was that horse? A fifth of a city block? Two hundred yards? A hundred? The width of an avenue? He was surprised that he was not more scared. It was as though until this moment she had been a zoo bear, resigned to being watched through bars, fed and cared for by keepers in cage space, all she had ever known from birth or capture as a cub. She was in no hurry to get to that horse. Nothing could frighten with a paunch like that, those short hind legs, those forelegs like human arms hanging loosely before her, miming helpless and headback laughter at something unbelievably funny. Ursus ridiculus.

In a fraction of a second she was no longer that. She was catapulted with such swiftness an eye blink would have lost her. The ravens did. She zigged; she zagged instant and unpredictable as lightning flash all the way down the valley and to the horse. *Now* he was scared! Considerably!

He felt Archie's hand squeeze on his right arm, turned his head. Slowly Archie lifted a finger, looked towards the bear below, then to the Weatherby magnum. The sign meant wait. But for what?

He meant, Get her in the scope! Of course!

Circled horse guts jumped out to him, a hoof, then a resting head with an empty eye socket.

"Cougar goes for the belly first," Archie had told him. "Coyote for the asshole. Ravens and crows an' magpies—the eyes."

Now he had her. "Heart's no good," Archie had explained. "Just the brain."

He'd lost her. He looked over the scope. She had moved to their side of the grey and red cadaver now. He could clearly hear her now, grunting and whooshing over it. She rose to her hind feet again, her back to them, her head turned over her left shoulder, her arms down in front of herself—fur giant at a urinal. She lowered herself half-way. The great rump worked and strained and very slowly she came full upright once more. Garland entrails hung from the entire horse she had lifted and now held cradled in her arms.

Eye to the scope, he moved the circle up.

"Now!"

He had the back of her head in the cross-hairs as he began the slow trigger squeeze. And now he was scared! Shitless!

Years ago Archie had given him those elk hoofs for the gun rack, already kinked and tied with sinew so that rigor mortis would freeze them at right angles.

"For the fishin' rod—rifle—handy on the wall."

He had shellacked the cloven hoofs till their licorice gleam was like oriental lacquer. He had tapped in dowelling and hung them on Sarah's line over the laundry tubs. She had objected, but he had argued that since the invention of the automatic drier, the days of clothes-lines, in or out of a house, were over. Not for her; she still needed it for small loads. They smelled, she said, disgustingly. She'd had to wash her hair after she had run her head into them when she reached for the light cord. He had admitted they were faintly rancid, then had removed the dowels, taken a screwdriver to the marrow high up in bone hollow, and filled them with concentrated bleach. Sarah did not care to verify that it had worked.

"Just keep them in your den!"

They'd been so right for the Weatherby magnum and for the graphite rod he'd bound and for the Parker-Hale double-barrel. Now he would have to get the rifle to a gunsmith, and it was going to be more than a fill and finish needed on the rosewood inlay, the cheek piece. Those claw marks. Archie had said something about the scope, too. No hurry. Ever. Probably. Now.

All the same, he'd got *her*. And she was magnificent! That explained Archie's exclamation when she had come out of the jack pine on the other side. During one of Archie's visits to the hospital, he had asked him what it was he'd said in Stony then. It had been easy to see that Archie hadn't cared to translate, had become noticeably more uncomfortable under further questioning, then had said he couldn't remember.

"Big, isn't she, Archie."

"Hey-up."

"How big?"

"Big."

"What did she measure?"

"I seen a few of them."

"How big?"

"I never seen one like that before."

"Length . . ."

"I never measured it out."

"How heavy do you think . . ."

"I didn't weight it neither."

"Couldn't you guess?"

"Hey-uh."

"Eight hundred?"

"Hey-uh." He shook his head again.

"Thousand?"

"Hey-uh."

"More! Twelve hundred!"

"Not so easy to guess the weight of it right. It was spring, you know. Been fall—maybe more than that. When I took it in for you, to tan for you and do the head the way you said you wanted, there was another fellow come in with a brown one."

"Uh-huh."

"'Merican. He said he come from Minneapolis for what he just brought in there. Maybe two year old. I guess they don't shoot many in Minneapolis."

"So?"

"In the back when we laid them out, they were together there. Out of the grizzly would make three of his brown one."

"God!"

"Four maybe."

"That big!"

"They let it come in here to visit you, Dobbs, and it stood up, it couldn't." He shook his head. "The colour of it isn't right."

"Huh!"

"Don't even look grizzly hair to me. The head on it is different-coloured from the rest of it."

"What colour!"

"Yellow. And the paws too."

"Yellow!"

"Hey-up."

"Well, what colour were the—"

"From the paws up—foot—foot an' a half—black.
That isn't all that was wrong with it."

"What else?"

"Claws on it. White ones. That bear wasn't local,
and that's the whole situation."

"But you said she was spring thin, didn't you?"

"Hey-up."

"So she couldn't have travelled very far. When
you gutted her, how was her stomach?"

"Squoze up." He had put his two fists together
and held them up. "About like that."

"Well, there you are."

"Hey-up."

"What the hell does that mean?"

"The bear come from somewhere else. I think."

"Other side of Devil's Thumb."

Archie shrugged.

"Western slope? Kootenays?"

"Hey-up."

"Yukon?"

"Hey-up."

"Alaska, for God's sake!"

"Hey-up. Somewhere else. For God's sake."

# CHAPTER 5

Annie had let him out at
the west entrance to Wapta Tower.

"Want me to come up with you, Poppa?"

"Uh-uh."

"I'll pick you up here at four-thirty."

"Fine."

"Sure you don't want me to—"

"I'll be all right."

"There's no rail to those steps."

He had dreaded coming out here for the first time

since Daisy Creek, his apprehension so intense it smelled of regression; he'd felt much like this when his mother had taken him to kindergarten and abandoned him there. Pretty unhealthy of him, to be remembering how Ray Beischal had sailed Clara Baker's tam over the fence at recess, how soft Miss Finlay's cheek had been the morning she had caught him chewing gum in class and he'd told her he'd forgotten to brush his teeth after breakfast and was chewing the Juicy Fruit on purpose to clean them. She had hugged him, and he knew she knew that was not the true reason he had been chewing a full package of Juicy Fruit gum. Her cheek had been so soft against his own, and the soap she used smelled so nice, and he had felt so dirty.

As soon as Annie had turned off Poundmaker Road and driven through the campus entrance there had been a feeling of sad *déjà vu*. Now a summer of dalliance must end. Repent! Prepare to meet thy Dean! With preparation and counselling, instruction and committee meetings, by working out schedules, ordering texts and supplies—prepare, in class and seminar and tutorial, to convert the young to the love of truth. Again.

"How did your summer go?"

"Grace and I have split."

"My, you've taken off weight."

"Jesus, she's put it on!"

"Enrolment's way up."

"How did your summer go?"

"I had measles."

"I learned to do the jack-knife."

"My gramma died."

"Enrolment's about the same as last year."

"How did your summer go?"

"Rotten! I didn't get tenure last spring!"

"I got a new baby sister."

"Enrolment's way down."

Because Livingstone University had not adopted the trimester system, its activity and metabolic rhythm resembled that of certain snails and crabs, torpid and dormant under the heat and dryness of summer. Except for the six weeks of summer school, this academic aestivation lasted from June convocation to September registration, administration brain centres kept alight mostly by secretaries. Each fall students wakened the university with their corpuscular flow across the campus from building to building, through halls, cafeterias, and common rooms, to offices, labs, and classrooms.

A dozen of them waited in front of the elevator now, but they were far too concerned with schedules and course selection to pay much attention to him, and the jammed cage gave him anonymity all the way to the fifth floor. He kept it as he walked down the hall between waiting students, who stood and leaned and sat on the floor with their knees up and their backs against the wall. At Herbie Stibbard's door a long queue began and continued to the English Department office, curving finally into the reception counter. He could see Bev bent over there.

"I have to take an English course," the young man was saying to her. "Without too much reading."

"Why is that?"

"I have four Chemistries—labs—I got no time. What course is 106?"

"Expository Writing. It's filled now." She looked up to the student and handed a paper to him. "Don't worry. They may add another section. You check back with me tomorrow and we'll work something out for you."

When you came right down to it, Bev was much more than the Chairman's secretary, she *was* the English Department, the caring and loving-hearted part of it. He moved on past the waiting students without her noticing him.

"532"

He hung the cane on his elbow and grabbed the knob while he reached for the keys in his jacket pocket.

"Dr. C. Dobbs
OFFICE HOURS
WINTER TERM 1983/84"

Which was incorrect, of course. Wrong term. Wrong year. It was now another Dr. C. Dobbs.

"Monday–Wednesday, 10:30–11:30
or by appointment"

He fitted the key into the slot.

SHAKESPEARE
IN
BRITIAN
July 9 to August 4, 1984

She'd screwed up that one for him. Wrong key.
While he played in a Comedy of Terrors, Herbie Stibbard
had taken over the shepherd role and gone to Stratford
in his place. Right key.

Turn it, Dobbs. Turn it! He released the knob and
let his hand drop to his side. Grab the knob again.
Unlock. Turn. Open.

All right now. Lift your left hand and close it on
the knob. That's all I want you to do. Just hold it there.
Now you can release it, drop your hand. Grab the knob
again. Hold. Turn. *Pull!*

Step inside.

Close the son-of-a-bitch! And lock it!

Good going, Dobbs! I told you that you could do
it, and if you pull out the bottom left-hand drawer
you'll find a box of Kleenex and you can wipe the
sweat off your hands and face. But first open that
window. It's been closed since April.

He leaned back in the chair behind his desk, looked
up to the opposite wall.

"LIFE AIN'T ART." Charlotte had made the ban-
ner for him three years ago, the white cut-out letters
stitched against red felt. Maybe she'd do another for
him: "IT'S JUST HELL!" If he had to see somebody
today he hoped it would be Charlotte or Herbie or
Alistair. Not Tait. Or Liz Skeffington—

There was a knock on his door.

"Come in!" Oh, hell! He'd locked it. "Just a minute!"

Let it be Charlotte or Alistair or Herbie. Please, not
Tait or Skeffington!

It was in fact a six-foot, thin, blond Iroquois! "I'm
looking for 352."

"This isn't it. Are you sure you're in the right
department—Native Studies?"

"Political Economy."

The high, curving roach of hair was bleached al-

most to white. He must have to shave both sides of his
skull daily. "You're two floors too high."

"Oh. What happened to your—"

"Adam Smith and John Stuart Mill are on the third
floor."

"How did you—"

"Fuck off, Hiawatha!"

Hobbling back to the desk chair, kindly Mr. Chips
thought testily to himself, "Caning's much too good for
cheeky Mohawk boys."

Bev had done a conscientious job of sending important mail on to him in the hospital and then to
the house, yet the stack to the left of his typewriter
must be a foot high. There'd be more in his mail
stall.

THE PRESIDENT AND CHANCELLOR
LIVINGSTONE UNIVERSITY
invite you to hear
SIR CÉCIL BROWN-WALTERS, F.R.S.
Scientist, speaking on
"SCIENCE AND THE CATEGORICAL IMPER-
ATIVE."
Tuesday, April 17, at 8:00 p.m.
Kathleen MacNair College
Reception following, Cougar Lounge.

Sorry, Sir Cecil, conflict with an earlier ursine imperative up Daisy Creek—waste-basket.

PRO AMORE MUSICAE SOCIETY
A RENAISSANCE CONCERT
Playing and singing English music of the seventeenth century . . . sacred and secular . . . recorder
and gamba . . . coffee, tea and fruit punch . . .

That too.

PAPERS AND CONFERENCES
. . . Dr. F. X. Kelly (Chemistry): "Synthetic Uses of
Indium (1) Halides." Annual Inorganic Conference,
Queen's University.

. . . Dr. Guy W. Fisher (Political Science): "Britain's Liberal-Social Democratic Alliance." Hollins College, Roanoke, Virginia.
. . . Dr. Peter Badger (Psychology): "Defining Fuzzy Systems for Different Periods of Life Span." Memorial University, Newfoundland.

Next one:

## GUIDELINES FOR GRADING WRITTEN ASSIGNMENTS

Teachers in the Department of English do not assign grades which are based on a predetermined pattern or "curve." Written assignments in the form of connected discourse (as opposed to factual answers on a quiz) are always graded in accordance with general criteria, which may be applied to the individual piece of work submitted.

What are being presented here, in fact, are "Guidelines": since it would be impossible to set forth standards which would be completely objective, comprehensive, and categorical. Not only are the elements of good writing many and complex, but the discourse of each student will have a personal style, which should be judged, in part at least, on its own merits. Indeed, each new assignment and each different course level may involve particular requirements and expectations, which should be judged accordingly.

On the reverse of this sheet, then, will be found a guide to the generally recognized characteristics which belong to work at each grade level, under headings which represent the four major components which form our judgments. . . .

By actual count, in six sentences there were seven of them; obviously the writer had fallen under the evil spell of the which witch. No, by God, eight! Simply had to be Tait's writing. Some day that Great Rhetorician in the Sky might forgive him his trespasses against clarity and grace.

He crumpled "Guidelines for Grading Written Assignments" and tossed it into the waste-basket, pulling over the next sheet in the pile.

LIVINGSTONE UNIVERSITY
*MEMORANDUM*
TO: All Expository Writing Instructors,
    Department of English.
Subject: Meetings re Expository Writing Program.
    Two meetings which have been scheduled for Wednesday, 5 September, are being held for discussion of this year's Expository Writing Program. The first of these meetings will be held at 11:00 a.m., the second of them at 5:00 p.m. Both of these meetings will be held in 510 Wapta Tower. Attend either session.
Agenda:
    (1) Beginning-of-Class Procedures
    (2) Registration and Class Lists
    (3) Discussion of Course Objectives
    (4) The Role of the Expository Writing Teacher

> Cameron A. Tait
> Acting Head
> Department of English

Shit!

They'd kept it from him! Deliberately! Herbie, Dr. Lyon, Alistair, Charlotte. Not one word about it in their hospital visits. The whole goddam English Department in a conspiracy of silence! Back in November he'd been nominated for Department Head and the selection committee had included him in their list to go to the council. He had himself nominated Herbie and Alistair. Who in hell could have nominated Tait! Who had let *him* onto the short list! Acting Head! Two years of Tait! When that grizzly sow had denied him the chairmanship, it was the least of what she'd done to him. To be replaced by Tait was the turn of the screw!

Herbie owed him an explanation! Somebody did! He got up, grabbed the cane, started for the door.

\*    \*    \*

The line of students had shrunk by almost half. As always, Herbie's door was ajar. He looked up from his desk. "Colin! Enter, pursued by a bear."

"Not funny!"

"Great to see you back! No." He pointed to the yellow upholstered chair. "Take the easy one."

"Not to get out of."

"How are you feeling?"

"Tait's our new Head!"

"*Acting* Head. A little brief authority."

"Not little and not brief enough! Two years! How the hell did it happen?"

"The usual machinery. Nomination . . . selection committee . . . council . . ."

"I assumed it would be you or Alistair."

"I had to decline it to finish solving the Hamlet riddle."

"Why not Alistair?"

"Didn't you hear? They picked him second; he accepted, but in July he found out he'd won the Edinburgh chair for this year. He floated in here and handed me the letter to read so I could tell him it was true. Faculty Association voted unanimously to give him a year's leave with two-thirds pay. Nice for Alistair, and for Livingstone."

"It is. But Tait! What about Primrose?"

"His sabbatical this year."

"Who nominated Tait?"

"Livingstone's antidote to desire."

"Liz!"

"Could have been worse."

"How!"

"*He'd* nominated *her*."

"She hasn't made Associate yet!"

"Just an unpleasant fantasy to ease the pain. Her promotion to Associate is imminent now."

"You're kidding."

"Could be the reason she nominated Tait. I think they came to an understanding, and he better not forget it. Something I'll never understand; as teachers and scholars we are in such good company every day—"

"Tait and Skeffington!"

"—the company of all the great minds and hearts of all literary time and of the entire world. More than anyone else we can share their distilled love and proper hates and angers. How is it so few of us stand on the shoulders of the giants?"

"Not so easy to climb up there."

"Not publication. I mean being accountable—decent."

"Aw . . . Herbie, you are—"

"I didn't level with you, Colin. The imaginary relish was sweet for me, too, and I didn't really want to turn it down. Once you were out of it, I knew it would be Alistair, so I took myself off the short list. Then Alistair got the Edinburgh chair, and I couldn't go back to them and tell them the reason I'd given for refusal was specious."

"I'm sorry."

"I was disappointed. Unselfishly. There were things I wanted to do for the Department. Sweat money out of the budget for a writer-in-residence. Set up that all-art-is-one-and-indivisible course you came up with two years ago."

"That was the first thing I wanted to do."

"You would have. I could have, too—persuaded Fine Arts to put down their flutes for a minute and get off their painted asses long enough to marry the music, writing, painting of each period—Chaucerian, Elizabethan, Restoration, Victorian . . . I came up with a great title for the calendar: Polygamy 322. Oh, Colin, fortune hath cruelly scratched us both. How are you feeling?"

"I'm not sure. Liz, eh?"

"Yes."

"And Tait'll make sure she's crowned Associate."

"It would have happened anyway."

"No, it wouldn't—"

"Yes. Her novel's been accepted."

"It hasn't!"

"Yes."

"Harlequin!"

"Doubleday."

"I don't believe—"

"Spring list."

"Shit!"

"I'm sure it is."

"Oh—I hope I don't run into her for—"

"She won't be back till next week. She's in New York."

"That's nice."

"With her publisher."

"Not so nice."

"Up to now she has shown us some mercy."

"I hadn't noticed. What mercy?"

"Quantitatively. Stuck pretty well to poetry in the past."

"But her poetry was prose—her right-hand margin locked way over to the left."

"Evidently it's come loose."

At least he wouldn't have to face Skeffington for a week. When he and Sarah had separated, Liz had been the first girl off the mark. It had taken him some time to realize that he was running into her much more frequently than he ever had before. Mornings when he checked into Bev's office for his mail, she was there. Whenever he went into the faculty room for lunch or coffee, she was in the faculty room for lunch or coffee. It had got to the point where he was apprehensive even about going to the can; once inside he was safe, but going and coming in the hall there was a lot of open ground to cover before reaching sanctuary. He had tried avoiding action; he did not go for his mail as soon as he got out in the morning; he moved his lunch hour from noon to one, then back to eleven, then ahead to one again.

It was easy to say this was ridiculous, because it was. He couldn't tell her to leave him alone, for all he really had to go on was circumstantial evidence, which she could easily deny, and he'd end up looking like a vain fool. He must wait until she did make a clear pass at him. Knowing that it was only a matter of time until she made her move did not help, for then he would end up a heartless son-of-a-bitch who had led her on only to humiliate her. A sex-linked dilemma usually reserved for women. Why the hell him!

After two celibate years he still ached for Sarah, and Liz was built almost as lovely as the woman who'd left him. Her skirts were tight; her buttocks were often denim intimate; her blouses were loose and open damn near to her belly button, so that it was all too evident that she wore no brassière. God, how he wished they'd never discovered the birth control pill!

He kept telling himself that some day he and Sarah might get back together again; he reminded himself that half of Skeffington's one-year instructor appointment was over and that her contract might not be renewed. That passionate hope died when it *was*. He enjoyed the summer respite from her, then braced himself against the opening of an ardent winter term. Her eyes bothered him most—or rather, as well. She had a heavy hand with shadow on the upper lids. Lime, as though severe verdigris had set in. For the entire winter term it seemed those eyes had never left him.

But in the fall he found he need not have worried after all, and everybody except the Dean's wife knew why. Phyllis should have asked some questions. Why had her husband suddenly let his hair grow long and started having it professionally styled? Why had he begun wearing young and sporty jackets, robin's-egg blue or canary or cherry slacks, white shoes, and a great deal of gold? Did decanal duties demand all those evenings away from home? Why had he suddenly become vegetarian? Liz was. Were avocados aphrodisiac? Or spinach? Carrot juice? Bean sprouts? Alfalfa? Did Professor Skeffington whinny when she came? Nobody ever bothered to ask the Dean.

The following spring the P and T Committee had given Liz Skeffington an assistant professor's contract and put her on tenure track. At the Dean's insistence. It had been a foolhardy affair for him; her promotion could be justified only as the result of screw-and-tell blackmail. With Liz you didn't ask what was in it for her, but who was in her for what. Soon after Liz had been made Assistant Professor, the Dean gave up being a vegetarian.

That same spring Colin had a return of an old

childhood allergy he thought he'd outgrown. It baffled both him and his doctor, for tests showed that he was not sensitive at all to the cat dandruff and tomatoes that had once caused him high nose-bridge tickle, stuffed nasal passages, eye itch, shortness of breath, and paroxysms of sneezing.

"It's definitely not a food allergy. Probably some spring pollen," Dr. Lehmann said. "I thought we might be on to something with female cottonwood. This is a bad year for it. But it isn't that. Are you—now—going through an unusually tense . . . emotional time?"

"Maybe."

"Your work."

"No."

"Mmmmh." He did not ask about another, the most obvious, possible cause of emotional tension. "Let's wait a few weeks—say, early June—see what happens. This is an antihistamine prescription, which should give you some symptomatic relief."

The little yellow pills had worked. By the end of the term he was no longer getting the prescription refilled. It must have been pollen of some sort. The doctor could be correct about emotional tension's being the villain, for there was no doubt that Sarah was softening. If he played it right, he might even be able to move back into the house with her and Annie, if only on platonic terms.

Why the hell had he done it! No use telling himself Liz had put a strong move on him this fall. Took two to do it, damn it! He'd been marking his mid-terms; in his office at night, rather than back at the bachelor apartment. She'd knocked on his door, and even before he opened it he'd known who it was. He could recognize that musk smell at twenty paces.

Did he by any chance have instant coffee in his office; there wasn't any in the faculty room. He had. He gave it to her. She was sorry to interrupt him at work, but it looked as though they were the only two people in the whole English Department who didn't have a good home to go to. Even when she'd left to make her coffee, the office held on to her wild scent. From now on he'd better correct at his apartment. He sneezed.

He had just got back to the papers when she returned with his jar of instant coffee and her cup of coffee, and a cup of coffee for him.

"I remembered you take it black. You getting a cold?"

"No." He sneezed again. "An old allergy."

When they had finished their coffee, she got up, and he thought she was headed for the door. He was wrong. She turned back upon him just as he came round the end of the desk to let her out. They collided front to front and stayed that way until he backed up. She stepped towards him, but he was now against the desk. He put his hands out behind himself for support. He sneezed. His hand swept the pile of mid-term papers off the corner of the desk, and they fanned out over the floor. She stepped back from him.

"Oh. I'm sorry!"

"It's all right." He got down on his hands and knees. She got down on her hands and knees to help. They were facing each other and when he sneezed this time, it startled her. One of her breasts—whether the left or the right one, he could not clearly remember—came out. All the way. Pink. His attention was no longer on the mid-terms and neither was hers, if it ever had been. He sneezed again and papers lifted and drifted over the floor. She had not replaced the breast.

"I want you!"

He sneezed again and evidently she took this for consent, for she rose, reached up under her skirt and came out with her pants, tossed them aside, and knelt to throw her arms around him. Her tongue entered his mouth, searched, came out, and took his in. For a moment he thought he might lose it. She fell back, pulling him down with her. He managed to get his tongue back.

"Got to lock the door!"

"I did!"

"Let me get my pants off!"

Though there had been very little foreplay, she was quite wet. With one eager and convulsive movement she took him all the way in. It had been such a long time!

He sneezed and then he sneezed again.

"Oh, God! Oh, God!"

This time he sneezed himself right out of her.

"No! No!"

He was having trouble finding his way back in there, but she grabbed him. She knew much better than he did where it should go.

He sneezed three times in quick succession.

"That's it! That's it! That's it!"

The next ones came in a cluster of five.

"You are *great!*"

She was too! With the next paroxysm he lost his place again. As he re-entered he felt her legs circle and lock in a scissor lock around his waist. With each sneeze they had moved in short spurts over their bed of mid-term papers until now her head was against the bottom drawer of the filing cabinet, "O to Z." This seemed to increase the thrust power of the sneezes, which now exploded in one long and unbroken chain. She screamed and went limp.

He had gone back to Dr. Lehmann and more patch tests.

"Aha! Plus four! Florentine Lily!"

"What!"

"Source of orris root, a sweet and aromatic ingredient used quite often in cosmetics—face powder, the oil for perfumes in hair shampoo. Charmella Belle Products are the worst offenders, but Lady Kitty's not far behind. Food and Drug Administration—Consumer Protection Branch—should have banned orris root years ago. Can you think of—have you been in close proximity with anyone who might be using—"

"Yes."

"Then you'd better let her know. Tell her to change her brand of face powder—"

"Perfume."

"Perfume. Simple as that."

Simpler.

"No, Liz, don't come any nearer. You've got to stay away from me!"

"What's wrong!"

"Now I know what's causing my allergy. I'm moving to a new office—as far away from yours as possible—the last one at the far end of the hall—"

"Colin!"

"I'm sorry it's that way, but it is, and there's nothing we can do about—"

"Are you trying to brush me—"

"You must keep a good distance from me—in the hall here, the faculty room, the elevator, committee meetings, all Department functions—"

"Just you hold on a minute! You're not dropping me like a—"

"I have to. We have to. What happened the other night in the office—was—was what proved it."

"Proved what!"

"That—hah . . . As soon has high—as soon huh—as—ah-ah-hahyah-haah!" Thank God, it had finally come! "I start to—I st-huh—I can't help—hah—hah-haara—huh—AH—YAAAAAAH—SHOOOOOO!" He hadn't had to encourage that one at all! "I am allergic to youuuu-chOOOOOH!"

It was so goddam ridiculous she shouldn't have bought it, but his red eyes, stuffed-up nose, and explosive sneezing must have been convincing. She did keep her distance for quite a while, but then she must have noticed that whenever they were inadvertently close, he was not sneezing any more. She'd probably changed her perfume brand.

"You're pretty well over your allergy, Colin."

"It comes and goes."

"Maybe we ought to give it another—"

"No!"

"I've been thinking about it and—people simply can't be allergic to each other—"

"I am."

"That's not true!"

"To you."

"No—you're not—"

"Take my word for it."

"You're not sneezing now."

"I've got a bad rash."

"Bull-shit!"

"I cannot stand being near you. I don't want anything to do with you—allergy or no allergy!"

"And you said you were allergic to me—just so you could—"

"That's right!"

"Leading me on! Letting me think—"

"I did not! I didn't let you think anything! I've been trying to stay clear of you for over a year and a half! Stay away from me!"

"You bastard! Nobody plays ball-and-drop with me!"

"From now on stay away from me or I will bust your jaw!"

"Dobbs, you are going to be very sorry for this."

She had been right. Up until then there had been a chance for him and Sarah to get back together. In early January she had moved out to the Island, and a month later she went ahead with the formal divorce proceedings, Elizabeth Skeffington named as co-respondent. He had moved back into the house.

That evening in his office he had not even come close to going off!

They must have cut the day short; there were no students waiting in the hall now. English Department offices were closed, so Bev must have gone home early. The Chairman's door was open a crack. Tait!

"DR. VAL UNDERHILL"
"DR. HERBERT STIBBARD"
"PROFESSOR STANLEY PALMER"

All closed. With luck he wouldn't run into anyone in the hall on his way to the washroom and back.

"DR. CHARLOTTE ROBBINS"

Children's Literature. Dear Charlotte!

"DR. MACKENZIE LYON

Distinguished Professor Emeritus"

"DR. ELIZABETH SKEFFINGTON"

Virgin Emeritus!

## "DR. LLEWELLYN BROWN-EVANS"

Neo-Classical Literature. University of Bristol. Blue-label, prime-beef teacher. Wants his literary meat well aged, only. Has a dear friend who knows a fellow who knows a fellow who knows a fellow who was a chum of Evelyn Waugh.

## "DR. PETER ROBITAILLE"

Semantics. Here comes Peter Robitaille, hopping down the conference trail.

## "MEN'S WASHROOM
STAFF"

He had often wondered if any faculty member had ever entered without his *Bartlett's*. Much of the graffiti was plagiarized, but he liked to think that some of it was original, particularly the one on the left of the first toilet: "I came. I saw. I concurred. Caesar's Chinese Wars." The best one in the second stall had to be: "They also surf who only stand and wade. Milton at Pismo Beach." Probably an import. "Beware of Limbo Dancers" with the arrow pointing down. He'd seen that one before in the British Museum washroom. "Wait here for me. I'll be right back. Godot." University of Toronto. He couldn't remember which college.

"Guilt without sex" was new since Daisy Creek and "Byron is a sister-fucker," which had inspired someone to write under it, "Frank Norris is a wheat-fucker," beside which had been added, "and a real word-fucker." Scrawled above the middle urinal were the simple words: "Bloom was here."

Many of them had been edited with professorial symbols for common errors in usage:

"CS"
"AWK"
"?"
"AGR"
"AMBIG"
"FRAG"
"GR"

and, his favourite; "INC."

Some of the finest writing done at Livingstone University was on the toilet walls.

Over the silver paper-holder in his stall: "Livingstone University is an ivory shit-house." He had his red pencil with him. Just before he got up, he leaned over and wrote: "Then you must push harder."

On his way back from the washroom, he stopped to rest his hip, then realized he had just sniffed the air. Not the faintest smell of cigar smoke, so it must have been some time since Dr. Lyon had been out here. How he owed that man! Would have been nice to have visited with him today.

What a good guardian! At Toronto Lyon had been his supervisor for his Master's. Without him there would have been no Woodrow Wilson Fellowship. After Colin's doctoral years in London, he'd got him into Queen's as an assistant; then he'd sent for him after coming west to be Dean of Arts at Livingstone. He'd taught him to write. He'd taught him to teach. And what a tricky teacher *he* was! With what cunning sleight-of-hand he palmed truths and insights and hid them in his students without their knowing it, to appear magically years later.

"Restraint is the mother of obscurity."

"Never confuse ease of effect with ease of achievement."

"Brilliant image, Colin. Clever of you. I wonder what Katherine Mansfield would have thought of it."

"All art is one and indivisible."

"Let's have your *living* life, not your *reading* life."

"All fine writing is regional, whether the illusion happens on the not-so-devout road to Canterbury or floating down the Mississippi or the Congo or on a moor in Wessex or in a winter doorway in Copenhagen or the land of the Yahoos or a country churchyard or in the darkest heart of Bloomsbury."

Oh, how that dear old son-of-a-bitch could teach!

" 'To weet their cork-heel'd shoon.' There's denotation for you, Colin. 'I saw the new moon, late yestreen,/ Wi' the auld moon in her arm.' That's what they call connotation."

"Every single bit must be the truth—the whole thing a more meaningful lie."

And they picked a man like Tait for chairman! How he hated him! Maybe more than he did Skeffington. The feeling had become incandescent a year after Dr. Lyon's retirement. That fall the Faculty Council had just named him Distinguished Professor Emeritus and the announcement had been made on his birthday. The English Department had celebrated in the common room. Tait had not shown.

"I didn't see you there, Tait."

"Where?"

"Common room. To honour him. Bev baked him a birthday cake."

"I must have had a class."

"No. You didn't."

"Tutorial."

"You didn't have that either. You never come out to the university Thursday or Friday."

"Then I guess that must be why I didn't know about it."

"Bev put notices in all the mail slots."

"Must have slipped my mind."

"He started the whole creative writing program here."

"Before my time, I guess."

"He's done a lot for this university."

"Mmh."

"He excited students in a way that—"

"More to teaching than excitement."

"Of course."

"And I don't think the brighter students—the ones who wanted a greater challenge—were all that enthusiastic about him. They're not so easy to fool."

"What the hell do you mean!"

"He's a dear old fellow—charming old performer. That's all."

"And you, Tait, are an illiterate prick!"

At least Tait had been considerate enough not to show up in the neurological ward during those four months in the hospital. Dr. Lyon had been faithful. And Archie. Hard to say which one of those two he owed more.

*    *    *

He shouldn't have let that happen; sleeping in an office
chair was not what his back and neck needed. How
this day had taken it out of him. Tait to be Head; Liz to
be published! What time was it, anyway? If Annie had
phoned, surely it would have wakened him.

There was the sound of a key in the door. It opened.
Clyde.

"What did you do to yourself?"

"A bear."

"Aw—wondered why you wasn't 'round for a
while."

"Since last April."

"Yeah. Nobody tells a janitor anything. You was
campin' in the mountains?"

"Hunting."

"Grizzly?"

"Yes." Must be four-thirty. At exactly the same
time for five years, Clyde had ended his teaching day
for him. He would materialize, tall and loose and aimless-
seeming, wheeling his great garbage can on castors as
though he were walking a pet down the halls, into and
out of each office, where he swirled his mop in lazy
figure eights. It took relaxed grace to turn janitorial
work into a slow and absent-minded ballroom dance.

"I had a close call once. You want that?" He pointed
to "Guidelines," which had missed the basket.

"No."

"Isn't in the basket, I leave it. All they seem to do
is leave stuff on the floor. Pick up—fill up—dump out.
Every night, four to two, for thirteen years now. Just a
job. Like everybody else in here, I guess. Any of these
people do anything?"

"They teach."

"Anything *besides*."

"I guess they do."

"You do. Bear-huntin'. Me—it's bird-watchin'. I
meant like make somethin'—do somethin'. Are they
any good at anythin' important like that?"

The phone rang. It was Annie. They'd asked her to
do a shift at the Saddle and Sirloin. Could he take a taxi
home? Could he make his own supper? He had little

choice, for she was phoning from the restaurant. When he hung up Clyde was still by the door.

"New boss, eh."

"Yes."

"Dr. Tait."

"Yes."

"I hope you get better quick."

"Thanks, Clyde. What about Tait?"

"I was just wonderin'. How do they pick somebody for somethin' like that? To be the boss."

"A committee does it. Why do you—"

"Just curious. I'm a curious man. Grade seven education, but I'm curious."

"That's half the battle, Clyde."

"That committee should have looked underneath the top of his desk."

"Huh?"

"His chair seat. Beneath his book shelves."

"Gum?"

"No."


The breakfast dishes were submerged in the sink. She'd be tired after a long day at the university and six more hours at the Saddle and Sirloin on top of that. He'd do the dishes for her, but first the heating pad and the frozen peas. He took off his jacket and shirt. Thank God for frozen peas that could remember the morning application so the plastic sack would conform to the shape of his aching neck and shoulder. And the ice cake with the bottle neck sticking out of it. Thank God for Aqua Vite!


"That's just great for your spine, Poppa. Sleeping on the couch like that."

She looked tired.

"What did you have for supper?"

"Ham and eggs. I meant to do the dishes for you."

"Just leave them. I'll do them in the morning. How did your first day go?"

"All right. Annie—"

"I'm one tired cowgirl. I'm going to bed."

"Why don't you forget working at that place? I can—"

"Just stake me to my board and room, Poppa, that's all."

"But you've got your fees and materials—"

"Not really. My student loan came through. See you in the morning."

He did the dishes. He put the peas back into the freezer. He turned on the TV. Horror night. Must be Friday. Too bad she'd gone to bed.

"Remember, Poppa, *The Mole People*—all those lumpy, grotesque things coming up out of all that bubbling grey snot!"

Friday and Saturday nights she'd been allowed to stay up and watch.

"*The World of the Undead*! Dracula with sombrero! Mantillas and castanets! Blood-sucking with margarita chasers!"

She had ached to see them, but she could not bear to watch alone, so he'd spent hours and hours here on the couch with her tense beside him, her hand clutching his. If she hadn't gone to bed early, he could have held her hand again. But now it would be for his own protection against horror. He turned off the set.

Well, he'd made it through his first day at the university. Finding out that Tait was the new chairman, that Skeffington had found a publisher, hadn't been all bad. Both events had counter-irritant value. They had taken his mind off the neck and the shoulder and the elbow and the hip for a while. When it came to pain, anger was quite useful. Not against the bear and Tait and Skeffington so much as against this body he was trapped in. Mortification of the flesh wasn't what it was cracked up to be. The logical destination of stoicism had to be self-destruction, for only then could there be freedom from the tyranny of this too, too solid flesh.

You're at it again, Dobbs. Good thing Sarah isn't around any more.

"You never look *out*! You're always looking *in*! Anything outside yourself doesn't interest you! Anything or anybody! You are a selfish son-of-a-bitch!"

She had probably been right.

# CHAPTER 6

Passing Dr. Lyon's office had made him ask himself again, as he had done so often during the last few years, had there ever been, in all the history of marriage, a divorce based on canine grounds, the co-respondent a little dachshund bitch? Not very likely. Or a Seville orange? Just possibly. It was probably a universal human tendency to pick over the past like this, looking for one definitive event after which an unfortunate destination had become inevitable. No such search if the outcome had been a happy one, though.

That was something you never forgot, the time you'd first met the girl you married. Fall of 1957. Toronto. Late November of his honours year, Dud Moore had introduced them in the Tuck Shop. She'd been a Brocklebank girl and a close friend of Dud's sister, who had probably twisted her brother's arm. By spring they were going steady, in spite of her father.

Ralph Halstead turned out to be an alcoholic, proud of his Cabbagetown childhood, his grade nine education and the company he had built single-handed: Prestige Packaging Products.

"You name it, we got it. Corrugated, skin and blister, high- and low-density polyethylene . . ."

"Dad, I don't think—"

". . . shaped, round bottom, drawstring and handle bags . . ."

"There are other things we can talk about—"

"Over four hundred sizes of stock bags for immediate delivery."

"You promised, Dad. Not everybody's as interested as you are in boxes and bag—"

"You should be. They built this house and they
sent you to Brocklebank."

"Not Colin. He's not interested in—"

"That right, Colin?"

"Ohhh . . . I . . ."

"Guess they don't teach packaging in the university. Let me get you another drink."

"No thanks."

"I'll just get you . . ."

"Dad!"

Ralph sank back into his chair. "What are you
studying there?"

"English."

"Good money in that?"

"Dad, he's not going to university to make money—"

"What other reason is there? I'll tell you something. Greed. There's a good reason. There's the whole
key to your fellow man. Once you know that, you're
well on your way to success in this life. If I had ever
gone to university, God forbid, that's what I'd have
studied. They teach a course in greed there?"

"I think they call it Business Administration,"
Colin said.

"Well, good for them. Your glass is just about
empty. Let me—"

"I'll do it for him."

"I'll do it, Sadie."

"Sarah!"

"That's right. Don't ever call her Sadie, Colin. If
you know what's good for you. Here, Sarah, might as
well freshen up mine for me while you're out there."

Sarah looked at the glass he was holding up to her,
turned away. Ralph lowered his empty glass to the
table by his chair arm. "And what's your father do,
Colin?"

"I don't know."

"How's that?"

"I have no idea."

"How come?"

"I—I'm not in touch with him."

"Your people divorced?"

"No."

"He's dead."

"Possibly."

"Either he is or he isn't."

"I never knew him, Mr. Halstead."

"Aawww—took off—left your mother and you . . ."

"In a way."

"What do you mean—in a way?"

"Before I was born."

"Your poor mother. How did the two of you make out? Not welfare."

"No. She was able to support us."

"How?"

"Housekeeper."

"Good, honest work. She must be a fine woman."

"Yes. She is."

"You hear that, Sadie—Sarah. Colin's mother . . . ."

"Yes, Dad."

"Isn't easy for a single parent. Sadie and I know. We lost Olive when she was eight years old."

"That's young." Younger still to have been Sarah's mother.

"Accident." He lifted his glass, then realized it was empty. "Just the other side of Ajax. Before the Oshawa turn-off. Labour Day weekend. We were headed for Rice Lake. . . ."

"All right, Dad."

"Big Champion Diesel pulled out in front of me. He walked away from it without a scratch. They brought me into Hotel Doo. Two days later I come to with nuns and bleeding hearts and crucifixes. They didn't tell me for two weeks about Olive." He stood up. "She's in Mount Pleasant."

"Where you going?" Sarah sounded anxious.

"You be good to your mother, boy. She's the only one you got."

"Where are you—"

"The kitchen." He picked up his glass.

"Not for another—"

"Yes. I need it!"

Before the eleven o'clock news he had needed four more, and had fallen to sleep in his chair.

"All right, Dad." Sarah leaned over him. She shook him. He opened his eyes. He straightened up. "Time."

"Sure, sure. Halstead's cut off."

"I'll help you upstairs."

"I c'n make it."

"I don't think so."

". . . y'r 'pinion . . . ask for it. Who's he?"

"Colin Dobbs. He's just spent a nice evening with us. Let me help you—"

"Don' wan' help—f'm you, I wan'—you ne'er, ne'er gi'n me."

"Please, Dad!"

"Respec'! F'r y'r father . . ."

"Help me with him, Colin."

"An' mmmmmh gonna get it! Respec'! Have y'r respec'!"

On the chesterfield, after they'd gotten her father upstairs and onto the bed, she had cried in his arms, and then there had been some pretty heavy groping and he knew that he truly loved her. Two years later, when they were married, she told him her father had been drunk the Labour Day weekend she was eight and they were on their way to Rice Lake.

The first year they'd known each other she had been a knockout at the spring formal, with a three-gardenia corsage that said "I love you" against the black velvet gown edged with white lace. Look, Ma, no shoulders, no straps, but with plenty to hold it up all the same. The fraternity had taken over five linked suites in the St. Regis, one of them just for coats and liquor and mix and ice.

More drinking than dancing, really; he and Sarah had danced only the first one because her plantar wart was killing her. Steve Enright had done his French-Canadian thing about Prime Minister Diefenbaker and the St. Flore bull and the steamboat whistle, followed by "The Shooting of Dan McGrew," in spite of interruptions by Dud Moore coming through every five minutes and yelling, "Into the saddle!" followed by the brass assault of his bugle. Sarah put on her Livingstone River mink jacket, which had once been her mother's, and they'd gone out onto the fire-escape, and he had read her all of the Song of Solomon from the Gideon Bible.

Then he had pinned her with onyx and gold over her heart. They made it down to the ballroom just in time for the last dance, and then he joined his brothers with hands on each other's shoulders as they circled, singing:

A band of brothers in DKE
We march along tonight
Two by two,
With arms locked firm and tight.
We sing in honour of the tie
That binds our hearts in one,
Singing Dellltuh Kaaahpuh Epsilon!

As Brother Beta, Dud usually led them in the traditional march ceremony, but this time he was up in Room 515, immersed to his dinner-jacket armpits in water while he sang "The Volga Boatmen" and tried to pole the bathtub with a window-blind roller.

So merrily sing we all
To Deee Kay EEEE,
The mother of jollity,
Whose children are gay and free . . .

By the end of the song all the brothers had reversed the flow of their circle, tighter and tighter in upon itself, clinching into a mass of bodies that finally fell to the dance floor.

The girls all watched from the sides of the ballroom.

With a T.A. and the Woodrow Wilson Fellowship that Dr. Lyon had recommended him for, they were able to get married in September, almost a year after Dud had introduced them. Ralph had come to the wedding in Trinity College Chapel, unenthusiastically, but with a wedding gift of five hundred dollars, which paid the rent for half a year on their basement apartment. His mother and Aunt Nell, for whom she worked, had come down from Ottawa. Aunt Nell's wedding cheque had paid the other half of the apartment rent.

The only flaw he could remember in the first years of their marriage was caused by Ralph's visits to the apartment when Colin was at the university. He was usually gone by the time Colin got home, but an upset Sarah was a pretty good indication that her father had been there. Getting the Canada Council Doctoral Fellowship had given them their years at King's College, London, for his doctorate and, just as important, had placed the Atlantic between them and Ralph.

God had intended him to be a teacher; he knew that before the end of his first year at Queen's, when they had come back from England. He was more and more sure, though, with each passing year, that He had not intended Sarah to be a teacher's wife. It was not simply that she had found his colleagues and their wives uninteresting, or as she put it, "brainy and dull." She could not forgive them—at Queen's, at Livingstone—for using every opportunity they were given to put down "anyone who hasn't gone to university to make theirself into a genius like them!" She had a point. "And you're getting to be just as good at it as they are!"

He hoped not! Oh God, how he hoped not! As a little girl had she been one of the outcast, had she stood forlorn just outside the circle, uninvited and wanting to be invited and knowing she was never going to be invited? Was it true that he and Annie had excluded her? The year the Annie link had been broken and they'd sent her away to Brocklebank, just as Ralph had done with Sarah after he'd killed her mother on the highway, Colin had made up his mind to do something about it.

He had plotted it so very, very carefully, prepared a paper, "Autobiographical Impulse in Fiction," and had it accepted for the Commonwealth Literature Conference to be held during the Easter break by the University of Barcelona, at Sitges. He had applied successfully both to Livingstone and to the federal government for funding. The travel grant turned out to be generous; the peseta, low. Easter on the Mediterranean would be lovely and warm after a particularly bitter winter in a house that had seemed so empty and still, without Annie; he had even missed the scenes and confrontations that had once spilled pain over everybody. All the sounds of family had died away.

But it was not just to ease the Annie ache that he had set up the Spanish trip; now he knew that Sarah knew that both of them were wondering if this relationship could be saved. It was a little like discovering the marriage body's metabolic rhythm had changed without one's knowing it, overweighted with pounds and pounds of silence and impatience and annoyance. Pity there was no marriage scale to tell people when a deliberate diet was needed.

A week together under the Mediterranean sun would be a fresh beginning. Sitges was not new to them, for at the end of the years in London, and after he had successfully defended his doctoral dissertation on William Blake, they had flown to Barcelona before returning to North America. It had been such a warm and loving and brilliant three-week postcard. He had rented two bicycles, one of each sex, his with the carrier on the handle bars. Annie in a basket. She had been four that year.

The most beautiful of all the after-images he had of that May in Sitges belonged to their last day. He had walked along the edge of the playa, looking over the rail for Sarah and Annie, searching the line of sun-bathers on towels and striped deck-chairs in the shelter of the wall. One in five of the women was topless. He had stopped and marvelled at one with her head in her arms, a real water-winger! Then he had seen the golden little girl with a black ponytail staggering up the beach, with a blue sand pail held out by both hands in front of her plump belly. The proud and uncompromising arc of that back belonged to Annie.

She stopped at the figure of a woman supine on a blanket and lifted the pail high to spill her water load. The woman sat up, nude. They were the loveliest tits in all of Spain! Or the known world! They belonged to Sarah!

"How fair is thy love, my sister, my spouse! How much better is thy love than wine!"

It had probably been the closest and warmest three weeks of their life together. He had even done fiction again and written much of the short story "Roses Are Difficult Here," accepted by *Queen's Quarterly* and listed on the honour roll of Best American Short Stories. His first published work except for critical stuff. God intended him to be a writer as well as a teacher!

He had sent a copy to Dr. Lyon, by then out west at Livingstone University. He had liked it.

This time he had gotten a reservation at La Pinta, the same pension where they had stayed ten years before. It was the only thing that was the same. Six hours to New York, seven more to Lisbon and two more to Barcelona, then thirty vertiginous kilometres to Sitges had been too much for Sarah. She went to bed for a day, got up and out of her nightgown and into her bikini to go down to the beach to sunbathe, but instead ran her face into a superbly clear glass door and returned to bed for another day. Without her, he went up to the palace, ascending past Iberian stonework, then Visigothic, then Moorish, then into the Cistercian Chapel, where the conference papers were to be given.

His had seemed well received, certainly with more enthusiasm than the one by the Australian nun, Sister Moody, who had probably been taught to research and to pray well but not to project. The man from Leeds had given a dandy, illustrating well and with wit how the first colonial writers were generally the wives of generals and Anglican bishops, slumming with their hallmarked silver in a savagely new world, doing needlepoint and water-colours and poetry-writing by neo-classical numbers. In the following paper, a man from Bombay used the word "paradigm" seventeen times. Could have even been more of them, for Colin might have started counting late. "Syntagma" surfaced fifteen times. A paradigm, the Bombay professor felt, was vertical, a syntagma, horizontal. Or was it the other way round? He fondled the word "hermeneutical" five times only. True, he was not a bishop or a general's wife, but he was a prime example of what the man from Leeds had been talking about. There'd always be an England, and colonial literature would never, never die.

The man from Leeds, another from Michigan State, and one from the Canary Islands had expressed interest in publishing his paper if he'd cut it in half. Only the Canary Islands made good on the offer.

With the conference over and Sarah out of bed, the weather turned rotten. When he had suggested they go for a walk, she was not interested.

"Just going to rain again."

"It's stopped. Hasn't been raining for over an hour."

"You go. If I do, it'll pour."

"Nicer if you came with me."

"Not for me. I am never going to be warm again until I get back to North America. You go."

"I wish you would—'

"Please, Colin! Go!"

The whole Costa Dorado had been weeping, and the concrete walkway reflected like dark, wet glass. People were not even taking their dogs out to shit on the walk, in the flower-beds, or on the deserted beach, where deck-chairs were stacked and covered with canvas staked down against the wind. Land and sky were one without horizon, the same shade of pewter with a long white scribble of surf out there. Two days ago had been a sunny Palm Sunday with people carrying amber fronds tied with brilliant ribbon bows to church to be blessed for another year, and in front of the hotel, industrious children had all six of the swings arcing and chirping in unison. Now only the wind idled them.

He walked in the opposite direction from the palace, saw a lone figure up ahead. Nearer, he saw it was a thin and elderly woman with a sort of toque pulled down over her ears. She had urged her Yorkshire terrier into a flower-bed. The little mop had finished and moved ahead to spurn and cover, dirt and grass and portulaca and marigold heads flying.

When he came to the first stone breakwater, he saw a man half-way out, his back to the wind, crouched with both hands at his crotch; had it not been for the red kite dancing high, you might have thought he was urinating into the Mediterranean. At least.

How many silent breakfasts had there been? When had they stopped asking each other how the day had gone, or what they might do this weekend for fun? When had he realized that Annie came home from school to an empty house, her mother at the Winter Club for bridge and martinis daily? And maybe for the blond young squash instructor, though he could not be sure of that. He did not wish to be.

He was well away from the sea, had left behind the vacation homes, like pure mausoleums with blood roofs, empty of life, since the summer season had not really begun. The man up ahead was taking a leak by the side of the road, a little old fellow with a walnut face and an acorn beret. When Colin reached him he had finished. He said something in Spanish and Colin shook his head. The old man leaned down and lifted his bicycle, and that was when Colin noticed the tree just around the bend of the road, a citrus Christmas tree hung with orange globes.

Colin pointed to the tree, then to himself, mimed picking an orange and then peeling it. The old man grinned understanding, made a wide and permissive sweep of his arm, bowing as though to say, "Be my guest, Señor." He threw a leg over the saddle and took off.

Two into each topcoat pocket, one each for his jacket and pants pockets. He would put them in the blue bowl on the low dresser at the foot of her bed. Sorry, much too early for pomegranates, Sarah, but I picked oranges right off the tree and I made myself lumpy to carry them all the way home to you!

By the time he had reached the sea and the summer homes again, the sun had started to come out. He took off the topcoat with its load of oranges. Halfway down the walk he stopped in front of a high wrought-iron fence and through the black lace of it saw a white marble deer in the garden beyond. Someone opened the glass door on the balcony and released from within the house the sound of *The Messiah*, the final chorus taken as a joyous dance. "Amen! Amen! Amen! Amen! Amen! Amen . . . !" Exactly timed to the last "Amen!" a dove glided to land on the balcony rail.

The sun was now quite cleared of cloud. There was a child on one of the swings.

Sarah was not in the room. He put the oranges into the bowl and went out to look for her. The playa had come to full life, with people and bicycles and scooters and dogs. There were three children on the swings now. Giddy and silly, a black Afghan hound bounded into him, nearly knocked him over; the young girl owner apologized for it in Spanish or Portuguese or Italian, but he had already forgiven her anorectic bitch.

He walked all the way to the palace and back with no sign of Sarah. Try the room again.

The door was slightly opened. " 'For, lo, the winter is past, the rain is over and done,' " he called into the room.

She was standing before the dresser and looking down at the oranges he'd brought her.

" '. . . And the voice of the turtle is heard in our land.' " Half-way to her he caught the smell of brandy. "Where were you?"

"Out." She picked up one of the oranges.

"I couldn't find you anywhere. I picked those right off a tree for you."

Her attention was only for the orange. She began to peel it.

"On my walk I met a little Iberian leprechaun and the tree belonged to him."

She tossed the half-peeled orange back into the bowl. "Let's go home."

"But we've got another five days!"

"I don't want to stay any longer."

"The conference is through. Last paper this morning. Just the banquet tonight."

"I've had it."

"We've got from now on all to ourselves—"

"I don't want it. I'm not going to the banquet. I'm taking the train to Barcelona."

"Why!"

"To have a bath. To wash my hair—"

"You can—"

"In water that isn't loaded with salt!"

"Aww—come on, Sarah—stay and be my sea Cybele—"

"If that means washing with what comes out of those taps—no!"

"All right. After the banquet tonight we'll both go in to Barcelona. I'll come with you—"

"I don't want you to. I also want to be by myself for at least a day."

"Oh."

"I'm sick of this room and I'm sick of Sitges and I'm sick of Spain and I want to go home!"

"All right."

"And it wouldn't be a bad idea if you came home—"

"We'll talk it over—"

"—five days later!" She had picked up the orange again, had been tearing at it and dropping the peel on the floor. She pulled it into halves, loosened a segment. "What we needed was a holiday—from each other!" She bit into the segment. Her face contorted with revulsion and she spat out orange. "You bastard!" She threw the rest of the orange at him. "On purpose! You did that on purpose!"

He had not done it on purpose. The old man had known, but he had not, that what he had picked from the tree by the side of the road was a Seville orange, bitter as gall and fit only for marmalade. She had not believed him.

Nor had she believed him about Polly. Within a week of their return from Spain, Dr. Lyon had told him that he was beginning his sabbatical at the end of the spring term, and would be away in Louisiana for the whole year. His mail was no problem, for Bev would be forwarding that to him, but he was concerned about the dog. She was getting old and quite likely could not survive an unloved year in a dog kennel. Because he could never ever repay the debt he owed his old mentor and because he knew how much the dog meant to Dr. Lyon, especially since Mrs. Lyon had died the year before, he said Polly could stay with him and Sarah.

"That's very kind of you, Colin. You talk it over with Sarah and let me know."

"I don't have to, Dr. Lyon. She'd just love to have Polly with us while you're away."

Which turned out to be a goddam lie.

"Why didn't you check with me first before you promised to—"

"I didn't think you'd mind. The dog means so much to him and he means so much to me."

"And I mean nothing to you—you couldn't be bothered to tell me we're taking in a dog for a whole year!"

"I'm sorry. I thought you'd like to have her—"

"No. You did not! If you'd thought I'd like that,

then you would have asked me if it would be all right with me. You had no right to do it—promise something that's going to be dumped onto someone else! She won't be your responsibility! She'll be mine! You get her out of this house—put her in a kennel!"

"I can't do that."

"You certainly can!"

"She wouldn't survive. She'd die of a broken heart."

"No, she wouldn't."

"Dr. Lyon said—she's very important to him—he left her with us—"

"He did not leave her with us! I know you! You *offered* to take her!"

"He didn't come right out and—"

"I know he didn't! 'I'll take her for you, Dr. Lyon, and dump her on Sarah so she can ruin the rugs and stink up the whole house and upset the routine!' "

"She won't do that. She's a dear little thing."

Lie number two. She had been badly spoiled. Whenever she was told to sit, she stood; to come, she stayed; to shut up, she barked.

"Also, she's got bad breath!"

That was not all she had; there must have been some chronic yeasting process going on within her, producing prodigious volumes of gas for such a little dog. Wraith silent, she would come unnoticed to curl up at one's feet and to release a long whisper of sound so faint there was no warning of the decay smell that would very soon rise from her.

"My whole house stinks! Why should you care! You're out at the university all day! *I'm* the one that's getting gassed, not you! *And* all day long I keep tripping over her. She trips people!"

"She's deaf. She can't hear you coming."

"I'm telling you—even before she got deaf she tripped people. Deliberately!"

She also whistled. Mostly after midnight. Urgent and plaintive, the tea-kettle sound made it all the way from the kitchen to their bedroom to waken Sarah, who would dig him in the ribs. "She's whistling again!"

The first time it had happened, he had gotten up and gone down and let her out and waited for her to bark to come in again. She hadn't, and when he had gone out to see how she was doing, he discovered that she had left the yard. Barefoot and in his pyjamas, he searched the neighbourhood for over an hour before he found her. From then on he not only let her out, he went with her and stayed while she squatted to do what she must do, then brought her back into the family room. During the day, though, if she had to go, she did not whistle.

"She has not even been house-broken!"

That was not quite true. She must have once been house-broken; age had made her incontinent. Now they had a card table blocking the doorway from the kitchen to the hall, to keep her out of the dining room and the living room, and newspaper laid down over the family room and the kitchen floor. Precaution had come too late. When Sarah pulled out the couch in the living room to clean, she found a great yellow stain in her British India rose rug, precisely the shape of Australia. It could only have been accomplished in the past two weeks. Polly's urine seemed to have all the bleaching power of chlorine!

"Get her out of my house!"

"I can't—we promised Dr. Lyon—"

"*You* promised him!"

"We can't—where can we—"

"I don't care! Get her out!" She was trembling with frustration and rage.

"We can't put her out—"

"Outside! Now! She's not to come into my house again!"

"You know she won't stay inside the yard. She's homesick—"

"*I* am homesick! Close the yard off! Tie her up!"

He had done the latter with a long leash, one end snapped to her collar, the other attached to a pulley that would slide along the clothes-line and give her room to move. It generally took her less than half an hour to loop the leash round and round the clothesline pole or the weeping birch trunk.

It did solve the Polly problem until mid-October.

"She can't make it through a bitter winter outside, Sarah. She's never been hardened to it."

"She's not coming in the house."

"She's an old dog! Fifteen."

"Board her."

"She's a hundred and five in human terms!"

"Put her in a senior citizen kennel."

"I can't do that! Dr. Lyon entrusted her to us—"

"You! Not me!"

"She's got to come inside by November!"

"Make her an insulated doghouse. With central heating."

She had intended it as unfeeling sarcasm, but he did build a house, and he did insulate it. In one corner he made a nest of old blanket for her. He ran an extension from the outside plug by the back door, looped it around a low branch of the birch. When the weather turned extremely cold in a couple of weeks, he would hook up the circular electric heater.

It turned out to be a long Indian summer, lasting almost to the final week of November. He connected the heater before going to bed. That night Polly chewed through the rubber extension cord and electrocuted herself.

"Oh, Colin, at her age she probably had a heart attack or a stroke—"

"Her mouth is burnt!"

"What did you do with her?"

"She's on the back porch."

"What are you going to do with her?"

"Dr. Lyon—I'll have to write him. She was very important to him."

Half-way out to the university he knew he must phone. He got through to Dr. Lyon easily. The old man's voice was very even as he said it was thoughtful of Colin to phone him. It was not too great a surprise to him. He had been preparing himself for this sad eventuality for the past four years. He was grateful, he said, that if she had not spent these last months with him, she had spent them with someone who loved her and cared for her. Colin and Sarah. "When did it—how did she . . ."

"Some time last night. She might have had a heart attack—stroke seizure—quite likely just went off in her sleep, Sarah thinks, Dr. Lyon."

"Thank you again for looking after her for me and

for going to the trouble of phoning me. I have another
favour to ask you."

Bury her for him.

". . . by the river bank behind the Grounds Department building. There's a clump of black birch. Do
you know it?"

Colin did.

"We used to take our morning and our evening
walks together out there and sit and rest under the
birch before we walked back to the house. She loved
the river and I used to throw out sticks and twigs and
she'd run up the bank and follow them as they drifted
downstream. She'd never retrieve them, but she'd come
back to me and sit and wait for me to throw another
one for her."

"I'll do it."

"Thank you again for looking after her and for
going to the trouble of phoning and telling me."

He felt like a proper shit!

During the night it began to snow. After breakfast
three days later, when he looked out and saw it had
stopped, he went into the kitchen closet and got a large
garbage baggy, went out to the porch and lifted Polly
to put her inside. She was frozen into several stiff and
uncooperative angles, one hind leg at full length, the
other drawn up, both front ones extended. One last
electric spasm must have left her in this grotesque and
awkward shape. He made holes so her legs could stick
out, slung the bag over a shoulder and carried her out
to the car. He lowered the station wagon tail-gate,
swung her inside, and threw in the round-nosed shovel.

He parked by the Environmental Design and
Grounds Care building, took Polly and the shovel out
of the car, and made it down the steep slope to the
river. He found the clump of black birch easily enough,
but when he had cleared away a foot of snow, the
point of the shovel could not make a dent in the frozen
earth. He'd need a pick and a bar. He started up the
hillside to borrow them from someone in Grounds Care.
The building was closed; there wasn't a commissionaire
in sight or a car in the parking lot; he had an Advanced
Creative Writing seminar at one o'clock. Briefly he considered going back down the slope for Polly and the

shovel, decided there was no point in lugging them back up here. He started up the car.

Sarah needed the car because it was Saturday and she always did the week's grocery shopping on Saturday morning and it had not been easy to get her two o'clock hair appointment with Rita and why didn't he do the dog on Sunday.

"Because I'm up to my ass in mid-terms I've got to do Sunday."

"Do the papers today and Polly tomorrow."

He had agreed to that before he realized that there wouldn't be a tool rental place open tomorrow, on a Sunday, so he could get the goddam pick and bar he needed to dig Polly's grave under the goddam black birch by the river she had loved so well. He spent both Saturday and Sunday on the papers. Monday he had an examination to supervise in the morning and another in the afternoon. By Tuesday the jet stream had changed and the blizzard warnings on the eleven o'clock weather report proved accurate. Wednesday so few people were able to make it out to the university that classes and exams were withdrawn. Thursday he gave his last exam and, after gathering papers, headed for the river.

He could find neither Polly nor the round-nosed shovel under the five-foot bank of snow drifted from the river edge to the black birch. At dark he made it up the hill with the bar and pick. It took him three sessions over the next week to uncover the shovel handle and then Polly. The ground was now utterly impervious to the pick or the bar. He floundered back up the slope with the shovel and the bar and the pick, then back down for Polly, then back up with Polly.

Sarah went out alone to the airport to pick up Annie, home from Brocklebank for the Christmas holidays, because the doctor had sent him to bed with the flu, which had graduated to a secondary infection of viral pneumonia. He lay in bed coughing and reflecting that none of this would have happened to him if only he had married a dog-lover!

Polly in the plastic bag was under the back porch. She would be all right there, but only until the first March chinook thaw.

\*      \*      \*

The sound of the eaves dripping awoke him. The house was like a sauna. He got out of bed; went downstairs, opened the front door, then the back one, then the kitchen window. He was half-way up the stairs when he remembered Polly. Outside, it was spring lovely. He reached under the porch. She had not thawed.

Back in the house with her in his arms, he turned on the light switch at the head of the basement stairs. He carried Polly through the laundry room and past the furnace to the freezer chest. As he lifted the lid, the interior light came on. Shit! It was three-quarters full!

In the freezer half of the upstairs refrigerator, he was able to free a full shelf by rearranging packages. Now he could take stuff out of the basement chest and transfer it to make room for Polly. Downstairs again, he lifted out frozen meat till he had cleared one end of the freezer chest to the floor. He laid Polly down in there, replaced the packages over. He closed the lid.

The house had cooled down. He shut the back and front doors. He was able to slide into bed without waking up Sarah.

He supposed he should have told Sarah what he had done, but there had never seemed to be a time quite right to tell her she had a frozen dog in her freezer chest. As time went by, he thought of it less and less frequently; indeed he had forgotten about it completely. Early in April, just before his last Criticism seminar, she called him at his office. She was hysterical. She had opened the freezer to get a package of filet mignon for the beef Wellington she wanted to do. She had found Polly! How could he do a thing like that to her!

When he got home, her emotional storm was still raging. She had been busy, for she had moved everything of his out of their bedroom—socks, shoes, shirts, underwear, suits, downstairs and into his basement den.

"Don't you tell me it wasn't deliberate! You did it out of pure contempt! You've never respected me! And you never will!"

He never had buried Polly, for when he had explained on the phone to Dr. Lyon the difficulties he'd run into, the old man had decided to have her stuffed. He asked Colin to put her into *his* deep-freezer until he got back from Louisiana.

So—there had been two years in the basement den, and then he had moved entirely out of the house and into the furnished bachelor suite near the university, the one with the stove that had two of four burners that worked, a fridge without a freezing compartment, and a twelve-inch black-and-white TV. Most people probably assumed that he had been responsible for the breakup, crediting him with exotic extra-marital infidelity. Graduate students mostly. There were others who found it surprising, even shocking; they had yet to learn that more marriages than they realized were being cunningly simulated for an audience outside the family. When the partners had reached their early or mid-forties and their young had left the nest, that seemed to be the time to come out of the closet. With his and Sarah's marriage, it had happened a little sooner than most. That was all.

Very early in the two years of their legally required separation, he had become wary of women, mostly faculty wives working through their husbands to set him up with close friends whose marriages had foundered. Invariably these women wanted to confide in him more than he cared to hear about what dreadful men they had been married to, and the dreadful things their mates had done to them. All men were disloyal and selfish and cruel and not to be trusted. How long they had suffered and how foolish they had been to put up with what they had put up with as long as they had, until the children were old enough for them to get a divorce. He wondered if Sarah were telling some fellow about the bitter Seville orange and the frozen dachshund under the filet she needed for the beef Wellington. Every goddam one of them, instead of feeling they were well out of marriage forever, still had only one thing in mind: to marry again.

In retrospect he knew that if it hadn't been Polly, it would have been something else. The fuse had been lit years before; the dog in the freezer had not been a cause, just a detonator.

Theirs had been a paper divorce. No litigation. No court ceremony. Just pain. He had lost Annie. He had lost Sarah. No—Sarah, then Annie. Sarah had quickly found a husband who was not brainy and dull, a gynaecologist, Colin had heard. She'd moved out to the Island with him.

Several times he had tried to return to his writing for surcease. It hadn't worked. He had taken up something less dangerous than marriage: bear-hunting.

# CHAPTER 7

So—he'd made it through the first day, and, given time, his guts would stop knotting up as soon as he left the house. The office doorknob was now a conquered enemy and with willpower and luck would stay that way. Next challenge: Tait. He really must not put it off. Tomorrow he should walk right in there and explain that he couldn't handle a full teaching load this session, and possibly not during the next one. Sorry, but that's how it is, Tait. Congratulations on becoming Acting Head. Delighted to have my next two teaching years in your capable hands.

God damn that bear!

Come on, Dobbs. You grabbed the doorknob; same thing with Tait. By the balls!

Two days later there was a memo in his slot. "I want to see you, Colin."

God damn Tait!

"Nice to have you back." He had not got up from his chair behind the desk. "How are you feeling?"

"All right."

"Terrible thing."

If he meant his appointment as Head, he was right.

"Sorry I didn't get out to see you in the hospital. Been a pretty busy summer for me. All this—after Alistair got the Edinburgh thing. Meetings. The Dean—Academic Vice-President."

His right little finger had begun to twitch on him; he clenched it in his left hand and felt it trying to escape.

"Enrolment's up surprisingly and with Alistair taking off, things are pretty tense. They'll ease off hopefully when we get classes rolling."

Depended upon how hopeful the classes were, of course.

"What do you think you can manage, Colin?"

"Not a full load."

"I didn't think so. What do you think you can handle?"

"In the winter session—a third."

"Off."

"No."

"In what?"

"The Advanced Creative Writing seminar."

"And the spring session?"

"The second session of Creative Writing and maybe Literature in Process."

Tait had pulled over a pad and was making notations.

"That comes to a half-load altogether."

"Could be more in the spring session. Depends on what shape I'm in."

"Of course."

"I'll know that better by Christmas break." He'd forgotten Kleenex. "Maybe I could take on Expository Writing as well and then pick up a sixth in the intersession."

"Uh-huh."

"What did *you* have in mind?"

"The way we're set up it's difficult. Got to be either a third or two thirds. In a session you can't divide three by two."

"That's right."

"We've got one hell of a student enrolment and

we've lost a big chunk out of Romance Literature with Alistair gone. Primrose is on sabbatical. . . ."

"I know."

"Which damages Victorian Literature and Literature in Process—"

"You got any Kleenex?"

"Sure. And we've got two extra sections of Expository Writing."

Now that he was Acting Head, Tait was not calling it Bonehead English any more.

"You can see the spot we're in."

He had finished wiping his hands and forehead. "The wastebasket."

Tait shoved it over with a foot. "You want to do the Creative Writing during the winter session."

"Only so I'll be looking over their shoulders for the spring session."

"How about doing Expository Writing in the winter session as well?"

He had also called it Suppository Writing before becoming Head.

"I don't know."

"Just twelve in the Creative Writing seminar. No exams. Just twelve of them."

Which explained clearly how little Tait knew about creative writing, as well as syntax. "I would just as soon do the Creative Writing this fall by itself."

"You know best what you can handle. I can't be sure how the Dean and Academic Vice-President will feel about it."

Tait was learning fast.

"It's really up to them."

"And that is really bull-shit, Tait!"

"Hold on, Colin—"

"You hold on! Twelve students writing an average of fifteen pages a week at the very least comes to two hundred a week. And each of them has a tutorial every two weeks, and that adds up to six hours a week. Now you know, and you can explain that to the Dean and the Academic Vice-President. They already know the Head is closer to department matters than they are and they will listen to you, and in fact leave the decision to you—"

"Regulations and department rules say the Dean and—"

"And Socrates says regulations and rules are for fucking fools!"

"What does Socrates have to say about salary?"

God, he hadn't even thought of that!

"Which is entirely a matter for the Dean and the Academic Vice-President to decide."

He couldn't reach back into the waste-basket to retrieve the Kleenex and he'd be damned if he'd ask Tait for more. "If I have managed by the end of the intersessional—to do five-sixths—full salary shouldn't be asking too much."

"I'll see what they have to say about it."

"That would be decent of you. If you will."

"I said I would."

"And *hopefully* they will go along with it."

Tait must have kept his promise, more or less. It was to be at full salary, but he would be teaching a section of Expository Writing as well as the Creative Writing seminar in the winter session. In spring it would be a full load if he could manage Literature in Process. Stand-off.

Thank God the seminar would be the first one; facing twelve was better than facing thirty-five. He had mentally rehearsed a couple of scripts for it. He'd wear his coloured glasses, of course. He might begin by telling them a bear had done this to him, so that there would be no whispered conferences as they asked and told each other what had happened to him. No—better to act as though nothing were out of the ordinary; mut be hundreds of professors returning to classes after they'd been savaged by highway accidents, muggings, surgeons, bears.

But go early. Get into Canterbury Lounge well before anyone else. Take a couch farthest from the light. No—a chair. Keep the good side towards them and, as much as possible, head down as though he were working from his notes. Remember the goddam Kleenex. Cut it short. Probably just after the coffee break. An hour and a half would do.

*    *    *

He knew none of them; they were Alistair's people.
Most of them were admitted before it was known he
was going to Scotland. If they were all right with Alistair,
they were all right with him.

So far so good. They'd trickled in and he'd been
able to keep his head down naturally, attention on the
class list as they handed him their admit-to-lecture cards
so that he could check them off. Actually there were
fourteen, not twelve. After tonight there might be a
couple of triflers dropping out.

"Important things first. I don't, but you may smoke.
Tobacco. We're going to be together here for three
hours every Monday night from now till next spring."

No sweat yet. Right arm and shoulder and neck
behaving.

"In spite of what the course description in the
calendar says, you do not have to complete for me four
short stories, chapters of projected novels, or twenty
poems before Christmas break. Please keep this quiet.
After Christmas we will behave more responsibly, and
by next April you may have completed a short story or
two or three scenes for a longer work, or maybe ten
poems worthy of being shared with others who are not
friends, lovers, or blood relatives. Sounds great, doesn't
it?"

They were agreeing with him.

"All I want you to do—during the winter and
spring sessions—is write. I want you to write every
day, every week, every month, of every term."

Now a few of them were not agreeing.

"Correction. Type. How many of you type?"

All but two raised their hands or nodded. He looked
to each of them: the older woman and the bearded
young man. "You do poetry?"

Both nodded.

"All right. It shouldn't be too difficult for you to
get someone to type it for you so I can read it. No
quills, please. Sorry. You're going to have to forgive
me for that sort of crack often during our year together.
Actually, down deep I am not a shallow person, the

professor explained defensively. I try to be honest. It is the most helpful thing I can be with you in your writing. You will have my caring ear and honest tongue and you may find that painful. There will also be times when you will be delighted. Both the pain and the delight can be trusted.

"Now. Here's an invitation to you that will make it easier for you. Every day for an hour—two—three—try to capture whatever floats to the surface of your consciousness. That's all I'm asking you to do. It isn't really writing. It's finding. Each of you has a unique, stored past. Until you prospect it you cannot know how artistically valuable it may be."

He had them! By God, he had them! Except for the older woman and the burly young man with denim legs stretched full out and his head on the back of the couch.

"Wilder Penfield, a fellow Canadian, made a great discovery while he was stimulating a patient's cortex with an electric probe. He was searching for the precise location of a genetic flaw or tumour lesion that might be causing her seizures. While he was doing this she heard her mother singing; she heard the lyrics; she recognized the tune and she also felt again the emotional context of the forgotten experience. Dr. Penfield and the patient pinned down when it must have happened—before she was three years old. That was the day Penfield discovered that the brain loses nothing it has received. That was the day that understanding of the bicameral structure of the brain became much clearer. Penfield also hoped to find the exact physical location of the soul; during his childhood his mother had coloured him Methodist."

After the coffee break he asked if any of them had ever done this sort of self-indulgent writing to no known thematic or narrative destination. Four of them said they had, but not with any consistency, and only when they'd had nothing to write about.

"That's what I mean—you deliberately do it without a blueprint of a poem or a story or a scene."

"Just doodling?" That was the slender little chain-smoker with the straight blonde hair.

"Mm-hmm."

"Improv."

"Pardon?"

"In acting. Stanislavsky. Lee Strasberg."

"Yes! That's exactly it! Well, almost. Do you act?"

"I try."

"Ah-hah. You must be the fifth columnist from Fine Arts."

"I guess."

"I've kept a journal for years," said the older woman beside the young girl. "Everything that's happened during the day."

"Mm-hmm."

"From the time I get up in the morning, till I go to bed."

"And have you found it helpful? From that material have you built poems or . . ."

"No. I suppose it's just a diary."

"What I'm suggesting is not really a day-to-day account of what has just happened. Most of what turns out to be useful seems to come after a time lag. Often out of childhood. The early years of your life—the first ten—are the litmus years, the ones that seem to stain us most vividly. I'm not sure why that is."

"First time round," the little smoker said.

"Probably. First-time-in-a-lifetime freshness. Sights and sounds and tastes and smells and touches. Let's try something. Starting to my left—just give us whatever you think of. You start it off."

"Uhhh—pickles."

"What kind?"

"Aaah—nine-day."

"Where?"

"Our kitchen—in the fall—my mom—vinegar."

"Next."

"Bread baking."

"Next."

"Wolf willow."

"Crows calling."

"Sweet peas."

"Little Daisy air rifle."

"I don't know."

"Next."

"Jerking off." That was the almost prostrate young man.

"Next."

"My grampa."

"Next."

"Cruel nun."

He looked down at his seminar list. Judy MacDermott, Drama Department. "How cruel?"

"Made us play marbles with her. Sister John of the Cross."

"What's cruel about playing marbles."

"She always won. Cleaned us out. Finally got my agate that had fire inside it."

"That was cruel."

"We had to buy them back from her. She put the money in the poor-box."

"What else did she do?"

"Told us when we got older and were in a car with a boy to put a Chicago telephone directory on the seat between us."

"Where did you spend your childhood?"

"Cape Breton. Fourteen hundred miles east of Chicago."

Everyone laughed.

"There you are, then, that's the sort of thing that comes out in free-fall thinking. We could call it the innocence of childhood. It was once natural for each of us. Now it's become unnatural, and I'm inviting you to make it natural again. Not quite the same thing, though. Call it the innocence of experience. It's not an easy hurdle for you to take, but if you're serious about writing, it's the first one you must take. Just the first.

"Try it the way we've just done it. Tell the left side of your brain—the assessor, the critic—to bugger off. You are not writing something to be shared for approval. You are simply finding. Whatever floats to the surface of your consciousness, get it outside yourself. No win—no lose; succeed—fail. High mark in English 319. Publication. Nobel Prize for Literature. Whatever declares itself.

"If you want to fool your reader, your poem or play or novel or short story must seem to be in the world of the many. They are illusions that can be smelled and tasted and heard and touched and seen. You find sensuous fragments in *your* past—emotions, people that you remember—then your creative partner reads through a sort of minefield with your words for triggers. He sets off explosions of recognition, and then gives you total credit for them when, in fact, the charges were already set in his own past. If the reader and the writer together do not manage such recognitions, there is no life resonance and they might better use their time in some clever, cerebral game—say, chess."

He stopped and looked around. He really did have them now! Every one of them!

"Now—for some necessary mechanics. When you've done a week's work, drop it off to Mrs. Sidorsky in the English Department office. She'll stick it in my slot. At some time convenient for both of us I'll have tutorials with each of you—probably turn out to be every two weeks. We'll go over your work and make guesses about it. During our interviews I may ask you if I may use something of yours in the next seminar. Indeed, the seminars will be made from the fabric of your work. I'm the one who will read it aloud, not just because I'm a better reader than most of you, but because it gives you a chance to observe the response of the others to your work. I won't tell them whose it is.

"I've found this effective. Supposing it's a piece of yours I'm reading and the others laugh, or they are moved almost to tears. That tells you that what you have written has bridged, has reached over to them. This is a sort of inadvertent criticism. It is a most important kind of criticism. It dispels the loneliness of writing much more than articulated criticism can. We'll do a lot of that too. Now—questions?"

The reclining young man who had jerked off lifted a hand.

"Yes?"

"Every week you want us to hand in this stuff?"

"That's right."

"How much of it?"

"Different for different people. Say you came up with two pages a day, then it would be fourteen. Five—thirty-five. Or if it's the week the dam busted—seventy."

"And you're going to read it out loud to everybody."

"Yes."

"Here. In the seminar."

"If it's illustrative—useful."

"Bread and pickles and sweet peas and rosy-fingered dawn and golden sunsets and nuns that play marbles—"

"Oh—sorry! Some of what you find may not be very nice. The seven deadly sins are just a good beginning. There are lots of dirty bits lying in the dark down there: shame, guilt, hypocrisy, hurt, greed, selfishness. . . . Don't say no to any of them if they float up, because each time that left-hemisphere judge says 'No'—or right if you're left-handed—it closes off the flow. If it turns out too painful to show me, don't. You're doing this for yourself, not for me or anybody else. At this point. When something like this happens, just stick in a sheet saying—ah—'What I did Friday and Saturday and Sunday is too private.' I hope you will do that. It would be most considerate of you, for I have led a sheltered life."

"I don't write that way."

"How do you write?"

"Well—I get a good image—it comes to me and I turn it over in my head and then I sit down and I write out a story around it and then I do another draft of it and then another one. Works even better for me with poetry. Turn it over and over and think about it and think about it. Until a person's done that there doesn't seem to be much point in writing it, does there?"

"Yes. There does."

"Why?"

"It's hard to explain in a few words. It's just that putting it *outside* yourself by writing it as well as thinking it—somehow makes it easier for what you've found, to tell you what it is, and what to do with it. But not too quickly."

"I still don't see why a person should go to all the trouble of writing it. Just rough crap."

"Because then you can tell better if it *is* just rough crap. It is much easier to fondle it in your mind than when it is on a page. Writing it makes it easier for you to step back from it later and assess its worth, its effect. Just try it. Doing it will explain to you much better than

I can. Beginning next week you will also have a chance to hear what has happened for the others."

"I still don't get it."

"Do you paint?"

"Huh!"

"What would you think of a painter who has his images rise for him and he just turns them over and over in his mind and then—bang—instant paintings?"

"He's looking at what he's painting."

"That's what I want you to do. But your land-scapes and still lifes and models have to be found inside yourself first and be put outside yourself so that you'll be able to write from them. They don't come ready-made; they rise bit by bit to the surface for you. With some of you it may turn out to be a chaos of fragments, incomplete sentences—run-on diarrhoea. The findings of others may be so beautifully balanced and meaningful and moving and dramatic, the rest of us will hate them for it. Don't let it bother you. I promise you they will be in trouble later on. It will tyrannize them when they try to move from life to art. Any more questions?"

Evidently not.

"Now—this is just a first hurdle you must learn to take, and the less civilized you are, the easier it will be to take it. Once you've learned it, you'll do it again and again and again throughout your writing life—at the beginning of each poem and play, short story and novel. Take my word for it, Keats did it. More often than Shelley. Wordsworth, almost never, which was a shame, for God wasted a lot of beautiful insights on him. Chaucer always cleared it. So did Shakespeare and Mark Twain, Hardy, and Conrad. Henry James went round one side or the other, but Katherine Mans-field didn't, nor did Virginia Woolf, Steinbeck or Eudora Welty or Elizabeth Spencer or Alice Munro. . . ."

"What about Kerouac?" the young man said.

"He never got off his goddam motorcycle."

# CHAPTER 8

He had hoped Annie would be through by the time he had done the bicycle, but as usual she was trying to prove up a homestead in there; also, before the odometer window had brought up the second, reluctant 0 to begin a new kilometre, his right foot had begun to flutter. When he increased his pumping speed to fight back and the needle crawled up from twenty to thirty, the twitching had become imperative, then the whole leg had begun to dance. Before the third kilometre had come up, his foot had jumped right off the pedal twice. To hell with it!

He had just hooked the traction bracket, with its pulley and dangling nylon, over the bedroom door when he heard the shower start to rain on the other side of the wall. She'd be in there another hour! He finished buckling on the bridle harness, then sat in the chair and lifted the yellow pail with its forty-pound load of bricks into his lap. With the usual difficulty he reached up and managed to get the loops above his ears caught into the hooks of the hanging yoke. He spread his knees and eased the pail down between them.

One, and two, and three, and four, and five, and six . . .

Within the first three minutes, the muscles would begin to relax, the neck and shoulder pain to soften as he counted out one hundred and eighty to himself. He would lift on the pail for one hundred and twenty, then lower it for the next three minutes of tension. He was getting pretty good at it, and his self-whispered minutes generally came out within a few seconds one way or the other of the set alarm clock on the floor beside the chair. Annie had figured the system out for him. Some day she might even discover a way to time herself in that bathroom.

He had almost finished the twenty minutes when he heard the door open.

"Hey, Poppa. Going to end up a real tall guy if you keep this up." Meadowlark-cheerful in her yellow terry cloth kimono that came just to her knees. "How many kilometres did you race this morning?"

He could not nod. He could not shake. His jaw hinges were locked.

"I don't want to see that speedometer still reading seven hundred and thirteen." She reached into her robe pocket. "When do you think you're going to need me today? To drive you out to the university?"

She knew very well he did not go out to the university on a Saturday.

"What about this?" She was holding out a square envelope rimmed with black and gold.

Till he was out of traction, she must resign herself to soliloquy.

"University colours. Remember? An invitation, looks like." She turned the envelope over. "Addressed to you. Don't you read your mail?"

"Junk," he said through his teeth.

She opened the flap.

"My mail!"

She took out a card. She read: "'The Master of Kathleen MacNair College invites you to a wine and cheese party, Saturday, September the seventeenth, to be held in the close—' What's a close?"

Since all he really could manage was sign language, definition would have to wait.

"Master's wine and cheese party invitation is junk mail?"

The alarm went off. He grasped the pail and lifted it. "I am not going to the Master's wine and cheese party."

With his muscles tired now, it was difficult to balance the pail on his knees and at the same time reach up for the loops in these yoke hooks to free himself.

She read from the invitation again: "'To honour the new President of Livingstone University.'"

"A president is not without honor, save in his own university." He had stopped trying for the hooks so that he could balance the teetery pail of bricks. "And I am allergic to cheese and university presidents." The alarm stopped. He'd just rest his arms a minute.

"That's no answer, Poppa."

"It's mine."

"*I'd* like to go."

"Then go."

"With *you*. I really think you ought to. Nice way to start things off. With a bang."

"Just let me whimp—"

"Chance to see everybody again when you've been away from them so long. Get it over all at once."

"No."

"Why no?"

"I told you why."

"No you didn't tell me why. You just gave me a smart-ass answer. You did not tell me at all. Aw—come on, Poppa!"

"I—I just don't want to. Unhook me."

"Let's go back to the beginning. Why don't you want . . ."

"Unhook me, please."

"*Why* don't you want—"

"Turn me loose, God damn it!"

She reached up. "—want to go to the Master's wine and cheese party? It is the finest wine and cheese party in all the land. Well—*biggest*, anyway. There."

"That's just one thing that's wrong with it."

"Ah-ah! Neck exercises."

He sat back, clasped his hands behind his head, and strained against them for a count of four. He released the pressure and dropped his chin to his chest. "I'm not sure I could take it."

"I see."

He tipped back and pushed and held again. One-two-three-four. "Aaaah! Huh. Too soon. Much too soon. I'd like to do it by degrees."

"Not the way, Poppa."

"It's my way."

"Slow self-torture—"

"What do you think I'm doing right now, for God's sake!"

"That's what you used to tell me. Remember?"

"Huh?"

"At Peggy Lake. 'Just close your eyes, Annie, and hold your nose and do it. Jump right in and get it over with.' "

"Well, I am not holding my nose and jumping right into any wine and cheese—"

"Can't you—ever—*level with me!*" Shrill as any osprey over Peggy Lake.

"All right! I would not care to inflict this half-clown face upon the army of the American Revolution—"

"It won't be that—"

"—if they were gathered this very afternoon in the close of Kathleen MacNair College—"

"I don't think invitations were sent out to the—"

"—to honour the new fucking president of the brand-new United States of America!"

*"You don't have to scream at me!"*

*"I sure as hell do!"*

*"At least you've given me an honest answer—finally!"*

He heard the slam of the bathroom door.


Push back and hold, one-two-three-four. Release and down, one-two-three-four. God damn the wine and cheese party, one-two-three-four! The university and all those who teach in her, one-two-three-four! That grizzly up Daisy Creek, one-two-three-four! Piss himself before she let him get in to that toilet, one-two-three-four!


He should have known that would not be the end of it.

She set down his orange juice and cereal before him, then sat down herself. "Poppa—think of it as part of your—"

"I do not want to talk about it."

"So you said, but I do."

"Did you put any salt in this porridge?"

"Try tasting it." She lifted her coffee cup, tilted, drank, then lowered, her eyes steady upon him. "There are two kinds of therapy."

"There's not enough in it."

"There is. Your bicycle, traction, pool lengths, exercises. That's one kind—*physio*-therapy. There is also—"

"Interference in the lives of others."

"—*mental* therapy, and it is time you applied yourself to doing some of that."

"More salt next time." He shoved away the bowl and reached behind himself for his cane.

"Poppa, this thing is just the thing—the chance you need to—"

"Quit pushing me around!"

"Damn it, Poppa, nobody can do it for you! I don't want to push you around! I want you to push yourself around."

He put the percolator back on the stove, picked up the cup and saucer, moved down the counter. "Where's the goddam cream and sugar?"

"Left of the goddam sink. I know how you feel, Poppa, and that's why I think you should go."

He poured in the cream, pulled over the sugar bowl.

"God—when you want to, you sure do succeed in being one stubborn, rude bastard! Where are you going?"

"Living room. I intend to drink my coffee in the living room—"

"Why not give it a try, Poppa? If it's too much for you, just give me the signal—we'll leave."

"—by myself."


He had picked up the letter from the floor under the mail slot; he had read it in the hallway and had known instantly he would not be going to the Master's wine and cheese party to honour the new president of Livingstone University. He should not have left the invitation on the butler's helper by the front door. He should have been less trusting and more careful.

Filled it too full again! There was a dark patch where some had sloshed onto the corner of the rug, just inside the living-room doorway. He laid the cane up against the couch end, and managed, without spilling more, to tip coffee from the saucer back into the cup. He carefully set it down on the coffee table with the Eskimo carvings there.

A gentle apple scent perfumed the whole place. Acrylic paint! Now he saw what had happened in the far end of the living room since he had last been in here. This was a two-storey house of twenty-three hundred square feet, not counting his basement den. There were three bedrooms, a dining room, a family room, a sun-porch—and she had to turn his living room into a goddam studio!

She had pulled the padded fireplace bench over to the six-foot teepee that was her easel, in front of the French doors opening onto the sun-porch. Here, in the corner, stood the brass tree that used to be properly and conveniently in the hallway for coats and hats. Now it was draped with the log cabin quilt she had taken off the colonial maple bed in the spare room. There too, frozen in full gallop, was the dappled hobby-horse of Shetland size, which had been stabled in the basement ever since she'd outgrown it two decades ago. Under and around the card table against the right wall were leaves that had fallen from the small May Day tree she'd uprooted and leaned against the rusted iron wagon wheel.

She must have spent the entire night before, setting this up, and if she had done it to surprise him, she had been successful! Why not her own bedroom? The spare bedroom? The basement? The sun-room? Why in here, for Rembrandt's sake!

That would have to be her reason: the light. The large front window at this end of the room and the eight-foot French doors at the other were generous with it. The sun, coming in from behind him now, was printing the coffee table top with slender shadow bars and light squares. He stared down at the otter holding the white arc of an ivory fish in its mouth, at the black bulb with inadequate tail and flippers, floating on its back, head held up so that it could look down at its belly-button, and at the Eskimo hunter embracing the upside-down seal with its head protruding through its captor's legs.

"All right now, Poppa." With her hands behind

her back she stopped in front of the coffee table and looked down to him.

"Why didn't you warn me you were going to trash up my living room?"

She bent down, and still with one hand behind her back, lifted the otter and placed it in one of the light squares. "Only room in the house with a decent light." She slid the walrus over to another square. "If you can't have north, then east-west is always best." She shifted the hunter and seal. She straightened up. "Your move, Poppa." Both hands were behind her back again. "Eskimo chess."

"I'm not interested in cute games."

"Okay. No more cute games. What about that meeting with the Dean you were supposed to have that you did not have?"

"He called it off."

"But you did turn down the invitation to high table last week."

"You have a very nasty habit of coming back over old ground again and again."

"Maybe I do. You have a very nasty habit of being querulous again and again."

"I am not querulous!"

"See what I mean?"

"I am annoyed!"

"Same thing."

"No. Not the same thing at all. The word querulous is not nearly strong enough to carry my feelings about high table at Kathleen MacNair College!"

"What have you got against—"

"It's colonial!"

"Come on now! High table originated in Oxford—Cambridge. . . ."

"That's the source, all right."

"So? How come colonial?"

"Ritual plagiarism. By the new of the old. The worst kind. Colonial."

"So what would you put in its place? Once-a-week prairie chicken mating dance?"

"Preferable."

"Senior and junior fellows in sleigh bells and bear claws and porcupine crests?"

"Sure."

"Muskrat steak Diane, followed by kinnikinnick cigars, hazelnuts, Madeira, and snuff?"

"No snuff. I never want to see that silver snuff mull again, even if the Master took a pinch from it himself. That would be refreshing. He should be forced to snort some so he'd sneeze his ass off. God knows how long it's been since he's had a reflex that hasn't been calculated."

"Well, good on you, Poppa. But about that wine and cheese party today—"

"There is integrity in the prairie chicken mating dance—"

"It was you brought up the prairie chicken mating—"

"I don't give a fuck about the prairie chicken mating—"

"The prairie chickens do. Right after. The Stonys, too. But high table at the distinguished Kathleen MacNair College has bugger-all to do with anything: learning, teaching, scholarship, or fellowship!"

"Poppa—you and I are going to go to that wine and cheese party—"

"Long before now high table has revolted me. That is the reason I have not attended one for the past six years! I don't intend to go to one for the rest of my life!"

"Now look who's going back over old ground? Let's return to the matter of today's wine and cheese party—"

"I am not taking this Hallowe'en face to any—"

She had brought her hands from behind her to drop it on the table. It lay there now among the soapstone carvings. An eye patch. Flesh pink!


So—it was to be another nice day after all! She did not need any help with the breakfast dishes. She had no idea where the *Globe and Mail* was. She preferred to go to Foodvale and the dry cleaners alone. She did not feel like driving into the foothills to see the hills and coulees all aflame, because she had better things to do and fall colour, for its own sake, pissed her off! By noon, her anger might be cooled down, but only to be replaced probably by one of her hibernating sulks. That would be too much!

He found her in the living room, dabbing at a four-by-five-foot yellow and green and rust painting. Not of the hobby-horse, May Day tree, and wagon wheel, though. A portrait, perhaps.

"All right, Annie." Female one; winking her left eye. "The wine and cheese party. All right." Or her nipple.

"Oh, Poppa!"

God, how she swung! Born with no emotion gyroscope!

"You'll see! I'm right. You won't regret it."

"There's one condition. We leave early."

"Sure we do."

"On our way out to the university—"

"Okay by me."

"—we stop in at Wild Trophy World and—"

"Oh, shit!"

"Look, this has to be the third time I've asked you. You always come up with some excuse for not going there. You don't seem to be able to accept how important it is for me to find out where they are with my bear hide—"

"You could phone."

"I have. I get the same guy each time and he refuses to give me any specific information. Now, there can be no possible reason why we can't drop by there today. We just leave half an hour early. Otherwise— forget the goddam wine and cheese party! And quit shaking your head!"

"It's not negative, Poppa. Realization. Just this moment I've come to know what kind of little boy you were."

"We put in an appearance—that's all."

"Whatever you say. Stubborn. Impatient. Always had to have your own way. I bet you pulled temper tantrums all the time. I mean real dandies—lying on your back and kicking your heels on the floor—"

"*You* certainly did. Almost daily."

"I wouldn't have been your mother for the world."

"Then quit trying to be—God damn it!"

"And so tricky smart. I'll bet she was so frustrated she wanted to belt you so bad she could taste it."

Even before they left the house, he made a pact with himself: no matter how capricious it turned out to be, he would not criticize her driving. She could exceed autobahn speed and he would keep his mouth shut.

"Could you put your window down?"

"Sure."

"And your purse over—"

"Just about to. You going to wear that thing I got for you?"

"No."

"That's nice."

"I have sun-glasses."

"That's not so nice."

"If you say so."

"I just did. Aw, come on, Poppa, let's be kind to each other, shall we?"

"I'll try."

"Me too. Where is this Wild Trophy World?"

"At 3431 Meadow Lark. Right on our way to the university, at Thirty-second or Thirty-third, you turn east for four or five blocks. I'll direct you. I can't manage the end of this—"

"Let me. Ever wish you could get your hands on the guy who designed all seat-belts?"

"Frequently."

"He also did the keys for sardine cans, you know. Plastic pouches for airline cheese . . ."

"Teapots that dribble."

"Panty hose that runs."

"Razor blades that shave your face exactly two and a half times."

"Maxi-pads that stick to your—"

"Same fellow responsible for those, too?"

"Sure is. Son-of-a-bitch should have been drowned at birth!"

"Held under with Kahlil Gibran!"

"I love you, Poppa."

"That's nice."

"I only wish it were as easy to like you."

"Can't have everything, Annie."

"There's something I've been meaning to tell you."

"What?"

"I started to a couple of times. Then—I didn't. Chickened—now what do you suppose she's got in mind?"

"Huh?"

"In front of us! Her! Last three blocks her left turn signal's been on! Make up your mind, you silly bitch!"

"I don't think she can hear you." He should never have said that, for she punched the horn, startling the Volkswagen over the centre line and into the path of a truck, which veered just in time. The truck driver blew his horn. So did Annie again as the frightened beetle cut back across the centre line and across the nose of their car, canted with both right wheels up and over the curb, but came down again in time to miss the corner mailbox, and, with left tail-light blinking, make a right-hand turn.

"Disgrace to your whole sex!"

"Annie."

"What!"

"Cool down."

"You see what that bitch did!"

"Yes. I saw what she did after you blasted your horn at her. That last street was Thirty-ninth. We wanted Thirty-third."

"So we circle round and we come at it from the other direction. You said you'd direct me."

"Sorry. Something must have distracted me."

After entering a one-way the wrong way and backing out again, then a street that died at the railroad tracks, they made it to Wild Trophy World.

"Aren't you coming in with me?"

"Nope."

"Suit yourself."

"Unless you need me."

"I'll be all right." He straightened up, then leaned down to the window again. "You might find it interesting."

"I don't think so."

"It's a very old craft. Taxidermy."

"Sure. I'd just rather not, Poppa. I get reminded often enough of—what that—"

"Oh, come on, Annie!"

"—as it is."

"I'd like you to see her."

"I'm—no. I'm not fussy about open caskets at funerals, either. I'll wait here while you go on in. Take your time. No hurry."

WILD TROPHY WORLD said the high sign covering almost half of the two-storey building. A bounding cougar, snarling timber wolf, rampant grizzly, and couchant Rocky Mountain sheep were menagerie melodramatic as a circus poster up there. FUR—FEATHER—FIN. FOUR GENERATIONS TAKE PRIDE IN THEIR WORK.

The sign on the door warned: BEWARE OF THE DOG.

He went in anyway.

There was no one behind the long counter or in front of it, but the place was not empty. Wire-strung snow geese, a pair of Canada honkers, several mallard ducks and green-necked drakes migrated across the ceiling, all of them flying for the right wall. Some of the leaders with umbrella wings and lowered feet prepared to light, others already had landed on shelving where pheasant, spruce and blue grouse, and prairie chicken waited. On lower ledges stood full mounts of weasel, mink, otter, badger, red fox, and coyote. Above the counter, the wall he faced was hung with head-mounts: bearded goat, prong-horned antelope, elk, mountain sheep, moose, and, dominant in the very centre, a musk-ox with its bone turban and sickle horns.

Through the glass front of the counter, in its lowest region, he could see cream bodies like abstract ghosts for the departed, and on the next level just head forms with labels: Bear Sm.—Bear Med.—Bear Grizz. Polar—Cougar—Timber Wolf—Lynx. Why in hell should he be wishing his colleague Herbie Stibbard were here to see this?

"May I help you?"

He looked up to the man who had appeared behind the counter. "Yes." Senior citizen. "I came in about a bear."

"I'm Mr. Munro."

It was not the voice he remembered hearing on the phone. If it were the owner, he might get somewhere this time. "A friend of mine brought it in to you—for me—early in May." Three-piece dark blue suit any branch bank manager could be proud of. "Nicotine."

"Go right ahead. Most of my staff smoke."

"No—his name. My Stony friend, Archie Nicotine, who brought it in for me."

"Frankie must have handled that one. He isn't here, but perhaps I can help you."

"I hope so. I haven't been able to get here till now. I've been in hospital. I haven't even seen her hide. Except *on* her—when I shot her. I'd like to find out what stage—"

"Pretty nearly have to check that with Frankie. He's not here right now."

Hell! Now he'd have to get her to stop on the way back. "We can come back later when he's—"

"Sorry. He's up north. When they thin the buffalo herds—"

"But it's been four months! I've phoned here five times! All I get for some reason is a run-around—"

"Frankie won't be back for another two weeks."

"—from Frankie!"

"Let's just see what I can do for you. Come with me."

In the office, he went behind the desk, sat down. He moved an erect falcon with beak turned disdainfully to one side, pulled over a ledger-sized book. "I hope you've quite recovered from your illness or surg—"

"Well as I can expect."

"Would it likely be under your name or the Indian's?"

"Mine."

"You haven't told me what that is."

"Dobbs. Colin Dobbs."

"In May, you said."

"Yes."

He turned back several pages. Had to be Frankie's fault. Wasn't fair to dump on the old fellow. No reason, really, that a man consorting with hunters, performing life illusion on wild game, *shouldn't* dress and speak like a bank manager.

"Here we are." His thin finger had stopped. "Dr. Colin Dobbs." He looked up. "You're a doctor?"

"Not really."

"How's that?"

"I teach. The university."

He was looking down again. "May third. Number thirteen. Just as soon as they're brought in—raw—we tattoo them right away. In two places. Enter them in this."

"Then could we—could I see it?"

"Afraid not, Dr. Dobbs." He moved his finger along. He tapped it. "Because this notation says it is not here."

"Where is it?"

"At the tannery. Matter of fact, it was in the batch Frankie sent away just before he left."

"Could I go to the tannery and—"

"Not unless you went to Montreal."

"Montreal!"

"Fournier Frères. They're the best. We've dealt with them for years now."

He'd like to send Frankie's hide to Fournier Frères! Tattooed in two places! Raw!

"Four months! Just to get her tanned!"

"It's been a very busy year for us—for them."

"Perhaps I should tell you why I have been in hospital for three months. That bear almost gutted me last spring. She is the reason I now have a ball joint in my right hip—probably made from the same goddam plastic in those animal forms out there. Look!" He took off the sun-glasses. "How's this for a head-mount job."

"I—I don't know what to—"

"Get on the phone—to Fournier Frères! Tell them to get my bear tanned and get her the hell here! Before Frankie comes back from his goddam buffalo!"

"I'm awfully sorry—"

"Before she rots!"

"Now, don't you worry, Dr. Dobbs. Well salted and sloughed—ears turned inside out—kept cool—even as long as a full year's delay cannot hurt anything. I will phone them and I will ask them to get to it right away. If they haven't done so already."

"Thanks."

"I can only tell you that this is not the way we usually do things at Wild Trophy World. I quite understand how you feel about it. When Fournier Frères have done the wet tanning and returned your bear, we will repair any bullet holes or tears. We will patch or dye thin or bald flank. I will select the right size urethane foam head form, eyes, teeth. Rest assured that your bear will be—her head will be museum natural, just as you would like to remember her."

Not a banker. Annie had been right. Funeral director. "That's very comforting."

"We're hunters too, Dr. Dobbs. I don't so much these last few years, but Frankie—my grandson—never misses a season. For anything. He got his first bighorn at fourteen. Wild Trophy World appreciates what a hunter feels. Large, medium or small, a wild game trophy stands for a vital experience, such an important part of the hunter's past given back to him every time he looks at a head or full mount or rug. For four generations we have practised our art with a craft we have learned well."

He could just as well have been a university president.

He closed the book, sat back in his chair. "We do no pets. You will find our work in the finest natural history museums—worldwide." He leaned forward, took a pen out of its socket in the head of the winter weasel beside the desk blotter. "I will phone Montreal. Let me have your home and business number, Dr. Dobbs."

# CHAPTER 9

"Well?"

"Your purse."

"Sorry. How are they coming along with Trigger?"

"Hasn't even been tanned yet."

"You did see it, though?"

"No."

"Why not?"

"She's in Montreal. Your Tenth Avenue turn-off is next."

"Why is she—"

"Frankie sent her there."

"Who's Frankie?"

"Annie—generally you can tell well ahead of time if a light is red or green."

"If you don't want to talk about—"

"I don't. Anticipate light changes. Take your foot off the gas and let deceleration do the rest. It saves wear and tear on the brake bands, and it is one hell of a lot easier on my back."

"Look! Isn't my fault your goddam bear hide's in Montreal!"

"When the light changes—"

"So quit dumping on—"

"—and you take off, gas pedal restraint—"

"—my driving!"

"—saves rubber!"

"Save your criticism of my driv—"

"Both starting and stopping—since we left the house—you have squealed at five traffic lights! Why hurry to a wine and cheese party?"

"I am not responsible that your goddam grizzly's bilingual! I am not exceeding the speed limit! So quit front-seat driving and mind your own business!"

"It is my own goddam business! I'm inside this goddam car! I am sitting in the goddam death seat!"

"Good!"

She swerved the car over into the exit lane for Whoop-up Trail. He said nothing about her failure to use the turn signal light. Their silence held almost to Poundmaker Road.

She stopped the car at the Kathleen MacNair front gates. "I'll let you out here, Poppa. Save you walking. You go on in while I park the car."

"I'd rather you drove around and let me out at the back."

"Oh, come on—"

"Just do it, Annie!"

For a change, she did.

"Shit!"

"What's the matter now?"

"I'm trapped again. Undo the button on this thing for me."

"Okay, Lear."

"Where's my cane?"

"Here."

"I'll wait for you. We'll go in together."

"Whatever you say but—oh, now I get it! The reception line inside the front, you don't want to face—"

"That's right."

Every time he looked at it, he wondered why so much fuss had been made over Kathleen MacNair College, from coast to coast. How could so many consider this design a happy result of the competition won six years ago by the nation's leading architect. The college was, as Herbie Stibbard and Milton put it: "The cynosure of neighbouring eyes." A three-storey rectangle of native sandstone blocks, with squat towers at each corner, it did not suggest academe so much as a late-eighteenth-century Hudson's Bay fur-trading post, well secured against rum-crazed Indians. Without his key, even the Master couldn't breach it from eleven at night to six in the morning, when the porter had locked the great wrought-iron gates at either end.

Must be a good turn-out to honour the new president. No deathless hush in the close today. Shouldn't take this long for her to park and get back to him. That architect responsible for Kathleen MacNair had to have been Western-born; only way to explain the half-hoop vault of plastic over the interior, now loud with merriment within. He had ingeniously designed it to be retractable, so that it could be open to the foothills sky during spring and summer and early fall, and closed for the winter months. Covered-or-uncovered covered wagon. How Western could you get! What the hell could be keeping her this long!

He really should go through those gates, find a bench just inside, sit down, and wait for her, but he didn't care to face them any sooner than he had to. The sun-glasses would shield his eyes from them but could not hide the corrugated fish-belly skin below the right lens. The side-show could just wait till the alligator skin lady was good and ready! Soon enough their eyes would be drawn to his face; even when they were outside his sight field he would be able to feel their gaze trained on him, catch them at it, surprise them in curiosity, make them turn away in embarrassment.

He hoped they'd extracted every one of the two sets of croquet hoops and stakes. Be hell to balance wine in one hand, plate of cheese and crackers in the other, then catch a toe! Annie would get him to a bench. She'd bring stuff to him. He'd make it all right. If she ever showed up!

"What kept you?"

"Wasn't easy finding a parking spot. The car's way over—behind SUB. How are you doing?"

"I'm all right."

"Why didn't you go on in?"

"Nicer out here."

"Want my arm?"

"Not yet."

"Well, take it easy. Whenever you want to leave, you just let me know. I'll go get the car and bring it here."

"Thanks. There are going to be a few people I'd rather not—that I'd like you to—"

"Kick 'em in the nuts."

"Only if you have to. The following: Liz Skeffington—"

"I thought she was straight."

"We're not sure. The Master, of course. Cam Tait—"

"I don't know him."

"I'll let you know which ones. Whyte—you'll recognize him. He's Native Studies—"

"Indian."

"Just wishes he were. He'll be well fringed and beaded, wearing a bear's-claw necklace—maybe his doeskin shirt with elk scrota breast pockets."

"I might just be able to spot him."

"Felix Schlitgen—"

"Jawohl."

"He will probably be the only clinical psychologist there, wearing a monocle."

"I don't believe it!"

"Oh, he's from Psychology, all right. I can't think of anyone in Sociology I'd care to talk with at any length. Or Religious Studies . . ."

"Anybody you *would* like to talk—"

"Dr. Lyon—if he's having a good day. Charlotte Robbins, Alistair Black, Molly Skidmore . . ."

"I'll keep my eye peeled, Poppa, and I'll be able to read your face. Now—grab your nose and let's jump right in."

"Stick by me, Annie."

"I will, Poppa."

"In case I don't come up."

"I haven't lost a swimmer at a wine and cheese party yet."

Well, she had. Within fifteen minutes, and before they'd even got to the wine and cheese table, she'd said she had to go to the can, then abandoned him here in the tropics, where passion-flower climbed the walls, hibiscus and bougainvillaea flourished, where tubbed bamboo and frangipani, fish-tail, Neanthe bella and date palms had been exiled. By Christmas break the blue and orange blossoms would be poised for take-off, all at precisely the same forty-five-degree angle. The Master of Kathleen MacNair and all her junior and senior fellows would be well advised to get themselves inoculated against malaria, elephantiasis, yellow fever, and yaws.

Five times he had explained to strange people what had happened to him up Daisy Creek last Reading Break. One of them had introduced himself as a professor of physical geography. As opposed to spiritual geography, no doubt. Another admitted he was in human kinetics. So far he had avoided Cam Tait, but Herbie Stibbard had got to him. Even before Daisy Creek, talk with Herbie was sometimes just too much scholarly dessert imbedded with quotation and allusion like raisins in rice pudding. Although he hadn't once taken his eyes from the scarred cheek, Herbie wasn't so bad, really. He could teach.

He may well have thought it, but he hadn't aptly said: "Out, vile jelly!"

Several times he had caught sight of Molly Skid-more, always with concern, near apprehension, upon her face. His heart went out to her, for they were comrade skulkers: he was worried about his face; she, about her flower-beds, near the brutal feet of all these intruders, whose attention was for each other and not her plants. She was a pretty nice human, had to be as the Master's secretary; it was remarkable that daily intercourse with him (in the old meaning of the word) had never turned her bitter. Her plants must have made the six-year association bearable; if a person loved them as much as Molly did, flowers might ease pain. Given a chance to talk with her in this wine and cheese maelstrom, he'd tell her the babel and milling bodies might drive the squirrels out of the close. At least they would be distracted from excavating her new fall plant-ing of crocus and tulip and daffodil bulbs. Briefly. Nei-ther mustard nor kerosene nor pepper had worked for her, nor the buried moth-balls he had once suggested to her.

He hadn't caught sight of Dr. Lyon yet, which wasn't so surprising, for he'd had a feeling the old man would not show up. He'd seen Charlotte at a distance and through bodies, then lost her. God knew when Annie would drop her skirt and come back to him, so he'd better get to the wine and cheese table by the common room entrance on his own, then find an out-of-the-way bench and sit down, preferably behind foliage. That had been a very close call with Whyte on silent moccasins and with an eagle feather hanging in front of his left ear.

A few shots of white wine would be just what the doctor ordered; the trick was to get to it without being accosted, to keep his face from telegraphing messages of pain to people, who would stop him and pretend to listen to him, nodding and agreeing and staring, but actually wondering and guessing at the meaning of some inadvertent grimace or frown or tightening of the corners of his mouth. "Poor fellow! He's in pain!" Goddam right I am! And none of your goddam busi-ness, and nothing is to be gained by explaining what exactly had happened, where it had happened, why it had happened, or what it was in the first place that

would drive a man to hunt grizzly bears! I do not care
to be reminded of what she did to me up Daisy Creek
last Reading Break! It is an old nightmare tape I do not
want to play over again! And again and again and
again . . .

Oh, God! Liz Skeffington! Goddam ungulate all in
scarlet! Heading right for him! Where was Annie when
he needed her! By screening himself with all the skill of
a James Fenimore Cooper Indian, first with human
bodies, then a Neanthe bella palm, a skinny dracaena
marginata, and two birds-of-paradise, he finally made
it behind a tall convocation of tubbed bamboo. Gave
her the slip! Feral vegetarian! Probably had a double
stomach!

Escape had taken him in the wrong direction, at
least doubling his distance from the wine and cheese
table. Now he was between two of the three kidney-
shaped ponds with their synchronized fountains, at the
front gate of the close. Through the second fountain he
saw the deans of the Faculty of Education, Arts and
Science, Native Studies, Business Administration, Social Sciences, Drama, Music and Visual Arts, the Academic and Financial Vice-Presidents, the Chancellor, the
Master of Kathleen MacNair College, and next to him a
very tall man wearing a black and gold freshman beanie.
The reception line was still alive, and the stranger with
the beanie had to be the new president of Livingstone
University. His very first sight of him was through
rising and falling water; Herbie could tell him what sort
of omen, good or bad, that might be. Athena was the
wrong sex and she sure as hell wasn't seven feet tall.
And Poseidon would not wear a freshman beanie to a
wine and cheese party!

He'd better head back for that table and the white
wine! Quick!


Most of the people must have already come and loaded
and left, for he was alone at the bar end of the table,
and there were only a couple further down to his right,
making their cheese decisions. Evidently the bartender
had taken a break or gone to restock, but he had

thoughtfully left opened bottles: Cinzano, sherry, Dubonnet, red and white wine. No sign of Annie yet.

He picked up one of the stemmed goblets, found it surprisingly light even after he had filled it with white wine. He knocked it back, then refilled. Sherry. He took his paper plate and glass down the table to the yellow and orange and cream cubes of cheese, each one pierced by a green toothpick fletched with what looked like clear, dead grass. He made a selection, drank the sherry, returned to the bar end, refilled twice. One white wine; one Cinzano. Back for square and triangular crackers, Stilton, Camembert. He drank the Cinzano, revisited the bar, refilled and drank and poured a sherry—or a Cinzano, then down the table for smoked salmon. He passed over the pigmy penis sausages in foreskin pastry. On his last visit to the bar for his fifth or sixth glass of sherry or Cinzano or Dubonnet, he felt someone looking at him. To his right. Or the seventh. He turned to see the young man at the other end of the table, and for a moment did not recognize him. Slaughter! He had not seen his former student since last October, when he had asked him to discontinue the graduate writing seminar, after he had told him his short story of a school-yard gang rape was a careless piece of specious realism, that it was dreadfully flawed with authorial intrusion, and that it had such a confused point of view, it was hard to be sure the writer wasn't one of the boys on top. Slaughter had disagreed and told him to wipe his ass with his King's College doctorate.

When Colin had risen from his chair, Slaughter had lifted both fists. "You step round the end of that desk and I am going to tear your fucking arm off and beat you over the head with the bloody end of it!"

He had come round the end of the desk. Slaughter started for him, lifted both arms up and out, then suddenly dropped them, turned, and ran from the room.

·He was sitting in his chair and still telling himself it had not happened when there was a knock on the door.

"What happened?" It was Herbie.

"I'm not sure."

"I heard the shouting—down in my office!"

"Slaughter."

"What was it all about—"

"You ever had a student threaten you?"

"Not since I was one. Did he?"

"Pretty nasty. He came at me, then just turned and ran out of here. It was close. He meant it. Right till the last moment."

"Why did he—"

"I still can't believe it! I told him his short story was a piece of crap. He told me to take my doctorate and wipe my ass with it. I told him I didn't want him in the seminar. He threatened me and then charged me. He really intended to tear me apart!"

"Colin." Herbie was pointing towards the door. "He's still out there—sitting at the bottom of the stair well."

"Jesus!"

"He's crying."

"God!"

"He needs help."

"You've got it twisted, Herbie. I need protection!"

How had he failed to recognize that hulk instantly! Even with the beard he'd grown since that morning in the office! Very black. Very trim. He was coming down the table to him.

"Surprised to see me?"

"Yes."

"I made my honours year after all. B plus."

"Congratulations."

"In spite of you." He reached out, with fingers partly curved, stirred at the radishes, sent one rolling off the platter. "Should have been A." The thick fingers scooped black olives. "So—you nearly bought it with a bear, I hear." His head went back; all the olives went into his mouth. "And see." The other hand went out and came up with a cheese-stuffed stalk of celery. "I hope you're fully recovered."

"Your beard suits you."

"How long did it put you in the hospital?" He continued to chomp on the celery stalk.

"Quite Mephistophelian."

"Oh—dropped your paper plate! Here." He replaced the cheese and crackers that had fallen off it and handed the plate back. "About the beard. You really ought to grow one yourself."

"Colin . . ." An English voice intruded.

"Can that side of your face still grow hair?"

He turned away towards the voice.

"Colin, I don't think you've met our new president. Have you?" He had never thought he'd be glad to hear that British tenor. The Master was quite donnish in grey flannels, probably held up by his old school tie, under the brass-buttoned blue blazer. The ascot was paisley. He was in fine high-table voice today.

"Nice to meet you, Colin."

The man must be over seven feet tall!

"Dr. Dobbs is one of our creativists, Dr. Donaldson." The best of Waugh, indeed.

"I may call you Colin?"

Under the black freshman beanie with its quartering gold stripes, the eyes were large and dark and steady; they held a sad and dignified concern.

"Surnames get in the way and I don't like formality."

The lower parts of the cheeks were full, just a touch of basset.

"Most people call me Cal."

The President's eyes were not really on his own; they were probably aimed under the right lens of the sun-glasses. No doubt at all, he had told! "Sure, Cal."

"And specifically what is your discipline, Colin?"

That impossible beanie! "Criticism." He could not take his eyes off that beanie way up there! "Creative writing." The President had no intention of taking his eyes off the scarred cheek either.

"Prose," the Master explained.

All right—if it's the stare game you want to play, you're on!

"Fiction or non-fiction?" Telephone pole with a black and gold beanie on top!

"A little of both." I'll bet you flinch first.

"Even in the short time I've been here, I'm impressed with the very fine English Department at Livingstone."

I can beat you at it any day.

"Heavy on creative writing, Dr. Tait tells me."

I'll keep my eyes on your fucking beanie just as
long as you keep yours on my scarred, fucking face!

"I'm interested in creative writing myself."

"It's the only kind of writing that's worth while."
Nyah, nyah, nyah—you gave up before I gave up!

"Cal."

Annie had been wrong; he'd been right: coming here
had been a bad mistake. It had turned rotten before
Slaughter. He'd been on his feet much too long; the
wine and sherry hadn't helped all that much; his right
elbow was at it again, and the spine would join in
soon. Like a goddam hurt symphony; if the elbow was
the flute, then the neck was the violin and the spine—oh,
that deep ache like a cello refrain of pain echoing down
and out under his shoulder-blades and all through the
body band-shell. Come on, Dobbs, isn't all that bad or
you wouldn't be reaching for smart metaphors like
that. But if you don't find a place to sit down, it will get
worse! Soon!

Too bad there wasn't a spray against humans on
the market yet, gentler acting than mace, somewhat
like the one that discouraged dogs from lifting a leg.
Pocket or purse size, suitable for use at wine and cheese
parties, brand name: PISS OFF! That's the stuff, Dobbs!
No more self-pity, and don't forget to laugh when that
rock rolls right back down again. Feeling better already,
aren't you. And cursing always helps too. Feeling fucking better already! And you'll feel a hell of a lot better
when you find that goddam bench and sit down and
take the weight off that fucking hip too!

And he had found one, against the south wall,
under the second-floor balcony. It was hung with bas-
kets spilling spider plant, shielded by a twelve-foot
ficus benjamina, and empty so that he could put the
paper plate and the wineglass down beside himself and
be alone.

People seemed to have drifted towards the fountain end where he could see the Master with the new

president and the Dean of Graduate Studies and the Chancellor. He couldn't find Annie anywhere.

From the loudspeaker behind him came the Master's voice, saying how fortunate Livingstone University was that Dr. Donaldson had chosen to leave his post as financial vice-president of the nation's most distinguished university in the east to come west to Livingstone University. The Master stepped aside and back under the frangipani tree.

"Hi," Dr. Donaldson's deep voice came through the spider plants, "though as I look around this lovely place, I might have more fittingly said, Aloha." He waited out the short stir of laughter.

"I do appreciate the warm Western welcome you have given me. Nor has it been too warm, and I am truly grateful that you have excused me from hell week." He touched the freshman beanie with a finger. "Even though I am just a freshman to Livingstone University." He waited through another brief sprinkle. "I hope you will be as charitable to me later on during my tenure here." This time the response was longer and stronger. "I would like to say just a few words about this university's vital role in regional and national development, a role even more essential in these times of fiscal restraint, making it especially difficult to carry out rational plans for expansion and development in a young institution like Livingstone University. Preoccupied as we will be with budgets and expansion problems, we must fulfil all obligations and guard against erosion in the quality of our programs. I hope that together we may achieve flexibility and imagination through a positive and forward-looking self-definition. Not so much a *new* self-definition as one of changed emphasis on the vital importance of the humanities and the arts. I could not agree more with Shelley when he said, 'Poets are the unacknowledged legislators of the world.' "

In the next five minutes he mentioned few specifics on how the university would accomplish the changed but not new emphasis, beyond reference to a rare books and papers collection he considered vitally needed, the removal of asbestos from the walls and ceilings of the Crowfoot Gallery, and more musical performances and poetry readings. Colin guessed that most of those gathered in the close of Kathleen MacNair College already knew that Livingstone University was the third-largest employer in the community, with 900 employees, had 12,561 full-time and 292 part-time students upgrading their career skills or expanding vital life interests, that 10.1 million dollars per month in salaries flowed back into the community, and that 11 million dollars was spent annually from research grants.

"I am sorry that my wife cannot be with us here this afternoon. She is down with the flu, which is going round, and she has asked me to give you her regrets. Dell wants to meet you too, and she intends to do that next week when we will hold open house at our place, the presidential palace, 482 Cariboo Crescent, from ten o'clock on in the morning next Sunday. Bring your spouses with you—or your mistresses. For a pancake brunch. Suffice it to say we both look forward to our association with this great university."

"Do we bring our own maple syrup?" Cam Tait had sat down beside him on the bench.

"Seems to have a good supply of that on hand." Out of all the people here, why did it have to be Tait to sit down beside him! What an unrepentant Wordsworthian he was, with his constant air of excitement, as though he were on a never-ending scavenger hunt. Now that he had become Head, his tally of academic spoils in *Scholarly Briefs*, published by the Office of Information Services, would rise even higher in Addresses, Committee Appointments, Participations.

"Think he'll be good for us?"

"I have no idea."

"His university is the greatest. Trinity."

"Oxford?"

"No."

"Dublin?"

"Toronto—for his undergraduate years. Then Harvard."

"Law?"

"Political Science. Neiman Fellow. Henry's class."

"Henry?"

"Kissinger. Also Fine Arts, I understand."

"With Kissinger! In Fine Arts! In Harvard!"

"St. Andrews. He's well published. Most recent

issue of *Art Forum:* 'Corporate and Governmental Involvement in the Arts.' "

"Could do worse."

"Sure. 'Vital Values to be Found in Dance, Mime, and Abstract Finger Painting.' "

"You armed yourself ahead of time, didn't you?"

"I always do."

"I've often suspected that. Be a good fellow and bugger off, will you, Tait."

"I shall." He stood up.

"Will," Colin corrected him. "It was a promise. Mustn't let old North Dakota down, must we?"

Drew blood with that one. Tait's face had hardened. He stood up abruptly. "The speech of even English Department chairmen ought to be unflawed," he called after him, "grammatically."

Annie had been right. Coming here hadn't been such a bad idea after all. Some more of the Stilton now. And another sherry. Several more sherries.

By leaning his good hip against the bar end of the table, working with the cane, he was able to move the bottle closer to the edge, then slide it over and get it into his right jacket pocket, just the neck and shoulders showing. Nobody had noticed.

"Let me help you."

Slaughter!

"This one's much fuller."

Pain shot to the tip of his little finger as Slaughter grasped his right shoulder with one hand, and kept it there while he removed and replaced the sherry bottle.

"There you are, Dr. Dobbs. It's called heaping coals of fire on your head."

"Didn't expect to see you here."

Dear little teapot! "Charlotte!" She sat down beside him. "You can hug me if you're very careful."

Funny—he didn't mind telling her about what the bear had done to him up Daisy Creek.

"I'm glad you made it. Can't afford to lose a good teacher like you."

That was Charlotte; she envied no one his degrees, position, publication. She knew what a university was all about. Too bad she was diabetic. "Early onset. I'm no juvenile," she'd once told him. "Wouldn't even have it if I didn't teach. I'm going to have to quit doing morning seminars. Every time—half-way through—if I could test my urine, my sugar would show way up. Teaching triggers it."

He watched her, bent forward now, with her elbows on her spread knees.

"The only other person I know who rolls his own is my Stony friend, Archie Nicotine."

"At least half your students do."

"I meant tobacco." Whatever it was, every one of them must have better rolling skill. Her cigarettes looked as though they'd never heal up. Again and again and again her students would wince, explain to her that she was rolling them backwards; again and again she would let them show her, with their hands over hers, how it was properly done, then return to the loose and crippled things she seemed to have chain-smoked from the age of ten. She was sure as hell deft in handling Children's Literature, could teach rings around Tait, who always called it Kiddy Litter.

"You got crumbs and shreds all over you."

Squinting against the smoke, she pinched her skirt with both hands and flipped it up. "Presto."

"You always do that?"

"Sometimes I may let a young man brush them off for me. If he's a hunk."

"Whatever that is."

"Should keep your vocabulary updated, Colin."

"Annie sees to that. Go get a glass, Charley."

"You want me to get you a glass of wine?"

"No. Just reach down and you might find a bottle of sherry behind the bench. Get yourself a glass so we can drink to the new president."

"Diabetes won't let me."

"Guess I'll have to drink yours for you then."

"Looks to me as though you already have."

"Surprised to see Charles Slaughter a while back."

"Oh, he's still with us."

"Behaving himself?"

"No. Came close to being kicked out in April—just before classes were withdrawn."

"What saved him?"

"So near the end of his honours year."

"What did he do?"

"When the secretary said he couldn't barge right in on the Dean he jumped up on her desk, threatened to urinate all over her graduate files."

"Did he?"

"No. She screamed. Somebody called Security."

"Good enough reason to—"

"He also got angry at the stacks librarian when she reminded him of his overdue books. For the third time. He dumped a cup of coffee over her head."

"*Threatened* to."

"No. He did carry out that hot promise."

"Then why wasn't he—"

"A lot of people have wondered why. It seems Whyte and the Master here and Schlitgen—may have been others on the discipline committee also—felt expulsion would be too harsh just before his finals. He was given another chance."

"He's a dangerous young man."

"I know that, but—"

"Could be their support wasn't exactly voluntary."

"Oh."

"He did his exams. No more incidents."

" 'Nother sherry?"

"No thanks. Anyway, no more incidents on campus."

"Huh?"

"The apartment he shared with that clever and rather ugly girl—"

"Brenna McLean."

"Her kitchen cupboards—drawers, doors, counter, ironing board. He chain-sawed them."

"And they still let him back in!"

"Well. It did happen outside the university community. She didn't lay charges."

"Afraid to."

"I guess."

"Like Whyte—the others."

"He's doing a creative thesis."

"Whaaat!"

"He's writing a—"

"He couldn't write—home to his mother for money!"

"A novel he's been working on all summer."

"Who the hell okayed that?"

"Our new head."

"Tait!"

"One of the first decisions he made when he took over."

"Out of fright?"

"Possibly."

" 'Nother sherry?"

"No, thanks. I think I've really had enough, Colin."


"You were gone long enough."

"Sorry, Poppa."

"Where you been?"

"I ran into Vicky in the can—"

"This is Charley Robbins."

"You're Annie."

"She can teach."

"Professor Robbins."

"Childern's Litter—she stayed with me. Where were you?"

"Vicky wanted to show me what she'd done with her pink and cream collage. . . ."

"Shouldna left me."

"I think he's right, Annie."

"Alone."

"He smells like he just climbed out of a wine vat!"

"Sherry. Not much left in that bottle—"

"I was carryin' it to my sick gramma, but on my way through the wine an' cheese—your idea."

"Not to get boiled!"

"Not boiled."

"You sure as hell are!"

"I agree with Annie, Colin."

"She made me come here. Said she'd stick by me. She didn', but you did, Charley. Grateful for that."

"Think you'll need any help, Annie?"

"I've had some practice with him."

"You leavin' me too, Charley?"

"Annie's here now."

"Le's go home."

"That's what we're doing, Poppa. If you can stand."

"I can stand."

"Let alone walk! How's your balance?"

"'Smy balance."

"We'll take it slow and careful to the porter's office." She handed him his cane. "You can wait in there while I get the car."

"'Snot make a spectacle out of me. Front of the new presiden'. Want to go home."

"Not any more than I do."

"He's just a frenshman, you know."

"Here's how we do it. The crowd's thinned out some and we'll take it easy and we'll work our way—"

"For his beanie told me so."

"Take your cane in your other hand—your *other* hand. Now—your arm over my shoulder. Ready. Steady. When we get to the fountains . . ."

"Lead on, Leon."

". . . we're going to go round the left end one. . . ."

"Make end run roun' left end."

"Watch out for the curbing. Really careful round the pond."

"An' don' kiss any strange—"

"Straighten up."

"—frogs."

"And shut up and help me! Oh, my God!"

"Y'all right, Annie?"

"The first fountain!"

"End run round the end—careful the curb . . ."

"Hydrophobia!"

"Sorry to hear that."

"And now the second one! They're foaming! Third one too! All three! Spilling froth all over!"


"Party's over now."

"You could say that."

"Take me home."

"We are home. Now your shirt."

He pushed her hands away from his collar. "Cap'ble."

"Not with your shoe-laces or your socks or jacket you weren't."

"Go on downstairs. Paint something."

"You'll have trouble with your pants."

"Paint the Last Supper."

"Judas!"

" 'She snarled.' "

"You can't manage your pants."

" 'She r'iterated.' "

"Damn it, Poppa!"

" 'She 'jac'lated.' "

No trouble whatever. He just left them on and climbed under the covers. Oh, God! Shouldn't have rolled over to his back. Whole head straining to lift off like a hot-air balloon! Stomach too! He fell twice in the hall, making it to the toilet bowl, but just once on his way back to the bedroom. Annie's! He corrected that.

Little better now. Not much. Some. Should have stuck with the white. Should have stayed home. Her idea. Chipping and chipping at him till it was easier to go than to miss it, as he had wanted to in the first place. Wasn't my idea, Cal. Please understand that. Wanted to stay home and self-define myself. Tell Dell for me. Can't make it next Sunday to the pancake brunch. Sorry, Chip and Dale. Sorry to you too, Molly, and all your poor plants, but you should never have dropped mothballs into the sherry!

Sorry, Annie. Poppa's turn now. Held your head for you when you unloaded all that chocolate birthday cake. Remember? "Oh, Poppa, I wish I wasn't true!" Now Poppa's boiled and skinned and sloughed and salted and tattooed in two places. Poppa's very, very, sherry sick and all too true!

Sick of academe, where magpies, crows, and ravens in their black gowns hook their hoods, set their mortarboards, then glide off and alight before that stuffed ground owl in black and gold chancellor robes, to carry off rolled and ribboned B.A.s, M.A.s, and Ph.D.s in eager beaks while learned head-mounts look down on solemn ceremony. Master Bear presides, as learned moose and caribou, scholarly elk and deer and sheep and goats gather in their department herds. Clever, prong-horn Herbie's harmless, but look out for timber she-wolf Skeffington and that weasel Tait.

In our wild trophy world we don't do pets. One exception: that basset head-mount in the freshman beanie.

# CHAPTER 10

He had known he would be hung over, but not this bad; at both temples and across his forehead, the blood was blacksmithing. When he sat up so did his stomach. His head and the bedroom swam.

"And how are we feeling this morning. I hope."

"Oh, Annie! Annie, Annie, Annie!"

"You've answered my question. Here's some coffee."

"It wouldn't stay down."

"Drink it and get dressed and come down for your breakfast."

"Food is a four-letter word!"

"So is fool!"

"I wish I wasn't true!"

"It's a problem for both of us."

"What time is it?"

"Quarter after seven."

"Oh, God!"

"Yes. He's in His Heaven and all's—"

"Please—just leave me—"

"When you've drunk your coffee and after you're dressed. I see you've already managed to get your pants on by yourself. I'll help with your shoes—then downstairs."

"Be nice to me, Annie."

"It's not easy."

The smell hit him at the head of the stairs.

"Oh, no! Not bacon and fried eggs!"

"Grab the banister."

"Cruel!"

"And watch where you put your feet. You've had nothing on your stomach since yesterday noon. Except for what you ate at Kathleen MacNair. Mostly cheese."

"Don't mention—"

"I see by the toilet bowl this morning that some time last night you threw everything up."

"I think I'm going to—"

"From the look of it—mostly Camembert puke. You blew it."

"Couldn't we discuss something else besides vomit!"

"The wine and cheese party, after I got you there for your own good. You blew it. Deliberately."

"Not deliberately."

"Look—when you came out of that place, it was all over your face. Whatever it was you found out about your goddam bear hide. I don't care how disappointed you were—it was no excuse for what you did."

"I'm sorry."

"Okay. Let's get in there and you get those eggs and bacon inside you."

Foolhardy as it was to try, he did get them down and they stayed there. She poured him a third cup of coffee and set four pills beside it. "Take two of them now. In about a half an hour, the other two. That will be when we leave for the university."

"Huh!"

"What you need now is about twelve pool lengths—then a sauna."

"What I need is to get back upstairs."

"Suit yourself."

"If I need you . . ."

"You can phone the university. I'll be working till two in the studio. You want to stay here alone, it's okay with me, but I really think you should come out with me, work the poison out of your system in the pool, and sweat it out in the sauna."

"The pool and sauna are crowded as hell on Saturdays."

"Today is Sunday."

"Worse."

"Not this early. Right to noon I'll bet you'll have that pool and sauna all to yourself. I leave in half an hour."

"Give me some quarter."

"Sure. There's one other possibility."

"What?"

"I could drop you off at the drug and alcohol abuse centre."

On their way out there she delivered what must have been a well-prepared lecture, an ironic one for her generation and for her. She told him she had little patience with people who gave away control of their lives to others, to drugs, to alcohol, which was just a liquid cop-out favoured and forgiven by parents, who criticized the young for their new ones.

"Getting high is not funny, Poppa—whatever kind of high it is. I know what I'm talking about."

"I'm not arguing it is, Annie."

"I run clean."

"Did you have a bad experience?"

"Not my own. Remember I started to tell you something on our way out yesterday?"

"I'm not remembering very much."

"Just before that Volkswagen. She was probably pissed too."

"Yes."

"I started to tell you something—two things, actually. You got it coming to you. I owe you a more detailed explanation than I gave you that first day in the hospital. Like—why I split. Middle of my first semester at Victoria."

"To find yourself, your mother told me."

"Mmmh. That was very in then."

"It still is. I do teach, you know."

"All that time I knew you were worried for me but I couldn't—I didn't want—I didn't know how to . . ."

"How to what?"

"Explain. And it isn't any easier now."

"Then wait till it is."

"That's what I've been telling myself, but it isn't going to get any easier."

"I guess you'll never stop lowering your frightening gangplanks, Annie, but—please—just tell me."

"Well—when she left you she made a real bad trade back there. Loyalty is not one of his strongest qualities. Mother is not going to live happily ever after with her chiropractor."

"Chiropractor! He's a gynaecologist!"

"So she likes people to believe. I guess he's a gynaecological chiropractor and he does indeed specialize in women. I think, Poppa, you could have been better informed about him."

"I didn't care to be!"

"I know that, Elmer."

And he knew now! This was going to be a bad one!

"I couldn't tell Mother why—then—either."

"You don't have to tell me now, Annie, if you—"

"Oh, I have to. For quite a while I couldn't be sure it wasn't just my horny adolescent imagination. Maybe the signals were false signals. Then I knew they weren't. Then I explained to him that even though he was only my stepfather, doing it with him would still be incest. Then I kicked him in the nuts. Then I left."

He had not anticipated it would be this bad!

"That's why I haven't seen Mother. I've never told her. Maybe I shouldn't have told you."

"You should have."

"Any questions from the audience?"

"One. Did you get him good?"

"His face went white. Oh, Poppa, I am so blue!"

"You said there were two things—you wanted to tell me."

"Mother's the bad experience, Poppa. She's why I don't use—anything. She does. Too much. Or did. I feel sorry for her. I feel sorry for you."

"Poor Sarah!"

"I guess I feel sorriest for myself."

"Chiropractor!"

"I really shouldn't be surprised that you didn't know. You always did have a sort of innocence, Poppa."

"Not 'sort of.' "

"Yes, you have."

"Don't qualify superlatives. Innocence. Virginity."

"I have neither of those. But you do have a tough innocence."

"You too, Annie. Tougher than I thought."

"Oh, you saw to that. Not so innocent, though. Most women aren't."

"I must have missed that survey."

"At least, not nearly so innocent as men are."

"Could you—pull over."

"Men *think* women are innocent."

"Stop the car!"

"Best thing we got going for us. Never have made it other—"

"That bacon and eggs you forced me to—"


"Feeling better?"

"Not sure."

"There's Kleenex in the glove compartment. How's your head now?"

"Still there."

"Left side of your chin—"

"Pay attention to your driving."

"You must be feeling better when you start criticising my driving."

"It comes and goes now. The new president was wearing a freshman beanie, wasn't he?"

"Yes."

"And there was some confusion around the fountains."

"A lot of it."

"But I'm not clear what it was all about."

"That's because you passed out in the porter's office while I went for the car."

"Seemed to be a lot of—looked like foam."

"That's what it was. We nearly went down in it. Others did. Trying to capture goldfish."

"Were they that drunk!"

"No. They were trying to save them."

"From what?"

"Death by detergent."

"Detergent!"

"Somebody dumped it into each pool and let the fountains do the rest."

"Oh, don't, Annie. I've told you I'm sorry—"

"Somebody did. The guy in the flannels and the blue blazer."

"The Master!"

"Up to his knees in the first pool, yelling at people to forget the ones floating on top and rescue the ones under water. He kept shouting 'Bloody engineers!' "

"There were over two hundred goldfish!"

"Not any more. You feeling better now?"

"I shouldn't after what you've just told me. But I do."

"You think it might have been somebody from Engineering? Why should the Master—"

"He's got a Matthew Arnold complex. Considers Engineering and Education faculties the worst of the barbarians, unfit for either junior or senior fellowship in Kathleen MacNair. He's positive it was engineers did the plants last year."

"Plants?"

"Three new tubs showed up last spring inside the close. He probably didn't even notice them. Molly would, because along with everything else he leaves that sort of thing to her. Each tub was labelled. *Elegantissima*."

"What's that?"

"Common name: threadleaf or false aralia. Each must have thought the other had ordered them from Plants and Grounds."

"What about them?"

"They were about a foot high when they first appeared. By fall, maybe five foot. Very graceful, feathery umbrellas of slender leaves."

"Oh, no!"

"False indeed. Late September somebody harvested them."

"Marijuana!"

"According to the people from the Botany Department he called in for help. He's sure it was engineers then. And now with the goldfish, I guess."

"You think it was?"

"He was wrong about the false aralia. General opinion is that it was an inside job. Three of the junior fellows—one from Biology, another from Drama, the third from either Anthropology or Environmental Design. All pretty heavy users."

"They're two different things!"

"Can't argue with you."

"One's stupid! The other's vicious. It took a pretty sick person to do in all those goldfish!"

"I agree."

"You know anybody who would—"

"Right now, I don't want to think about it. Like the Master. Just conjecture."

"Which you don't care to share."

"I think I'm going to be sick again."

It had been a false alarm, but only because there were no bacon and eggs left down there. When she let him out at the entrance of the Human Kinetics Building, to go to her studio, she had still not forgiven him.

"Have a nice day, Poppa."

There was nobody in front of the counter when he picked up his towel and left his watch and wallet with the attendant. He had the locker room to himself, was just as lucky when he left the shower and went out to the pool. All lanes stayed empty while he willed himself to fifteen lengths, the last three languid and on his back. He had just climbed out when a young boy came out of the men's door and did a racing dive from the shallow end.

The sauna blessed him; as he worked his hotter and hotter way up, he could feel the ache diluting in his back and hip and shoulder and elbow. The nausea and headache were almost gone. If his luck held, he'd be finished in here and out and dressed, without curious eyes tracing scar tracks over his back and chest and stomach. There had always been annoyances when he had company in here, somebody trying to turn the place into a steam-bath by dippering water again and again on the lava rocks so that breath intake could almost sear, or faculty young in search of parents, popping in and holding the door open. Last year, some fellow had relieved himself on the hot rocks so that the place would be public-lavatory offensive for later occupants, and for days after, it smelled like a sour citrus grove in hell.

He moved up another bench. Carefully. Years of

contraction and expansion had levered nail heads out
from the cedar planks so that a first-time or careless
user had simply to touch hot metal to inflict an instant
buttock brand. Or, if male, much worse. He could feel
the sweat gathering on his forehead, then a run starting from his left eyebrow to tickle down his cheek.
Probably the right one too, though the nerve the surgeon had imported from the back of his knee could not
let him know about that. He looked over to both doors.
God, he hoped no one came in! Of either sex! The bear
had made him modest.

Seven years before, when Human Kinetics had got
its pool, gymnasium, indoor track, and squash courts
building, it had not been its intention that the sauna be
used heterosexually. But with cost overruns and the
provincial government's unwillingness to increase its
contribution, a second room had become a casualty of
necessary budget compromise. Since then the university had made a vital, extramural contribution to the
sex education of neighbouring Livingstone Heights
youngsters as they watched both sexes running and
rolling in snow-drifts. Occasionally during a chinook in
early spring, some daredevils broke the ice skin at the
river edge to immerse themselves in the therapeutic
interest of shocking the heart, contracting blood vessels
and genitals, erecting nipples, and slamming shut academic pores. Now one heard hardly anyone suggest
another facility be built; mixed sauna bathing had become a well-established Livingstone University tradition.

For almost the only time since he'd abandoned the
novel, his first visit to the sauna had tempted him to
try a short story, one that would happen in this promising setting. Naked, people said so much about themselves. Unwittingly. Body language became more articulate. Negligent towels were dropped over privates. A
casual leg was thrown over a knee; men leaned forward
on their elbows, heads down in the thinker pose;
women kept their legs together, arms folded across
their breasts, or if they had long enough hair, they let it
fall over both shoulders and hang down in front. Not
all that effective a curtain if the breasts were large;
nipples that peeped stimulated. Comparative Literature
had taken one look at Classics in Translation's magnifi-

cent knockers and found himself evidently excited. How did you forbid an erection? He had draped his towel over it but the teepee still told on him. He had never returned.

Head of Drama always leaned back against the second level, flung one leg out, foot on the floor, and drew his other up on the bench beside himself, to display all he had. Which was considerable. Tait generally lay flat out on his stomach so he could hog the top level. Herbie Stibbard often read the *New York Times Book Review* and left with print on his thighs. All the news that's fit to imprint. Just might do that short story some day.

Chill surprised his ankles. He looked over to the women's door on his wrong side, then quickly away, but not before he'd seen her soft, dark triangle and one breast. The gold and black towel over her right shoulder hid the other. Brown-eyed Susan. With great willpower he kept his gaze consideratley ahead of himself. It had to be the first time since Daisy Creek he'd averted his face for someone else's sake.

Eye slide let him see that she had seated herself on the far corner of the lowest planks. She had a most articulate back, shoulders level and well squared. When she moved her arms a shoulder-blade declared itself, the other still under the towel. The high edge of her hip was distinctly young. Rodin's *Danaïd*. Seated. She must have just left the pool or shower, for her hair was a black calotte. Cardinal Wolsey.

He was running with sweat now. He ought to move down a couple of notches, but that would bring him closer to her. If he slid further along to his left, she might interpret it unfortunately. Maybe not, if he were to move away and down at the same time. His chest and stomach scars were livid red and purple. God only knew how the eye and cheek were. He'd better just get out of here!

She'd turned towards him. The breast with its chocolate aureole was not adolescent. Champagne glass! Goodbye, Cardinal!

A cold blast hit him.

"I forgot the combination!" The child was holding it wide open.

"Shut the door, Robin!"

The weather moderated.

"What's the right combin—"

"Four-eight-three."

Brief winter again.

"I'm sorry."

"That's all right." Now they'd spoken to each other would be rude to leave.

"He always forgets the number."

"So do I," he lied again.

Blizzard!

"I tried that one and it doesn't work!"

Continuing cold!

"Try it again! Four-eight-three!"

"It won't work!"

"Try it anyway and shut the bloody door!"

He was not going to have to come down now to cool off, after all.

"We haven't met before."

Naked or otherwise. "Colin Dobbs. English."

"Helen Sweeney. Philosophy."

Just what the hell did he say to her now?

"You're new to Livingstone?"

"Three months. Exchange. Lausanne."

"Sweeney's a very Swiss name."

"My ex was Irish. Is. I've kept his name. Not for myself so much as for—"

And we shall have snow.

"Jeezus H., Robin!"

"I told you! Four-eight-one doesn't work—"

"Three! Four—eight—three!"

"You said four-eight-*one*!"

"I said four-eight-*three*!" She looked up to him. "Didn't I?"

"Several times."

She said she was sorry again and he said it was all right again. Four-eight-three must have been the corrct combination for her son's locker because he did not return to freeze them again. She explained that she was not a sauna frequenter; indeed this was her first time in one, and just how long should one spend in one? He said half an hour.

She moved up a level. He came down one. A drop

of sweat had gathered and trembled from the tip of her nose. She wiped at it with the back of her wrist. Perspiration was usually well started in about five mintues, he told her; until then, it helped to capture it where it first appeared—the forehead—cheeks—and transfer it to drier and hotter skin areas.

"Guess I'll take your advice." She lifted her breast, put her hand under it and brought it out cupped to spread moisture over her left shoulder, then underneath the towel still hanging over her right side.

"I've just about had it. My half-hour." He lowered himself to the first level and his cane.

Her whole body gleamed now. Quite lovely!

He stood. Too quickly for heat-slackened muscles. His hip gave out underneath him. He fell back and down, but only onto the planks.

"You all right?" She came down to him. The towel had fallen from her shoulder.

"Okay. Okay." Now he understood the towel. She had only one breast.

"You're sure?"

"Yes." He had made it to his feet again. "I'm all right."

She handed him the cane. "I—" She looked down at herself, then up to him. "I thought I'd have it all to myself."

"So did I."

"If there had to be someone else, I'm rather glad it was you."

"Me too."

"My being here bothered you?"

"At first."

"Until?"

"At first."

"Do you mind if I ask you . . ."

"I was mauled by a bear."

"Oh, dear!"

"About four months ago."

"So—you're an Ursus."

"They left that one off the zodiac calendar." He started for the door.

"Not mine."

He turned back to her. She had not replaced the towel. "Nice meeting you." In all your naked candour. "And Robin." Glorified by sweat!

She was grinning, for God's sake. "We must see more of each other."

CHAPTER **11**

He had known for some time through supper, and as they sat over their coffee, that there was something she wanted to bring up with him. Once she very nearly had, but then had backed away from it. Whatever it was, he knew that engineering mood, when she was blueprinting and gathering arguments and persuasions to construct something unfortunate for him. He'd had years and years of experience in reading the surface of hundreds of student young; with his own Annie recognition came almost always too late.

"What's on your mind?"

"Just wondering. When I was little, Poppa, I felt sort of gypped."

"How?"

"No grampas—no grammas."

True, but *not* what was really on her mind. "I didn't have any, either. Grampas and grammas seem to be a disappearing commodity. Along with the two-storey house and the upstairs room to put them in. Lodges for the awkward elderly in their sunset years."

"Don't write a book about it, Poppa. Mine all died before I was born, except for your mother, right?"

"Your grandmother—my mother—died when we were in England. You were three, so I don't suppose you'd remember her. You saw each other only once, on our way over. She approved of you. She was Irish."

"I know that."

"Ballymena."

"And my grampa?"

"I never knew him."

"Did he come from Ireland, too?"

"I don't know." It might not be what she had on her mind, but it was something he had often put out of his own. "There was just my mother."

"Didn't your mother ever . . .?"

"There was just my mother."

"Really!"

"You were named after her."

"You told me that when I was little, too."

"At the age of thirteen she went to work in the mills. In the thirties—when she was eighteen or nineteen—she emigrated. Over here she got work as a hotel chambermaid. Until—she had me."

"Oh."

"What I've never told you before is that my father is an unknown quantity."

"Oh, Poppa!"

"It's all right. It was a very classy CPR hotel. The Château Laurier, in our nation's capital."

"And you never knew him."

"He could have been some travelling pharmaceutical or drygoods or fountain pen or encyclopaedia salesman. I've wondered. I know he could not have been Catholic. I have devoutly hoped all my life that he was not our prime minister at the time, the Right Honourable William Lyon Mackenzie King or the leader of His Majesty's Loyal Opposition, the Right Honourable R. B. Bennett."

"Sorry I asked, Poppa."

"Don't be. No big deal."

"I think it was. Then. Has been. For you."

"Perhaps."

"You mentioned an aunt."

"She wasn't really. My mother was her housekeeper. Aunt Nell."

"What was Aunt Nell like?"

"Eminent Victorian from a most élite Eastern family that went back and beyond the United Empire Loyalists. Her money was very old, too. Belleville furniture factory. Mostly bedsteads, I think. So—ironically enough—I was mansion-raised."

"That was the aunt that went crazy?"

"Yes."

"Poor Poppa."

"Not really. They both loved me. My mother, Aunt Nell. I had a red CCM two-wheeler at eight, and tube skates for the Rideau Canal. They made sure I didn't go into the mills at thirteen—or the bedstead factory. Aunt Nell was as proud as my mother when I won the Governor General's Medal in grade nine. So you did have a grandmother, and a great-grandmother as well."

"What about Mother's . . .?"

"They did not approve of me. I did not approve of them. My last conversation with your maternal grampa, I told him that at least I'd been *born* a bastard."

"Good for you! Tell me more about Gramma."

"She was a dark Celt like you. Your hair—your eyes, skin—that nose you hated when you were little."

"I still do."

"All hers. She was very loving-hearted and she used snuff."

"Hah!"

"Mother Gallagher's Eucalyptus Snuff. In the mills they couldn't smoke. Dark, granulated stuff that looked like tiny mouse turds. Strong."

"How do you know?"

"When I was little, if I had a stuffed-up nose she'd give me a very small pinch of it. There'd be instant sting, then a cold wind blowing through my nostrils, my sinuses, my whole head. My eyes would water and I'd sneeze and sneeze and sneeze and be able to breathe again. Had modern antihistamine nasal sprays beat a mile."

"I'll bet."

"We never used it in front of Aunt Nell. And you were right when you guessed I had tantrums and drummed my heels on the floor, but mostly after she'd knocked me down there."

"I think I know how she must have felt."

"Once, when I was about five or so, I asked her for a dime and she wouldn't give it to me and I whined and I whined—"

"And she drove you one."

"She told me she would not piss in my ear if my brain was on fire. I accepted that. Got the dime from Aunt Nell."

"Who would give you—"

"Who *would* piss in my ear if my brain were only lukewarm."

"What else?"

"You were three and we were in England when she died."

"I think I can remember."

"You and your mother stayed over there while I flew back for the funeral. She was fifty-one. There'd been a mastectomy she never told me about. I visited Aunt Nell in the mental home, but she was not recognizing anyone. Do you remember much of when we were in Orpington?"

"A blue donkey."

"Chagall's. In the Tate Gallery. You loved it. I used to take you in there with me and to the British Museum when I was doing my research for my Blake dissertation."

"She must have been proud of you."

"Very. And without really understanding what I did."

Annie got up. "And you always dried the dishes for her."

"Never."


"Poppa."

"Mmmh."

She pulled the sink plug, and with her cloth began slow and absent-minded circles in the water. "I've been wanting to do something for some time."

Here it was. He took up a handful of cutlery, began to dry them one by one. The last of the water slurped down the drain. She turned on the tap and started wiping at the sides of the sink. "I need you for it."

Brace yourself. "For what?" He slid a fork into its slot.

"I'd like you . . . to—when neither of us has a

class and I don't have a shift at the Saddle and Sirloin—to sit for me."

He threw the last knife in. He shut the drawer. He shook out the dish-towel and laid the end over the counter edge.

"I'd like to paint you."

She hadn't said that!

"Will you—sit for me?"

Shift! Sit! Shit! "You don't mean it!"

"I really do. You're quite important to me, Poppa. You have been as long as I can remember."

"You could not possibly be serious!"

"I am!"

"It is the most unfeeling—how could you ask—even think of—"

"I could because I—"

"—heartless—"

"—love you and I—"

"—selfish—"

"It isn't!"

"It sure as hell is! You're not using this face in oil, gouache, acrylic, or water—"

"I am not interested in your surface! I'm interested in *you*. I don't give a damn about your—"

"I do!"

"That's right! And maybe that's why I want to paint you! The guy I've built inside of me all my life! The person I don't think is scarred—*inside*—"

"No!"

"—of me! Please, Poppa—please listen to me, to what I am trying to tell you! Not about painting you—"

"Which I won't let you do!"

"Okay, Poppa."

"Even if that bear had sliced off my left ear!"

She'd shifted from the living room to the sun-porch with all its glass. Where she should have been doing her painting in the first place. Moving up to the Battle of Waterloo with all his impedimenta must have been a simpler undertaking for Wellington. Now that she'd struck camp in the end of the living room, he could be grateful it was a living room again. The log cabin quilt was back on its bed in the spare room; the dappled horse cantered once more behind the furnace; she had rolled the wagon wheel out of the living room, hooped it down the hall, through the kitchen, the family room, and outside to lean against the back fence. Once more, coats and hats and scarves could be hung from the brass clothes-tree by the front door, though she still preferred to use the end of the banister for that.

Everything she touched seemed to turn to chaos: the bathroom, the kitchen, her bedroom. She had control over nothing but him! Oh, she knew so well how to use his vulnerability to her for her own selfish purposes! She had known long before first mention that he would cave in. He had been so certain that he wouldn't. This time.

God, she was good at it! No argument about taking down her earlier studies and drawings and finished paintings, Scotch-taped to the living-room walls. They did make the family room more interesting. Yes, it was too bad she had done the first-of-term paper for her painting master, declaring her intention to do studies and nine finished paintings, all of her own father. Even though the key project for the whole semester had been enthusiastically accepted, and it was too late now to find something else and go all through the difficult process all over, she would not even mention the matter again. She kept that savage promise till he could stand it no longer.

He leaned back in the swivel chair that would probably never see the basement den again, as he watched her down on her knees before the fireplace bench, by the easel, squeezing out paint blobs onto the Laura Secord Ice Cream lid she was using for a palette.

"Exotic turds for colourful birds."

"Hail to thee, too, blithe Poppa. Nice image."

"I thought so."

"Let's hope we don't come up with bird-shit paintings, though." She finished screwing on its top and returned the tube to its case on the bench. "While I'm getting ready you can pray for me."

"I always have." Cobalt. And now for himself. "I still don't like the idea. How long do we have to do this?"

"The whole semester."

"You never told me that!"

"Yes, I did."

"I don't remember."

"That's because you don't listen very well. In that paper I promised nine paintings."

"Of me! Couldn't you do some still lifes—landscapes?"

"I do those at school. But my main target is you, just as I promised it would be! Portraits of Poppa." She had begun mixing with her palette knife.

"Is that one of my shirts? That was white. Initially."

"It's just an old one. I found it in the basement."

"In the den."

"Yes."

"Where I used to live the last couple of years I was married to your mother. More or less."

"So—there you are. Ten years old."

"But not ten years used. Please—ask me first."

"Sure."

"I suppose I could still use it for a sports—"

"I said I would, Poppa."

"If I ever go to Hawaii—"

"God damn it, Poppa!"

"Sorry."

"Have you noticed you always say 'your mother'? You never call her Sarah any more."

"I guess not. Except to myself."

"Sorry. Now—try to stay just like that. If you want to move, tell me."

"Okay."

"And I may or I may not let you."

There was more behind all this than she was letting on, and he couldn't find a clue to what it was. It was there, all right, and she did not intend letting him know what it was. She'd said something about surface and her image of him inside herself. Or his—inside himself. It was not simply that she wanted and needed him to sit for her. Good enough reason, but not the main reason at all and he would probably never know that reason until she wanted him to.

Actually it really wasn't all that bad, sitting here while she dipped and she stroked and she dipped again. In time he relaxed into a limbo state, vaguely aware of the peripheral mouse movements of her hand and brush off to the left or the right or behind the easel. They were removed from each other, yet they were quite close. The old camp-fire magic.

"Let's knock it off, Poppa."

When he'd made it to his feet and around the easel, he found she'd dropped a cloth over what she'd done. She said it was too soon for him to see.

That was all right with him.


"Why didn't you promise your teacher you'd do portraits of yourself instead of me?"

"Because doing you is just about as subjective as I care to get."

"Don't all painters do self-portraits?"

"When they've got nothing better to do." She came round the easel. "Why?"

"Wouldn't it be interesting if two artists were friends and they set up their easels—both of them did—one at each end of a studio, and then they did portraits of each other. One painter painting a painting of the other painter painting a painting of the other doing the other. . . ."

"Mmmh. That chair doesn't look quite right to me."

"Don't you think it's an interesting idea?"

She set her palette down on the bench. " 'La Composition en abîme.' Plenty of that clever shit floating around as it is. Doesn't seem the same angle it was."

"I'm a little disappointed. I thought I thought of it."

"All kinds of painters painting what other painters are painting—"

"That isn't what I was getting—"

"Or else a painter paints what he painted from what he painted, repeating what he painted right back to what he painted that worked for him the first time."

"That wasn't my point at all!"

"You sure you didn't turn this chair on the swivel?"

"Yes. Nice to know from the start we're going to have a friendly session this morning."

"Oh, Poppa, I didn't mean to be unfriendly at all! I just meant—it's a trick. Like the cereal package with the old Quaker on it, holding up his oatmeal box that's got an old Quaker holding up an old guy holding up an old guy. . . . I guess it could happen in writing, too."

"Don't you poach on my territory. I won't poach on yours."

She went to the easel. "I was thinking about a hell of an idea I had this morning."

"About what's happening with your painting?"

"No. I've noticed something about you."

"Have you?"

"More to the left. Your head."

"What about me?"

"And your chin down a little. I think it's your main problem. From the first day in the hospital I've thought about it. This morning the answer came to me while I was washing my hair. I guess that's why it did—washing my hair made me think about hair."

"Whatever this problem may turn out to be, I have a premonition I am not going to like the solution much. I never do when you take so long to get to the point."

"I thought Why didn't I think of that before?"

"Yes?"

"And why didn't *you* think of it before? Then—I thought—maybe you *did.*"

"What?"

"Think of it before."

"This answer to this problem you think is my main problem—is it animal or vegetable or mineral?"

"Quit it. I'm serious, Poppa."

"If you are, then get to it!"

"Your face."

He had not been ready for that one at all! "The— answer you—to that . . ."

"The way you feel so uptight and sensitive about your face. A lot more than you ought."

"It is my face! This is worse than Grandfather's old ram! You still have not got to what the hell this is all about!"

"All right, Poppa. If you're so concerned about what that grizzly did to your face—the way you think it

looks to other people—then why in hell haven't you
grown a goddam beard to hide it?"

"Oh, Annie! Do you think I didn't think of that!"

"You did?"

"The very first gang-bang conference on me.
Neurologist—neuro-surgeon—internist—psychologist—
physiotherapist—commissionaire. I asked the plastic
surgeon when the hair would start to grow on that
cheek. He said it would never grow hair on it and I
asked him why wouldn't it grow hair on it and he said
it wasn't hair-growing skin they'd used on it and I said
why wasn't it and he said because skin taken from
your thigh or the cheek of your ass did not generally
grow hair and I said what the hell's wrong with the
skin from my armpits! from the back of my head! from
my crotch!"

"Oh."

"They do it all the time for baldness."

"Not pubic hair!"

"Quit it! I'm serious! He admitted it would have
been possible, but the skin texture—the hair density
would be wrong. He said something about axillary
sebacious glands. . . ."

"He ought to know."

"Sure he should. He can't help it if he belongs to a
rationalizing profession."

"Oh, God, Poppa!"

"He didn't give the actual reason why he didn't do
it. The usual one with doctors. That it wasn't convenient!"

"Okay, Poppa."

"For *him*!"


"I'm through with men."

"Forever?"

"A while. Taking a sabbatical from guys. Some
time I might tell you why."

"I've led a sheltered life."

"So you say. Often. Lean forward the way you
were." She stepped around the easel and towards him.
"They have a way of turning into frogs when I kiss
them—every time."

"You used to like frogs. When you were little."

"You seem to forget I'm not little any more. Too old for frogs. You—ah—had a bad one last night. I heard."

"You heard right."

"Same one?"

"Mmmh."

She moved out and to the side of the easel and turned to face him.

"But this time it wasn't closing in on me. I was being sucked from the centre and thrown out and away. Falling."

"Other than that, the nightmare was a success." She turned the easel and stepped away. Her attention shifted from him to the canvas and back to him again as though she were a spectator at a tennis match.

"I guess."

She looked down to the yellow and white and black and raspberry pudding paint on her plastic lid. She stirred and dabbed and looked up. Her face was not so much intent as sad. He felt his own sun go under cloud.

"How many times did you fall this week?"

"Just twice."

"That's nice. Lean forward the way you were."

"I'm trying to ease my neck."

"And I'm trying to get crease and shadow detail inside your elbows. You didn't shave this morning."

"It's Saturday."

"Get back the way you were, damn it."

He leaned forward.

"That's better."

"How bloody long does it take to do elbow creases?"

"Please, Poppa. And, if you can—shut up."

"You're doing all the talking."

"I am trying to get a touchy bit done with your forearms—your hands. If you talk, it distracts. Painters don't talk. They paint."

He managed to keep from telling her she was sure as hell an exception to that rule. Actually his neck was not killing him.

"This is the most frustrating session I've had. Started out to be so good. Now it's turned to shit!"

Why had he ever agreed to sit for her!

"You know, Poppa, I'm a little—disturbed. I'm serious about painting."

"You said painters don't—"

"And I don't know how to put it. I don't like what I often turn up. Inside myself."

"Like what?"

"Unpleasantness. No. More than that. Real dark stuff. I'm not all that nice a person, Poppa. There's a lot of black shit in there."

"There is in most people, Annie."

"It's pretty upsetting. Selfishness. Meanness. Violence . . ."

"You haven't got a monopoly on it. Any writer knows that. I didn't realize painters did, too."

"How the hell would I know! I'm no painter!"

"Yet."

"Thanks!"

"I've looked over the shoulder of a lot of young writers. Would it surprise you to know that I've had this conversation before?"

"I guess so."

"With the promising ones. The ones committed to more than smart-ass performance. Up on the high wire, 'no life net' time."

"The worst is . . . finding out how—unstable you really are."

"Mmmh."

"What a mess you are."

"Uh-huh."

"No real value. Do you know when most child-battering occurs?"

"No."

"Onset of the mother's period."

"I'll watch out for it now you've warned me. I take it that is also true of father-battering. You want to miss this session?"

"No."

"I do."

"Tough. Every day, every week, every month, every year. I've heard you say it often enough about writing. Lean back this time. Turn your face towards me."

"My bloody elbow's killing me."

"Let it kill you a while longer." She lifted the brush and made three long, downward strokes, let her arm drop and hang. She stepped back. "Now that you've brought it up."

"My elbow?"

"Writing."

"You brought it up."

"Last ten years or so—you been doing any?"

"No."

"Every day, every week, every year."

"I said no."

"That novel you worked on—back there—what were you going to call it?"

"Titles are generally the last thing you find."

"Guess I should have known that. Tell me, just how many pages did you get done on it?"

"Annie! Why don't you just paint!"

"I do. Every day, every week, every—"

"Let's talk about something else."

"Sure. We will. After you tell me—how many pages?"

"One hundred and nineteen!"

"That's quite a few, isn't it?"

"No."

"Almost half a book—"

"It isn't."

"Any reason I couldn't see it?"

"Yes."

"All the same, I'd like to."

"You can't."

"Oh. I'm to show you mine, but you won't show me yours. Why won't you let me—"

"I threw it away."

"That bad, eh?"

"I thought so."

"Maybe not."

"It was."

"Maybe you shouldn't have thrown—"

"I should have. You mind if we talk about something else?"

"Yes. I do. What was your novel all about?"

"That's something else people who don't write
always ask people who write."

"All the same."

"A teacher."

"Autobiographical, eh?"

"I guess. He was a loser."

"Aw, Poppa!"

"A funny one, though."

"If it was good enough for Cervantes, then it should
be good enough for you."

"Novel of the absurd. The central character's name
was Sissons."

"Wow! How existentialist can you get!"

"Mmmh."

"I guess you did right to throw it away, Poppa."

"I did right."


She had moved back and stood now with one foot out
while she looked at the canvas. She laid down her
palette and brush. "O.K., come and take a look at it,
Poppa."

"Shove it."

"Impossible. It's two and a half by four feet. Take
a look and tell me what you think."

He had finally got his weight over his left knee in
order to pry himself out of the swivel chair. "Take your
hands off me."

"Just helping—"

"By myself." He straightened up with his hands in
the small of his back, squared his shoulders and lifted
his chest, felt the stretch ache that was not true pain in
his neck. He walked to the easel and around it.

His first feeling was surprised relief. The seated
figure was mercifully impressionistic. It was headless.
It was crouched. The hands were not resting on the
thighs as they'd been while she painted him. They
were almost crab-clawed and held turned down and
forward and close to each other.

"What you think, Poppa?"

He was not able to pin the reason he was feeling
slightly sick.

"Poppa?"

"I feel sick."

Now there was unfortunate recognition.

"Your back?"

"Your painting."

"Oh, Poppa!"

The lifted hands hung above no keys. The type-writer was missing!

"It makes me feel sick! Was that your intention!"

"No!"

"It had to be!"

"It wasn't! Whatever it is that—"

"Look at it!"

"Whatever's upsetting you, it was not deliberate at all!"

"A writer with his hands frozen in mid—"

"That isn't what it is, for God's sake."

"It sure as hell is!"

"It's just an exercise, Poppa—a finding exercise! Don't lay your emotional—goddam literary trip on me!"

"Not any more, I won't!"

"Well—can't be all bad. Must be saying something. Don't look at me! Look at the painting—God damn it! Tell me what you think about—"

"It would be only a literary opinion." He turned away. "Of the worst kind!" He began to walk to the door. "From a non-writer!"


"Annie. Why does it have to be me—all the time—to make the loving allowances?"

"I make them, too!"

"The score looks pretty one-sided to me."

"*You* say!"

"Look. I told you I didn't want to sit for you. In spite of that, I did, so that you could do what you'd promised you would do for your course."

"I didn't ask you to do it just for myself."

"What's that mean?"

"It means I had other reasons, which were not selfish ones."

"Like what?"

"Understanding better."

"Understanding what better?"

"You. Us. Seemed like a great idea that I though
you'd—hell, I wanted to do it as much for you as fo
me!"

"I see."

"No, you don't."

"That painting—"

"Is bloody good evidence of what I'm talking about.
Even if I didn't intend it. Consciously. I guess I do
think of you as something besides my father. A writer
I didn't plan it that way! What you saw wasn't selfishly
done for a goddam assignment. Sure—I paint for myself. But in what—when you sit for me, I'm painting
for you, too!"

"It would have been nice if you'd told me that in
the first place."

"I thought I had. I have now and it doesn't seem
to cut much ice with you, and if you think what you
seem to think about me and about why I asked you to
sit for me, then you're badly informed and you can
forget it!"

"Hold on. Let's back up a bit."

"Yeah. To that crack about loving allowances!"

"All right."

"So?"

"I take it back. Maybe the score is not one-sided."

"I know that. I also know you didn't really mean it
when you said it."

"Thanks."

"I'm not so sure you really mean that. Will you
continue to sit?"

"I'll take it under consideration. If you will."

"Will what?"

"Take it under consideration to continue—to paint
me."

"I shall."

"Will."

"Why not give me a morning off?"

"Because it's panic time." She had begun mixing
with the knife. "Also some nice things are beginning to
happen for me with the way I'm working the paint. He
said I wasn't just drawing with it any more."

"When did that happen?"

"The one you hated so much."

"The headless—"

"No."

"The last of the mole people?"

"The one when you said, 'Jesus Christ, I haven't got jaundice!' "

"He liked that one!"

"He sure did." She went behind the easel, looked out to him, then back to the painting. "More towards me. Yeah." She picked up her brush and dabbed at the palette. "How come—all of a sudden—you got interested in hunting big game?" She leaned forward and made a stroke. "Late in life."

"Not so late."

"Okay. Early. In middle age."

"I just did."

"But why?"

"Person doesn't have to have a reason for everything he does. Does he?"

"Something like that, he does. I mean—didn't you ever ask yourself, why the hell am I—"

"No."

"You must have."

"You ever ask yourself why you wanted to fish—tie your own flies?"

"No, really."

"Ski?"

"No."

"See. People do a lot of things simply because they want to. Tennis . . . hockey . . . marbles . . . hopscotch."

"Games."

"Get into politics . . . make money . . . make women . . . travel."

"Kill."

"I suppose."

"Didn't like that one so much, did you? That's where I have some difficulty with you."

"Where?"

"Bear-hunting. How come—all of a sudden—you decide to—"

"Not all of a sudden."

"Looks that way to me."

"Well, it wasn't."

"Oh. How was it?"

"All the years I've gone up Paradise Valley. Camping, fishing—ducks, geese . . ."

"Not big game, though."

"Getting to know Archie. I think it was a perfectly natural thing for me to do."

"Go out five seasons—to kill a bear."

"Annie—"

"Which you won't even eat."

"People do not always have a clear, didactic reason for absolutely everything they—"

"That's what you keep saying, but this seems so unusual for you—to me."

"Well, it isn't. I wanted to. I did it. You'll just have to accept that."

"Evidently you have. I don't have to."

"Yes, you do."

"Why?"

"Because it's none of your goddam business."

"Oh, great! Just great! None of little Annie's business if Poppa wants to get Archie Nicotine to shoot an old grey horse and leave him to rot up Daisy Creek—"

"That's right!"

"—so a bear will come out of her winter den and catch the smell and come to him, so Poppa can draw a bead on her and drop her so he can have a skin for *his* den. You want to know what I think of that!"

"Not really!"

"Not very goddam much! For some strange reason cheating comes to my mind—"

"You don't know what you're talking—"

"—loaded dice! Frequenting a whore-house!"

"Damn it, Annie!"

"I simply cannot understand it at all!"

"So shut up about it!"

"And I'll tell you something else. You haven't bothered to understand it, either. You don't care to even begin to examine it!"

"That's right!"

"Well, good for you, Elmer. I do care to because I don't think you're the kind of guy who has to win at any cost. Go for the cheap score. I won't accept that bout you! Yet. If I have to, then, boy, have I been wrong about you! I never wanted to be wronger in my whole life!"

"I think we've pretty well explored this topic."

"Shit!" She threw down the brush. "Now look what you've made me do!" With a cloth she began to rub at the painting.

"Annie, Annie, Annie—you haven't changed a bit."

"That supposed to be good or bad?"

"Neither. When you were little—"

"Which I am not any more."

"All right. Not any more."

"Which you keep forgetting. Constantly!"

"I'll try harder not to. But when you were . . . thirteen on—you were always digging into why people were what they were, why they did what they did. You were always fond of problems. Other people's."

"So what."

"Had a lot of sleepless nights over how you might turn out. 'Dear Annie: Advice to the Lost and the Losing.' Or worse: I might end up as father of yet another analyst."

"Nice diversion, Poppa." She dropped the stained cloth to the floor, picked up the brush and palette. "Don't lose any more sleep over that. I did not end up—"

"Not professionally, but you still have the same old amateur zeal. Still using your Freud and Sears catalogue psychology for the salvation—"

"Okay, Poppa."

"—of all others. Aim at yourself for a change."

"Mother was right. You are one sarcastic—" She pulled up short.

"Sarcastic what?"

"Uh—fellow."

"Sarcastic what?"

"Guy." She leaned forward, intent now on the painting.

"I'm still waiting, Annie."

She straightened up. She bent down and laid the palette on the floor. "Remember a while back when you told me a lot about your mother?"

"Yes."

"Aunt Nell?"

"Yes."

She came round the easel and towards him. "I do aim at myself and I guess I miss a lot. So maybe I haven't had enough practice at it and you're probably right. As right as anybody can be—about me—any father about his daughter."

"What about my mother—Aunt Nell?"

"Since you told me about them and about—I lost some sleep over you, too. It's funny how you think you're so close to somebody, you think you know everything about them. They're very clear to you. Then all of a sudden they aren't—so clear."

"Yes?"

"I never knew about your father, Poppa."

"I never told you."

"Yeah. Why not?"

"I don't know. Guess it just never came up."

"Do you wonder about him? Who he was—what he might be like?"

"No. Oh—when I was a child maybe. Even then— just curiosity."

"Not much later on, though?"

"Nope."

"When did you quit?"

"About the time you were born."

"I think I would have."

"It's no great matter, Annie."

"The hell it isn't!"

"Lots of people lose their fathers one way or another. If it's going to happen, then I guess mine was as good a way as any."

"Mmmh. There's something you haven't noticed."

"What?"

"Ever since you told me about my gramma—Aunt Nell—your father, who wasn't—I haven't called you a bastard."

"That's nice."

"Even though you are—sometimes."

The last five minutes had been silent and intent for her, a juggling act as she traded brushes between her mouth and her working hand. She straightened and stepped back. She looked down to her lid palette, then up to the painting, then to him, then back to the painting again. She took the handle from between her teeth, then stuck both brushes into the untidy black nest of her hair, bristles straight up.

"I can get up, Pocahontas?"

"Yep. This one sure ain't porcupine quill on birch bark, Poppa."

"Done?"

With a wrist flick she sailed the lid aside in a Frisbee glide.

"As much as it ever will be. Remember what you once told me? Nobody ever finishes. They just abandon. Let's have our crit. now."

Only head and shoulders this time. The eyes were closed. Half the face or slightly more than that was in full light but the right side lay in dusk. She had gone heavy on the paint so the face had a stroked strength it probably did not deserve. The head slanted to the right and down, almost in sleep. Of course. He had dozed off a couple of times when she was painting him. Both eyes were closed. The shadow line fell down the forehead, then distinct as a blade edge along the nose, the lips, the chin.

*Both* eyes were closed!

There was no meat obscenity, for there was no red rocker under the closed right eye he could never close again. Distortion was not being denied. The eye was simply sad in shadow.

"Well, Poppa?"

The cheek scars too.

"It's what they call the *ténébriste* school technique."

"It's what you had in mind when you asked me to sit for you."

"Not clearly, Poppa. What you think of it?"

"Hey-up, Annie. Hey-up!"

# CHAPTER 12

They were thankful to have made it through the fall session, both of them; her drawing and painting criticisms had gone well and she might just end up with an A average; he had marked a good third of his papers. If it was all right with her, he proposed, they could just float through the Christmas break and gather strength for the new term. She seemed to agree with him; it meant she'd have more time to paint; she wanted to do landscapes, so they'd go out to the university and she would drop him off at his office to do his papers while she sketched along the river. He might even, if he felt up to it, come with her a few times and get in some walking. He said it would be better for him to stay home and work down in the den. She said, no, it wouldn't be better for him to do that, because if he didn't get off his ass and out of the house and moving, his hip and back would freeze up on him.

"Who knows, you might even loosen up and get some muscle tone in a week or so and try some cross-country skiing with me."

"Oh sure, after we've done our pairs figure-skating."

"I'm serious."

"So am I. Let's just settle for walking."

Too late, as usual, he realized that walking was all that she had intended for him in the first place. It had worked out pretty well, though, paying off noticeably in his hip and, surprisingly, in his neck and shoulders, too. The Friday before Christmas he was even a little disappointed when she stopped the car to let him out at the south entrance of Wapta Tower and told him she was driving back, in order to get some Christmas things done. He had just got the seat-belt unbuckled by himself, and without his right shoulder or elbow squealing, when she asked him what he wanted for Christmas.

"My two top vertebrae."

"Come on. Give me a clue, Poppa."

"You know what I want for Christmas. Just one thing."

"Besides that, damn it."

"Just that. You said to leave it all to you."

"It's come back from Montreal."

"Two weeks ago! You said! Have you seen it?"

"No, I haven't seen it."

"Then how do we know it isn't still in Montreal! If they didn't let you see it!"

"Because I did not *care* to see it. Not until I have to. You know how I feel about—"

"You persuaded me to let you handle it. You said I'd blow up at them and louse it up."

"Poppa, you will have it for Christmas. Evidently they've been flooded with stuff and Frankie's managed to foul up their whole operation. His grampa is a nice old man and I feel sorry for him. Frankie's all he's got. Frankie is one bad Boy Scout."

"I know that."

"The sad thing is—so does his grampa, who is giving your bear his full attention. You will have the damn thing for Christmas. He promised me that. I think he is a promise-keeper. It will be delivered just as soon as it's done. Also the others."

"What?"

"Head-mounts. Donner and Blitzen and Rudolph with a goddam alternating two-hundred-watt—I'll pick you up at five."

"Drop into Wild Trophy World—"

"On my way back out, I will, if I get everything done I have to get done. Careful of the ice on those steps. You be down here at five."

The chill kissed him as soon as he opened his door. Two spoken requests and four memos to Tait and still no move to a new office that was not in a north-west corner! He left the door ajar so some of the hall heat might creep in, then got his cup from the shelf and went down to the faculty lounge.

Closed and locked, but there was light showing under Bev's office door. He knocked.

Tait!

"Haven't you got a good home to go to, Dobbs?"

"No. And I haven't got an office yet that won't give me hypothermia!"

"I'm working on it."

"I want to get into the faculty lounge."

Tait got the key out of Bev's desk, went down the hall, and unlocked the door for him.

"Be sure to lock it after you."

" 'Yourself.' Reflexive."

Tait jerked out the key and turned away.

"The first 'you' is understood." That had fixed it if Tait had intended having coffee in there, too.

He pushed the button so the door would lock after himself, and returned to his office. Still cold. While he drank his coffee, he managed only two and a half papers before his right hand began to cramp on him. He gathered everything up and went back to Bev's office. This time he simply went inside and to the desk and got her keys and let himself into the lounge. He made himself another cup of instant coffee and held it tight in his hand till the cramp had melted and the little finger had stopped twitching.

He was on his fourth paper when Tait came in. With *his* cup! He said nothing while he mixed his coffee. Then the son-of-a-bitch sat down with it, on the couch by the door. He opened a brown paper bag and took out a plastic yoghurt container. Raw carrots, green onions, celery.

Maybe, if he were to concentrate very, very hard, he could will him out of the room and back to his office.

It did not work.

"Do you mind not slurping?"

Tait had pried up the yoghurt lid and began to excavate. Raspberry or strawberry.

"How is Slaughter coming along with his creative dissertation?"

"No idea."

"Shouldn't you have? You okayed it."

"Primrose is his supervisor." Slurp.

"Isn't that nice for Primrose."

"Whyte's riding shot-gun, too."

"Whyte's Native Studies."

"That's right. The novel concerns native people. He's calling it *The Red Messiah*." He pulled over the paper bag and looked inside.

Shit! He began to gather up his papers. An apple was too much!

The office was still cold. He shoved his right hand into his crotch and held it there to borrow heat. When he thought Tait might be through, he went back to the lounge. Now there were papers on the coffee table and Tait, crouched over them.

"My office is freezing."

"So is mine." Tait did not look up. "They've turned down the heat for the Christmas break."

"How the hell can I—"

"Look, Dobbs, I've got to get this budget done, so go find someone else to practise your sarcasm on!"

He went back to his office. He managed one more paper before his hand cramped again. He phoned for a taxi.

As well as his car, there was a truck parked in front of the house. Annie must have been out with the snow shovel and a broom, from the look of the steps and the landing. He'd forgotten his key again. She took her time answering the bell.

"Poppa!"

"You took your time answering—"

"Yeah. All the time you camped on that doorbell. What the hell are you doing—"

"They've turned the heat off out there."

"Why didn't you phone for me?"

"I didn't want to bother you. All the way out and back. You going to let me through?"

She stepped aside. "How much did that taxi cost you?"

"What are all the dining-room chairs doing out here in the hall?"

"Polishing them. I don't want to spill lemon oil on the rug. Light mushroom shows stains and you've warned me often enough it's genuine Peking oriental."

"Why the red table-cloth and the candles on the dining-room—"

"Just three days left. I told you I had a lot of Christmas things to do. I thought I'd set up the dining room ahead of time."

"You promised. We're not making a big thing out of it."

"That's right."

"Whose blue half-ton is that out in front?"

"I have no idea."

He set down his briefcase on the butler's helper. "I can get it off myself." He almost did, but the right shoulder grabbed him. She freed him, then she hung the coat up on the brass tree.

"When I got out of the taxi I smelled something burning. Seemed to come from the back of our place. Is the heat on in the garage?"

"No."

"I smelled smoke from out that way"

"Somebody burning trash in the alleyway."

"Wood smoke."

"How you coming on your papers?"

"Eighty-seven left. It smelled like wood smoke."

"So. It's December and there are fireplaces and people use them in December and when we get chinook conditions we can also get inversions. What's made you so jumpy, Poppa?"

"It's not fireplace smoke. Smelled like somebody barbecuing."

"In December! Come on."

"It did."

"Okay then. Some neighbourhood idiot wants to barbecue in the middle of winter and he can't do it inside, because he doesn't want to kill off all his family, yet, with charcoal carbon monoxide, so he's doing it outside and the wind carrying the smoke—"

"Didn't you smell it when you opened the front door?"

"No."

"Go to the back door."

"What do you want me to do about it! No law against barbecuing in winter. And if our garage is on fire, it is not likely to smell like barbecuing. Go on down to your den with those papers you haven't marked and let me get my work done up here."

"All right." He sighed.

"Your neck?"

"Not so good. And my shoulder and hip and—"

"Change in the weather? Atmospheric pressure—"

"And the goddam administration turned off the goddam heat in the university. Cold does it every time. How long till supper?"

"It sure as hell isn't now. Four-thirty."

"What are we having?"

"Elk roast and bannocks and deep huckleberry pie."

"Huh!"

"While you were supposed to be doing papers at the university, I went out and dropped a five-point bull, skinned and gutted and quartered him myself. Then I picked a pail of huckleberries. Want me to give you a rub?"

"Oh God, I always do, Annie, but first I think I better get the heating pad and the frozen peas."

"I'll get them."

"I can do it. You do what you have to do." He started for the refrigerator.

"The heating pad's on the couch."

"I noticed that. And the frozen peas are in the freezing compartment."

She had come by him, opened the top door, and reached inside. "Here." She shut the door. He took the plastic bag from her.

"When are we having this roast elk and bannock and huckleberry—"

"Late. I've got a lot to do. Around seven, seven-thirty. Will you get out of my refriger—"

"Just some cheese and crackers. Glass of orange juice."

"You'll spoil your supper!"

"Three hours from now!"

"No, Poppa, please!"

"You're coming on awful strong, Annie."

"I have a nice supper planned."

"Okay. I'll settle for a spritzer."

"Sure. Carry down your pad and peas and papers and try to balance a full glass—"

"I'll drink it here before I go down."

"I'll bring it down to you."

She turned around. She reached inside, her body still between him and the refrigerator. "Take your stuff and go on down, Poppa."

What the hell was up, anyway! "Were those champagne bottles in there?"

"That's right. Mumm's."

"How come?"

"Christmas—New Year's."

"Four magnums!"

"Or is it magna."

"Lot of champagne for just two of us."

"Over the holidays there'll be—"

"You promised me it would be low key."

"Sure. But we'll be having *some* people in. I did not promise to nail up a quarantine card on our front door."

"What people?"

"Whomever you want. Dr. Lyon. Dr. Stibbard . . . Professor Robbins . . ."

"Not Tait!"

"No."

"Skeffington!"

"Just friends. Informal. Anything wrong with that? Mine too. Vicky. Harry."

"Who the hell is Harry?"

"My painting master."

"Oh."

"That's all. Unless there's somebody else you might want to—"

"Let's not get carried away. North and South Armies of the Civil War."

"I promised you, Poppa."

"That's the trouble. Whose truck is that parked out in front?"

"I told you. I have no idea. Get to your papers. I'll bring your spritzer down to you."


He had long ago made a compact with himself never to put off grading papers; the example of teachers like Tait had helped him keep that promise. The first year he'd taught at Queen's he had announced to his classes that if he ever failed to return papers on the date he said he would, he would cancel lectures for two weeks. He had not had to pay them that impossible reward for his own crime.

Because of his own fear of failure, he hated doing papers. He was not good at succinct criticism and always tracked them up with red ink. If he overlooked a crippled sentence, piece of confused thinking, or unintended same-word echo, or purple writing; if he failed to congratulate a fresh insight, a sensuous fragment, a fine connotation, or clean logic, he would be letting the student down. More than that, he was uncomfortable with judgement power; a student had so much riding on a teacher's decision for success or failure. He had never forgotten his own apprehension when he entered an examination theatre, with printed sheets and foolscap booklets on the polished oak of fattened chair arms. It was not so different from the tension he'd felt when the bear had shouldered her way in that slow saunter out of the lodge-pole pines across the valley of Daisy Creek.

A judge should have the same concern; if Justice is blind, then Our Blessed Lady of Education must also be, but not unfeeling. Look at Tait. Look at Skeffington. Look at the print-outs of mid-term or final grades on doors all down department walls, anonymous numbers shielding vulnerable young, and after each, the A's and B's and C's and D's, and in one cruel instance last year, the mortal F– given by Skeffington.

He hoped he never lost compassion. Liz had never lost it—she'd never had it! He remembered how she'd told him once that it was impossible to teach and at the same time relate to a student beyond a totally objective relationship. What lazy and heartless shit! The only worthwhile relationship must be subjective as well, total human to total human.

He managed ten more, looked at his watch: six-twenty. Annie had said supper would be late, seven to seven-thirty, but with her that could be eight. He'd just take a lie-down on the couch. . . .

\*     \*     \*

Somebody had stirred up the camp-fire. He looked up to Archie, standing over him.

"Hey, Archie!"

"Annie wants you upstairs now, Dobbs."

He sat up. "You staying for supper with us?"

"Hey-up."

"What's going on up there!"

"You better ask her about that."

He listened to the sound surf above, voices, foot-steps, chair scrape. The front door chimes began to play. He should have known she was pulling something off! He started up the stairs after Archie.

But not this! She must have invited the whole English Department! All of Livingstone University! There were people in the hallway; there were people sitting on steps clear up to the landing, with plates on their knees and wineglasses down beside themselves or in their hands. For all he knew, the upstairs was infested, too.

Skeffington!

Tait!

Whyte!

So much for her promises!

"Surprise, Poppa."

"God damn you, Annie!"

"I love you too, Poppa!"


He had not seen Annie anywhere for some time, then he caught sight of her through the hallway door, talking with Archie. She left Archie and came into the living room.

"What are you two reds plotting against us whites?"

"Hold it a minute, Poppa." She went on past him and to the fireplace.

"Now! Everybody got their glasses filled? Please move back as far as you can." Herbie Stibbard had joined her. "And don't anybody drink that champagne until I tell you." She crooked a finger to summon someone from the sun-porch end of the room. "I would like to introduce my two partners in this crime against my father tonight." Now Whyte had come to her side. "Dr. Stibbard and Professor Whyte."

And Archie had to be in on it, too, whatever it was.

"The Head of Native Studies has promised me he will not do the prairie chicken mating dance or the Montana foxtrot for us. So far he has kept that promise. He also delivered and barbecued with alder the eighteen-pound elk roast of which there is nothing left. As well, he fried for you almost a gross of baking-soda bannocks and boiled the cauldron of pineapple-weed tea you have drunk. Along with the chokecherry wine, he supplied the cigarette papers and the dried kinni-kinnick, which was such a disappointment to some of you. All this was accomplished in spite of my father, who did his very best to spoil the surprise."

How beautiful she was tonight in that sheath dress of gold and green, standing before the fireplace flame. Without a line or a colour flat or sharp to her, she was lovely as a salmon fly, and that was not all! How valuable and tough his ring-a-ding child had grown up to be! When Sarah had been wheeled shuddering from the Wellesley Hospital delivery room, looked up to him, and said, "She's a girl, Colin!" he had been so right: "She'll be better than any damn man!"

Now Archie had rejoined the party, entering backwards and bent over as he dragged a large paper-wrapped bundle across the floor and to the centre of the room.

"Dr. Stibbard has a few words to say."

Herbie stepped forward and looked down at the brown-papered hulk, then lifted his head and cleared his throat. " 'Some revelation is at hand.' We are all gathered for a ceremony of surprise."

Look, Ma: no notes. Herbie has a-hunting gone.

"So watchful Bruin forms, with plastic care,
Each growing lump, and brings it to a bear."

Tracking Pope through Book I of "The Dunciad." And now he's found relevant Dryden spoor as well, in "Absalom and Achitophel":

"Got, while his soul did huddled notions try,
And born a shapeless lump, like Anarchy."

Let he who is without scholarly sin cast the first
footnote. I absolve you, Herbie, for none of yours were
mortal and I am just as guilty too.

>"... and the head of a man,
>A gaze blank and pitiless as the sun,
>Is moving its slow thighs, while all about it
>Reel shadows of the indignant desert birds."

They were ravens, Herbie. Indignant Daisy Creek
ravens, dear colleague. Your words were never few but
I forgive you that, for you will always hear the voice of
the falconer. Annie, too! Annie, too!

Herbie had finished and stepped back, but Yeats's
voice echoed on through "the sea-wind scream." His
own Annie had been

>"... granted beauty and yet not
>Beauty to make a stranger's eye distraught,
>Or hers before a looking glass ..."

She had done all this for him and so much more
ever since she had rescued him from the hospital. Oh,
Annie, dear Annie, fine Annie: "Do not eat crazy salad
with your meat!"

"... As all of you, except my father, know, Professor Whyte drives a half-ton blue truck. Do not drink
that champagne yet, Professor Skeffington."

Liz, on the couch beside Tait, lowered her glass.

"Professor Whyte."

Shit!

"Man is a hunter," Whyte began, "and the bear is
his master animal, man's life-giver, the source that
must never fail. For hundreds of thousands of years
they shared the cave, Neanderthal man—"

"And woman." That was Skeffington.

"Hear! Hear!" That was Annie.

"Of course. Probably deliberately, early man chose
a cave where bears were hibernating and killed them
when he needed them."

"First deep-freeze pantry." That was Tait.

"Obviously a feminine decision."

"Perhaps, Liz. A decision made some time when

she was not busy interrupting. Bear has also given man religion and art. The cave was man's first shrine, with the bear totem his first icon, and bear-killing his first guilt. The atavistic echo of the hunter persists—"

"In Lebanon. In Ireland. El Salvador, Guatemala. In Georgetown. In Watergate. In—"

"Even though you may very well be right, Professor Skeffington, shut up!"

"Thank you, Ms. Dobbs. Even today, north of Japan, a bear cub is captured and the women put it to their breast and suckle it until fall sacrifice. Each villager whispers in its ear, asking it to tell Master Bear they treated it kindly. They thrust thigh bones into the eye sockets after killing it so that it cannot identify them or testify against them for what they have done to it. Ceremony of killing guilt, the genesis of religious ritual.

"In the cave he shared with bear, man saw the claw marks on the walls and stencilled his own oxide hand-prints beside them, saying, 'I am in here too.' From that to pictographs was no great step. Bear gave man art."

Whyte lifted his champagne glass. All around the room the other glasses rose.

"To bear. To Colin."

Annie had choreographed it well. Whyte and Archie and Herbie stooped as one, cut cord, tore away paper, and spread out the hide, then straightened up and stepped back. The others had closed in to the centre of the room. All were looking down.

Now he knew how a drowning man must feel as he hung aslant in dark water with no above and no below!

"May I drink my champagne now?"

He heard someone behind him say, "Is *that* what did it to him?"

Tait, open-mouthed, lifted his attention from the hide and stared at him. His mouth closed. A slight smile dawned.

"It's not grizzled," someone said.

Tait's smirk had become a full grin. He looked down to the hide spread-eagled on the floor, then back

at him again. He lifted his champagne glass and drank
without taking his eyes away.

Charlotte, to his left, had a cigarette in her mouth
and compassionate concern upon her face. Her response
hurt even more than Tait's.

He heard Archie say, "It's the wrong one."

He looked down to the small brown bear hide
again and felt a hand at his elbow, then an arm around
his waist. "Oh, Poppa!" Her arm tightened. "I have an
important announcement to make. This is not my father's bear. Archie."

"Hey-up."

"Let's get this brown son-of-a-bitch out of here!"

As Archie bent down with her and they began to
fold it up, he muttered something to Annie. It must
have been Stony. It sounded like: "Minneapolis."


It would be a long time before he would get to sleep
tonight. How often he had lain in the dark and waited
and waited and waited. Especially since Daisy Creek.
All over again this was the year he had been ten, the
rheumatic fever year when he had been taken out of
school. Gypped out of Pee Wee and Little League.
Important only to his mother and to Aunt Nell.

When Annie had asked him about his father, he
had not been completely truthful with her. He had not
informed her that his mother and Aunt Nell had explained to him that his father had died before he was
born. Nor had he told her his mother had said she
didn't know what a "catch colt" was, either, and that
Aunt Nell had fired Andy Spinks, the chauffeur and
gardener, when Colin had asked her why Andy had
called him that after he found all the pulled-up tulip
bulbs. During the bed-rest year he had wondered often
and dreamed a father to knock out flies to him and to
tighten skate-laces for him.

Sometimes, when he was angry enough with her,
he had told himself that his mother was not really his
mother at all, and during the year he was the only
child alive in the world, he had not only wished it so;
he had come easily to believe it true, promoting himself
from half to full orphan. They levelled with him when

he reached fifteen and he graduated to bastard. Parva cum laude.

Maybe it had been inevitable that he should end up a teacher, the father he'd been denied—to others.

The phantom drum—the one he'd so often heard since Daisy Creek—had begun as soon as he had lain down, the false sound that was more than amplified heartbeat. Arrowsmith had told him that damage to his right ear caused it. Now it was as though, somewhere in the darkened bedroom, a derisive child was humming while he flipped his lips with a fingertip to make the silly flutter sound.

He pulled down three deep breaths, just as he had when the bear had stood with the lifted horse in her arms. He expelled the last one to hold the lungs quite empty, slowly, slowly squeezed the hair trigger, gun steady and snug to his shoulder. He felt the butt kick of it and heard the crack of it.

Horse and bear dropped.

He fired and he fired and he fired again with firecracker smell lingering in his nose. She was half-way across the valley by the fourth shot when her great rump went out from under her and she sat, and she turned, still seated, in one full, barber-chair circle. Only then did he realize that he had not used the scope for any of the shots after the first one. Also, that Archie had not even lifted his rifle.

She disappeared into the pine on the other side. Somewhere behind and above them, a spruce grouse began to drum.

"Just wounded it, Dobbs." Archie was looking out and across the valley. "In the ass, maybe." He stood up. "So now we got to go after it."

Once they had got down the bank and onto the flats, it was easy going, for the chinook wind had shrunk and licked up snow to only ankle depth. They stopped at her skid circle and looked down.

"No blood."

"What do we do now, Archie?"

"We got to make sure."

As soon as they entered the pine bush on the other side, the snow was up to their knees. Archie stopped. Her tracks had brought them to a large depression saucer in the snow a few yards inside. From its centre lifted a breath of steam from three black lumps. Archie stepped down and turned, then crouched and looked back towards the flats.

"Hey-up." He stood up.

"What, Archie?"

"Watchin' us all the time we was comin' over to it." He pointed to the centre of the packed snow. "Then it took a recent shit. Then it left here." He turned and pointed to the tracks going further into the bush. "We got to follow it."

"But there wasn't any blood back there, Archie."

"Hey-up."

"Or here."

"Hey-up."

"So she's probably taken off and up over the ridge into the high country—"

"If she isn't wounded you would be correct."

"But there's no blood showing. Can't be a wound without some traces of blood."

"Very seldom."

"What's the point in—"

"We got to follow it, and that's the whole situation."

Now the snow had deepened, her tracks leading them higher and then through deadfall they must go up and over and down and under. They came out of it, but into still deeper drifts plunging them over their hips. His thighs were aching now and inside his down jacket he was running with sweat. He sent up panting prayers for second wind, but they were not answered. The third time he floundered and fell, he did not try to get up right away, just lay back for blessed rest in the soft snow.

God only knew how far ahead Archie was now. It didn't make sense! No blood! He'd missed her four times, so no blood bled from her. She had simply taken her merry-go-round ride when she lost her footing in slippery snow and skidded about at precisely the same moment he had let that last one go. By now she was out of the country and on her way to the Yukon, for God's sake!

He sat up. He reached and grabbed a small spruce trunk for purchase and made it to his feet. When he had found solid ground underneath, he began to brush the snow from the Weatherby. My God! Lucky he hadn't blown himself apart! All that flailing and stumbling with the safety off! He snicked it on.

No use trying to catch up with Archie now; have to back-track and wait for him at the tree edge. It was just as bad getting back there, except that he didn't have to keep up with Archie and he could rest often.

Just as he came out of the pine he heard the blunt beat of a spruce grouse again. Daisy Creek Valley was urgent with early spring and they must be all over the place, with blood bubbles at their throats. He heard the ravens indignant again, looked out and across to the dead horse.

He heard crashing behind himself, and turned to see her coming at him from the lodge-pole pine!

As a child, he had known fear quite often: of the dark, of thunder, of lightning, the strap, teachers, other boys, thin ice, exams. Fear was probably the young's most underrated emotion. He'd had his fair share of nightmare panic: his body falling and falling, faster than his stomach could, his mind awaking helpless in a prison of still sleeping flesh, finding himself naked in a public place, impotent flight.

The circle dream that returned to him again and again was a new and dreadful one. Inside meant to be destroyed by suffocation; outside meant he no longer was. He had been a bastard child, an adolescent, become a teacher, an almost-writer, was now a middle-aged cripple. All of these should belong to each other and they no longer did, for he seemed to keep losing the self key and was locked out from them. Never before had he experienced this dreaming detachment when he no longer had great concern about himself. Or rather, about *him*. At such times he did feel sorry for him, but not as deeply as he should, not so sorry as he would have, had it remained himself.

All his life, fear and delight had helped him to assume himself to be axiomatic, and it was now a wrong assumption. I feel, therefore I am. Examine that false premise: I. No I, then nothing felt and therefore: am not. Death does not mean I end, for there was no to die.

Just him . . .

# CHAPTER 13

Archie had stayed overnight, was having breakfast with them before taking off for Paradise. He looked up to Annie, her lips making counting movements as she watched Archie spoon sugar into his third cup of coffee. "I got a sweet tooth."

"Jaw. That was seven teaspoons, Archie."

"Hey-up. I could use another your tailor-mades, too."

She shoved the package over to him.

"Too bad it happened like that last night, Dobbs."

"My fault, Archie. Making it a surprise—"

"No, Annie."

"All them people after all them nice speeches lookin' at it to make you ashamed about it."

"I'll get over it, Archie. Soon as we get the right hide."

"Hey-up. I think I already seen that wrong hide before I seen it last night."

"Huh!"

"I told you about it."

"You did?"

"Back there in the hospital when I made many frequent visits on you. I think it's the same one."

"As what?"

"When I took yours in for you the same time and the American was in there with me too and we spread both them out on the floor in the back of their place."

"Yes."

"Right size. Right colour for it. Looks like his one to me. Yours and his got mixed up somehow."

"Really!"

"Hey-up."

"There are all kinds of brown bears, Archie," Annie said.

"Hey-up."

"So—how can you be sure?"

"It wasn't difficult. I turned it over last night and it was sewed in four places."

"What did that tell you?"

"Where he showed me he never missed any of his four shots, and the right flank of it had a patch they put in it for him where he fucked it up from skinning it out. You got the Minneapolis one, Dobbs, and that's the whole situation."

"Great! I hope you're right, Archie."

"Me, too!"

"What do you remember about him?"

Archie took a swallow of coffee. "Fat."

Annie jumped up.

"Where you going?"

"Phone."

"You'll just get a recording. They're closed till after New Year's."

"You already . . . ?"

"Before you and Archie came down."

Annie sat again. "What else can you remember about him?"

"Minneapolis."

"Did he tell you his name?"

"You don't need his name, Poppa."

"He didn't tell it."

"Doesn't matter, Poppa. They just check their records for the fellow from Minneapolis brought in a hide the same day Archie did. After New Year's we get it all straightened out."

"Hey-up. Then you can throw another bear party for him."

"One was enough, Archie."

"Thanks for invitin' me to it anyway and for stayin' over. Merry White Christmas to you people. I'm pickin' Magdalene up on my way back."

* * *

When she had come back from seeing Archie out, she said, "I'm so sorry, Poppa."

"It wasn't your fault."

"It was."

"No."

"I feel like it was. I set it up. I set *you* up and I'd give anything if I hadn't."

"It was very thoughtful of you. You went to a lot of trouble and I appreciate—"

"I wanted to make it a dandy for you."

"You did."

"The timing was so important. It had to be after the mid-terms were over and before Christmas so I could get the people you'd want. Because it was to be a surprise, I couldn't check with you whom you'd want or you wouldn't want."

"You don't have to explain."

"That's how come I invited the whole department. I knew you wouldn't want Dr. Tait, but I couldn't invite everybody *except* the Head. I saw his face when the skin was unwrapped and that Skeffington woman—"

"It's all right, Annie."

"The hell it is! I'll make it up to you. You'll see."

"When you do, please warn me ahead of time."

"Quit being so decent about it!"

"Okay. But why Whyte? He isn't English Department."

"That was Dr. Stibbard's suggestion when I told him Archie would be there."

"Whyte's the wrong tribe."

"All the same, he's the one came up with that elk roast. He took over and barbecued it, made the bannocks. I thought it was great what he said about Master Bear and religion and art—"

"Please, Annie! Don't try to make me appreciate Whyte!"

"That's more like it."

"Right now let's drop it."

"Where you going?"

"Down. Papers."

* * *

Just before noon the next day, Annie came to him in the den.

"How are they coming?"

"Nineteen left."

"How you feeling?"

"Not bad. Physically."

"The—other?"

"Well as I can expect. One thing can be said for marking papers. It does anaesthetize."

"Damn it, Poppa, we are not going to let that party spoil the first Christmas we've had together in eight years! What do you say we use this afternoon for something important?"

"Like what?"

"Two days till Christmas and we haven't got a tree yet. That's my fault, too. Just wasn't going to be room for one in here with all those people. It's a lovely day out. What do you say we—"

"Sure."

They had driven west through chinook sunshine and into the hills to find and to argue and to decide. At the sun-porch end of the living room, they lifted the perfect pine they'd picked, spent the evening decorating it, then laying their presents beneath it. This ceremony had gone well.

Christmas morning by the time he had finished five kilometres on the bike, done his traction and exercises, and made it downstairs, she had breakfast ready. Special. Eggs Benedict. They moved into the living room to have their coffee in front of the fireplace.

"Let's open, Poppa."

The dressing gown was nice. It fitted.

"Blue goes with your eyes and walking around in your undershorts isn't classy."

The freesia-scented soap proved he had not forgotten her favourite flower.

"Oh, Poppa!" Seated on the fireplace bench, she looked down at the present she'd just unwrapped. "What is it?"

"A mull, for snuff."

"It's beautiful! The two little birds! Is it an apple branch?"

"Cherry, I think."

"Their wings out. They're just landing on it." She turned it over. "What's it made of?"

"Ram's horn. The lid's pewter."

"Hey! Hey! Around the side of the rim—my name!"

"Your gramma's too."

"Aw—she brought it over with her all the way from Ireland!"

"Mmmh."

"Let's you and I have a fix!"

"I forgot to load it."

"And anyway you haven't got a head cold."

"From now on I'll come to you if I have one. You've got one more present left. That envelope on the tree."

She got up, went over, picked it off, and opened it. "Four hundred!"

"There's a condition tied to it, though. How you spend it."

"How?"

"Airline ticket to the Island. Return."

"Oh."

"It's also a present to your mother."

"Aw! I don't know about—"

"Yes, Annie."

"But—"

"She's your mother. She probably misses you as much as I did."

"No way!"

"I can stop payment."

"Not with that goddam chiro—"

"Annie, Annie."

"I don't need any horny adjust—"

"He won't offer you one. This is something a man understands better than a woman. Take it from me. One good kick in the nuts is generally all that's needed."

"It would still be a tacky situation."

"It would mean a lot to your mother."

"But it would leave you alone."

"A bonus."

"Aw—Poppa!"

"I can make out by myself now. She needs you too. Spend New Year's with her."

"I wanted to get a lot of work done during the break."

"You can. Take your charcoal and pad and brush and paint with you."

"I suppose . . ."

"Do her."

She looked up from the cheque. "You know, Poppa, you're turning out to be a half-decent guy."

"I always have been. You just didn't notice it."

She had got up and lifted the padded lid of the fireplace bench. She turned back to him and held out a flat parcel. "I saved your main present till the last, too."

She'd had it matted and framed for him, the shadow and light portrait.

"Merry Christmas, Poppa."

"It is, Annie. It is!"

God would forgive him, he told himself as he dropped off to sleep, for letting her think that the young mill girl had brought the snuff-box over from Ireland with her. Some day he might tell Annie that she hadn't, that it had been a Christmas present years ago from Aunt Nell, who had given up hope of ever breaking the other Annie Dobbs of the filthy habit. He might even tell her how he'd arranged for Herbie to take it into the jeweller's to have the name engraved on the pewter rim.

He doubted he ever would, though.

"You sure you'll be all right?"

"Sure."

"It's over a week."

"Herbie's promised to look in on me regularly."

"You'll keep at the bike and exercises and—"

"I will. Be nice to your mother. Even if he doesn't make a pass at you, kick him in the nuts for me."

"I will."

"Wish your mother well for me. When's your taxi?"

"Noon. My flight doesn't leave till one-twenty.

One thing, Poppa—while I'm gone, try not to—don't you worry about that bear hide."

"That I cannot promise you."

"We'll get it all straightened out after I get back."

"What I still can't understand is how they could get switched. They tattoo them—"

"I know."

"They enter them in a ledger—"

"After I get back—"

"What worries me—"

"Shit! I'm sorry I brought it up!"

"How could it just happen? How could anybody confuse a small brown bear hide with a grizzly?"

"I never even saw it. It was already wrapped when I picked it up."

"Who wrapped it?"

"Frankie, I guess. He's got to be the one responsible for what happened. I should have checked. I could just kick myself."

"No."

"I had that Frankie pegged from the first time I met him. It's an old habit of mine—sizing people up as soon as I meet them."

"A lot of us do."

"I do it a funny way, though. I'll meet someone and I'm right back in grade four with Edna Signer across the aisle from me, and this new person's a boob like her. Or a squealer like Gertrude Graham was. Or else she copies all the time, the way Keitha Harris did. Guys, too. I'm dropping a valentine again into the cardboard box by the window, for Harvey Jolley—"

"Which category does Frankie—"

"Or Aub Taylor's going to twist my arm up between my shoulder-blades. Soon as I met Frankie, I thought, oh boy!"

"Oh boy, what?"

"Don't you ever take your eyes off him, Annie. He'll knock the ice cream right out of your cone and onto the sidewalk. The very first time—after you said you'd let me handle it for you and I went in there, Frankie put a move on me. Open season for our Frankie on everything. His gun is always—"

"Okay."

"—out for mounts all the time."

"I've got the picture, Annie."

"Champion pussy-hunter of them—"

"You are repeating yourself—unpleasantly!"

"So I was. But I want to make an important point. When I get back after New Year's, Frankie's our main target."

"Mine."

"Huh?"

"I'm handling it myself."

"You need me to—"

"No, I don't."

"You can't get the thing into the car and out of it—here or out there—"

"Herbie's already agreed to do that."

"Oh."

"And you'll be on the Island with your mother."

"Wait till I get back."

"I'm doing it the day after New Year's."

"I have a good reason for wanting to go in there with you. I have a confession to make. They had the hide ready three weeks before the party and I told them to hold it. Frankie's grampa and I plotted together."

"That's all right."

"No! It isn't! Maybe if I hadn't stuck my big nose in it—"

"They did it."

"*Frankie* did it. Not the old man. That's why I want to be there so you won't be too hard on him!"

"I won't be."

"He's pretty nice, Poppa. I fell for him. He told me all about how he lost his only son, Frankie's dad. I told him about you, and he thought it was great the way I wanted to throw a surprise party with your friends and champagne to celebrate your bear. He's like me. A real gut-spiller. He invited me to come out there any time and use their specimens for models if it could help me in my painting, and I said maybe I might. What I'm getting at, Poppa, is I don't want you to fly off the handle at him for something Frankie did."

"All right, Annie. Just Frankie."

"I'd still like to be there."

"I've promised you."

"Not just for his grampa's sake. I'd like to bust Frankie's jaw!"

The front door chimes sounded.

Herbie had been able to manage the bear hide alone, both at the house and then out at Wild Trophy World. Colin held the door open for him.

"Just drop it on the floor, Herbie."

But he stopped just inside and stood with the parcel in his arms as he looked up to the ducks and geese flying overhead, the antelope and deer and moose and bear and wolf head-mounts on the wall behind the counter. His gaze stopped and stayed on the dominant musk-ox with its halo of bone.

"Put it on the floor, Herbie." He went to the counter and rang the bell.

Now Herbie had come to the counter, was bent over and staring down at the shelves holding cream shapes rampant and couchant, fanged animal dentures with candy tongues. He looked up with disbelief then back down again. He released a sigh of wonder. "The levels, Colin! The white ghosts!" He looked up again with incredulity. "Those labels! Could be the seven deadly sins!" His eyes lifted to the musk-ox head, dropped back to the shelves. "Only the mouth of hell is missing!"

"If you say so, Herbie."

"The reproduction on the wall above my desk! 'Painting on the West Face of the Wall which divides the Nave from the Chancel of the Trinity at Stratford-upon-Avon in Warwickshire.' You've seen it!"

"Yes." He hit the bell again.

" 'The Last Judgement'! In three dimensions!"

"Dr. Dobbs."

"Mr. Munro—my colleague, Dr. Stibbard."

"Mr. Munro," Herbie said, "this counter with these forms and that musk-ox looking down—"

"Just a minute, Herbie. I—I've had to bring the hide back, Mr. Munro." He pointed to it. "There's been a mistake. Herbie, would you lift it up and open it. It's been a very embarrassing one for me."

"Oh, I hope our work hasn't been unsatisfactory!"

"Not that. Thanks, Herbie. It's the wrong one."

"Pardon?"

"This hide is a *brown* bear hide. Belongs to somebody else. It's not my bear. See?"

The old man looked down at it.

"Mine was a grizzly—full grown. An unusually
large one."

"Oh."

"It may not even be a Rocky Mountain grizzly. I
talked with Dr. Heron, our head of Environmental Design, and he told me it could possibly be one of the
plains grizzlies that used to follow the buffalo. . . ."

"Grass grizzly."

"I guess. It certainly isn't this—brown—adolescent."
He wished he hadn't said that, after promising Annie
to take it easy on the old man.

"Excuse me, Dr. Dobbs. I'll just get Frankie. He's
moulding in the back, working on the clam forms."

"Is that right, Colin—about the buffalo!" Herbie
said.

"Possible. Heron says he'd have to see it. He guesses
it's more likely related to Kodiak—"

"This is my grandson, Dr. Dobbs."

So this young man in his late twenties or early
thirties, wearing brown coveralls and removing yellow
plastic gloves, was Frankie. With those almond eyes of
startling olive grey, Frankie was falcon handsome.

"There seems to be some trouble about Dr. Dobbs's
bear—"

"His daughter picked it up."

"No, she didn't!"

"Over three weeks ago."

"Not mine!"

"Sure."

"No—it isn't! That isn't a grizzly!"

"It's the one that was brought in."

"Archie didn't bring this one in to you!"

"He did."

"Now, just a minute—"

"I tattooed it. I entered it in the book."

"I want my hide!"

"That's it, Dr. Dobbs."

"It is not! I ought to know! This one did not come

out to the horse! This isn't the one I had in my scope!
did not shoot this!"

"That's the one the Indian—"

"Bull-shit! It was not a brown bear did this to me!
It was a grizzly. I want *my* bear!"

"You've got it. This is the one the Indian brought—"

"No—it is not!" There was not a flicker of those
cold, innocent eyes.

"Mr. Munro, your grandson is suggesting something very nasty here—that Archie Nicotine delivered
to you this brown bear hide instead of mine. Instead of
the one he skinned out and salted and sloughed and
kept in the agency root house till he brought it in and
handed it over to your grandson—"

"Dr. Dobbs—"

"—who is standing behind that goddam counter
and lying in his goddam teeth!"

The son-of-a-bitch had lowered his eyes, but only
because he was pulling on his yellow gloves. He left.

"Let's put it this way, Mr. Munro. I know Archie
Nicotine to be an honourable man. Can you say that
you know the same to be true—of your grandson?"

Suddenly the old man looked much older. He
dropped his eyes to the hide, then looked away from
it.

"You've known him since his birth, haven't you."

Almost imperceptibly the old man nodded.

"So. You ought to be able to answer my question
without too much difficulty."

So much for the promise he'd made to Annie.

# CHAPTER 14

It had been a nice visit with her mother; she had got a lot of work done out there. As he had assured her, the one kick had been enough for the ardent chiropractor. It was great that he had done his bike and traction and exercises regularly.

"And how did you make out with the bear hide?"

"Not so good."

"What happened?"

"You were right. Frankie's the problem."

"You didn't go hard on his—"

"I tried not to. Frankie insisted there had been a mistake—"

"He didn't!"

"Yes. He did. He said the hide we got was the one Archie brought in to him."

"The son-of-a-bitch!"

"I'm afraid there was a deliberate switch, Annie. I think after Archie left, the man from Minneapolis slipped Frankie a little something to do it."

"Oh, no!"

"It's the only explanation."

"What are you going to do about it?"

"I don't know."

"Frankie's grampa had nothing to do with it!"

"You're probably right."

"Frankie's grampa won't—he wouldn't—he'll do something about it."

"I don't know."

"I do. I got to know him. He's not the kind of fellow would—would—"

"I don't know."

"He'll straighten it out. Now he knows. He'll do the right thing."

"I hope so."

"Just give him some time."

"That's what I'm doing, Annie. Right now it's all I can do."

Three days later, just after supper, Annie had answered the phone.

"For you, Poppa. It's Frankie's grampa. I told you."

After he'd hung up, she said. "What did he say?"

"Wants to talk with me."

"See."

"I'm going out there tomorrow morning."

"I can miss my—"

"No. I think I'd better go alone."

"But—"

"Annie, if you'd been in there before—if you'd seen his face after I'd explained. . . . I think it would be considerate of you not to be there."

"Oh."

"Somebody I cared about took a bribe, I'd want as few people in on it as possible. This is just between me and Mr. Munro. And Frankie."

"I wish to hell you hadn't gone after that bear in the first place!"

"I've had the same wish."

"Maybe you ought to just drop it."

"No."

"It's only a hide."

"It's much more than that, Annie."

"According to you."

"Yes."

"And Frankie's grampa."

"I think so."

"Jesus, am I ever glad I'm not a man!"

Annie had dropped him off at Wild Trophy World, on the way to the university. When he'd finished he'd call a taxi.

"I don't know what to say," Mr. Munro said after they'd gone into the office, "except that I am sorry for what has happened. I would give anything if there hadn't been this—misunderstanding."

"It's not a misunderstanding."

"I'm afraid it is."

"I got the wrong bear hide!"

"Frankie says the head-mount and rug you—"

"Frankie is lying."

"—was made from the raw hide brought in—"

"Get him in here!"

"—the one he tattooed and entered in your name."

"I want him in here!"

"Frankie has told me—"

"That he was paid to switch those hides?"

"Let's say we don't know how—"

"I know!"

"—the mix-up—"

"I don't know how much he was paid to do it, but he was! A couple of hundred! Three! Five! Let's have him in here and he can tell us!"

"Please, Dr. Dobbs—"

"He can also take back that shit about Archie! Get him in here!"

"He's not here today."

"I told you on the phone I wanted to talk with *both* of you!"

"He's not in."

"All right. Your ledger *is*. I think it will tell us whose the brown one really is. Archie thinks he recognized it. The same afternoon he dropped mine in here there was another hunter. All we have to do is look up the entries in that book for that same day and see if there was a grizzly head and rug mount shipped out to Minneapolis."

"Dr. Dobbs, I've lost quite a bit of sleep over this—"

"By mistake. If you wish."

"I've tried to find a way to make it up to you. There is one possible—"

"There certainly is. Get the name of that fellow in Minneapolis—"

"Possible. For me." He got up. "Will you come to the back of the shop. I want you to see something."

In the middle of the floor there was a great mound of fur. Resting on top of it was a grizzled head with jaws opened, teeth and tongue bared. The old man bent down and began to open out the skin. He straightened up and came to Colin.

"There."

It took up almost all of the cleared centre of the shop floor. "That isn't mine."

"I know. I shot it myself in the Kootenays the spring of 1937. I would like you to have it."

"But—it isn't mine."

"Please."

"I can't. If I took it from you—I'm no different from that corrupt son-of-a-bitch in—"

"There is a difference."

"Not for me."

"Dr. Dobbs, you were right when you said I have known Frankie ever since he was born. His father was my only son. Till the Korean War. Frankie was just nine months, and he and his mother moved in with me. She married again when Frankie was three. He stayed with me."

"I'm sorry, Mr. Munro. I can't take it. It would still be the wrong one."

"All right. All right." The resignation in his voice suggested he had known all along that his offer would be rejected. "In spite of what the bear did to you, Dr. Dobbs, you are a lucky man. You have your daughter." He bent down and began to fold up the hide.

"My hip won't let me help you—"

"I understand."

When they had returned to the office, he said, "May we look at that book now?"

"No."

"The name of the hunter who did get my—"

"No."

"—get my bear."

"I won't do that."

"Wait a minute. Suppose it were you, not me— nearly gutted—had half your face ripped off—would you accept *my* offer?"

"Perhaps not. But tell me something, Dr. Dobbs. If your daughter were Frankie, would you go along with what you're asking of me?"

\* \* \*

Once he'd made up his mind, he had kept his decision secret from Annie. Hard enough to explain it to himself. There had been few times during his life when he had needed legal help: his mother's simple will and the more complicated probation of Aunt Nell's, dragged out for three years by the master procrastinator who had been her lawyer. After their move out west, an expert in real estate contracts, with a double-martini breath, had almost lost him a ten-thousand-dollar deposit on his house purchase. With the separation and divorce he had learned that half a lawyer is not better than none. Now—reluctantly—grizzly litigation.

He had told only Herbie that he must take Wild Trophy World into court and asked him if he thought his daughter, who had just articled, might recommend someone to handle the case. Herbie had promised to shut up about it and to tell Elsie to do the same. He had phoned the suggested law firm and explained his problem, and they had asked him to come in. Mr. Terry Kinistinick looked forward to seeing him.

To avoid argument with Annie, he had called a taxi to take him to the Monarch Trust Building. He looked up to the four columns of business firms listed alphabetically on the wall in the foyer and wished to hell he hadn't left the goddam name and office number behind. He could not remember which partner came first, and knowing it was either the thirteenth, the fifteenth, or the seventeenth floor was no help at all. Nothing under "K." Ah—there it was: "Partridge, Martin, Woodcock and Cardinal." No Kinistinick, though. An understandable exclusion from that aviary of lawyers. "1903-1915. 19th Floor."

He had just taken off his sun-glasses when the elevator stopped and two girls got on. Thank God, they left at the next floor; for they had looked away from him too quickly. Room 1903 must be the main office. He found it just down the hall, went inside. The receptionist at her desk glanced up to him, almost coyly, for her head was cocked to hold a receiver against her shoulder while she listened and made notations.

She looked down to her pad again and he waited. She hung up.

"Dr. Dobbs. I think I'm a little early. For Mr. Kinistinick."

"Just take a seat, please." She picked up the phone. He went over to the leather couch.

She replaced the receiver. "Mr. Kinistinick is coming right down."

Twenty minutes later Mr. Kinistinick entered and came over to him.

"Dr. Dobbs."

Serious. Fit. Tanned in February!

"Let's go up to my office."

Young. Was he articling with Partridge, Martin, Woodcock and Cardinal?

Out in the hall he said, "My office is up a floor. We can take the elevator—"

"I can manage one flight of stairs."

Generous size. Fine broadloom. Five-foot Kentia palm. Inoffensive prints. Onyx pen set. Pipe-rack. Rosewood desk. Actual leather easy chairs. Young Terry Kinistinick was not articling with Partridge, Martin, Woodcock and Cardinal.

"Now." He pulled over a pad. He took the pen out of its socket. "I understand this concerns a grizzly bear hide, which—ah—" He looked down to the pad. "—Wild Trophy World—taxidermists—were to prepare for you. Right?"

"Yes."

"Would you like a coffee?"

"No, thanks."

"Let's get some more particulars. Shall we go back a way. . . . You shot and killed a grizzly bear. When?"

"April. Third of April."

Kinistinick took it down.

"Last year."

Kinistinick looked up to him. "That's quite a while ago."

"Yes."

"Does it take that long to do something—like that?"

"I don't think so."

"Then why would—oh—you shot it early last April but you didn't get around to . . ."

"The delay was theirs. It wasn't delivered until Christmas—just before. I received the wrong one just before Christmas."

"But that's almost . . ." He held up a closed hand, released one finger after another. "April, May, June, July, August . . ." He set down the pen and lifted the other hand. "September, October—"

"Seven and a half months. The delay was theirs. They sent it away to Montreal to be tanned. They were very busy. They said."

"Uh-huh. And instead of your grizzly bear they delivered a young brown bear hide."

"Yes."

"Which was not the grizzly hide you took in to them—"

"I didn't take it in."

"Who did?"

"Archie Nicotine."

"Who is he?"

"My guide. He was with me when it happ—when I shot it. Up Daisy Creek."

"And he took in the grizzly hide to Wild Trophy World for you."

"That's right."

"So. You were not there when—"

"I was in the hospital. Archie skinned the bear and salted the hide a couple of days later. He kept it in the agency root house until he took it into Wild Trophy World."

"Agency?"

"Archie is a Stony Indian."

"Oh." He laid the pen down. He leaned forward, took a pipe out of the rack, then a pouch from his pocket. He unzipped the pouch. "Who did he hand it over to?"

Whom. The briar bowl was quite shiny. "Frank Munro."

"The owner? An employee?"

"I guess he runs the place. It's a family business. His grandfather seems to be looking over his shoulder."

"This Indian guide. You know him pretty well?"

"Very well."

He tamped tobacco with his thumb. "Anyone else

in there at the time? When Mr. Nicotine took the hide
into Wild Trophy World?''

"Archie says there was another man, a hunter
from Minneapolis, who'd just brought in a hide of his
own. Archie thinks it's the hide that was delivered to
me.''

"Uh-huh." He struck a match, drew the flame
down into the bowl. "This—Mr. Nicotine. Ah—tell me—
more about—about him." He shook out the match and
laid it in the ashtray. "How long have you known
him?''

"Eleven—twelve years.''

"Young? Old?''

"Middle-aged.''

"Oh. Do you mind? My pipe?''

Only because it smelled like a hairdressing salon.
"No.''

"Has he ever, to your knowledge, been—ah—
involved with the law?''

"I have no idea.''

"We must find out, Dr. Dobbs. He is Indian.''

"I believe I said he was.''

"Mmmh. Now. Where?''

"Wild Trophy World is on the corner of Meadow
Lark and—''

"No. The bear hunt.''

"Daisy Creek—about forty miles west of Shelby.''

"Mm-hmm.''

"Roughly.''

"That is where you shot the bear and where the
bear . . .''

"Mauled me.''

"Mmmh. You say Mr. Nicotine thinks the hide
you got was the same hide he saw when he brought
yours into the taxidermists'. How could he tell that?''

"He examined it and there were four places they'd
stitched it, and the man from Minneapolis had told
Archie that he'd shot at his bear four times without a
miss. Also, Archie said there was a patch in one of the
flanks—same place he'd noticed skinning damage when
he took my hide into Wild Trophy World.''

"I see." He sat back in his chair. "Couple of weeks
ago . . ." He puffed on the pipe. "I noticed a for-sale

ad in classified. . . ." He drew more deeply. "Polar
. . ." He sucked again. ". . . bear rug." Out, thank
God. He laid the pipe on the blotter. "Six thousand
dollars. Would the market price of a grizzly run the
same as a polar bear?"

"I don't know."

"A small brown bear would be much less, of course.
We can find out easily enough and when we have the
difference between them—"

"I'm not interested in monetary difference between—"

"Nor am I—*only*."

"I want the skin of the bear that did this to me!"

"I was coming to that. Justice is not concerned
only with material values. Those which cannot be
weighed, priced, measured, calibrated are also important in a judgment sense."

"I'm glad to hear that."

"Your injury, pain, suffering, both physically and
spiritually, must be taken into account. I find this an
intriguing case, and I think we'll go for Supreme rather
than County or District. Before our next meeting I'd
like you to get me a list of all the expenses incurred in
going after this bear: travel, payments to Mr. Nicotine,
medical or hospital expenses, loss of income. Oh—and
we must have Mr. Nicotine come in."

"All right."

"If he has a record, we must know it." He picked
up the pipe, turned it over in his hand. "You ever
smoke a pipe?"

"Briefly. When I stopped smoking ten years ago."

"How long till they quit scalding your mouth and
tongue?"

"I don't know. I decided to make a clean break
before I found that out."

"Yeah." He stood up. "Give me a couple of weeks
on this. Next time let's have Mr. Nicotine, too."

"Sure. You have a very fine tan."

"Hawaii. I dive. I just got back."

# CHAPTER 15

Just before and just after sleep, it seemed, insights came to him most often; he had been just about to drop off when he had perceived that truth years ago. Since then he had lost count of the number of times after the lights were out that something great had floated up, and he had rolled over to switch on the reading lamp and reach for the pad and pencil on the night table by his side of the bed. Sarah had kept careful score, though. For her, gang rape was preferable to broken sleep; he had discovered that about her while he was shaving one morning.

The sea caves might also float treasures up to him when he was having a cup of coffee, staring into a fire, or walking, if it were not in the city. And while tying flies, of course. Yet he could not recall anything of any worth that had ever been granted to him while he had been angling; hour after hour of iambic back cast with final spondee, simply lulled thought. Human metronomes don't think. That one, too, had happened while he was shaving. Never used it, though.

And now as he looked in the bathroom mirror, another good one: how considerate God could sometimes be—only head and facial hair, unchecked, could grow to any length. Damned awkward otherwise. Hey, hey! Since Daisy Creek he'd had only *half* a face that needed shaving! And hey again! If he could be that derisive about it, maybe he was no longer so sensitive about that cheek and that eye! He must tell Annie at breakfast!

But as soon as he saw her face, he knew it was not going to be one of their good mornings. Last night, too, she had been preoccupied, as though she had something to tell him. Something that would not be heart-warming. He had waited for it, but for her own reasons she had not brought it up. Whatever it was.

"I had a great insight while I was shaving, Annie."

"Eat your breakfast before it gets colder."

"The hair on your face and the hair on your head is the only hair on your body that keeps on—"

"Pass over the toast."

"—growing."

"Before it mildews."

He shoved the plate towards her. "Means all you got to worry about is getting haircuts and shaving your face."

"If you're a man."

"Wouldn't it be awful if the other hair kept getting away on you."

She went right on buttering the piece of toast.

"Stop and think about it."

She reached for the raspberry jam.

"Coming out of your armpits and right down and out of your sleeves so you'd have to keep stuffing it back up your shirt cuffs."

"We shave ours."

"Even if you didn't, it wouldn't grow very long. And the other. All down your legs so you'd have to tuck it inside your sock tops."

"We shave our legs, too. There was a phone call for you yesterday."

So! "Who was it?"

She bit off a corner of toast—chewed—swallowed. "Just who is Mr. Kinistinick?"

"Why?"

"Because it was his secretary phoned. He wants to see you."

"When?"

"Next Tuesday."

"What else did she—"

"You have an appointment with him for one-thirty."

"He's a lawyer."

"She said *another* appointment. You didn't tell me you'd already gone to a lawyer."

"I guess I didn't."

"Why not?"

"What else did she say?"

"Why not?"

"I didn't want to bother you with it. Do they want Archie to come in, too?"

"Yes. Why not?"

"Because I wanted to handle it myself. My own way."

"Wouldn't it have been nicer if you'd told me?"

"Maybe."

"Instead of sneaking off to see a lawyer. Did you think I might try to talk you out of it?"

"Maybe."

"Did you think I might think retaining a lawyer and going into court over that goddam bear hide was carrying a bad thing too goddam far?"

"Yes."

"Well, you were goddam well right!"

"There you are. You've got jam on your chin."

"And you got jam all over your face!"

"I guess I have."

"You don't have to pull stuff like that on me, Poppa."

"You telling me you wouldn't have tried to talk me out of it?"

"No. But you know I wouldn't have got anywhere with you. You hired him?"

"Yes."

"To really give it to Frankie."

"To help me recover my proper bear hide. He says it's an intriguing case."

"That's nice."

"He thinks we can win."

"I wish you success. One thing, though."

"What?"

"You and Kinistinick make sure it's Frankie you got in your peep-sights. Not his grampa."

"We will."


He had tutorials with Mrs. Humphrey at ten and with Griffin at eleven. He'd managed to shove Judy MacDermott's ahead to Friday, so that meant he had plenty of time for lunch and getting down to the offices of Partridge, Woodcock, Martin and Cardinal by one-thirty;

then back to the university for his Expository Writing class at four.

He was concerned for both Mrs. Humphrey and Noel Griffin. He guessed Mrs. Humphrey to be in her mid-sixties. She had wanted to write ever since she'd been a little girl, she had told him, and after her son and daughter had grown up and left, and her husband, Alex, had died two years ago, she had come to university as a special student. She had never lost her desire to write during all the years of bringing up children and being a wife to Alex. Indeed she had never relinquished her membership in the Canadian Authors' Association and had kept up her journal for over fifty years. Very early in the course she had asked him if he would like her to make selections from her journal so that he could read them. He had told her that he was more interested in what she was writing now.

She had made perceptive and helpful comments about others' writing during the seminars, but it had been difficult for him to find anything of hers to use. For her sake. Up to bat only twice since the course had started. He began the interview by telling her that he rather liked the stuff about her grandmother living in a sod house on the prairies at the turn of the century. Her grandmother's saying that when it rained outside for three days, it had rained inside the house for five days, had been a nice find.

"I liked the cobwebs in the high corners of the front porch and your grandmother knocking them down with the broom and your concern for the baby spiders; and there's the raspberry vinegar your older brother splashed on the front of your birthday dress and you let your mother think it was blood and he got a good whipping for it. You're not running past as much as you did before Christmas."

"Dr. Dobbs—I have listened to a lot of impressive stuff in the seminar."

"Yes?"

"Some pretty fine writing."

"Finding."

"All right. Finding. It will be even better when they go back and polish it."

"Perhaps."

"My stuff doesn't even come close."

"Mrs. Humphrey—"

"I know it and you know it. What happened to that honest tongue you promised us the very first seminar? Cat got it?"

"Oh."

"Supposing I were forty or so years younger, would you be congratulating me on homesteader sod huts and baby spiders and raspberry vinegar?"

"Maybe not."

"That's better. What do I do about it?"

"That's a tough one, Mrs. Humphrey."

"You want me to drop out?"

"No."

"What do I do, then?"

"What you have been doing. You've hung in—right from the beginning."

"That's all I've done."

"If you'd waited a little longer I might have turned honest."

"And told me I was wasting my time."

"You aren't."

"And yours."

"You aren't."

"I think so."

"Look. We all write *for* somebody. Long before publication that person is standing in the shadows— listening—watching—feeling. You have such readers."

"Name one."

"How many grandchildren do you have?"

"Six."

"Okay. There's six. I think what you are finding about your pioneer gramma, and the little girl you were, ought to put you on the top of your grandchildren's best-seller list."

She was not looking at him at all, her head back and turned towards the window. He heard her catch her breath.

"Mrs. Humphrey."

She faced him. There were tears in her eyes. Had he hurt her that much! "Are you all right?"

She wiped her face with the back of her hand, and nodded.

"If you want to drop out—"

"Dr. Dobbs—I—I wouldn't d-drop out of a seminar of yours if you were teaching a course in child abuse!"

"How long did it take you to write this?"

"That one went great." Griffin was sitting in the chair Mrs. Humphrey had just left. "Just happened. Happens a lot like that for me. Sittin' in the can . . . in a bar . . . I can remember exactly how this one happened."

"How?"

"I'd parked my car just the way he did in the story. After I'd been walkin' late at night in the ravine the way he did. Fall. Dead leaves and squirrels and all that shit. I parked my car the way he did that night and I went in to the typewriter and I sat down and I wrote that story. It just wrote itself. I know it's a short one, but it took less than forty minutes. Came just like shit off a shovel."

"I can see that."

"Take that mirror."

"The full-length, hallway—"

"Louis Sixteenth. I got no mirror like that or like the one in the hallway he comes into after he was walkin' in the ravine and this old girl-friend, he thinks of her. I used to live in a house on Dougall—high, narrow house—like the one he passes and he recognizes it's the old girl-friend's house and he thinks of her and he wonders if she still lives in it because of this unanswered question that's kept buggin' him and buggin' him so he goes up the steps and he rings the bell but she doesn't answer it. Nobody answers it but he goes in there anyway and there's that mirror in the hallway and she's there and it happens."

"She does the blow job on him."

"Oh—wait a minute. *Did* she. Actually. Did she really do it? In retrospect he isn't sure she did."

"All in his imagination."

"No. In the mirror. The magic mirror. Look at the title."

"I did."

" 'Caverns Measureless'—almost named itself for me. And a week after, something else occurred to me."

"What?"

"Happened the same way for Coleridge. That was how he wrote 'Kubla Khan,' you know."

"He said it was. You accept that?"

"Sure. Don't you?"

"No."

"You sayin' Coleridge is a liar."

"Yes."

"I believe him—he did opium and passed out and woke up in the morning and wrote 'Kubla Khan'—"

"I do not believe in the 'lightning stroke of genius' approach to writing or to painting or to any art. I do not believe in romantic horse-shit! And I've had to make a reluctant decision. I think it would be wise for you to withdraw from the second session of 327."

"I already made the same decision."

"Oh, you have! No hard feelings?"

"No. You gave me a pass for the first session. I already talked it over with Dr. Tait."

"He advised you to drop out."

"He suggested I hang in, but I decided not to."

At the door he turned back. "I sent it away."

"*New Yorker*?"

"*Playboy*."

"Let me know what they think of it."


"He said he'd be here and he will be. He didn't promise not to be late."

"They seem to have no understanding of time."

"Oh, Archie does. He looks on it as simply an arbitrary white convention not to be taken too literally. My daughter holds much the same—"

"Well, we don't. We won't wait any longer for him, Dr. Dobbs. Let's you and I get some things out of the way. . . ." Kinistinick leaned over sideways, pulled open a bottom drawer and brought out a clock. "First thing on our agenda—writ of summons." He turned the clock over, gave it a short wind, consulted the face while he set it, pushed in its start button, and placed it on the corner of his desk.

Young Terry Kinistinick certainly took it literally. "Coffee?"

With that inexorable hand sweeping up every twenty-four-carat second! "No thanks. How long do you think it will be—"

"Oh, this time—depending on when Mr. Nicotine shows up—half an hour should do us."

"For the case. How long does something like this generally take?"

"The actual proceeding itself, not long. Depending on the court's case-load when we come to trial, you might have to allow a full day for it—or two—three at the most. We're going to have to have several meetings."

"I meant how long till we *get* into court with it?"

"Three months—"

"That long!"

"—to three years."

"Oh, come on! Where's *her* clock!"

"Good question."

"I knew she was blind, but not paraplegic!"

"She is, Dr. Dobbs. She is."

"What do you have to do to make it the three months?"

"Depends on which writ of summons we get. It can be a generally endorsed writ. That's the long one. Or it can be a special endorsement. Special one contains considerably more details about the plaintiff's claim against the defendant. When the defendant has been served—personally—he must make an appearance within fifteen days. After he's done that, within thirty days, we must file a statement of claim against him."

"Then we go to court."

"No. Pleadings. Discovery. We can suck up some time by filing the complaint with the writ of special endorsement."

"And *then* we—"

"Not yet. Pre-trial."

"What's that?"

"The counsels—not you or the defendant, normally—meet with the judge in his chambers. That can be a time-shortener—one last chance to reach a solution agreeable to both parties. It works in quite a few cases."

"Still be three months, though."

"At least. And only if we are successful in getting a special endorsement, which will depend on Rule 33." He pulled over a thick brown book, *Rules of Practice*. He opened the book, set aside a folded paper marker. " '(1). At the option of the plaintiff, the writ of summons may be specially endorsed with a statement of his claim where the plaintiff seeks to recover a debt or liquidated demand in money (with or without interest and whether the interest be payable by way of damages or otherwise) arising—' "

"I'm not after *money!*"

"I know. I know that. (C), under (1) . . . 'Work done or services rendered . . .' " He turned a page. "(K): 'In an action for recovery of chattels . . .' " He put the marker back in place, closed the book, glanced at the clock. "I think we can be optimistic about a special endorsement. But not about Mr. Nicotine."

"Archie will be here."

"All right. Until he does show, something else we can discuss, which doesn't need him. The defendant or defendants in this action. We have to decide that for the writ of summons."

"Frankie. Frank Munro."

"Yes." He wrote it down. "And just to be sure about actual payment of damages and costs if we win— the company, Wild Trophy World. Now—the other one, the grandfather, I believe you said."

"I don't know about—"

"I think so. We must cover all bases. Frank Munro. Wild Trophy World. The other owner or partner."

"But Frankie's grandfather was not—I don't think he was involved—"

"Oh, he is—"

"No. Not responsible for what happened."

"He is still liable."

"He may be, but I don't want to include him as a—a—whatever you call it—"

"Defendant."

"In the—"

"Action. In order to get a special endorsement, we must be quite specific and detailed. Sufficiency is important. Among other things, we must be particular about the defendants."

"I want to be particular. Frankie. Wild Trophy World. That's all."

Kinistinick laid down the pen. He sat back in his chair. "I am not advising a shotgun approach. That can damage a case as much as anything."

"Okay then. Leave Frankie's grampa out of it."

"For now, think it over. We can always come back—"

"For good."

"You may regret it."

The phone rang.

"Tell him I'll be right down." He replaced the receiver. "Mr. Nicotine." He pushed back his chair. "Finally. If you'll excuse me, I'll go down for him."

"Sure."

He did not stop the clock.

When he had come back with Archie, he said, "The first thing I want to explain to you, Mr. Nicotine, is that this is a civil action for damages and for recovery of Dr. Dobbs's bear. It is not a criminal action, you understand."

"Hey-up. No Queen."

"That's right."

"Bein' a bear."

"Pardon?"

"Not a fox."

"Not bad, Mr. Nicotine." Kinistinick was grinning slightly. "Not bad at all." He looked at the clock. He discarded the grin. "In this case you will not be a defendant. A witness. But you will still be under oath when you testify. I have to point out to you that a witness guilty of perjury gets into a lot more trouble than a defendant would. You understand that?"

"Hey-up."

"You are a prime declarant. As a matter of fact Dr. Dobbs's only declarant, his only witness."

"I guess you are correct. The bear bein' dead now."

"Dr. Dobbs has told me that the bear is—was—a unique bear."

"Hey-uh?"

"Quite identifiable. Unmistakable. You could easily recognize it."

"Hey-up."

"*Ursus horribilis.*"

Archie looked over to Colin.

"Latin name for grizzly, Archie."

"Hey-up."

"Besides being a grizzly, what other distinctive—qualities?"

"The size of it. The colour of it."

"What about the colour?"

"Wrong."

"Yes?"

"Wasn't like grizzly hair colour." He pointed to the light cocoa broadloom. "Like that is."

"Mmmh."

"The face of it was yellow."

"Yes?" He pulled over his pad and was making notations.

"The feet was different, too."

"How?"

"Black ones. The claws was white."

"That is certainly specific."

"It was an unusuable bear," Archie said.

"Yes. And you say it was a large one."

"Hey-up."

"How large?"

"I never seen one that big before."

"How large have you seen?"

"Large ones. I been around bears a lot. It was larger than all of the ones before."

"Now. The day you took Dr. Dobbs's hide—the bear's—into Wild Trophy World, I understand there was another hunter there at the same time."

"Hey-up."

"With *his* bear."

"Hey-up."

"What was his like?"

"Like the one Dobbs got from them."

"Uh-huh."

"Brown. Small."

"With identifiable—uh—marks."

"Four bullet holes. Belly—shoulder—neck. The flank been tore bad."

"Now." Kinistinick turned over to a new notebook sheet. "Mr. Nicotine, you have a record." With the pen he tapped photocopied sheets on the desk. "It's—not a short one."

"Hey-up."

"Goes back quite a few years. What—exactly—charges have you faced?"

"You went and got it." Archie jerked a thumb at the charge record. "Didn't you read it?"

"I have, but I'd like to know what *you* have to say."

"Hey-uh?"

"About these charges."

"I got arrested on them. Drunk to disturb the public. Destroyin' property several times. Tables—chairs—beer glasses. Drunk when I was drivin'. I paid for them if I had the money fine, or else I went in the bucket."

"Assault."

"Hey-up."

"With a deadly weapon."

"Hey-up."

"Knife."

"Norman Catface."

Kinistinick had run a finger down the first sheet. He flipped it over.

"Sarcee," Archie explained. "He sold his sister, Gloria Catface. Before she did that, she got crowned Miss Fish and Game one year. Her brother tried to sell a Stony girl, too, so I cut him so he would learn not to do that any more."

"I don't seem to have that one listed." Kinistinick looked up to Archie. "Did he not lay a charge?"

"He was too smart for that."

Kinistinick consulted the record again. "The assault charge which I do have here—with a deadly weapon . . ."

"Charlie Standin' at the Door."

"Yes. That's the one."

"In '76. Frontier Days Rodeo. In the Number Four horse barn. He started it first."

"Yes?"

"When he hit me with his deadly weapon."

"Uh-huh."

"Chuck-wagon stove. The judge found for me that time."

"I see that. Something else. Nothing listed here the last few years."

"That's correct. Nine."

"Why is that?"

"Most those times you got I was influenced."

"Drunk."

"Hey-up. Except for Norman Catface. I was sober for that time."

"But why aren't there any charges after—ah—'76?"

"I successfully overcome my drinkin' problem."

"How did that happen?"

"It was difficult."

"Exceptionally?"

"Hey-up."

Kinistinick shoved the paper to the front of the desk. "I'd like you to take this with you, Mr. Nicotine. Back to the Paradise Reserve—"

"I don't think I got any room in my files for it."

"All the same. Go over it and memorize it."

"What for?"

"So that when you testify, and the other lawyer asks you to recall the times you've been in trouble with the law, you will be able to give him everything."

"Why?"

"Well. If he asks you about a certain day and year you'd forgot, you'll be able to remember it."

"What for?"

"To help your friend, Dr. Dobbs."

"How would that do it?"

"Well. If you are under oath on the stand and you didn't remember, the defence lawyer would be able to suggest that you were trying to hide something."

"What has me hidin' somethin' got to do with Dobbs's wrong bear?"

"It hasn't anything really, but the defence will try to make it look as though it did."

"Hey-up."

"You understand now?"

"Now I do. I come up an untrusted liar."

"Yes."

"Like most of us reds is."

"I'm afraid so."

"Then we better be more careful of that. You better get the other one."

"Other what?"

Archie indicated the record. "The Shelby one. When I had my drinkin' problem, it got me more trouble with the law closer to Paradise."

"There's another record?"

"Hey-up. It's longer than that one."

"Oh."

"But it's the same kind of stuff."

"I see."

"Mostly."

"What do you mean—mostly?"

"Rustlin'."

"No!"

"Christmas trees."

"You were charged with rustling Christmas trees, Mr. Nicotine?"

"Pettigrew, when I cut five hundred spruce off his lease without tellin' him about it. Little ones."

"Oh."

"I had to pay for damaging his lease, but still made a good profit out of them."

"What else?"

"Indecent exposure."

"Yes. We have that listed on this one."

"That time in the city is. It happened to me in Shelby, too. The same way, only between the Gateway Hotel beer parlour and the Sanitary Cafe and the Mountie discovered me when I was taking a piss the way I was doin' it behind the Empress the other time for the city piss I took."

"All right—"

"You see, when I had my drinkin' problem I was a chronic pisser—"

"Yes. Mr. Nicotine. Now—"

"I was ignorant it was against the law to piss outside the city, either."

"The next point on our agenda—"

"If the RCMP are getting after pissers everywhere

to cease pissing, they ought to put up some no pissing
signs, and that's the whole situation."

"Some day they may get around to it."

"The magistrate said it was not legal to spit, either."

"That one is not generally enforced. The next
thing—"

"Still legal to fart?"

Terry Kinistinick stared at him for a moment. "Archie, you are going to be one of two things when you
get up. Either you are going to be the best damn
witness I will ever have during my law career—or, if
we're unlucky in our bench draw, the worst."

"Hey-up." Archie reached down for his hat. "Let
me know which one of them it is." He stood up. "I
have had frequent experience at it in my life of crime."
He put on his hat. "I can keep my mouth shut, too."
He looked over to the door.

"Now, just a minute. I would like you to tell me—"

"I would like you to tell me where you got your
legal toilet."

"Third on the left beyond the elevator."

"Wait for me, Archie," Colin said. "Turn off your
clock till we get back."

"It's off, Dr. Dobbs. I have to come with you
fellows too."

## CHAPTER 16

There must have been un-
noticed clues that could have explained the President's
unusual interest in him. Before the Christmas break
there had been several invitations to come up to the
top of Wapta Tower for a talk. He knew that he was—
had been—the object of intense curiosity within the
university community, that people from other depart-
ments, with whom he had never before exchanged a

vord, found it necessary to approach him, to speak to
iim. Understandable. But that sort of thing had passed
iway, and now seldom did anyone take a second look
it the cheek or the eye patch. He was pretty sure the
grizzly had nothing to do with the President's joining
iim or inviting him to sit at his table all those times in
he faculty dining room.

Early in April the mystery was solved. Rosemary
ohoned and said the President would like to have lunch
vith him today and would meet him at whatever time
vould be convenient for Colin. Cougar Lounge.

The President was not wearing a freshman beanie;
ie was carrying a manila envelope. When they were
eated, he put it down on the floor, propped up against
ı chair rung. Why was this man seeking him out?
Maybe informal chats like this, to no destination, were
iis way of keeping in touch with those down in the
renches, but if he were doing it with everyone in every
lepartment in every faculty, he wouldn't have time left
o carry out his real presidential duties. The answer
came with their rice pudding and coffee, when Dr.
Donaldson leaned over, brought up the fat envelope,
and laid it on the table.

"I had an ulterior motive for wanting to have lunch
and a talk with you, Colin." He tapped the envelope
oetween them. "This."

Too thick for poetry. Thin for a novel.

"I wondered if you would do something for me."

Jesus! Not all that thin. *Could be* a novel.

"I know it's an imposition." Donaldson's dark eyes
were solemn with sincerity.

Novella.

"I need your skilled and experienced opinion. I
would appreciate it very much." There was a pulpit
resonance in his voice.

Seven or eight or so short stories?

"I don't even know whether I've written a novel or
I haven't. Would you read this and tell me if I'm wasting my time?"

Was there anybody anywhere in the whole world
who did not write!

"All I want from you is an honest opinion."

And did not really want an honest opinion.

"After you've read it, a simple answer will do. Ye
or no."

Before sending it to the publisher.

"I've titled it *Many Silent Thunders*. Will you read it
Colin?"

Did Socrates have any choice? "Dr. Donaldson—'

"Cal."

"Ah, Cal. I appreciate your confidence in me
but—my experience is—pretty well upstream with ou
young students—"

"I've heard great things about you. You've pub
lished fiction."

"It's been over ten years since I've done an
writing."

"I would value your opinion. Nobody else in ou
English Department—"

"*Yes!*"

"You will?"

"There is somebody else! We have a very fine—
well, it's her first—novelist. All I ever did was shor
stories. Her *novel* is due to be released within a few
weeks, I understand. Doubleday."

"Oh."

"New York."

"Really?"

"She would give—I'm sure she would—a truly ex
pert and helpful and honest opinion."

"What's her name?"

"Dr. Elizabeth Skeffington. You see—Cal—a nove
is such a large canvas. I'm not as qualified to handle i
as she would be. A few short stories was all I ever di
manage when I was writing, and that's ten years ago
You can hold a short story in your head, but you can'
hold a novel in there."

"True. Your very modesty increases my confidence
in your judgement. I would like your opinion ever
more now."

Shit! "Sure."

Dr. Donaldson had picked up the envelope. "
guess we'd both better get back to work."

"Yes. There's a dissertation defence early this
afternoon."

"And I have a meeting with the Chairman of the

oard of Governors. Looks as though we're getting a
rm commitment finally from the Gillingham Corpora-
on on the Chuck Wagon Dome." He tucked *Many
ilent Thunders* under his arm and picked up the check.
Thanks very much for your advice. And your gener-
us promise to read it, too. After Elizabeth . . ."

"Skeffington."

"Yes. I have only this one copy."

"I understand. Speak to Dr. Tait about her. He
nows her very well."

"I will. Unless you want to read it first . . ."

"No, really. Liz first, Cal."

It would be very interesting to see what kind of
riticism he'd get from Liz. Her promotion to Associate
/as coming up before the P and T Committee at the
nd of the month, and ever since she'd made Assis-
ant, she'd worked for it. In *Scholarly Briefs* her name
ppeared almost as often as Tait's or Robitaille's; you'd
hink they were all in Sociology or the Faculty of Edu-
ation. She'd done papers and attended conferences
vith the industry of a Girl Scout harvesting proficiency
·adges. She had an honest-to-God novel coming out.
·he had Tait on her side. Or on her. So what if she
ouldn't teach worth a shit; lecture plans were un-
nown to her; she just haemorrhaged for up to three
·ours. Capricious, witty, sardonic enough that many of
he students thought she was just great. Each year,
hough, in each class, there would be one student who
lidn't think so, a girl in almost every case, the one to
·e singled out as the weak or wounded chicken, and to
·e destroyed before all the others. Somehow he had a
·eeling that, much as she had at stake, she would be
quite honest in her opinion of President Donaldson's
·ovel, *Many Silent Thunders*.

He could hardly wait.

"Colin. You seen Liz Skeffington anywhere?" Whyte
rom Native Studies.

"Try the faculty room. One o'clock. She might still
·e browsing in there." Should have smelled him com-
ng; his charred scent travelled out from him always.
Vhat the hell was he doing in the English Department?

Actually there was something a little sad about
Harold. He'd been born Torontonian, one of the Rosedale

Whytes, so his surname must seem unfair to him whe
there were so many names it could have been: Eagle
sham, Redman, Wolfe, Foxe, Fenimore . . . He'd turne
red rather late in life; after the sixties years he'd worke
in the Queen East Distress Centre, where he'd unsel
ishly and sincerely dropped acid, smoked hash, an
felt the thrilling line of cocaine, the better to under
stand the plight of the vulnerable young.

He had brought his dedication west with him t
head up the new Livingstone Native Studies Depar
ment. Soon his hair was done in braids that hung dow
in front of his ears, and he wore a black felt ha
uncreased like a wide-brimmed licorice gum drop. Th
hat was as much necessity as costume, for he wa
finding more and more hair in his brush and comt
and there weren't that many bald Indians around. H
was zealous about his red mission. There had bee
four months of low-grade fever, fatigue, stomach up
sets, and lingering diarrhoea after his teepee summe
in the mountains near Paradise Valley, where he ha
fasted, done sweat baths, and for two months drun
only pure mountain water from a running stream—whic
meant that he had picked up giardiasis. Colloquial name
beaver-piss fever.

Poor Harold. Wonder what he and Skeffington
were plotting against the whites today.

Better check the time of that defence.

LIVINGSTONE UNIVERSITY
DEPARTMENT OF ENGLISH
ANNOUNCEMENT
Charles Slaughter
will read from his novel
THE RED MESSIAH
Friday, 7 April, at 1:15 p.m.
in
Room 594 Wapta Tower North.
In Partial Fulfilment of the Requirements
for the Degree of Master of Arts at
Livingstone University.

Tait's fault!
Cigar smoke. Dr. Lyon must be in his office today

No time to drop in on him before the defence. No time
after, either, for there was the appointment with Archie and Kinistinick at Partridge, Woodcock, Martin
and Cardinal at four.

Didn't smell like Lyon's cigars, though. Much
stronger out here in the hall, and not coming from the
direction of Dr. Lyon's office. The opposite. It got
stronger and stronger as he neared the T.A. room,
where Slaughter would defend. Couldn't be *wood* smoke!
Now too he could hear a wild and distant sound, a
rhythmic bumping under a thin ululation. Smell and
sound strengthened as he neared the T.A. room. He'd
heard that wild chant before, out on the Paradise Valley Reserve. Prairie chicken mating dance. And it *was*
wood smoke!

His eyes had to adjust to the dim light from the
candles. A good dozen of them were flickering from
the book and magazine shelves and the long table with
the cross rising from the centre. It had to be five feet
high and the crucified figure was red except for the
eagle feather war bonnet on the hanging head. He
heard clinking that was coming not from the tape recorder playing the chicken dance, but from the shadows at the far end of the table. Slaughter! In breech
clout and porcupine crest, with feathers at his rump
and harness bells circling his wrist, elbows and ankles.

He had identified the wood smoke now. Alder
shavings burning with a small token flame, in the metal
dish by the open window. All this explained why Whyte
was in the English Department this afternoon.


Even his knowledge of Tait's potential for idiocy had
not prepared him for this defence travesty!

Slaughter had read from the thing. As supervisor,
Palmer had led off the questioning, and with great
restraint Colin had held back as long as he could.

"Mr. Slaughter. The shooting of the old Indian
gathering kinnikinnick along the river bank. The rancher's motivation for doing that . . . Is this explained
somewhere outside of what you've read to us?"

"Thematically it is, Dr. Dobbs."

"How's that?"

"The red man is being executed. The rancher is white."

"The sodomy scene seems gratuitous—"

Part of the paradigm. "The red man is being sodomized."

"You seem to have left out being burned at the stake and being flayed alive."

"Actually not. I've covered that, too. The incident in which the trapper skins the beaver alive. It is clearly stated several times that the beaver is the totem of this tribe. Also it is the same white trapper who pushes the little Indian girl over the cut-bank where she loses consciousness and is burnt in the forest fire the trapper started. Have you read my novel, Dr. Dobbs?"

"Your outline. I've heard the excerpts you have read."

"Also there's the smothering of the nineteen families in summer camp tents at the foot of the mountain when the whole north side gives way and buries them in their sleep as a result of the decades of excavation of lime and cement for the concrete that went into the building of North American cities."

"The red man is being smothered by white civilization," Whyte said, nodding encouragingly.

"I missed that thematic connection, too. This red messiah, who worked as a boy with his father, carving totem poles, was carried across the Crazy Horse River by a placer miner named Kristofferson—"

"There's much more linking him to Christ. He has a follower who has a vision on the road to Tarsands," Whyte explained. "His coming is announced early in the novel by the Metis, Télésphore Baptiste, who ate grasshoppers—"

"I'd like to hear from Mr. Slaughter, Professor Whyte."

"My central figure feeds the entire Indian reserve with bannocks and Rocky Mountain whitefish," Slaughter said.

"And in one of the excerpts you read to us," Colin said, "he persuades his people to derail a CPR freight train hauling tanks of nitric acid from which fifty thousand gallons are spilled, and the resulting gas is

carried on the chinook wind to destroy twelve hundred
people—"

"*White* people."

"Yes. Also he incites his followers to dynamite an
oil rig so that it blows wild and sends clouds of hydro-
gen sulphide gas through the legislative buildings so
that the Premier and his Cabinet die, as you say, 'in
great, fart-smelling clouds of poison gas.' "

" 'An eye for an eye.' "

"And persuades them to 'decapitate all the village
virgins after disembowelling them of their wombs and
the fruits thereof—' "

" 'A tooth for a tooth.' "

"I can overlook the minor contradiction of virgin
wombs bearing fruit, but not the fact that both the
principles of justice you cite belong to the Old Testament and could hardly be messages given by a post-
New Testament messiah."

"If he were white," Whyte said. "Slaughter's is a
*red* messiah."

"Red or white, a delivering and rescuing messiah—"

"He's an avenger, too," Slaughter said.

"Then isn't your theme a contradiction in terms?"

"I don't think so."

"Would you explain why you think—"

"I don't care to."

"This *is* a thesis defence."

"I disagree. This is a piece of creative art. Art
doesn't have to be defended. It just is."

"Then what are we all doing here?"

"For you to answer. I've given my opinion."

"To whom else does it belong?"

"Oscar Wilde. If you're not familiar with it, read
what he said in the court case to Sir Edward George
Clarke, when Wilde was defending *The Portrait of Dorian
Gray* against charges of immorality."

"And you're suggesting the trial of Dorian—"

"I'm just saying—"

"Well, I'm saying you are not Oscar Wilde. Oscar
Wilde was not asked to defend a creative thesis in
partial fulfilment of the requirements for the degree of
Master of Arts at this university. The difference is not
slight!"

"I am quite aware that Oscar Wilde does not hold an M.A. from this university! I am also aware of the way you—"

They were never to find out what Slaughter was also aware of, for at that point in the defence, the alder and candles triggered the smoke detectors. Alarm bells began to ring throughout the department and on all seventeen floors of Wapta Tower. Thanks to the annoying fire drills that Dr. Donaldson had doubled as soon as he had been installed as president, the evacuation of Wapta Tower went off without a hitch.

Kinistinick had good news for him; they might go to pre-trial as early as three weeks from now. "Supreme Court has raised hell about the tremendous backlog of cases, and told counsel to get cracking. Four judges are coming in and they are staying to wind up two hundred cases. That means a lot of wheeling and dealing and bargaining to avoid days of hearings and arguments. Now, about the pre-trial. You are willing to give away damages—costs—for just the return of your bear hide?"

"Yes."

"It's a lot to give them. They might go for it."

."I doubt it."

"Don't be too sure about your doubt. All they'd have to give us in return would be the name, and address of the man from Minneapolis."

"More than that. He bribed Frankie to—"

"*If* he bribed Frankie."

"No if. Frankie did. Frankie took money—"

"Frankie could deny that. The man from Minneapolis would not be likely to admit he gave anything to Frankie."

"I'm thinking of the grandfather. For him it's all or nothing. He knows what Frankie did, and there is no way he will agree to anything that will lead us to the man who bribed his grandson to switch those hides."

"We'll just have to wait and see. At the pre-trial, Archie."

"Hey-uh?"

"When—if we do go to trial and you're up and

heir lawyer is asking you questions, just answer him
straight. Especially about your record. Every time. Tell
him only what he asks you."

"Hey-up."

"No more."

"Hey-up."

"Remember. You will be under oath."

"Hey-up."

"Can you say 'yes'?"

"Hey-up."

"And 'no'?"

"Hey-up."

"It would be much easier for the judge and for the
court reporter if you did that."

"Hey-uh?"

"Said 'yes' and 'no' instead of 'hey-up' and 'hey-
uh?'"

"Speak white?"

"Hey-up," Terry said.

"I will be careful to follow all of your very helpful
advice to me, Kinnikinnick."

"Kinistinick, Archie. And the lawyer they've re-
tained is named Leonard Farkus. You aren't likely to
have to use his name, but if you do, I want you to
pronounce it very carefully."

"Yes."

Kinistinick leaned across the desk and stopped the
clock.

"Could you get your secretary to call me a taxi?"

"Sure."

"I can ride you home," Archie said.

"University."

"I go right past to Paradise."

On their way out Archie said, "That bear hide.
You think he's going to get it back for you?"

"He seems to think so."

"Lawyers and judges get paid good wages."

"Yes."

"His clock keepin' time of what it's goin' to cost
you?"

"Yes."

"Seems like a lot of money and trouble to me for
one bear hide. Judge. Lawyers. Me comin' all the way

in and out from Paradise several times, and for the court, too."

"What are you driving at?"

"You whites go to a lot of trouble about a lot of things don't seem to be worth a lot of trouble, which is difficult for me to understand. You must have it in for that bear pretty bad."

"Huh?"

"The way you want that hide."

"It's mine."

"Hey-up. The bear's. Just because it's dead don't make it stop belongin' to it, and don't give me none of that old scalp shit again."

"I wasn't about to."

"You're civilized. I guess you hate it what it done to you up Daisy Creek."

"I might."

"You aren't goin' to use it for anything. Keep you warm—throw over the hood of your car in winter, or a truck seat maybe. It got you good and you want the right hide so you can look at it and you can tell it's the one is dead and you're the one is still alive, and maybe that's the whole situation."

"Maybe it is, Archie."

"It is difficult for me to understand."

"This court action to get the bear—"

Archie shook his head. "You white savages."

Archie let him out in front of Cougar Lounge, but couldn't come in for supper with him. He had to get back to Paradise for a band council meeting. As he watched Archie's truck drive off, he felt inexplicably sad. Why should he? Kinistinick had seemed optimistic enough about the suit. Although Slaughter's defence had been annoying, its climax had been an exciting one. He'd got himself cleverly out of reading *Many Silent Thunders*. He wished he didn't have to face them for three hours in the Creative Writing seminar after supper.

Sedge was withered on the lake tonight. Annie wouldn't be sitting in to audit the way she'd done lately. Whenever she'd been there the birds had really sung. Damn near the only times. There had been so few lessons that had gone really well—with his head back, his arm kinked to fire them straight up and up, where they paused, then knifed down and sliced the water with just a blip of sound. Cut-the-dead-man's throat. There had been few of them like that since Daisy Creek and that goddam bear. Tonight would probably be a kuh-lunker.

My God, he was a man of quick action! He spotted them over by the window, but they were so deep in conversation, they didn't notice him before he turned and got out of there. He'd just have a bacon and tomato sandwich in the Wapta Tower cafeteria. Good luck, Cal! You are going to need it with La Belle Liz!

"How'd your day go, Poppa?"

"Great! Had a wonderful seminar. I wish you'd been there."

"I wish I had."

"Yours?"

"So-so."

"Kinistinick's very pleased with the way our case is shaping up. Wood-shedding today."

"Huh?"

"Coaching me and Archie. His expression for it. What you reading?"

"Joyce Cary. *The Horse's Mouth*. When did you start writing, Poppa?"

"I don't know."

"You must. Was it when you were a little boy?"

"No."

"When then?"

"I told you. I don't know. Kinistinick says we might go to pre-trial within three weeks."

"Good for you guys. I know when I first painted—"

"Before you could talk."

"You're kidding!"

"Your play-pen in Willowdale. Your mother left you out there a lot. You had to hang onto the rungs to stand up."

"I painted then?"

"I came home from the university and it was time for your nap and I went out to bring you in and you'd stepped out of your diapers. On the floor of the play-pen like a white nest. Mostly white. You'd painted the rails, the floor—every single rung. . . ."

"Really!"

"God, your mother was mad."

"You too."

"Madder. I had to clean it. Kinistinick thinks at the pre-trial they'll agree to give us the name of the man from Minneapolis."

"Poppa—I am not very interested in the man from Minneapolis. I have had it with your bear hide. Why did you quit writing?"

Which was worse? A sudden assault like this or her long, preliminary approaches?

"You must have thought about it—you didn't just up and stop, did you? Did it trickle out on you? Did you have a block?"

"A writer always has blocks."

"Painters, too. Did you hit one big one that you couldn't get past?"

"I don't know."

"You must know."

"Look. I've had a long day. I don't want to talk about—"

"Just about that goddam bear. Last night I went downstairs and I found some of your short stories. *Harbour Press—Pelican Quarterly—Western Review*. . . ."

"Church basement time."

" 'Roses Are Difficult Here.' Atlantic First. That's not church basement time. They were good stories, Poppa."

"Blood relatives always say that."

"Damn it! I mean it! I'd like to know why you quit writing!"

"Because—I decided I wasn't very good at it, I suppose."

"I'll put it another way. Why did you start?"

"Because I felt like it."

"And you quit because you felt like it."

"I didn't say that."

"Let's try again. If you quit because you felt you couldn't, how come you started when you didn't know you could?"

"There is a hell of a difference between not knowing whether or not you can and—knowing you can't."

"Maybe you quit too easily. Too soon."

"I don't think so."

"How long does it take a writer to learn to write?"

"About as long as it takes to become an orthodontist. Possibly longer. Do you intend to try it?"

"No. I got enough trouble with learning to paint."

"Look, Annie—it is not unusual—whether they like it or not—for people to discover they have limitations. There came a time when I knew—clearly—that probably God did not intend me to be a writer."

"Does it bother you?"

"Not now. Some."

"When did you start hunting bears?"

"Annie. I stopped writing—because the well ran dry."

"When? 1974?"

"Around then."

"Pretty convenient."

"What?"

"'Seventy-four you quit writing. Was that when things went sour for you and mother?"

"Good night, Annie."

"That why you quit?"

"No."

"You sure?"

"I don't want to talk about it."

"I do."

"I don't and that's the end of it." He got up.

"You don't have to leave. I'll drop it."

"Thanks."

"For now."

# CHAPTER 17

Annie could be right; he was probably over the physical worst of it, and living much better with the remaining Daisy Creek pain. Just the mornings were awful. No surprises, please; it's hard to keep the survival thread unbroken; the most trivial annoyance might snap it. Easy to understand now—well ahead of his own time—why the old were so often cranky; age wounds fuelled the anger of the elderly.

"Done your traction?"

"Not yet."

"Exercises?"

"Later."

"Heat pad and the frozen peas."

"No."

"You've got to be consistent, Poppa."

"I got to have my breakfast."

"You'll just stiffen up if you don't. Your whole spine—"

"It's *my* goddam spine!"

"Exercise lubricates the joints."

"Shut up!"

"I will if you have some yoghurt."

"No."

"It's good for you, Poppa. There are practically no calories and it's natural and healthy—"

"I can't stand the goddam—"

"You've never even tried it."

"Yes, I have."

"Not strawberry you haven't."

"Get me a cup of coffee."

"This strawberry—"

"You have successfully made up my mind about

yoghurt for the rest of my life! Get me a cup of coffee before I wrap this cane around your neck!"

On their way out to the university, she said, "How well do you actually know me, Poppa?"

"We've been introduced."

"I'm serious. Don't you ever take anything seriously?"

"Only in the mornings."

"So I've noticed. How well do you—"

"Probably more than I care to."

"That's what I figured. You really should get to know me better. Don't you want to know your daughter better?"

"Sure."

"I was a year in San Francisco. Wouldn't you like to know what I did in San Francisco?"

"You've told me."

"Not everything."

"Thanks."

"Like in the song: 'I Sold My Ass in San Francisco.' "

"Quit it!"

"You don't even know what I did in Brocklebank. 'We are from Brocklebank. Brocklebank are we—' "

"Come on, Annie."

" 'We haven't lost our—virginiteeeeee—' "

"Deliberate vulgarity is childish."

" 'We don't like scandal. We use the candle . . . We didn't, you know."

"Glad to hear that."

"They licked each other. I didn't."

"I am also glad to hear that."

"And I did not sell my ass in San—"

"As it so often is, it has been nice having this nice talk with you, Annie."

"Pick you up at four?"

"Kinistinick this afternoon. The pre-trial is this morning."

"Don't wrap your cane around his neck."

"I'll try not to."


"Didn't work out," Kinistinick said.

"Frankie and his grampa have too much at stake."

"It was still worth a try. If they'd bought no damages for the fellow in Minneapolis we'd be well on our way to getting your bear back. Our Judge Hunter wasn't much help to us in the pre-trial and I think he is going to be a handicap when we get into court."

"Why's that?"

"He does not approve of young counsellors. He does not like the way I part my hair. Only way I can explain my bad batting average with him."

"Are you trying to tell me something besides the pre-trial?"

"Yes."

"What?"

"I'm not happy with Hunter."

"And so?"

"I think it would be wise to ask for a delay."

"How long?"

"The end of this circuit. Then there'll be a whole new batch of judges. None of them could be worse for us than Hunter."

"How long till that would be?"

"Month."

"Oh, no!"

"Look—pre-trial didn't work out, but we did get a special endorsement. With a delay for a new judge we won't be setting any speed record, but we'll still be making pretty good time. I advise the delay. The decision is yours."


"Hey, this isn't bad, Judy! It grabbed me. Emotionally. The old woman coming out on the widow walk whenever the children throw pebbles and taunt her and call her a witch."

She had great promise, Judy MacDermott from Fine Arts. Since the first seminar in the fall, how beautifully she had cleared that initial life hurdle.

"Remember that find of yours back in January some time?"

"What one?"

"The snail on the sidewalk?"

"Uh-huh."

"Why should I remember that one when I read this?"

"Search me."

Don't come on too strong, Dobbs. "I'm not sure. I just have a feeling; I think there might be a meaning link." Hold back. Hold back. "What's a widow walk like?"

"A little porch high up under the eaves on the front of the house. Generally faces the sea."

"Uh-huh. You know, that was a pretty good snail you found. Faint mucus trail on the cement."

"Clear snot."

"Nice, child's connotation."

"Back then you said it was interesting."

"Did I."

"You also said it was just a descriptive still."

"Mmmm-hmm. Children can be pretty cruel, can't they."

"Yeah." Wait for it. Wait for it. "Hey! Hey!"

"What?"

"You're right. When we came across a snail on the walk—a bunch of us, you know what we did?"

"No."

"How come I didn't—it was Florence's idea. She got this stick with a sharp end on it and she started poking at it. And the other kids—a couple of them, Jeanie and Mavis—found their sticks—and they were all poking at that snail." She'd got it! Oh God, she'd got it!

"And it pulled back inside the shell and they dug inside it to get at that jelly body. Just like the kids did to the poor old lady when she came out under that steep pitch roof over the widow walk. Like a pointy shell."

"Nice. Nice. Reminds me of a fine poem Irving Layton wrote. Called 'Cain.' About a frog a fellow killed with a BB gun. Don't read it, Judy. You going to take a run at—"

"I want to! Boy, do I ever want to! The kids do the snail stuff and then they go on and do the same thing to the old witch woman!"

The children do the old woman on the widow's walk *first*, dear Judy, and *then* they do the snail. And you keep your big, fat mouth shut, Dobbs.

"Oh, sorry."

"It's all right, Herbie. Judy and I are finished."

When she'd gone, Herbie closed the door behind her and came back to sit down. "Heard the news?"

"Tell me."

"Liz got turned down for Associate."

"No!"

"Council recommended it. Dr. Donaldson reversed it. Tait tells me she's taking it pretty hard."

"I wonder why the President turned her down."

"You know how discreet Tait is."

"Yes."

"It seems that our president has written a novel."

*Many Silent Thunders.*

"Oh. You know all about it?"

"I—ah, heard he—somebody mentioned it to me."

"Tait arranged for Liz to read it for him and tell him what she thought about it."

"Yes."

"She told him."

"And her criticism was not favourable."

"According to Tait, it was short and not sweet. You know our Liz."

"Fairly well."

"She said—when she'd read the manuscript—that it could not be called writing. It was typing."

"Pretty brutal."

"How come you knew the title?"

"Even for her."

"How come?"

"I told you. Somebody mentioned it—"

"Who?"

"I can't remember."


"We go the seventeenth."

"Finally."

"That's the good news."

"Hell! What's the bad?"

"Judge McElroy is the bad news."

"What about him?"

"We got him. He's pretty rough."

"Wouldn't that work in our favour?"

"Ordinarily it would."

"Why are we an exception?"

"Archie."

"How's that?"

"McElroy has a strong aboriginal bias. It can happen after watching a long Indian parade of assault, drunken driving, disturbing the public, break-and-enter, second degree, soliciting. When Archie takes the stand and the defence is able to bring out priors, I'm afraid Judge McElroy will see red. Archie's drinking—"

"He kicked it!"

"I know he did."

"So will judge McElroy."

"Which will aggravate our problem. His Lordship hasn't kicked his. He hasn't even admitted it to himself yet. I would have to be very careful with him up there. Not just for ethnic or alcohol reasons. There's his prostate."

"Huh!"

"Outside of earshot he is generally called 'Old Pisser.' With him on the bench there are frequent interruptions; there can be no long or complicated arguments after the last recess. His attention span is severely contracted by his sphincter muscle."

"Are we talking about justice!"

"No. A court of law. I really think we should try for one more delay and another judge."

"Without a prejudice."

"Yes."

"Against you or against Archie. How do we know it won't be my turn next—to give a fresh judicial ass the heartburn!"

"I advise—you instruct. If you want time to think it over—"

"I want to *get* it over. We've got the seventeenth. Let's keep it. If we give it up we might end up with the delay and *another* unfortunate judge."

"Your decision."

"That's it."


"Just how did you get started writing, Poppa? In school?"

"In a way"

"How?"

"About grade six or seven. In Composition when we were told to write a paragraph—by description—by example. God, there must have been seven different ways you could develop a stinking paragraph. I found myself doing my homework and instead of wishing I could get the thing done and over with, I found I *liked* doing it. I was spending three times more time developing one paragraph than I needed to, in order to get a good grade. Actually it must have started a lot earlier than that. Initial potential shows itself very early."

"How?"

"Child who's a loner. I was. Also one who wants to make people laugh. I did. Some people have an extra spectator–extra listener quality from birth. Maybe conception. There's one in my Creative Writing seminar. That Judy MacDermott. She's more interested in acting, actually, but I think that's going to change. Writers and actors are very close."

"I heard you say that in one of the seminars."

"I do repeat myself. Besides listening and watching, they have to want to share. You were bad that way."

"I was?"

"Anyone who teaches elementary school has a chance to see it happening early—in a little grade one or two child. Whether they pay any attention to it or not is another matter. Most of the time—not. Who needs to be bugged by a kid all the time telling you all about what just happened on the way to school, or at recess, that was exciting or funny or awful? You were always doing it—right on through junior high. In Social Studies when you were studying the empires of the Fertile Crescent and you were whispering and Miss Appleby said, 'What is it that's so interesting you and Geraldine are talking about that you don't care to share it with all the rest of us?' And afterwards on your way home with Geraldine you said wasn't Miss Appleby the most sarcastic bitch and Geraldine said she sure was, and you both agreed the empires of the Fertile Crescent gave your ass the heartburn."

"I remember that."

"And who put the horsehair in the crotch of the Health skeleton on Mr. Ray's desk?"

"It was me."

"No!"

"Wasn't horsehair. I got it off Mother's muskrat coat."


"We won't be going today."

"No!"

"Yes."

"Why not!"

"The break-and-enter took longer than anticipated so they weren't able to finish the rape before lunch recess. They've shoved a hit-and-run in ahead of us."

"Tomorrow—"

"Is Saturday."

"Monday, then."

"No. His Lordship can sit only half a day on Monday."

"Has he got haemorrhoids too!"

"He has to catch an early flight east."

"Then when do we—"

"Thursday."

"Thursday!"

"Wednesday is the soonest he can fly back from the Canadian Bar Association convention. It's a prior commitment he made. In Toronto."

"I made one of those too," Archie said. "In Fort Kamoose."

"I hope it's an important one," Terry said.

"Little Britches Rodeo."

"Oh well, if that's all it—"

"Gatine is in the bareback and the saddle bronc and the calf-ropin'."

"But you could spare Thursday morning?"

"Hey-up." Archie shook his head. "That's when he's helpin' his little sister, Nadine. First time for her. The wild-goat-milkin' event."

"Just a minute," Colin said. "When does this circuit end?"

"Another ten days."

"There's our answer. Damn near a week delay till

those lawyers finish flocking in Toronto and Judge McElroy flies back here, so why don't we just get another delay and another judge."

"We can't. Not now."

"You advised it before."

"That's right, and we could have done it then. We can't now."

"Why not?"

"Because once a judge has assumed jurisdiction over a case, that's your judge. We are stuck with Old Pisser."

"How can you teach and not do it yourself?"

"I can—I have."

"As the priest said to the group in marriage counselling."

"Just take my word for it. It is quite possible for someone who does not write to help people—"

"Or the eunuch to all the ladies in the harem."

"Damn it, Annie, I am not interested in playing the old target game with you."

"I am not playing any target game! I am—"

"I'm going to bed."

"You're still good at that—sleeping."

"No. I'm not. I find sleeping one of the most difficult things I've ever done—now!"

"And going to court over a goddam bear hide! That bear's pretty convenient for you, isn't it? Load everything on that bear. What a beautiful, romantic cop-out she gave you. Well, forget it! Before her you were in trouble! Bad trouble! Why the hell were you chasing after bears in the first place! I'll tell you why! It's because you'd quit writing. Sucking her out to that old grey horse you guys shot is one hell of a lot easier way than writing to make yourself important!"

"One of our president's degrees is counterfeit," Herbie said. "Everybody's talking about it."

"What do you mean—counterfeit?"

"Bogus. Phoney."

"How did they—who—?"

"Liz. She got Rosemary to show her Donaldson's curriculum vitae after she wondered about the St. Andrews fine arts doctorate. Unlike our Appointments Committee, Liz checked things out with St. Andrews University."

"And Donaldson had failed to . . . ?"

"St. Andrews has no record—undergraduate, graduate, postgraduate—of a Calvin Edward Donaldson."

"Really!"

"Nor does St. Andrews have a fine arts faculty that grants a fine arts degree. So when this came to light, the Chancellor and the Chairman called a meeting of the Board of Governors last week."

"Donaldson's resigned."

"No."

"They've asked for his resignation."

"No. They asked him for an explanation."

"He couldn't have any."

"He gave it a pretty good try, though. Said he'd had a lifelong interest in the arts. Been a devoted patron—served on the boards of the Toronto Symphony, National Ballet, Stratford Festival, Royal Ontario Museum, CRTC, Canada Council."

"Has he?"

"Must have. Wouldn't dare to name them if he hadn't. Now that he knows Liz. In his explanation he also named the North American corporations he's advised on their art collections: banks, trusts, breweries, distillers, oil and tobacco companies. He listed papers published in internationally respected and refereed art journals—"

"Still—"

"He pointed out that he had not claimed to be an alumnus of St. Andrews University in Scotland, and he was extremely sorry if they had mistaken the Scottish St. Andrews for his St. Andrews."

"Where's his? Cayman Brac?"

"Better than that. The classified section in the back of *Popular Mechanics*. Magna cum laude."

"Hah!"

"Well you might say, Colin. He expressed deep regret that this bit of parchment window-dressing might be an embarrassment to Livingstone University, but that in actuality he had left his post as financial vice-president of the nation's most distinguished university to come west to Livingstone, eminently qualified not only to make temporal decisions but also to help achieve the new fine arts dimension the Board of Governors wished for Livingstone University."

"God, he's good!"

"He reminded them of a couple of touchdowns he's made very early in his first quarter: persuading the Minister of Recreation, Physical Education and Culture and the Gillingham Corporation to fund the cost of the Chuck Wagon Dome; and he mentioned the firm commitment of private money to the projected Olympic-sized Muhlerberg Beer swimming pool."

"Jesus, he must have been thick with Kissinger back there at Harvard! Is he going to make it?"

"The Master of Kathleen MacNair backed him up."

"The Master hates his guts!"

"I believe you're right, Colin, but the Master seems to be able to swallow his distaste. Don't forget Donaldson suggested Kathleen might be house-mother of the rare books and papers collection he has planned. Understandable. It promises to hold more Canadian papers and attract more Can Lit researchers than the University of Texas."

"Are you telling me that he'll be staying on?"

"Fifty-fifty. Right about now Matthew Arnold must be turning in his grave."

"It's a pretty dirty business we're in, Herbie."


He had not shot her! Not only had he missed when she had risen with the horse in her arms, and missed each time he'd fired at her in flight across the valley, he had not killed her when she'd charged him!

"My God, Archie! Why did you wait till now!"

"Hey-uh?"

"To tell me!"

"I didn't wait—"

"Yes, you—"

"I already told it to you. In the hospital."

"No, you didn't!"

"Hey-up. Remember I said your scope was way off? I said it was sighted high."

"I know you said that."

"I tried it after I brought you in. It was off a good two foot and to the left also."

"You told me that, but you did not tell me I missed her again when she charged me."

"You are correct. I didn't tell you that, because you didn't miss it."

"But you just said—"

"I said you didn't kill it, Dobbs. I said I did that."

"Oh."

"It took four. The first one just interrupted what it was doin' to you and it come at me and I dropped it, but it got up and it come at me again and I dropped it again. It still got up and when I dropped it the last time it was down onto the top of you. I didn't tell you all of that in the hospital."

"No, Archie, you didn't."

"I didn't think you would be very interested at that time."

"It took *four* shots for you to kill her?"

"Hey-up. They were all placed good, too." He tapped a finger four times beside his right ear. "All of them was together." He held up his hand with thumb and fingers making a half-circle. "All of them would fit inside of your boot heel. When I skinned it out I found yours too. The left shoulder of it was just a bunch of gravel."

"I did not kill her."

"Your shot also blew the heart out of it."

"But you killed her."

"I had to do that."

"*You* killed her."

"Hey-up. I'm afraid I did."

He had not *killed* her! *Archie* had! Her charge on him had been no greater shock than this discovery! He had *not* killed her. Archie *had*! Each time he told himself this new and incredible truth, he felt another tremor of surprise. And another and another. He had not done it. Archie . . . Impossible! How could she live on after he had blown her heart out!

But Archie said she had! And there had been enough

life left in her to maul him. Heartless, she had almost killed *him*, and *Archie had killed her*! Once he had accepted that, he felt a strange relief. Why should he? Had he been in some guilt cage without knowing it? It was as though he had just received an unexpected parole. From Archie. What an ironic one it was, and what cruel penance he had paid since Daisy Creek, and must keep on paying for the rest of his life. Not a full pardon but lovely. From *her*!

And if he had not killed her, then what justifiable point was there in pursuing the action against Wild Trophy World? What honest reason did he have for going on to trial? Good question, Dobbs. Now ask yourself another. Do you want to go on? Yes! God damn it! Yes! One more question. *Should* you?

He did know one thing: he had never hated anyone else in his whole life as much as he now hated that Minneapolis son-of-a-bitch, who had bought false importance from falcon Frankie! What a glorious, Nimrodian fiction he must have built for himself by now. How carefully he must have rehearsed hunting bullshit, to shovel it out again and again and again! Somewhere in Minneapolis there sat a man in his male study, wicked with delight in possessing that magnificent grizzly spread before him. She yawned her fanged jaws for him and for him she combed the floor, with ivory claws that had torn off half the face of Colin Dobbs!

How many times had the phoney prick leaned back in his cowhide chair, probably with a neat bourbon in his hand, cigar smoke blue around his head, telling his cronies how she had charged him and charged him again, while he stood fearless, unflinching and alone, up to his fat ass in snow, risking his very life in the remaining wilderness of Canada! Did he tell them how he had shattered her shoulder and blown out her heart with one magnum shell from his Weatherby? No, sirree! He'd been way under-powered with just his .303. Had to get her with four brain shots, all grouped in just the space of a boot heel. She had finally fallen on him, bathing him in her own blood, smothering him in deep snow while his whole life past unreeled before him. Somehow, by calling upon superhuman strength hidden deep within himself, he had got himself out from under one ton of grizzly bear. He had gutted and skinned her. He had salted her. He had taken her into Wild Trophy World at the same time as a Stony Indian came in with a pitifully small, brown bear hide. And even though they'd heard him tell the story a hundred times, his listeners would shake their heads and say, "Bully for you, Ernie boy!"

Neither of them had killed her. Archie had. But she had almost killed *him*. She had not done that to the man from Minneapolis. She had not done that to Archie. Just to Colin Dobbs. He had the real right to her hide. This false hip, pinned elbow, broken spine, clawed eye, and raddled cheek entitled him! Colin Dobbs!

Dropping the action now would accomplish nothing; indeed it would let that infectious carrier in Minneapolis go unpunished. And Frankie. Annie was right; Mr. Munro was an honourable man, or had been. The corruption must stop somewhere.

He would not drop the action.


Deep in the bush behind him, a spruce grouse began to drum. He heard ravens calling, and looked out and over to the hide. They were circling and landing and taking off from the dead horse again. How had he ever missed her with the first shot, when she had risen with that grey carcass in her arms, and again three more times, when she took off over the valley!

The spruce grouse began to drum again. She had simply lost her footing in slippery snow at precisely the same moment he had let that fourth shot go.

He heard crashing behind himself, turned and saw her coming at him through the lodge-pole pine! He lifted the rifle, aimed, pulled. The goddam safety! He slid it off with his thumb, raised the rifle, got her in the scope, fired. She veered, but her glancing flank hit him with the shatter power of a wrecker ball.

He managed to get to his knees. He lifted the rifle to his shoulder as she lifted to her hind legs, then lowered to charge him again.

# CHAPTER 18

Annie had refused to come in. Archie and Kinistinick were waiting for him just inside the court-house. As they walked up the marble stairs, he realized that he had never before come to a court of law, even as a spectator. Even for the divorce proceedings. Kinistinick left him with Archie on one of the benches that circled the second floor, where their case room was. There were people on every bench, heads down, a leg over a knee, intent on papers and folders. They were here, most of them, for a purpose that seemed unusual, important, dangerous. Some appeared to be denying that, and pretending they were not here for any such purpose. They looked vulnerable, as though they had just been sent to the Principal's office. There were some uncaring people waiting, too, in black gowns, engaged in conversation, leaning against the walls or the high brass rail round the great stair well. There was a man with beautiful white hair and pink cheeks, in morning coat and pin-striped trousers, looking just like a floor-walker in a British department store. Somewhere in this court-house there simply had to be a costume and regalia room.

"What you thinking about, Archie?"

"Crows."

"All those black gowns. . . ?"

"From when I was a kid I been fussy about crows."

"Your totem."

"Hey-up." He shook his head. "I ain't pure Stony because I got some Blackfoot in me from my great-grampa. Chief Crowfoot. I am also thinkin' about Miss Wilkerson. I didn't get a good education like you got, Dobbs."

"You do pretty well."

"She was skinny. All she ever ate was seed-cake and tea. English. When I was in grade six, the two years of it, one spring I caught a crow just been hatched out and I fed it and it made it and it kep' close to me all the time. You know what a crow's tongue is made like?"

"No."

"They're stuck underneath. I cut it so it could talk, but it disappointed me."

"Wouldn't talk."

"It come out white. Just two words, but he said them real clear."

"What were they?"

"Easy ones for a crow to say. Close to natural, crow talk like they do when they take off into the bush."

"*Caw, caw.*"

"Miss Wilkerson didn't like what he said—him out there on the teeter-totter or the swings, waitin' for me in the school yard. Sayin' it over and over again, with the little kids listenin' to him and not to her readin' them about Peter Rabbit. She said it was a two-word obseem directif I taught him to say."

"Oh."

"Somethin' you people tell us reds to do all the time. That was her last year of teachin' us on Paradise. She did what the crow said for her to do. All right if I smoke here?"

"Others are."

"Way I feel, Dobbs, I wish I had that crow with me right now."

"I wish you did too, Archie."

"All right." It was Kinistinick in his black gown.

"We go in now?"

"You stay here, Dr. Dobbs. Archie comes with me first. They have a separate room for him. When I come back you and I will go in together. Archie."

"Hey-up."

"I want you to remember everything I've told you."

"Hey-uh?"

"Their counsel's name is Farkus."

"Hey-up."

"He's going to bring up your record, but not until

I've brought it up in the least damaging way we can
What's his name?"

"Whose?"

"Their counsel's."

"Fark-ass."

"See what I mean, damn it, Archie?"

"Fark-uss."

"Better. Now when I do bring up your previou
charges—the indecent exposures—the word sometime
used by whites for 'piss' is 'urinate.' "

"Hey-up."

"Judge McElroy, who does a great deal of it, mus
be respectfully addressed—not as 'Your War Ship' bu
as 'Your Lordship.' "

"Hey-up."

"Not as 'Your Lard Ship.' Or worse."

"I shall speak very clear and careful of everything
say when I am on the Bible."

"Good."

"Even though it will be difficult for me, not bein
very by-ling-you-all, Mr. Kin-is-tin-ick."

"You are very important to the outcome of Dobbs'
case. Put out your cigarette."

When Colin came back, Kinistinick said, "How
you feeling?"

"All right."

"All set?"

"I've had almost a year to get set."

"As plaintiff we go first. You can't overdo tha
cane. Save the face damage for the last. Keep those
coloured glasses on till you come to the end of the
injuries the bear did to you. The witness chair is to the
right of the judge, so the right side of your face will be
away from him. I want you to turn it towards him jus
before you take off the glasses."

"Do we have to do this kind of phoney—!"

"Yes."

There were already spectators in the case room,
possibly a dozen or more.

"No," Kinistinick whispered. "This end of the sec
ond row behind the rail. Front one's reserved for press
and people they don't think will jump over the rail."

He left Colin and went through to a chair with a

ectern beside it. There was another to the right of the
raised bench, also with a lectern. The young man intent on papers there must be Leonard Farkus. Colin
looked down his row and saw Frankie Munro at the far
end.

"Order in the court!" It was a young girl in a short
black gown. Everyone stood, Colin last to his feet, for
the bench was low and the cane had fallen to the floor.
No need for Kinistinick to have told him to ham it up.

Judge McElroy in his grey Supreme Court robes
came through a door over to the right and behind the
bench. He sat. He leaned over and said something to
the young woman below the bench, who handed papers up to him. He examined them for a moment, then
lifted his head and beckoned with a long finger first to
his right and then to his left. Farkus and Kinistinick got
up and came before him. While he spoke to them they
stood, looking up to him and nodding like two obedi-
ent young ravens. No. Magpies, for when they turned
from him, white flashed at the neck and breast.

Kinistinick came to Colin and made a great show
of helping him take up his position to be sworn in.

"Your name?"

"Colin Dobbs."

"Your occupation?"

"Professor of English. Livingstone University."

"You live where?"

"2943 Killdeer Boulevard. South West."

"Would you please tell the court, Dr. Dobbs, what
happened to you on the morning of April third last
year?"

"I was hunting grizzly in the first range of mountains in the Daisy Creek area, about forty miles west of
the town of Shelby. I shot a grizzly bear. She mauled
me."

"Would you describe to the court the nature and
extent of your injuries?"

"She almost disembowelled me. She destroyed my
right hip joint. She cracked two cervical vertebrae—
smashed my elbow." He could feel his hand starting to
jump on his knee; he tried to still it with his left hand.
The sweat had started. This was when Terry wanted
him to turn to Judge McElroy and take off the coloured

glasses to reveal the eye and all the cheek. He averted his face from the bench. "I had some plastic surgery done to my face. I spent three months in the neurological ward of Western General Hospital."

"And where is Western General Hospital?"

"The corner of Holy Cross and Rodeo."

"The name of the doctor attending you?"

"There were several but the main one was a Doctor Arrowsmith."

"You say you shot the grizzly bear before it did all this to you?"

"Yes."

"It mauled you *after* you had shot it?"

"Yes."

"What was the nature of the shot—wound—you inflicted upon the grizzly bear?"

"A Weatherby magnum shell. It destroyed her shoulder. It blew the heart out of her."

"You could tell that as soon as you shot it?"

"No. I lost consciousness when she attacked me."

"For how long were you unconscious after it attacked you?"

"Two days, after surgery—after my guide, Mr. Archie Nicotine, pulled her off me and took me out and into Emergency in Western General Hospital. When he skinned her out, Mr. Nicotine discovered that her shoulder was destroyed and that her heart had been blown out by my shot."

"If the heart had been blown out, would that not be a mortal wound?

"Yes."

"Yet after that, you have testified, the grizzly bear charged you. You have told the court the grizzly bear almost disembowelled you. It destroyed your right hip. It broke your neck, your right elbow, the right side of your face. With the heart blown out, it still charged and mauled you?"

"Evidently a grizzly bear may live on—effectively—from three to five minutes after such a wound."

"On what authority do you know that?"

"Dr. Claude Heron of Livingstone University Environmental Design Department, one of the world's leading authorities on bears, told me this. He also told me

hat the grizzly I shot was what they called a plains or
rass grizzly that once followed the prairie buffalo—"

"Objection. Hearsay."

"Sustained."

It was still escaping him, whatever it was about
udge McElroy that had been tantalizing him ever since
e'd taken the stand. The man's face itself? That full
pper lip? The way the grey hair, unparted, fell across
is forehead, the shaggy edge of it well above the
arge, dark eyes?

Kinistinick continued his questioning, now bring-
ng out the monetary costs of the five springs Colin had
one grizzly-hunting with Archie as guide, his loss of
ncome resulting from the injuries sustained in acquir-
ng the grizzly hide, hospital and medical expenses.
'otal: $12,562.00.

"And what price, Dr. Dobbs, would you put on
he anguish and the mental and physical damage you
ave suffered in order to obtain the grizzly hide Mr.
Nicotine delivered to Wild Trophy World for prepara-
ion and mounting?"

"I could not possibly come up with a price on
hat."

Under Kinistinick's questioning he described the
grizzly with its blond face and unusual body colour,
he black feet and the ivory claws and the unusual size.
Once more Kinistinick mentioned Dr. Heron as an au-
hority on this unusual subspecies and once more Farkus
objected.

"Sustained," Judge McElroy said. "Dr. Dobbs, your
bear authority is not in this court. He was not . . . " He
looked down, then up again. " . . . up Daisy Creek the
morning of April third of last year." He stood up.
"Five-minute adjournment."

When the court had reconvened, Kinistinick began
the final part of the questioning, interrupted by Judge
McElroy's bladder.

"The plaintiff saw and shot a grizzly bear. A *grizzly*.
It was not a small brown bear. He has testified that Mr.
Archie Nicotine skinned out a grizzly bear and salted it
and sloughed it and brought it into Wild Trophy World,
which seven months later delivered to him a small
brown bear hide instead of his unique plains grizzly

with a yellow face, black feet, ivory claws—the bea[r]
which the plaintiff shot and which nearly disembow[-]
elled and destroyed him, *Ursus horribilis*."

Kinistinick gathered his papers from the lecter[n]
top and went to his chair.

"Have you questions for this witness, Mr. Farkus?["]

"No, milord."

"Your next witness, Mr. Kinistinick."

Kinistinick stood. "Mr. Archie Nicotine."

As Colin left the stand, he was still trying to decid[e]
what it was about Judge McElroy that still haunte[d]
him. It was an unusually large face, broad at the eyes[,]
both the nose and the jaw extremely long. The ma[n]
was compelled by some sort of tic that caused him t[o]
flare his nostrils from time to time. About every thirty
seconds, Colin guessed.

A door at the back corner of the court room ha[d]
opened and Archie came through it, followed by a ma[n]
who had evidently gone to get him. The young woman[,]
who must have been the court clerk, held up a Bible t[o]
Archie and swore him in. When Archie sat, he wa[s]
slightly lower than Judge McElroy in his grey Suprem[e]
Court robes with the crimson band that flowed ove[r]
one shoulder, down and across his front.

Terry Kinistinick had left his chair and stood before Archie.

"Your name?"

"Archie Nicotine."

"Where do you reside?"

"Paradise Valley Reserve. Third cabin south of the[]
suspension bridge across Storm Creek."

"And where is Paradise Valley Reserve?"

"West of Shelby maybe forty miles."

"Your occupation, Mr. Nicotine?"

"I am a duly elected councillor of the Paradis[e]
Valley Bear's Paw Stony band."

"And as well as that?"

"I do several things."

"What things?"

"I am a civil servant of Her Majesty's Fed'ral
Gover'ment Department of Indian Affairs."

"In what capacity would that be."

"Beef."

"Would you please tell the court in a little more detail your duties for the Department of Indian Affairs?"

"Hayin'. Stackin' green feed. Fencin'. Seedin'. Cuttin' and brandin' and trailin' them up to the forest reserve in spring and back down out of there in fall. I am officially in charge of Agerculture and Cattle on the Paradise Reserve where the Bear's Paw band of the Stony Indians reside."

"Thank you."

"I also help several white ranchers when they need it."

"Mm-hmm." Kinistinick picked up papers from the lectern.

"Mr. Nicotine, the record I have here indicates that this is not your first appearance in a court of law."

"You are correct."

"It lists a number of charges and convictions."

"Hey-up."

"Here in the city and in the town of Shelby. Going back to . . ." He looked down to the lectern top. ". . . 1965."

Judge McElroy leaned forward. "May I see the record?"

As Kinistinick questioned Archie on the charges, from the Christmas-tree-rustling through the assault with a deadly chuckwagon stove in the Number Four horse barn at the Frontier Days Rodeo, Judge McElroy's eyes never left the sheets before him. The intensity of his interest faded noticeably when they reached the first indecent exposure and Archie began to describe how, after seventeen beers, he had relieved himself between the Sanitary Cafe and the Gateway Hotel beer parlour. Judge McElroy stood and called for an adjournment. This time his exit was almost at a lope. He took Archie's record with him.

When the proceedings resumed, he sat back in his chair and several times closed his eyes as Terry's examination revealed that the offences had been alcohol-induced and that the record contained no charges against Archie in the nine years since he had stopped drinking.

"Mr. Nicotine, besides being a band councillor and an agricultural adviser to the Indian Affairs department of the federal government on the Paradise Valley Reserve, are there any other activities in which you are engaged?"

"I do packin' and guidin' for big game in zone 4281, too. I got a licence for doin' that."

"And did you so guide Dr. Dobbs early in April of last year?"

"Hey-up."

"Would you please tell the court what transpired at that time?"

"Dobbs's grizzly bear come out to the horse."

"What horse?"

"The old one I took up Daisy Creek after I found the grizzly tracks and shot it up there for bait and the grizzly smelled it and it come out to it and we was in the hide I built there and we watched it."

"When you watched it at the horse's carcase, how far from this grizzly bear were you and Dr. Dobbs at the time?"

"Close."

"How close?"

Archie lifted his arm and pointed, "If the back of this court was the hide, then . . ." He cocked the thumb of his left hand at Judge McElroy. ". . . Your Honourable would be that dead horse's cark-ass."

Judge McElroy opened his eyes, jerked up his head, nostrils flaring.

"Mr. Nicotine," Kinistinick began.

"It was an old grey geldin'. . . ." Archie had lowered the arm pointing out the back of the court room, but his cheetah face and his cocked left thumb were still trained on Judge McElroy. "He was real long in the tooth so he would of gone for dog food anyway. . . ."

"Uh—yes, Mr. Nicotine," Kinistinick said, "the grizzly bear that—"

"Even when my daughter, Magdalene, was little and she rode him he was old then and he was hardmouthed too but she could handle him. . . ."

"Counsel! The court would appreciate it if you could keep your witness to the matter in hand!"

"Yes, milord."

"He was a fence-crawler too."

"If that is possible!"

"Yes, milord."

"Unless I am wrong in my understanding that this ...se concerns a bear, *not* a horse!"

"Yes, milord."

"Then will you have your witness stick to the *bear* ...atter! That is spelled b-a-r-e!"

There was an appreciative titter from the sprin-...ing of spectators and court members. This must be ...ne vintage judicial humour, Colin thought, without a ...ncture of feeling or compassion to sweeten the tribu-...tion of litigants. God damn Archie Nicotine! Whose ...de was he on anyway! Next urine adjournment he ...ust get Terry to caution Archie again.

"So," Kinistinick was saying, "as you have just ...stified, both you and Dr. Dobbs watched the grizzly ...ear at close range. For how long, in your estimation, ...ould that time be, Mr. Nicotine?"

"From when the bear got to the grey horse's cark-...ss to when Dobbs shot an' missed it and it dropped ...e grey horse's cark-ass and it took off across Daisy ...reek flats."

"How many minutes?"

"I didn't look at my watch."

"But—"

"I don't wear it all the time."

Damn it, Archie! Terry's on *our* side!

Kinistinick seemed about to pursue the matter ...me further, then changed his mind. "When the griz-...ly bear was at the horse carc—was being examined by ...ou and Dr. Dobbs, at a very close range, was this the ...nly time you saw it?"

"Hey-up."

"Would you tell the court when you had further ...pportunity to examine the grizzly bear?"

"Before or after?"

"Before or after what?"

"Dobbs shot it. I seen it several times close before ...hat and I seen it later."

"When?"

"When we tracked it across Daisy Creek after Dobbs ...issed and then into the bush and Dobbs went back ...ut of the bush and it come back out too and it charged ...im on the flats. I was right behind it then. Closer than ...e time at the grey horse's car—"

"You witnessed the grizzly bear charge Dr. Dobbs?

"And I witnessed Dobbs shootin' it. And I wi
nessed it guttin' him and the other things it did to him
and that is the whole situation."

"Thank you. May I have Exhibit Two, which ha
already been entered into the record?"

That would be the brown bear hide that had bee
so humiliating at Christmas time. They also brough
out, unfolded, and set up an easel, then draped th
skin over it. Judge McElroy leaned forward on his gre
elbows to look at the bear hide. He seemed to hav
recovered from his annoyance earlier in the Archi
exchange; indeed, judging from the quirking at th
corners of the long mouth under the heavy Roma
nose, he must be amused by it.

"Counsel for the plaintiff, looking at this bear skin
it does cross my mind—or rather, may I express th
hope that skins of the other two are not to be brough
into this court as exhibits."

"Milord?"

"Surely you do not intend at a later time in th
proceedings to call Ms. Goldilocks as a declarant in thi
case." Judging from the laughter, McElroy had really
scored with his audience. And with himself, for he wa
grinning and Colin was almost sure he had heard
gentle whickering from the bench.

Kinistinick turned the easel about to face Archie
He stepped back from it. "You have told the court, Mr
Nicotine, that you are a professional guide to big-game
hunters."

"Hey-up."

"What sort of big game?"

"Moose. Elk. Deer. Sheep. Goat. Bear. Cougar sev
eral times when I had the hounds."

"For how long have you been a professional, li
censed guide to big-game hunters?"

"Long time. Maybe thirty years now."

"And you have hunted for yourself, of course—
before becoming a professional packer and guide?"

"Us red originals generally do a lot of huntin'."

"Bears?"

"We hunt them. We also eat them too."

"Can you recall when you went on your first bear
unt, Mr. Nicotine?"

"I was seven. It was a grizzly my father wounded
nd he run out of shells and he sent me up a tree to be
afe and I watched him."

"Watched him what?"

"Kill it."

"If he had run out of shells, how could he do
nat?"

"With a fence rail. He learnt me to track and hunt.
Ie was better than I am but he was the only one."

"Only one what?"

"Better than me at it."

"Mr. Nicotine, will you please tell the court, in
our judgement as a licensed and professional guide to
ig-game hunters in pursuit of bear trophies, as a hunter
ourself of bears since the age of seven with your
ather as you have just testified, would you say this
kin once belonged to the grizzly bear you have testi-
ed that you and Dr. Dobbs saw on the morning of
.pril the third up Daisy Creek in the first range of the
locky Mountains?"

"Hey-uh."

"The grizzly bear that both of you saw again at
ven closer range when the grizzly bear charged and
nauled Dr. Dobbs?"

Archie shook his head.

"Mr. Nicotine?"

"Hey-uh."

"Mr. Nicotine!"

"No. It's the wrong one."

"Is it in fact a *grizzly* bear?"

"No. It is about a two-year-old brown bear. I seen
t before. This one.

"Where?"

"Wild Trophy World. When I took Dobbs's in for
im when he was in the hospital. That same time there
vas a fellow from Minneapolis and he had his in there
oo and it was that one."

"Mr. Nicotine, although I do not mean to question
our qualification and many years' experience as a guide
nd hunter of bears, would it not be difficult to identify

a given bear skin with accuracy—set it apart from all
others similar in colour and in size?"

"You are correct."

"How then, as you have just testified, could you
say that you have seen this one before, on the day you
took Dr. Dobbs's grizzly bear skin to Wild Trophy
World?"

"Easy."

"How?"

"Turn it over and look at the inside skin side of it.
You're goin' to find it sewed in four places. The belly.
The neck. The left shoulder of the bear. The ass of it."

"Who sewed these four places you have so accurately described?"

"Wild Trophy World."

"Then am I to understand that such sewed places
are a common indication of the taxidermist craft in the
preparation of bear-skin trophies?"

"No."

"Then what would explain such sewed places?"

"Bullet holes. Also there is a patch they had to put
in the right flank of it where the fellow from Minneapolis fuh—screwed it up skinnin' it out after he shot it in
the neck and the belly and the ass—"

"Objection!" Farkus had jumped to his feet.

"The fellow from Minneapolis said to me he shot it
four times in the neck and the belly and—"

"Milord, it is my understanding that the gentleman from Minneapolis Mr. Nicotine refers to is not a
party to these proceedings. It is not for this witness to
tell the court what some gentleman from Minneapolis
may have said to him. That is hearsay. The gentleman
from Minneapolis is not a declarant in this case. This
being so, the witness's evidence of what might have
been said to him is irrelevant!"

"Objection sustained. Mr. Nicotine, I caution you
to restrict your comments to that which is directly relevant to the case. The opinions of others who are not
party to these proceedings are *not* relevant."

"Milord," Kinistinick said, "the purpose of this
line of questioning is nothing other than to get to the
truth in this case—to get this other hunter to court. The
plaintiff has been trying without success in the further

pursuit of truth in this case to get the man to court. We have been blocked in our request for the Wild Trophy World ledger, which will contain the name and address of the man from Minneapolis and the two tattooed notations which are on this brown bear hide. We submit that the ledger will contain for the same date the plaintiff's grizzly hide and *its* two identifying tattoo marks. It is the plaintiff's submission that if the ledger evidence were tendered, the matter in issue could be quickly resolved."

"Court adjourned." McElroy stood up. "Five minutes."

Shit! Or more accurately—piss! This was the third time McElroy had interrupted the proceedings to get to the washroom. It could not be simply because of his sphincter muscle and chance that each adjournment had been damaging to Terry's presentation of their case.

The adjournment over, Terry Kinistinick did his best to repair the damage, refreshing the court's memory of what he had accomplished by questioning Archie as a witness with vivid recall of the grizzly bear and as an ursine authority without peer.

"Mr. Nicotine," he summed up, "this is a young brown bear hide. It did not once belong to the yellow-faced, cocoa-coloured, black-stockinged, and ivory-clawed plains grizzly which, as you have testified, you and Dr. Dobbs saw on the morning of April the third of last year up Daisy Creek in the first range of the eastern slope of the Rocky Mountains west of the village of Shelby. Which both of you also saw at even closer range again when that grizzly bear charged and mauled and almost disembowelled Dr. Dobbs, destroyed his right hip ball joint, cracked two of his cervical vertebrae, smashed his elbow, clawed his head and the right side of his face. Is that correct?"

"Yes."

"And Exhibit Two is, according to your earlier testimony, the skin of a two-year-old brown bear, which you saw in its salted, raw state when it was brought in to Wild Trophy World on the afternoon of May third by a man from—"

"Objection!"

"Sustained."

"By a hunter. It is really beyond belief that this skin of a dear, departed brown bear *cub* could have ambled into Wild Trophy World all by itself."

"You are correct," Archie said.

"I'm finished," Kinistinick said. It was an unfortunate choice of words.

Judge McElroy leaned forward.

"Counsel for the defendant. Do you want this witness?"

Farkus stood. "Yes, milord." He stepped over towards Archie.

"Mr. Nicotine, let's go back a way—for the purpose of clarification. In your testimony I believe you said that you are not a drinking man. Is that correct?"

"Hey-up."

"But you were once—a drinking man. You said you had a severe drinking problem?"

"Hey-up."

"Mr. Nicotine. It would be much easier for the court if you could answer my questions with a 'yes' or a 'no.' I am sure His Lordship would appreciate it if you did that."

"I most certainly would," Judge McElroy said.

"Now—you are, you have just said, not a drinking man."

"No."

"But you were, you said, once."

"Yes."

"And this is your explanation for the—ah—impressive record of charges and convictions I have here."

"Yes."

"Destruction of property, disturbing—"

"Objection!"

"You have already brought them up. They are relevant, Mr. Kinistinick," McElroy said. "Continue."

"Destruction of property—public, private—disturbing the peace, indecent exposure, assault with a deadly weapon. All of these because you were under the influence of alcohol?"

"Yes."

"Which you no longer—indulge in."

"Hey-up."

"Mr. Nicotine—I must remind you that this court has not been able to obtain the services of a Stony Indian translator."

Judge McElroy smiled.

"Fuh—caw."

Judge McElroy stopped smiling. "Mr. Nicotine!"

"Clearin' my throat," Archie said, "Your Highness."

"Mr. Nicotine, when did you stop your drinking?"

"Pretty long time now."

"How long?"

"Eight-ten years."

"Which one?"

"Nine."

"And you have never had a drink since—whenever it was that you stopped?"

"Yes."

"You have—or you haven't?"

"I ain't."

"Why did you stop drinking?"

"Caused me all that trouble back then. It's worse for us people."

Judge McElroy nodded his head in gentle agreement.

"So. You saw the light and took the pledge."

"Hey—no."

"You didn't?"

"I just quit."

"Whiskey? Gin? Rum? Vodka?"

"Beer mostly."

"So. Now you do not go into beer parlours."

"That is not correct."

"Oh! You do go into them?"

"Quite a few times."

"And would you tell us: when was the last time you went into a beer parlour?"

"Last Saturday night."

"Oh. Oh! That recently. Now—let me get this straight." He had picked up the record sheets from the lectern top and held them by one corner. "It is your testimony—given—that this record"—he held it up—"I hold here, all of it is the result of your drinking. This long record"—he waved it in the direction of the bench—"—destruction of property, disturbing the peace, indecent exposure, assault with a deadly weapon, to name a few—was solely the result of your drinking! You further testify that you do not drink any more. That you have not had a drink in nine years. You expect this court to believe that? After you have just testified that you *do* go into beer parlours frequently in this city and in the village of Shelby. That indeed only last Saturday night you did go into the Gateway Ho— aagh!" He slammed the record down on the lectern, held his hands up, then dropped them as though to say, What's the use! "No further questions for *this* witness, milord." He walked over to his chair and sat down.

Judge McElroy looked over to Kinistinick. "Counsel for the defence, is there anything else you want of this witness?"

Terry stood. "Yes, milord, a question or two, just for clarification."

"Go ahead."

"Mr. Nicotine, you have just testified, in response to my learned friend's question, that you are a non-drinker."

"Yes."

"That you have been a non-drinker for nine years—since 1975?"

"Yes."

"And you have not been in trouble with the law since then?"

"Yes."

"You also said to Mr. Farkus that you have been frequently in various beer parlours since you stopped drinking, that you were in the Gateway Hotel beer parlour in Shelby as recently as last Saturday night."

"Yes."

"Would you tell the court how many beers you drank while you were in there?"

"None."

"What did you drink?"

"Diet Pepsi."

"You went into the Gateway Hotel beer parlour and drank Diet Pepsi. Surely, Mr. Nicotine, Diet Pepsi is more easily available to you in other places."

"Cheaper, too."

"Does this mean that you did not go into the Gateway Hotel beer parlour for the purpose of buying a bottle of Diet Pepsi?"

"Yes."

"Then—what was your reason?"

"Like most the other times. To help get Carol Rollin'-in-the-Mud out of there before she duked any more people and kicked the livin' sh— kicked the bar and the hotel to pieces."

"And how long has it been—?"

"She's still got her drinkin' problem."

"How long is it—as you have testified in response to Mr. Farkus's question—since you had your last drink?"

"Nineteen seventy-five."

"No further questions, milord."


"And you were at Wild Trophy World on the afternoon of May third when a bear skin was brought in?"

"Yes."

"By whom?"

"An Indian."

"Named?"

"He said Archie Nicotine. He said the hide belonged to a Dr. Colin Dobbs. He said Dr. Dobbs wanted a head and rug mount done. Jaws opened."

Wearing a three-piece grey-and-brown-flecked suit, with white shirt and black knitted tie, Frankie Munro sat quite erect and perched well forward in the witness chair, both hands down with fingers half curled and their tips on his knees.

"You have seen Exhibit Two, Mr. Munro?"

"Yes."

"Today in this court room?"

"Yes."

"Have you seen it before?"

"I have."

"Will you please tell the court when that was?"

"When the Indian brought it in between two and three o'clock the afternoon of May third."

Throughout his examination of Archie and now with Frankie, Leonard Farkus had been quite active; he paced; he turned; he leaned forward; he leaned backward; he nodded his head; he shook his head; he shrugged, pointed, and chopped in a performance that was part karate and part ballet. As he moved from the lectern to the witness, the bench, the lectern, the witness again, Frankie's almond eyes never left him.

"I sent it away to Fournier Frères in Montreal."

"Who are Fournier Frères?"

"The tannery we use. I also saw the hide all the time I worked on it doing the head and rug mount."

Without hesitation or emphasis, Frankie gave all his answers in the same clear, flat voice, each time tilting his head slightly, now to one side, now to the other, almost as though he were trying to capture sounds beyond human hearing limit.

"There is no doubt in my mind that Exhibit Two is the hide given us by the Indian, tattooed by me for identification in two places, prepared by me, delivered to Dr. Colin Dobbs on December the twentieth."

"Thank you, Mr. Munro."

"Counsel for the plaintiff, do you wish to ask this witness questions?"

"Yes, milord. Just a few in the further pursuit of understanding. Mr. Munro, you have testified that you received a bear skin from an Indian, whose name, incidentally, is Mr. Archie Nicotine, on the afternoon of May third. You have also said that you tattooed this skin in two places. Is tattooing the only precaution for identification purposes taken when a trophy skin is brought in to Wild Trophy World?"

"No."

"Would you explain to the court what else you do to ensure that the proper skin goes to the proper hunter?"

"We enter it in a ledger."

"You enter what in the ledger?"

"The tattoo. The name of the hunter."

"And his address?"

"Yes."

"Is that all?"

"Yes."

"Not his telephone number?"

"That too."

"Is that all?"

"Yes."

"No description of the skin? Not even what sort of animal it had belonged to? That it was that of a lynx, mountain sheep, goat, cougar, bear?"

"Yes. We do."

"If it were a bear, for instance. The sex?"

"Yes."

"That it was brown, black, cinnamon, grizzly?"

"Yes."

"And would you tell the court in some detail what you do have in this ledger for Dr. Dobbs, Mr. Munro?"

"His bear with its tattoo marks."

"His *grizzly* bear?"

"His brown bear."

"With a yellow face, light brown fur, black feet, ivory claws?"

"His brown bear, which the Indian brought in to us and which we mounted and delivered to Dr. Dobbs."

"That afternoon of May third, Mr. Munro. Can you recall for the court if it was a busy day at Wild Trophy World? Were there many hunters who brought in animal skins to be mounted by you?"

"No."

"How many such people did come in that afternoon?"

"The Indian with Dr. Dobbs's brown bear hide."

"Mr. Nicotine has testified that there was another hunter, who brought in a small brown bear skin with the same four bullet holes as those in Exhibit Two. But you say no such person came in to Wild Trophy World that afternoon?"

"That's right."

"So—of course—the ledger you will not tender the court would contain—"

"Objection!"

"Sustained."

"No further questions, milord."

"Will you be calling more witnesses, Mr. Farkus?"

"Just one more, milord."

"It is getting close to the lunch break. Do you anticipate it will be a long examination?"

"No, milord."

"Proceed then."

"Mr. Andrew David Munro."

This was a surprise. According to Archie, he and Frankie and the man from Minneapolis had been the only people in Wild Trophy World that afternoon he'd brought in the hide. Terry had said he doubted Farkus would use Mr. Munro, Sr., for there could be no prima facie evidence the old man could contribute. Perhaps Farkus was calling him simply as a character witness to tell the court what a fine boy his grandson had been and what an honourable and trustworthy man he'd grown up to be, quite incapable of accepting a bribe to switch bear hides.

"And what is your occupation, Mr. Munro?"

"Taxidermist."

"Where do you practise the—craft of taxidermy?"

"Wild Trophy World."

"You work there?"

"I am semi-retired."

"You are still the owner of Wild Trophy World?"

"In partnership with my grandson."

"What is his name?"

"Franklin Russell Munro. He is the fourth generation of Munros in Wild Trophy World. It was founded by my father in 1902."

"So, since that time Wild Trophy World must have prepared quite a number of big-game trophies for hunters?"

"And for natural history museums world-wide."

"Has there ever before—in the eighty-two years of the existence of Wild Trophy World—has there ever been an instance of a prepared and mounted specimen of animal or bird or fish for hunter or museum going to the wrong hunter or museum?"

"Never."

"Now, testimony has already been given the court that a bear skin was brought in to Wild Trophy World on or about two o'clock on the afternoon of May the third. Will you tell the court what you know about the events of May third?"

"It was brought in by a Mr. Archie Nicotine—"

"Objection. Hearsay. The witness was not present in Wild Trophy World when the skin was brought in!"

"Is that so, Mr. Farkus?"

"I am getting to that, milord."

"Then do it a little more quickly."

"Yes, milord. Were you, Mr. Munro, present in Wild Trophy World at the time that the bear skin was brought in?"

"Yes."

"Where precisely were you at that time?"

"In my office."

"Then did you witness the arrival of the bear skin?"

"Yes. I went to the door and I saw Mr. Nicotine at the counter, but Frankie had already come out from the back so I went back inside."

"Did you see the bear hide at that time?"

"Not really. My office is at some distance from the front counter."

"How far from it, Mr. Munro?"

"Forty or fifty feet. I did see the bear hide later."

"How much later?"

"Right after Mr. Nicotine left."

*And* the man from Minneapolis!

"Spread out on the counter where Frankie had just tattooed it in two places."

My God, the old man was perjuring himself!

"Was this the only bear skin on the counter or near it that your grandson had just tattooed?"

"Yes."

"Would you describe for the court the bear skin you saw?"

"It was a brown bear hide with four bullet holes and with a tear in the left—*right* flank."

"That's all, milord."

From the look on Terry's face, Colin could see that it had been a shocker for him too. "I have a few questions I would like to ask this witness, milord."

"Yes, counsel," Judge McElroy said, "after the lunch adjournment. We mustn't let that porridge get cold." He stood up.

Kinistinick came to Colin and as they left the case room he said, "We've got to talk with Archie and get this thing straight!"

\*     \*     \*

"All right, Archie. It's not just your word against Frankie's any more. Now it's *theirs* against yours. How many times did I ask you if there was anybody else in there?"

"Several times."

"I'll ask you again. Was Munro Senior in there or wasn't he?"

"I didn't see him then. All I seen was Frankie and the man from Minneapolis."

"In the front. At the counter."

"And when we spread out the hides in the back on the floor. If the old man seen me from his office in front or out back, then he must of seen the man from Minneapolis and two bear hides there and if you are lookin' for a liar you better look for an old white one and that is the whole situation."

"Okay. Okay, Archie. After lunch I do my cross-examination and tear him apart. That bit about the counter and the back of the—"

"No," Colin said, "you don't."

"Whaat!"

"You do not tear him apart in cross-examination. There won't be any cross-examination."

"But he perjured himself! We've got him on the stand—"

"That's final, Terry."

"Maybe you're right. If I implied perjury, it's just possible he could bring a charge against us."

"I don't think he would."

"Bring a charge?"

"Perjure himself under your cross-examination."

"There you are."

"Yes. There I am."


"In this matter between Dr. Colin Dobbs and Wild Trophy World, the plaintiff, Dr. Dobbs, asserts that the bear skin he received from Wild Trophy World, taxidermists, is not that of the bear he shot and took in to them to be mounted. He also asserts that his skin was sent to some other hunter. In Minneapolis. The defendant, Wild Trophy World, acknowledges receipt of a bear skin but asserts that the bear skin delivered to the plaintiff was the one they had received from him.

"The plaintiff acknowledges the receipt of a bear skin, but asserts that the bear skin delivered to him was not the one Wild Trophy World had received from him. The evidence given before me is obviously contradictory but my finding on the facts is as follows: whether or not a Minneapolis Nimrod actually received by error or any other means Dr. Dobbs's bear skin is not in my view essential to the determination of this case.

"Therefore: I find for the defendant. No costs.

"In these circumstances, gentlemen," he flared his nostrils and looked first to Kinistinick and then to Farkus, "I find it difficult to understand why the matter was brought before this court in the first place. It belonged in Small Claims Court."

# CHAPTER 19

Terry Kinistinick had seemed almost light-hearted about the decision. "We haven't really lost it," he said to Colin. "Old Pisser blew it—not letting us bring up the ledger notations for the two skins and where they'd sent yours. He did not allow all the best material evidence going to the proof of our allegations. That's grounds for appeal. The remedy we could ask for would be to have it sent back for re-trial. There's a good chance with another judge that evidence would be admitted. I think you'll get your bear."

"I want to think it over," Colin said, "about appealing."

"What for!"

"I just do."

"If you had allowed me to cross-examine Mr. Munro, the decision would have been quite diff—"

"I know."

"With an appeal—"

"I'll let you know, Terry."

He did not, however, tell him what happened before leaving the court-house after the trial. He probably never would.

He had been on his way to the washroom while Archie brought the truck to the front to give him a ride home. Just as he was about to enter, Mr. Munro came out.

When he had taken the witness stand, the man had seemed older than Colin remembered him, but not *this* old! It was as though it had been ten years or more since their meeting, when Mr. Munro had offered him the magnificent silver-tip grizzly he had shot in the Kootenays in 1937.

"I had to do it."

There was a white, powdery, moth-wing quality to the skin, taut over the cheek-bones; the stalk neck looked so fragile, circled by a shirt collar that seemed sizes too large for it.

"Do you understand? I had no choice."

The eyes were charcoal stark.

"You did not give me any. You could have, when I said I would let you have my grizzly hide."

Colin felt an idiotic urge to offer the man a cigarette.

"Mine could have *stood* for yours, couldn't it?"

Colin lowered his gaze from those tragically earnest eyes.

"Couldn't it, Dr. Dobbs?"

There was a dribble shadow down the inside pant leg. "Mr. Munro, would you have accepted if it had been my offer to you?"

"You asked me that then. I've thought about it since. Yes, Dr. Dobbs, I would have." He looked away then back again. "I certainly wouldn't have taken it any further, brought it in here. Why did you?"

The old man waited.

"You should ask yourself that. Think about it, as I will think about perjuring myself today—till I die." He turned away, then back to Colin again. "Please give my love to your daughter."

It had been a sincere request.

\* \* \*

Archie was waiting for him in front of the court-house.

"You don't get it," Archie said as they pulled away. "Your bear."

"No."

"That judge didn't believe me."

"I guess not, Archie."

"He believed that old man."

"Yes."

"He wasn't in his office, you know, Dobbs—when I took your bear in there for you."

"I know he wasn't, Archie. He just told me."

"I guess he didn't feel so good havin' to do that."

"He didn't."

"For his prick grandson."

"That's right."

Archie had stopped for the light. When he spoke, it was with his eyes ahead and up, more to himself than to Colin. "I done it several times. You?"

"We all have."

"If he told you he lied on the Bible, then are you goin' to appeal about it? Maybe then you'll get your bear back from Minneapolis."

"Kinistinick thinks so."

"That's why everybody did all this, isn't it?"

"It's why *I* did it.."

"Shouldn't it be important?"

"What do you mean?"

"So a person has to do it."

"You trying to tell me something, Archie?"

"Hey-up."

"Okay. Let me have it."

"Not you. Me. I know how that old man is feelin'. He done it for his grandson."

"Yes."

"One time when she was sick, she was twelve years old, and my Magdalene got real sick on her chest—sweatin'—she was about ready to die out of it. So—I did it."

"What?"

"I made a deal for her so she wouldn't die out of it."

"A deal with whom?"

"Who I made the deal with when the Bony Spectre was hangin' around outside our place—just waitin' till it was time. Me. Inside of me. I made a deal there. I said it to myself and him. The rest of my life I won't do that no more."

"Do what?"

"He kep' his deal. Bony Spectre rode off. Her fever broke that night. All that shit come off her chest. Spring she was good as ever—which ain't any hell for a Stony kid, and that's the whole situation."

"She got better because you made a promise."

"Hey-uh."

"To the Bony Spectre."

"Hey-up." Archie shook his head.

"Well—to whom?"

"You're white. It'd be too primitive for you to understand."

"Whoever it was, she did recover."

"Hey-up."

"He kept his part of the deal."

"Hey-up."

"You didn't."

"When I found those tracks up Daisy Creek and then I said I would guide you and I took that old horse up there and I shot him out on the flats. I was goin' out on real thin ice doin' all that. Helpin' isn't so different from doin'—is it?"

"It's different, Archie."

"That's what I said to myself then, too. Just bendin' it. Not breakin' it. Happens to hay wire. You keep on bendin' it—it is goin' to break, you know."

"Yes."

"I broke it. I had to. When she was at you."

"I think I know whom you made your deal with, Archie. Master Bear."

"Some kind of superstitious horse-shit like that."


"Did you hear the geese last night, Poppa?"

"They woke me up."

"Me too. Have some of this nice yoghurt?"

"No thanks."

"Chocolate."

"I have a weak stomach."

"So—you lost your case."

"Everybody lost."

"But you said Kinistinick said when you appeal it—"

"I am not appealing it."

"Whaat!"

"I've decided to drop the action."

"Oh, Poppa! Whatever made you—?"

"Archie. Finally."

"How did he—?"

"Something he told me. That I didn't know about."

"What did he—?"

"It concerned his daughter, Magdalene. Some kind of vow—pledge that he made, and broke."

"Well—bless Archie. Again."

"To save me. I owe him. And I owe you."

"You generally pay back."

"Do you remember what your mother and I gave you for your twelfth birthday?"

"The glass fly-rod."

"The guitar."

"Oh—yeah. Yeah!"

"Your Leonard Cohen year."

"Sure!"

"You didn't do so much painting that year, did you?"

"I guess not—too busy driving you and Mother nuts."

"That's right."

"Why?"

"Oh, I've thought a lot about some lyrics you made up then."

"Which ones?"

" 'Please Let Me In, Sir.' "

"Oh, my God! Have you still got them!"

"No."

"I can't remember—"

"Not on paper, but I've never forgotten them. Listen!

'Please let me in, sir.
I'm all alone, sir.
I'm awfully hungry, cold and tired, sir.
Oh, won't you please, please
Let me in, sir.'

"Oh, Poppa! Don't!"
"It gets worse:

'I'll clean your house, sir,
Wash your dishes, sir,
And make your bed, sir.
I'll cook your meals, sir.
All for nothing, sir,
If you just let me in, sir.
Oh please, please, let me in, sir!
Let me in, sir!'

"You did, Poppa!"
"Annie, I never would have made it without you."
"You would have. And now I have to tell you something. My visa came through."
"Visa!"
"Uh-huh."
"Where?"
"Palo Alto. I'm going back."
"When?"
"Month or so."
"To what?"
"Waitressing. Unless I have to work at the Flower Path. Don't look so stricken. I've been accepted in Fine Arts down there. Summer school. With that and one more semester, I get my degree."
"And then?"
"I've been giving it some thought."
"Master's?"
"Maybe not. You know those times you let me sit in on your writing seminar?"
"Yes."
"The one when you told them how they'd hear a voice in what they found inside themselves. Their own voice. And then they'd find other voices."
"Yes."

"And another time—when you told them they should keep on trying to say yes to humans no matter how goddam difficult it was to say it—most of the time. Ohhh—Poppa!"

"Please, Annie!"

"No matter—*how* shitty they—"

"Please—"

"—they're still the only game in town. Never give up on—never quit . . ."

"Please—don't cry!"

"Oh—Poppa, you are—one hell of a teacher! And I am so proud of you! And I want you to be proud of me!"

'I am, Annie! I am!"

"I'm not going on to graduate work—in painting."

"No!"

"Isn't because the odds are bad against me. It's just for a while."

"Don't. Don't—"

"Could be something in the genes. I just might take a run at teachers' college."

"You'd make a dandy! But don't quit your painting."

"No way. I'll never. I'll never quit painting if you do something—after I've gone."

"What?"

"Get back down to that den and saddle up your typewriter. Quit the quitting you've been doing for over ten years."

"Wait a minute—"

"I paint. You write. Simple as that. It is hypocrisy for you to tell them to write every day, every week, every month, every year—when you are not doing it yourself. Deal?"

"We'll see."

"Wherever I am, I will be looking for your byline."

"God damn it, Annie!"

"And I better find it because that's what you owe me. And yourself. If I have to do it for both of us, I'll be so busy down there I won't be able to get up to see you."

"I could come down . . . ?"

"Sorry. I'd be too busy painting and teaching. I just wouldn't have time for you."

"That's blackmail!"

"Yeah. It is. Make good use of it."

"I just might."

"Where are you going?"

"Downstairs."

"Really!"

"Mmmh."

"My God! Not to write!"

"Tie up a few flies."

"You're taking up fishing again?"

"You could call it that."

"Come on, Poppa! Cut the cute games. You going to shove that rock back up there again or aren't you?"

"I said—I might."

"Get that old novel out—"

"Hell, no. Remember that morning after the fall wine and cheese party for the new president?"

"I remember how hung over you were."

"I did fifteen lengths in the pool. . . ."

"And went into the sauna to sweat the poison out."

"Uh-huh."

"What about it?"

"That morning in there I got rid of quite a lot of poison. I thought—I—I'd have it alone—"

"Oh, Poppa!"

"—but I—didn't—huh—"

"Are you crying, Poppa?"

"I guess I am, Annie. For a woman in a sauna and for a broken old man who asked me to give his love to my daughter."

## ABOUT THE AUTHOR

W. O. Mitchell was born in Weyburn, Saskatchewan, in 1914. Although he has lived most of his life in Alberta and Saskatchewan, he has travelled widely and has been a lifeguard, deckhand, salesman, and high school teacher. For many years he was the most renowned resident in High River, Alberta, but he and his wife Merna now live in Calgary. He is in great demand as a visiting professor (currently at the University of Windsor), as a creative writing instructor at the Banff Centre each summer, and as a performer reading from his works.

Of these, his best-loved book is *Who Has Seen the Wind*. Since its publication in 1947 it has sold over a quarter of a million copies in Canada alone, and is hailed as the great Canadian classic of boyhood. Complementing that book (as *Huckleberry Finn* complements the earlier *Tom Sawyer*) is his 1981 best-seller *How I Spent My Summer Holidays*, hailed by some critics as his finest novel. His other works include *Jake and the Kid* (based on his legendary CBC-Radio series) and *The Vanishing Point*, which introduced the unforgettable Archie Nicotine. He also adapted another novel, *The Kite*, for the stage, where its immense success matched that of *Back to Beulah*; he has also written three other plays, which are included in his collection entitled *Dramatic W. O. Mitchell*.

Mr. Mitchell was made an Officer of the Order of Canada in 1973 and has been the subject of a National Film Board documentary. He is, in Pierre Berton's words, "an original."

*Shirley Hanton*

# A STUNNING NEW WORK FROM "MASTER STORYTELLER"*
## W. O. MITCHELL

### *SINCE DAISY CREEK*

"Fast-paced, highly entertaining . . . artfully structured so that the suspense is maintained until the very last page. . . . SINCE DAISY CREEK could serve as a textbook for what a contemporary Canadian ovel should be about."—*The Vancouver Sun**

"W. O. Mitchell has done it again. SINCE DAISY CREEK is a wonderful novel, packed with action, emotion, and insight."—*Jamie Conklin*

"Honest, funny, and very moving. . . . SINCE DAISY CREEK tops HOW I SPENT MY SUMMER HOLIDAYS and ties with WHO HAS SEEN THE WIND as Mitchell's best fiction."—*Ottawa Citizen*

"Explosive . . . some funny moments . . . spicier than Mitchell's previous stories."—*Toronto Star*

"An outstanding raconteur . . . Mitchell has peppered SINCE DAISY CREEK with amusing anecdotes and some good comic characterizations. . . . But the real treat is the great bear that nearly takes Dobbs's life."
—*Macleans*